NEW AND
SELECTED
ESSAYS

BOOKS BY ROBERT PENN WARREN

NEW AND
SELECTED
ESSAYS

Robert Penn Warren

RANDOM HOUSE

NEW YORK

Grateful acknowledgment is made to the following for permission
to reprint previously published material:

Henry Holt and Company, Inc.: Excerpts from *The Poetry of Robert Frost,* edited by Edward
Connery Lathem. Copyright © 1962 by Robert Frost. Copyright © 1975 by Lesley Frost
Ballantine.

Alfred A. Knopf, Inc.: Excerpts from *Selected Poems,* Third Edition, Revised and Enlarged,
by John Crowe Ransom. Copyright © 1969 by Alfred A. Knopf, Inc.

Random House, Inc.: Excerpts from the *Uncollected Stories of William Faulkner.* Copyright
1942 and renewed 1970 by Estelle Faulkner and Jill Faulkner Summers. Copyright 1942 by
William Faulkner.

Charles Scribner's Sons, an imprint of Macmillan Publishing Company: "Introduction" by
Robert Penn Warren from Modern Standard Author's Edition of *A Farewell to Arms,* by
Ernest Hemingway. Copyright 1949 by Charles Scribner's Sons.

The University of Alabama Press: "The Use of the Past," originally published in *A Time
to Hear and Answer: Essays for the Bicentennial Season,* edited by Taylor Littleton. Franklin
Lectures in Sciences and Humanities, 4th series. Copyright © 1977 by The University of
Alabama Press.

The University of Michigan Press: "The Themes of Robert Frost" from *The Writer and
His Craft,* edited by Roy Cowen. Copyright 1954 by the University of Michigan.

Library of Congress Cataloging-in-Publication Data

Warren, Robert Penn.
New and selected essays.

I. Title.
PS3545.A748N4   1989   810'.9   88-26470
ISBN 0-394-57516-4

Manufactured in the United States of America
24689753
First Edition
Book Design by Jo Anne Metsch

To Arnold and Bess Stein

CONTENTS

SECTION

I

PURE AND
IMPURE POETRY

CRITICS ARE RARELY faithful to their labels and their special strategies. Usually the critic will confess that no one strategy—the psychological, the moralistic, the formalistic, the historical—or combination of strategies, will quite work the defeat of the poem. For the poem is like the monstrous Orillo in Boiardo's *Orlando Innamorato.* When the sword lops off any member of the monster, that member is immediately rejoined to the body, and the monster is as formidable as ever. But the poem is even more formidable than the monster, for Orillo's adversary finally gained a victory by an astonishing feat of dexterity: he slashed off both the monster's arms and quick as a wink seized them and flung them into the river. The critic who vaingloriously trusts his method to account for the poem, to exhaust the poem, is trying to emulate this dexterity: he thinks

Delivered as Mesures Lecture at Princeton University, Spring 1942, as "Pure Poetry and the Structure of Poems." First published in *The Kenyon Review,* Spring 1943. Included in *Selected Essays,* 1958.

that he, too, can win by throwing the lopped-off arms into the river. But he is doomed to failure. Neither fire nor water will suffice to prevent the rejoining of the mutilated members to the monstrous torso. There is only one way to conquer the monster: you must eat it, bones, blood, skin, pelt, and gristle. And even then the monster is not dead, for it lives in you, is assimilated into you, and you are different, and somewhat monstrous yourself, for having eaten it.

So the monster will always win, and the critic knows this. He does not want to win. He knows that he must always play stooge to the monster. All he wants to do is to give the monster—the poem—a chance to exhibit again its miraculous power, which is poetry.

With this fable, I shall begin by observing that poetry wants to be pure. And it always succeeds in this ambition. In so far as we have poetry at all, it is always pure poetry; that is, it is not non-poetry. The poetry of Shakespeare, the poetry of Pope, the poetry of Herrick, is pure, in so far as it is poetry at all. We call the poetry "higher" or "lower," we say "more powerful" or "less powerful" about it, and we are, no doubt, quite right in doing so. The souls that form the great rose of Paradise are seated in banks and tiers of ascending blessedness, but they are all saved, they are all perfectly happy; they are all "pure," for they have all been purged of mortal taint. This is not to say, however, that if we get poetry from only one source, say Shakespeare, such a single source ought to suffice us, in as much as we can always appeal to it; or that, since all poetry is equally pure, we engage in a superfluous labor in trying to explore or create new sources of poetry. No, for we can remember that every soul in the great rose is precious in the eyes of God. No soul is the substitute for another.

Poetry wants to be pure, but poems do not. At least, most of them do not want to be too pure. The poems want to give us poetry, which is pure, and the elements of a poem, in so far as it is a good poem, will work together toward that end, but many of the elements, taken in themselves, may actually seem to contradict that end, or be neutral toward the achieving of that end. Are we then to conclude that neutral or recalcitrant elements are simply an index to human frailty, and that in a perfect world there would be no dross in poems, which would, then, be perfectly pure? No, it does not seem to be merely the fault of our world, for the poems include,

deliberately, more of the so-called dross than would appear necessary. They are not even as pure as they might be in this imperfect
world. They mar themselves with cacophonies, jagged rhythms,
ugly words and ugly thoughts, colloquialisms, clichés, sterile technical terms, headwork and argument, self-contradictions, clever-
nesses, irony, realism—all things which call us back to the world of
prose and imperfection.

Sometimes a poet will reflect on this state of affairs, and grieve.
He will decide that he, at least, will try to make one poem as pure
as possible. So he writes:

> Now sleeps the crimson petal, now the white;
> Nor waves the cypress in the palace walk;
> Nor winks the gold fin in the porphyry font.
> The fire-fly wakens; waken thou with me.

We know the famous garden—the garden in Tennyson's "Princess." We know how all nature conspires here to express the purity
of the moment: how the milk-white peacock glimmers like a ghost,
and how like a ghost the unnamed "she" glimmers on to her tryst;
how earth lies "all Danaë to the stars," as the beloved's heart lies
open to the lover; and how, in the end, the lily folds up her sweetness, "and slips into the bosom of the lake," as the lovers are lost
in the sweet dissolution of love.

And we know another poet and another garden. Or perhaps it
is the same garden, after all, viewed by a different poet, Shelley.

> I arise from dreams of thee
> In the first sweet sleep of night,
> When the winds are breathing low,
> - And the stars are shining bright.
> I arise from dreams of thee,
> And a spirit in my feet
> Hath led me—who knows how?
> To thy chamber window, Sweet!

We remember how, again, all nature conspires, how the wandering
airs "faint," how the Champak's odors "pine," how the nightin-

gale's complaint "dies upon her heart," as the lover will die upon the beloved's heart. Nature here strains out of nature, it wants to be called by another name, it wants to spiritualize itself by calling itself another name. How does the lover get to the chamber window? He refuses to say how, in his semi-somnambulistic daze, he got there. He blames, he says, "a spirit in my feet," and hastens to disavow any knowledge of how that spirit operates. In any case, he arrives at the chamber window. Subsequent events and the lover's reaction toward them are somewhat hazy. We know only that the lover, who faints and fails at the opening of the last stanza and who asks to be lifted from the grass by a more enterprising beloved, is in a condition of delectable passivity, in which distinctions blur out in the "purity" of the moment.

Let us turn to another garden: the place, Verona; the time, a summer night, with full moon. The lover speaks:

> But, soft! what light through yonder
>   window breaks?
> It is the east . . .

But we know the rest, and know that this garden, in which nature for the moment conspires again with the lover, is the most famous of them all, for the scene is justly admired for its purity of effect, for giving us the very essence of young, untarnished love. Nature conspires beneficently here, but we may remember that beyond the garden wall strolls Mercutio, who can celebrate Queen Mab, but who is always aware that nature has other names as well as the names the pure poets and pure lovers put upon her. And we remember that Mercutio, outside the wall, has just said:

> . . . 'twould anger him
> To raise a spirit in his mistress' circle
> Of some strange nature, letting it there stand
> Till she had laid it and conjured it down.

Mercutio has made a joke, a bawdy joke. That is bad enough, but worse, he has made his joke witty and, worst of all, intellectually complicated in its form. Realism, wit, intellectual complication— these are the enemies of the garden purity.

But the poet has not only let us see Mercutio outside the garden wall. Within the garden itself, when the lover invokes nature, when he spiritualizes and innocently trusts her, and says,

> Lady, by yonder blessed moon I swear,

the lady herself replies,

> O! swear not by the moon, the inconstant moon,
> That monthly changes in her circled orb.

The lady distrusts "pure" poems, nature spiritualized into forgetfulness. She has, as it were, a rigorous taste in metaphor, too; she brings a logical criticism to bear on the metaphor which is too easy; the metaphor must prove itself to her, must be willing to subject itself to scrutiny beyond the moment's enthusiasm. She injects the impurity of an intellectual style into the lover's pure poem.

And we must not forget the voice of the nurse, who calls from within, a voice which, we discover, is the voice of expediency, of half-measures, of the view that circumstances alter cases—the voice of prose and imperfection.

It is time to ask ourselves if the celebrated poetry of this scene, which as poetry is pure, exists despite the impurities of the total composition, if the effect would be more purely poetic were the nurse and Mercutio absent and the lady a more sympathetic critic of pure poems. I do not think so. The effect might even be more vulnerable poetically if the impurities were purged away. Mercutio, the lady, and the nurse are critics of the lover, who believes in pure poems, but perhaps they are necessary. Perhaps the lover can be accepted only in their context. The poet seems to say: "I know the worst that can be said on this subject, and I am giving fair warning. Read at your own risk." So the poetry arises from a recalcitrant and contradictory context; and finally involves that context.

Let us return to one of the other gardens, in which there is no Mercutio or nurse, and in which the lady is more sympathetic. Let us mar its purity by installing Mercutio in the shrubbery, from which the poet was so careful to banish him. You can hear his comment when the lover says:

> And a spirit in my feet
> Hath led me—who knows how?
> To thy chamber window, Sweet!

And we can guess what the wicked tongue would have to say in response to the last stanza.

It may be that the poet should have made early peace with Mercutio, and appealed to his better nature. For Mercutio seems to be glad to co-operate with a poet. But he must be invited; otherwise, he is apt to show a streak of merry vindictiveness about the finished product. Poems are vulnerable enough at best. Bright reason mocks them like sun from a wintry sky. They are easily left naked to laughter when leaves fall in the garden and the cold winds come. Therefore, they need all the friends they can get, and Mercutio, who is an ally of reason and who himself is given to mocking laughter, is a good friend for a poem to have.

On what terms does a poet make his peace with Mercutio? There are about as many sets of terms as there are good poets. I know that I have loaded the answer with the word *good* here, that I have implied a scale of excellence based, in part at least, on degree of complication. I shall return to this question. For the moment, however, let us examine an anonymous sixteenth-century poem whose apparent innocence and simple lyric cry should earn it a place in any anthology of "pure poetry."

> Western wind, when will thou blow,
> The small rain down can rain?
> Christ, if my love were in my arms
> And I in my bed again!

The lover, grieving for the absent beloved, cries out for relief. Several kinds of relief are involved in the appeal to the wind. First, there is the relief that would be had from the sympathetic manifestation of nature. The lover, in his perturbation of spirit, invokes the perturbations of nature. He invokes the beneficent perturbation,

> Western wind, when will thou blow,

as Lear invokes the destructive,

> Blow, winds, and crack your cheeks! rage! blow!

Second, there is the relief that would be had by the fulfillment of grief—the frost of grief, the drought of grief broken, the full anguish expressed, then the violence allayed in the peace of tears. Third, there is the relief that would be had in the excitement and fulfillment of love itself. There seems to be a contrast between the first two types of relief and the third type; speaking loosely, we may say that the first two types are romantic and general, the third type realistic and specific. So much for the first two lines.

In the last two lines, the lover cries out for the specific solace of his case: reunion with his beloved. But there is a difference between the two lines. The first is general, and romantic. The phrase "in my arms" does not seem to mean exactly what it says. True, it has a literal meaning, if we can look close at the words, but it is hard to look close because of the romantic aura—the spiritualized mist about them.[1] But with the last line the perfectly literal meaning suddenly comes into sharp focus. The mist is rifted and we can look straight at the words, which, we discover with a slight shock of surprise, do mean exactly what they say. The last line is realistic and specific. It is not even content to say,

> And I in bed again!

It is, rather, more scrupulously specific, and says,

> And I in *my* bed again!

All of this does not go to say that the realistic elements here are to be taken as canceling, or negating, the romantic elements. There is no ironical leer. The poem is not a celebration of carnality. It is

---

[1]It may be objected here that I am reading the phrase "in my arms" as a twentieth-century reader. I confess the fact. Certainly, several centuries have passed since the composition of the little poem, and those centuries have thickened the romantic mist about the words, but it is scarcely to be believed that the sixteenth century was the clear, literal Eden dawn of poetry when words walked without the fig leaf.

a faithful lover who speaks. He is faithful to the absent beloved, and he is also faithful to the full experience of love. That is, he does not abstract one aspect of the experience and call it the whole experience. He does not strain nature out of nature; he does not overspiritualize nature. This nameless poet would never have said, in the happier days of his love, that he had been led to his Sweet's chamber window by "a spirit in my feet"; and he certainly would not have added the coy disavowal, "who knows how?" But because the nameless poet refused to overspiritualize nature, we can accept the spirituality of the poem.

Another poem gives us another problem.

> Ah, what avails the sceptered race!
>   Ah, what the form divine!
> What every virtue, every grace!
>   Rose Aylmer, all were thine.
>
> Rose Aylmer, whom these wakeful eyes
>   May weep, but never see,
> A night of memories and of sighs
>   I consecrate to thee.

This is another poem about lost love: a "soft" subject. Now, to one kind of poet the soft subject presents a sore temptation. Because it is soft in its natural state, he is inclined to feel that to get at its poetic essence he must make it softer still, that he must insist on its softness, that he must render it as "pure" as possible. At first glance, it may seem that Landor is trying to do just that. What he says seems to be emphatic, unqualified, and open. Not every power, grace, and virtue could avail to preserve his love. That statement insists on the pathetic contrast. And in the next stanza, wakefulness and tearfulness are mentioned quite unashamedly, along with memories and sighs. It is all blurted out, as pure as possible.

But only in the paraphrase is it "blurted." The actual quality of the first stanza is hard, not soft. It is a chiseled stanza, in which formality is insisted upon. We may observe the balance of the first and second lines; the balance of the first half with the second half of the third line, which recapitulates the structure of the first two lines; the balance of the two parts of the last line, though here the balance is merely a rhythmical and not a sense balance as in the preceding instances; the binders of discreet alliteration, repetition, and assonance. The stanza is built up, as it were, of units which are firmly defined and sharply separated, phrase by phrase, line by line. We have the formal control of the soft subject, ritual and not surrender.

But in the second stanza the rigor of this formality is somewhat abated, as the more general, speculative emphasis (why cannot pomp, virtue, and grace avail?) gives way to the personal emphasis, as though the repetition of the beloved's name had, momentarily, released the flood of feeling. The first line of the second stanza spills over into the second; the "wakeful eyes" as subject find their verb in the next line, "weep," and the *wake-weep* alliteration, along with the pause after *weep,* points up the disintegration of the line, just as it emphasizes the situation. Then with the phrase "but never see" falling away from the long thrust of the rhetorical structure to the pause after *weep,* the poem seems to go completely soft, the frame is broken. But, even as the poet insists on "memories and sighs," in the last two lines he restores the balance. Notice the understatement of "A night." It says: "I know that life is a fairly complicated affair, and that I am committed to it and to its complications. I intend to stand by my commitment, as a man of integrity, that is, to live despite the grief. Since life is complicated, I cannot, if I am to live, spare too much time for indulging grief. I can give *a* night, but not all nights." The lover, like the hero of Frost's poem "Stopping by Woods on a Snowy Evening," tears himself from the temptation of staring into the treacherous, delicious blackness, for he, too, has "promises to keep." Or he resembles the Homeric heroes who, after the perilous passage is made, after their energy has saved their lives, and after they have beached their craft and eaten their meal, can then set aside an hour before sleep to mourn the comrades lost by the way—the heroes who, as Aldous Huxley says, understand realistically a whole truth as contrasted with a half-truth.

Is this a denial of the depth and sincerity of the grief? The soft reader, who wants the poem pure, may be inclined to say so. But let us look at the last line to see what it gives us in answer to this question. The answer seems to lie in the word *consecrate.* The meter thrusts this word at us; we observe that two of the three metrical accents in the line fall on syllables of this word, forcing it beyond its prose emphasis. The word is important and the importance is justified, for the word tells us that the single night is not merely a lapse into weakness, a trivial event to be forgotten when the weakness is overcome. It is, rather, an event of the most extreme and focal importance, an event formally dedicated, "set apart for sacred uses," an event by which other events are to be measured. So the word *consecrate* formalizes, philosophizes, ritualizes the grief; it specifies what in the first stanza has been implied by style.

But here is another poem of grief, grief at the death of a child. It is "Bells for John Whiteside's Daughter," by John Crowe Ransom.[2]

There was such speed in her little body,
And such lightness in her footfall,
It is no wonder her brown study
Astonishes us all.

Her wars were bruited in our high window.
We looked among orchard trees and beyond,
Where she took arms against her shadow,
Or harried unto the pond

The lazy geese, like a snow cloud
Dripping their snow on the green grass,
Tricking and stopping, sleepy and proud,
Who cried in goose, Alas,

For the tireless heart within the little
Lady with rod that made them rise
From their noon apple-dreams, and scuttle
Goose-fashion under the skies!

But now go the bells, and we are ready;
In one house we are sternly stopped
To say we are vexed at her brown study,
Lying so primly propped.

Forbes Special Offer

12 ISSUES FOR $21.50

SAVE 52%

☐ Bill me.
☐ Payment enclosed.
☐ I prefer 3 years for $96— the lowest basic rate, only $1.19 a copy.

Name _____ (please print)

Address _____ Apt #

City _____ State _____ Zip _____

In Canada, 12 iss/$34.25 Can. 3 years/$172 Can.
Please allow 30-60 days for delivery of your first issue.
12 issues at the cover price are $45. Basic subscriber rate is $21.50.

F046

Another soft subject, softer, if anything, than the subject of "Rose Aylmer," and it presents the same problem. But the problem is solved in a different way.

The first stanza is based on two time-honored clichés: first, "Heavens, won't that child ever be still, she is driving me distracted"; and second, "She was such an active, healthy-looking child, who would've ever thought she would just up and die?" In fact, the whole poem develops these clichés, and exploits, in a backhand fashion, the ironies implicit in their interrelation. And in this connection, we may note that the fact of the clichés, rather than more original or profound observations at the root of the poem, is important; there is in the poem the contrast between the staleness of the clichés and the shock of the reality. Further, we may note that the second cliché is an answer, savagely ironical in itself, to the first: the child you wished would be still *is* still, despite all that activity which had interrupted your adult occupations.

But such a savage irony is not the game here. It is too desperate, too naked, in a word, too pure. And ultimately, it is, in a sense, a meaningless irony if left in its pure state, because it depends on a mechanical, accidental contrast in nature, void of moral content. The poem is concerned with modifications and modulations of this brute, basic irony, modulations and modifications contingent upon an attitude taken toward it by a responsible human being, the speaker of the poem. The savagery is masked, or ameliorated.

In this connection, we may observe, first, the phrase "brown study." It is not the "frosted flower," the "marmoreal immobility," or any one of a thousand such phrases which would aim for the pure effect. It is merely the brown study which astonishes—a phrase which denies, as it were, the finality of the situation, underplays the pathos, and merely reminds one of those moments of childish pensiveness into which the grownup cannot penetrate. And the phrase itself is a cliché—the common now echoed in the uncommon.

Next, we may observe that stanzas two, three, and four simply document, with a busy yet wavering rhythm (one sentence runs through the three stanzas), the tireless naughtiness which was once the cause of rebuke, the naughtiness which disturbed the mature goings-on in the room with the "high window." But the naughtiness is now transmuted into a kind of fanciful story-book dream world, in which geese are whiter than nature, and the grass greener, in which geese speak in goose language, saying "Alas," and have apple-dreams. It is a drowsy, delicious world, in which the geese are bigger than life, and more important. It is an unreal (now unreal because lost), stylized world. Notice how the phrase "the little lady with rod" works: the detached primness of "little lady"; the formal, stiff effect gained by the omission of the article before *rod;* the slightly unnatural use of the word *rod* itself, which sets some distance between us and the scene (perhaps with the hint of the fairy story, a magic wand, or a magic rod—not a common, everyday stick). But the stanzas tie back into the premises of the poem in other ways. The little girl, in her excess of energy, warred against her shadow. Is it crowding matters too hard to surmise that the shadow here achieves a sort of covert symbolic significance? The little girl lost her war against her "shadow," which was always with her. Certainly the phrase "tireless heart" has some rich connotations. And the geese which say "Alas" conspire with the family to deplore the excessive activity of the child. (They do not conspire to express the present grief, only the past vexation—an inversion of the method of the pastoral elegy, or of the method of the first two garden poems.)

The business of the three stanzas, then, may be said to be twofold. First, they make us believe more fully in the child and therefore in the fact of the grief itself. They "prove" the grief, and they show the deliciousness of the lost world which will never look the same from the high window. Second, and contrariwise, they "transcend" the grief, or at least give a hint of a means for transcending immediate anguish: the lost world is, in one sense, redeemed out of time; it enters the pages of the picture book where geese speak, where the untrue is true, where the fleeting is fixed. What was had cannot, after all, be lost. (By way of comparison—a comparison which, because extreme, may be helpful—we may think of the transcendence in *A la Recherche du Temps Perdu.*) The three stanzas, then, to state it in another way, have validated the first stanza and have prepared for the last.

The three stanzas have made it possible for us to say, when the bell tolls, "we are ready." Some kind of terms, perhaps not the best terms possible but some kind, has been made with the savage underlying irony. But the terms arrived at do not prevent the occasion from being a "stern" one. The transcendence is not absolute, and in the end is possible only because of an exercise of will and self-control. Because we control ourselves, we can say "vexed" and not some big word. And the word itself picks up the first of the domestic clichés on which the poem is based—the outburst of impatience at the naughty child who, by dying, has performed her most serious piece of naughtiness. But now the word comes to us charged with the burden of the poem, and further, as re-echoed here by the phrase "brown study," charged by the sentence in which it occurs: we are gathered formally, ritualistically, sternly together to say the word *vexed*. [3] *Vexed* becomes the ritualistic, the summarizing word.

I have used the words *pure* and *impure* often in the foregoing pages, and I confess that I have used them rather loosely. But perhaps it has been evident that I have meant something like this: the pure poem tries to be pure by excluding, more or less rigidly, certain elements which might qualify or contradict its original impulse. In other words, the pure poems want to be, and desperately, all of a piece. It has also been evident, no doubt, that the kinds of impurity which are admitted or excluded by the various little anthology pieces which have been presented, are different in the different poems. This is only to be expected, for there is not one doctrine of "pure poetry"—not one definition of what constitutes impurity in poems—but many.

And not all of the doctrines are recent. When, for example, one

---

[3]It might be profitable, in contrast with this poem, to look at "After the Burial," by James Russell Lowell, a poem which is identical in situation. But in Lowell's poem the savagery of the irony is unqualified. In fact, the whole poem insists, quite literally, that qualification is impossible: the scheme of the poem is to set up the brute fact of death against possible consolations. It insists on "tears," the "thin-worn locket," the "anguish of deathless hair," "the smallness of the child's grave," the "little shoe in the corner." It is a poem which, we might say, does not progress, but ends where it begins, resting in savage irony from which it stems; or we might say that it is a poem without any "insides," for the hero of the poem is not attempting to do anything about the problem which confronts him—it is a poem without issue, without conflict, a poem of unconditional surrender. In other words, it tries to be a pure poem, pure grief, absolutely inconsolable. It is a strident poem, and strident in its rhythms. The fact that we know this poem to be an expression of a bereavement historically real makes it an embarrassing poem, as well. It is a naked poem.

cites Poe as the father of *the* doctrine of pure poetry, one is in error; Poe simply fathered *a* particular doctrine of pure poetry. One can find other doctrines of purity long antedating Poe. When Sir Philip Sidney, for example, legislated against tragicomedy, he was repeating a current doctrine of purity. When Ben Jonson told William Drummond that Donne, for not keeping of accent, deserved hanging, he was defending another kind of purity; and when Dryden spoke to save the ear of the fair sex from metaphysical perplexities in amorous poems, he was defending another kind of purity, just as he was defending another when he defined the nature of the heroic drama. The eighteenth century had a doctrine of pure poetry, which may be summed up under the word *sublimity,* but which involved two corollary doctrines, one concerning diction and the other concerning imagery. But at the same time that this century, by means of these corollary doctrines, was tidying up and purifying the doctrine derived from Longinus, it was admitting into the drama certain impurities which the theorists of the heroic drama would not have admitted.

But when we think of the modern doctrine of pure poetry, we usually think of Poe, as critic and poet, perhaps of Shelley, of the Symbolists, of the Abbé Bremond, perhaps of Pater, and certainly of George Moore and the Imagists. We know Poe's position: the long poem is "a flat contradiction in terms," because intense excitement, which is essential in poetry, cannot be long maintained; the moral sense and the intellect function more satisfactorily in prose than in poetry, and, in fact, "Truth" and the "Passions," which are for Poe associated with the intellect and the moral sense, may actually be inimical to poetry; vagueness, suggestiveness are central virtues, for poetry has for "its object an *indefinite* instead of a *definite* pleasure"; poetry is not supposed to undergo close inspection, only a cursory glance, for it, "above all things, is a beautiful painting whose tints, to minute inspection, are confusion worse confounded, but start out boldly to the cursory glance of the connoisseur"; poetry aspires toward music, since it is concerned with "indefinite sensations, to which music is an *essential,* since the comprehension of sweet sound is our most indefinite conception"; melancholy is the most poetical effect and enters into all the higher manifestations of beauty. We know, too, the Abbé Bremond's mystical interpretation, and the preface to George Moore's anthology, and the Imagist manifesto.

But these views are not identical. Shelley, for instance, delights in the imprecision praised and practiced by Poe, but he has an enormous appetite for "Truth" and the "Passions," which are, except for purposes of contrast, excluded by Poe. The Imagist manifesto, while excluding ideas, endorses precision rather than vagueness in rendering the image, and admits diction and objects which would have seemed impure to Poe and to many poets of the nineteenth century, and does not take much stock in the importance of verbal music. George Moore emphasizes the objective aspect of his pure poetry, which he describes as "something which the poet creates outside his own personality," and this is opposed to the subjective emphasis in Poe and Shelley; but he shares with both an emphasis on verbal music, and with the former a distaste for ideas.

But more recently, the notion of poetic purity has emerged in other contexts, contexts which sometimes obscure the connection of the new theories with the older theories. For instance, Max Eastman has a theory. "Pure poetry," he says in *The Literary Mind,* "is the pure effort to heighten consciousness." Mr. Eastman, we discover elsewhere in his book, would ban idea from poetry, but his motive is different from, say, the motive of Poe, and the difference is important: Poe would kick out the ideas because the ideas hurt the poetry, and Mr. Eastman would kick out the ideas because the poetry hurts the ideas. Only the scientist, he tells us, is entitled to have ideas on any subject, and the rest of the citizenry must wait to be told what attitude to take toward the ideas which they are not permitted to have except at second-hand. Literary truth, he says, is truth which is "uncertain or comparatively unimportant." But he does assign the poet a function—to heighten consciousness. In the light of this context we would have to rewrite his original definition: pure poetry is the pure effort to heighten consciousness, but the consciousness which is heightened must not have any connection with ideas, must involve no attitude toward any ideas.

Furthermore, to assist the poet in fulfilling the assigned function, Mr. Eastman gives him a somewhat sketchy doctrine of "pure" poetic diction. For instance, the word *bloated* is not admissible into a poem because it is, as he testifies, "sacred to the memory of dead fish," and the word *tangy* is, though he knows not exactly how, "intrinsically poetic." The notion of a vocabulary which is intrinsically poetic seems, with Mr. Eastman, to mean a vocabulary which indicates agreeable or beautiful objects. So we might rewrite the original definition to read: pure poetry is the pure effort to heighten consciousness, but the consciousness which is heightened must be a consciousness exclusively of agreeable or beautiful objects—certainly not a consciousness of any ideas.

In a recent book, *The Idiom of Poetry,* Frederick Pottle has discussed the question of pure poetry. He distinguishes another type of pure poetry in addition to the types already mentioned. He calls it the "Elliptical," and would include in it symbolist and metaphysical poetry (old and new) and some work by poets such as Collins, Blake, and Browning. He observes—without any pejorative implication, for he is a critical relativist and scarcely permits himself the luxury of evaluative judgments—that the contemporary product differs from older examples of the elliptical type in that "the modern poet goes much farther in employing private experiences or ideas than would formerly have been thought legitimate." To the common reader, he says, "the prime characteristic of this kind of poetry is not the nature of its imagery but its obscurity: its urgent suggestion that you add something to the poem without telling you what that something is." This omitted "something" he interprets as the prose "frame"—to use his word—the statement of the occasion, the logical or narrative transitions, the generalized application derived from the poem, etc. In other words, this type of pure poetry contends that "the effect would be more powerful if we could somehow manage to feel the images fully and accurately without having the effect diluted by any words put in to give us a 'meaning'—that is, if we could expel all the talk *about* the imaginative realization and have the pure realization itself."[4]

[4]F. W. Bateson, in *English Poetry and the English Language,* discusses the modern elliptical practice in poetry. Tennyson, he points out in connection with "The Sailor Boy," dilutes his poetry by telling a story as well as writing a poem, and "a shorter poem would have spoilt his story." The claims of prose conquer the claims of poetry. Of the Victorians in general: "The dramatic and narrative framework of their poems, by circumventing the disconcerting plunges into *medias res* which are the essence of poetry, brings it down to a level of prose. The reader knows where he is; it serves the purpose of introduction and note." Such introduc-

For the moment I shall pass the question of the accuracy of Mr.
Pottle's description of the impulse of Elliptical Poetry and present
the question which ultimately concerns him. How pure does poetry
need to be in practice? That is the question which Mr. Pottle asks.
He answers by saying that a great degree of impurity *may* be
admitted, and cites our famous didactic poems, *The Faerie Queene,
An Essay on Man, The Vanity of Human Wishes, The Excursion.* That
is the only answer which the relativist, and nominalist, can give.
Then he turns to what he calls the hardest question in the theory
of poetry: What kind of prosaism is acceptable and what is not? His
answer, which he advances very modestly, is this:

> . . . the element of prose is innocent and even salutary when it
> appears as—take your choice of three metaphors—a background on
> which the images are projected, or a frame in which they are shown,
> or a thread on which they are strung. In short, when it serves a
> *structural* purpose. Prose in a poem seems offensive to me when
> . . . the prosaisms are sharp, obvious, individual, and ranked co-
> ordinately with the images.

At first glance this looks plausible, and the critic has used the
sanctified word *structural.* But at second glance we may begin to
wonder what the sanctified word means to the critic. It means
something rather mechanical—background, frame, thread. The
structure is a showcase, say a jeweler's showcase, in which the
little jewels of poetry are exhibited, the images. The showcase
shouldn't be ornamental itself ("sharp, obvious, individual," Mr.
Pottle says), for it would then distract us from the jewels; it
should be chastely designed, and the jewels should repose on
black velvet and not on flowered chintz. But Mr. Pottle doesn't
ask what the relation among the bright jewels should be. Not
only does the showcase bear no relation to the jewels, but the
jewels, apparently, bear no relation to each other. Each one is a

---

tion and notes in the body of the poem itself are exactly what Mr. Pottle says is
missing in Elliptical Poetry. Mr. Bateson agrees with Poe in accepting intensity as
the criterion of the poetic effect, and in accepting the corollary that a poem should
be short. But he, contradicting Poe, seems to admire precise and complicated
incidental effects.

shining little focus of heightened interest, and all together they make only such a pattern, perhaps, as may make it easier for the eye to travel from one little jewel to the next, when the time comes to move on. Structure becomes here simply a device of salesmanship, a well-arranged showcase.

It is all mechanical. And this means that Mr. Pottle, after all, is himself an exponent of pure poetry. He locates the poetry simply in the images, the nodes of "pure realization." This means that what he calls the "element of prose" includes definition of situation, movement of narrative, logical transition, factual description, generalization, ideas. Such things, for him, do not participate in the poetic effect of the poem; in fact, they work against the poetic effect, and so, though necessary as a frame, should be kept from being "sharp, obvious, individual."[5]

I have referred to *The Idiom of Poetry,* first, because it is such an admirable and provocative book, sane, lucid, generous-spirited, and second, because, to my mind, it illustrates the insidiousness with which a doctrine of pure poetry can penetrate into the theory of a critic who is suspicious of such a doctrine. Furthermore, I have felt that Mr. Pottle's analysis might help me to define the common denominator of the various doctrines of pure poetry.

That common denominator seems to be the belief that poetry is an essence that is to be located at some particular place in a poem, or in some particular element. The exponent of pure poetry persuades himself that he has determined the particular something in which the poetry inheres, and then proceeds to decree that poems shall be composed, as nearly as possible, of that element and of

[5]Several other difficulties concerning Pottle's statement may suggest themselves. First, since he seems to infer that the poetic essence resides in the image, what view would he take of meter and rhythm? His statement, strictly construed, would mean that these factors do not participate in the poetic effect, but are simply part of the frame. Second, what view of dramatic poetry is implied? It seems again that a strict interpretation would mean that the story and the images bear no essential relation to each other, that the story is simply part of the frame. That is, the story, characters, rhythms, and ideas are on one level, and the images, in which the poetry inheres, are on another. But Caroline Spurgeon, G. Wilson Knight, and other critics have given us some reason for holding that the images do bear some relation to the business of the other items. In fact, all of the items, as Jacques Maritain has said, "feelings, ideas, representations, are for the artist merely materials and means, still symbols." That is, they are all elements in a single expressive structure.

nothing else. If we add up the things excluded by various critics and practitioners, we get a list about like this:

1. ideas, truths, generalizations, "meaning"
2. precise, complicated, "intellectual" images
3. unbeautiful, disagreeable, or neutral materials
4. situation, narrative, logical transition
5. realistic details, exact descriptions, realism in general
6. shifts in tone or mood
7. irony
8. metrical variation, dramatic adaptations of rhythm, cacophony, etc.
9. meter itself
10. subjective and personal elements.

No one theory of pure poetry excludes all of these items, and, as a matter of fact, the items listed are not on the same level of importance. Nor do the items always bear the same interpretation. For example, if one item seems to be central to discussions of pure poetry, it is the first: "ideas," it is said, "are not involved in the poetic effect, and may even be inimical to it." But this view can be interpreted in a variety of ways. If it is interpreted as simply meaning that the paraphrase of a poem is not equivalent to the poem, that the poetic gist is not to be defined as the statement embodied in the poem with the sugar-coating as bait, then the view can be held by opponents as well as exponents of any theory of pure poetry. We might scale down from this interpretation to the other extreme interpretation that the poem should merely give the sharp image in isolation. But there are many complicated and confused variations possible between the two extremes. There is, for example, the interpretation that "ideas," though they are not involved in the poetic effect, must appear in poems to provide, as Mr. Pottle's prosaisms do, a kind of frame, or thread, for the poetry—a spine to support the poetic flesh, or a Christmas tree on which the baubles of poetry are hung.[6] T. S. Eliot has said something of this sort:

[6]Such an interpretation seems to find a parallel in E. M. Forster's treatment of plot in fiction. Plot in his theory becomes a mere spine and does not really participate, except in a narrow, formal sense, in the fictional effect. By his inversion of the Aristotelian principle the plot becomes merely a necessary evil.

> The chief use of the "meaning" of a poem, in the ordinary sense, may be (for here again I am speaking of some kinds of poetry and not all) to satisfy one habit of the reader, to keep his mind diverted and quiet, while the poem does its work upon him: much as the imaginary burglar is always provided with a bit of nice meat for the house-dog.

Here, it would seem, Mr. Eliot has simply inverted the old sugar-coated-pill theory: the idea becomes the sugar-coating and the "poetry" becomes the medicine. This seems to say that the idea in a poem does not participate in the poetic effect, and seems to commit Mr. Eliot to a theory of pure poetry. But to do justice to the quotation, we should first observe that the parenthesis indicates that the writer is referring to some sort of provisional and superficial distinction and not to a fundamental one, and second observe that the passage is out of its context. In the context, Mr. Eliot goes on to say that some poets "become impatient of this 'meaning' [explicit statement of ideas in logical order] which seems superfluous, and perceive possibilities of intensity through its elimination." This may mean either of two things. It may mean that ideas do not participate in the poetic effect, or it may mean that, though they do participate in the poetic effect, they need not appear in the poem in an explicit and argued form. And this second reading would scarcely be a doctrine of pure poetry at all, for it would involve poetic casuistry and not poetic principle.

We might, however, illustrate the second interpretation by glancing at Marvell's "Horatian Ode" on Cromwell. Marvell does not give us narrative; he does not give us an account of the issues behind the Civil War; he does not state the two competing ideas which are dramatized in the poem, the idea of "sanction" and the idea of "efficiency." But the effect of the poem does involve those two factors; and the reserved irony, scarcely resolved, which emerges from the historical situation, is an irony derived from unstated materials and ideas. It is, to use Mr. Pottle's term again, a pure poem in so far as it is elliptical in method, but it is anything but a pure poem if by purity we mean the exclusion of idea from participation in the poetic effect. And Mr. Eliot's own practice implies that he believes that ideas do participate in the poetic effect. Otherwise, why did he put the clues to his ideas in the notes at the end of *The Waste Land* after so carefully excluding any explicit statement of them from the body of the poem? If he is regarding those ideas as mere bait—the "bit of nice meat for the house-dog"—he has put the ideas in a peculiar place, in the back of the book—like giving the dog the meat on the way out of the house with the swag, or giving the mouse the cheese after he is in the trap.

All this leads to the speculation that Marvell and Mr. Eliot have purged away statement of ideas from their poems, not because they wanted the ideas to participate less in the poetry, but because they wanted them to participate more fully, intensely, and immediately. This impulse, then, would account for the characteristic types of image, types in which precision, complication, and complicated intellectual relation to the theme are exploited; in other words, they are trying—whatever may be their final success—to carry the movement of mind to the center of the process. On these grounds they are the exact opposite of poets who, presumably on grounds of purity, exclude the movement of mind from the center of the poetic process—from the internal structure of the poem—but pay their respects to it as a kind of footnote, or gloss, or application coming at the end. Marvell and Eliot, by their cutting away of frame, are trying to emphasize the participation of ideas in the poetic process. Then Elliptical Poetry is not, as Mr. Pottle says it is, a pure poetry at all; the elliptical poet is elliptical for purposes of inclusion, not exclusion.

But waiving the question of Elliptical Poetry, no one of the other theories does—or could—exclude all the items on the list above. And that fact may instruct us. If all of these items were excluded, we might not have any poem at all. For instance, we know how some critics have pointed out that even in the strictest Imagist poetry idea creeps in—when the image leaves its natural habitat and enters a poem, it begins to "mean" something. The attempt to read ideas out of the poetic party violates the unity of our being and the unity of our experience. "For this reason," as Santayana puts it, "philosophy, when a poet is not mindless, enters inevitably into his poetry, since it has entered into his life; or rather, the detail of things and the detail of ideas pass equally into his verse, when both alike lie in the path that has led him to his ideal. To object to theory in poetry would be like objecting to words there; for words, too, are symbols without the sensuous character of the things they stand for; and yet it is only by the net of new connections which words throw over things, in recalling them, that poetry arises at all. Poetry is an attenuation, a rehandling, an echo of crude experience; it is itself a theoretic vision of things at arm's length."

Does this not, then, lead us to the conclusion that poetry does not inhere in any particular element but depends upon the set of relationships, the structure, which we call the poem?

Then the question arises: what elements cannot be used in such a structure? I should answer that nothing that is available in human experience is to be legislated out of poetry. This does not mean that anything can be used in *any* poem, or that some materials or elements may not prove more recalcitrant than others, or that it might not be easy to have too much of some things. But it does mean that, granted certain contexts, any sort of material, a chemical formula for instance, might appear functionally in a poem. It also may mean that, other things being equal, the greatness of a poet depends upon the extent of the area of experience which he can master poetically.

Can we make any generalizations about the nature of the poetic structure? First, it involves resistances, at various levels. There is the tension between the rhythm of the poem and the rhythm of speech (a tension which is very low at the extreme of free verse and at the extreme of verse such as that of "Ulalume," which verges toward a walloping doggerel); between the formality of the rhythm and the informality of the language; between the particular and the general, the concrete and the abstract; between the elements of even the simplest metaphor; between the beautiful and the ugly; between ideas (as in Marvell's poem); between the elements involved in irony (as in "Bells for John Whiteside's Daughter" or "Rose Aylmer"); between prosaisms and poeticisms (as in "Western Wind").

This list is not intended to be exhaustive; it is intended to be merely suggestive. But it may be taken to imply that the poet is like the jujitsu expert; he wins by utilizing the resistance of his opponent—the materials of the poem. In other words, a poem, to be good, must earn itself. It is a motion toward a point of rest, but if it is not a resisted motion, it is motion of no consequence. For example, a poem which depends upon stock materials and stock responses is simply a toboggan slide, or a fall through space. And the good poem must, in some way, involve the resistances; it must carry something of the context of its own creation: it must come to terms with Mercutio.

This is another way of saying that a good poem involves the participation of the reader; it must, as Coleridge puts it, make the reader into "an active creative being." Perhaps we can see this most readily in the case of tragedy: the determination of good or evil is not a "given" in tragedy, it is something to be earned in the process, and even the tragic villain must be "loved." We must kill him, as Brutus killed Caesar, not as butchers but as sacrificers. And all of this adds up to the fact that the structure is a dramatic structure, a movement through action toward rest, through complication toward simplicity of effect.

In the foregoing discussion, I have deliberately omitted reference to another type of pure poetry, a type which tends to become dominant in an age of political crisis and social disorientation. Perhaps the most sensible description of this type can be found in an essay by Herbert Muller:

> If it is not the primary business of the poet to be eloquent about these matters [faith and ideals], it still does not follow that he has more dignity or wisdom than those who are, or that he should have more sophistication. At any rate the fact is that almost all poets of the past did freely make large, simple statements, and not in their prosy or lax moments.

Mr. Muller then goes on to illustrate by quoting three famous large, simple statements:

> *E'n la sua volontade è nostra pace*

and

> We are such stuff
> As dreams are made on; and our little life
> Is rounded with a sleep.

and

> The mind is its own place, and in itself
> Can make a heaven of hell, a hell of heaven.

Mr. Muller is here attacking the critical emphasis on ironic tension in poetry. His attack really involves two lines of argument. First, the poet is not wiser than the statesman, philosopher, or saint, people who are eloquent about faith and ideals and who say what they mean, without benefit of irony. This Platonic line of argument is, I think, off the point in the present context. Second, the poets of the past have made large, simple affirmations, have said what they meant. This line of argument is very much on the point.

Poets *have* tried very hard, for thousands of years, to say what they mean. Not only have they tried to say what they mean, they have tried to prove what they mean. The saint proves his vision by stepping cheerfully into the fires. The poet, somewhat less spectacularly, proves his vision by submitting it to the fires of irony—to the drama of his structure—in the hope that the fires will refine it. In other words, the poet wishes to indicate that his vision has been earned, that it can survive reference to the complexities and contradictions of experience. And irony is one such device of reference.

In this connection let us look at the first of Mr. Muller's exhibits. The famous line occurs in Canto III of the *Paradiso.* It is spoken by Piccarda Donati, in answer to Dante's question as to why she does not desire to rise higher than her present sphere, the sphere of the moon. But it expresses, in unequivocal terms, a central theme of the *Commedia,* as of Christian experience. On the one hand, it may be a pious truism, fit for sampler work, and on the other hand, it may be a burning conviction, tested and earned. Dante, in his poem, sets out to show how it has been earned and tested.

One set of ironic contrasts which centers on this theme concerns, for instance, the opposition between the notion of human justice and the notion of divine justice. The story of Paolo and Francesca is so warm, appealing, and pathetic in its human terms, and their punishment so savage and unrelenting, so incommensurable, it seems, with the fault, that Dante, torn by the conflict, falls down as a dead body falls. Or Farinata, the enemy of Dante's house, is presented by the poet in terms of his human grandeur, which now, in Hell, is transmuted into a superhuman grandeur,

> com' avesse l'inferno in gran dispitto.

Ulysses remains a hero, a hero who should draw special applause from Dante, who defined the temporal end of man as the conquest of knowledge. But Ulysses is damned, as the great Brutus is damned, who hangs from the jaws of the fiend in the lowest pit of traitors. So divine justice is set over against human pathos, human dignity, human grandeur, human intellect, human justice. And we recall how Virgil, more than once, reminds Dante that he must not apply human standards to the sights he sees. It is this long conflict, which appears in many forms, this ironic tension, which finally gives body to the simple eloquence of the line in question; the statement is meaningful, not for what it says, but for what has gone before. It is earned. It has been earned by the entire poem.

I do not want to misrepresent Mr. Muller. He does follow his quotations by the sentence: "If they are properly qualified in the work as a whole, they may still be taken straight, they *are* [he italicizes the word] taken so in recollection as in their immediate impact." But how can we take a line "straight," in either "recollection" or "immediate impact," unless we ignore what "properly qualified" the line in "the work as a whole"? And if we do take it so, are we not violating, very definitely, the poet's meaning, for the poet means the *poem,* he doesn't mean the line.

It would be interesting to try to develop the contexts of the other passages which Mr. Muller quotes. But in any case, he is simply trying, in his essay, to guard against what he considers to be, rightly or wrongly, a too narrow description of poetry; he is not trying to legislate all poetry into the type of simple eloquence, the unqualified statement of "faith and ideals." But we have also witnessed certain, probably preliminary, attempts to legislate literature into becoming a simple, unqualified, "pure" statement of faith and ideals. We have seen the writers of the 1920s called the "irresponsibles." We have seen writers such as Proust, Eliot, Dreiser, and Faulkner called writers of the "death drive." Why are these writers condemned? Because they have tried, within the limits of their gifts, to remain faithful to the complexities of the problems with which they are dealing, because they have refused to take the easy statement as solution, because they have tried to define the context in which, and the terms by which, faith and ideals may be earned.

This method, however, will scarcely satisfy the mind which is hot for certainties; to that mind it will seem merely an index to lukewarmness, indecision, disunity, treason. The new theory of purity would purge out all complexities and all ironies and all self-criticism. And this theory will forget that the hand-me-down faith, the hand-me-down ideals, no matter what the professed content, is in the end not only meaningless but vicious. It is vicious because, as parody, it is the enemy of all faith.

THE USE OF

THE PAST

*M*Y SUBJECT TONIGHT is the use of the past. I see the subject in the immediate context of the particular crises of the past two decades—political and cultural—for it seems to me that associated with those crises, sometimes as cause and sometimes as consequence, is a contempt for the past. But also, and more broadly, I see this subject in the context of impending celebration of our second centennial of nationhood.

On July 4, 1876, in an address delivered at Taunton, Massachusetts, Brooks Adams demanded: "Can we look over the United States and honestly tell ourselves that all things are well with us?" And he answered his own question: "We cannot conceal from ourselves that all things are not well." Almost a century later, looking forward to July 4, 1976, one does not stamp himself as a

First published in *A Time to Hear and Answer: Essays for the Bicentennial Season,* edited by Taylor Littleton. Franklin Lectures in Sciences and Humanities, 4th Series. University of Alabama Press for Auburn University, 1977.

prophet of doom if he predicts that on that date we will be forced to echo the answer that Adams gave to his own question.

But on July 4, 1976—in this age of adman blandness, public-relations images, and moral ambiguities—will anybody be ill-mannered enough even to ask the question? To play fair, we must admit that in 1876, Brooks Adams asked his question in Taunton, Massachusetts, not in Philadelphia, where, that year, from May 8 to November 10, a considerable segment of the population of the nation was busy sweeping embarrassing questions under the rug—including the great International Exhibition to demonstrate American progress, the august presence of Dom Pedro II, emperor of Brazil, and of his empress, the *Centennial Inaugural March* by Richard Wagner, "composed expressly for the occasion," a hymn by John Greenleaf Whittier, ditto, a cantata by Sidney Lanier, ditto, a speech by President Grant, ditto, and a prayer by a certain Right Reverend Bishop Simpson, ditto, who implored the Almighty, somewhat tardily it may have seemed, to guide the officials of the nation that they might "ever rule in righteousness."

There were, of course, some malcontents about. Walt Whitman, for instance, who, though still clinging to a faith in the future of democracy, could say that American society, in the moment of the great victory of the Civil War, was "canker'd, crude, superstitious, and rotten," and that in the nation, to "severe eyes," there appeared only "a sort of dry and flat Sahara," with "cities, crowded with petty grotesques, malformations, phantoms, playing meaningless antics." And Melville could remark the possibility of America's becoming a "Dead level of rank commonplace," a sort of "Anglo-Saxon China . . . In the Dark Ages of Democracy." But if Whitman, the erstwhile poet of democracy, and Melville, a staunch Unionist, now had dire forebodings, those forebodings were not on the program at the opening of the Exhibition or at the Celebration of July 4, 1876. They were buried somewhere in *Democratic Vistas* and in *Clarel*.

What I am getting at is this: Americans, by and large, have had little use for the past except for purposes of interior decorating (early American pine is expensive), personal vanity (it is nice to have the *Mayflower* or the Declaration of Independence in the family), or pietistic and self-congratulatory celebrations, such as our recent well-bred little hubbub about the Civil War. Henry Ford, sage and philosopher, spoke for many of us when he said, "History is bunk," and there is the force of parable in the fact that the house at Seventh and Market streets in Philadelphia, where Jefferson wrote the Declaration of Independence, was torn down, in 1883, to make space for a bank, and when the bank was torn down, in 1932, a hot-dog stand, more appropriate to the period, replaced it. Now, for a more cheerful if somewhat retarded note, in 1963, Congress approved the purchase of the site, and at last a more-or-less accurate replica of the Graff house will be visible to patriots on tour.

Thomas Jefferson did say that "The land belongs to the living generation," but he also said, in his *Notes on the State of Virginia,* that history should be the basis for the education of the free citizen. A sense of the past, according to Jefferson, was necessary to nurture a self capable of exercising judgment concerning the present and the future, a self, that is, with a feeling for destiny. Jefferson would have seen no contradiction between his two utterances. But now, alas, what often passes for the free citizen in our land would see nothing but a walking contradiction.

So it is not likely that we, looking about us, shall take the impending national festival as the right occasion for reflecting on the nature of our national past, for indulging in a little self-scrutiny, or for an exercise in humility. Is it likely that in Philadelphia, on July 4, 1976, some poet will be on the program to read another "Recessional"? Which, in parody of the poem (not read by Kipling), might appropriately run:

> Home-called, our navies slink away
> From Asia, stilled their futile fire,
> And all our expanding GNP of yesterday
> Is one with Nineveh and Tyre.
> Lord God of Hosts, be with us yet,
> Lest we forget, lest we forget.

I may be on the wrong track here. It may be that Americans, after all, do meditate on the lesson of their past. It can be argued that the lesson of the American past is that the past has no lesson, and that the burden of American history is that history is, indeed, bunk. In a deep sense, the mission of America has been to make all things new. This continent was a new Eden in which man would miraculously assume his prelapsarian condition, and the movement westward was a perpetual baptism into a new innocence—or at least a movement into a territory where the sheriff couldn't serve his warrant. For the sense of guilt and the pangs of conscience are an index of Time, and in the beckoning, golden distances of the great new westward continent, the dimension of space redeemed man from the dimension of time. This was as true of seventeenth-century New England, where the new arrivals dreamed of a City of God set on a Hill, as for nineteenth-century Texas, where it was not only bad manners but downright dangerous to ask a man where he came from.

The sense of being freed from the past, of being reborn, of being forever innocent, did give America an abounding energy, an undauntable self-reliance, and an unquenchable optimism, and we should be lacking in gratitude to Providence to deny these obvious benefits. But sometimes virtues have their defects, and sometimes, even, the defects tend to run away with the virtues. If, in America, the past was wiped out and Americans felt themselves to be—to adapt a phrase from Emerson—the "party of the Future," they also felt themselves to be a Chosen People, who, unlike the Jews, could never sin in God's sight. Furthermore, they came to feel that God's will and their own were miraculously identical. In fact, they were inclined to feel that even their whims, appetites, and passing fancies were an index of God's will.

So we have what Daniel Bell, in *The Cultural Contradictions of Capitalism,* has recently called the "end of the bourgeois idea"—with nothing to put in place of its notion of society but "self-infinitization," the gratification of whims, appetites, and passing fancies—some of which we didn't even know we had until we saw the slick color ad or the blue movie. This represents, to continue with Mr. Bell, a culture of "immediacy, impact, sensation and simultaneity"—and he might have added "authenticity" as this word is frequently used. The culture of the "impulse quest" is one that denies both the sense of community and the social obligation. And, as it denies such relations, this culture denies, too, a relation to time; we live in a "society without fathers."

The "society without fathers" is a logical projection of an impulse old on these shores, and one that, in a paradoxical way, has contributed to our success.* We began our great project with the notion that with the past wiped out, perfection and universal prosperity were just around the corner. The American's basic gospel was millennialism. The disciples of a certain William Miller might leave all their earthly possessions and gather on a hill to await the Second Coming (slated, according to Mr. Miller, for March 22, 1844) and get laughed at for their gullibility. But the final comedy was that most of the laughers, then and now, were—are—members in good standing of the Cult of Quick Perfectionism: tomorrow all will be redeemed, the bank of the future will be broken, every man will be king. Our millennialism had roots in certain aspects of Christianity, but it survived the passing of the Old Time Religion, with its promise of other-worldly salvation, and has prospered most exceedingly with the New Time Religion of Technology, with its promise of this-worldly salvation. But here we should notice that whereas the millennialist of the new dispensation pays lip service to the dreamy-eyed fellows with equations on the blackboards and chalk dust on their unpressed lapels, he finds his real high priests among the social scientists and the psychologists, for these are the fellows who really have the know-how to stamp out evil in both slum and human heart and who can guarantee virtue and happiness, willy-nilly. The thread runs true from Emerson's drip-dry Christianity, with no Blood of the Lamb required, to B. F. Skinner's *Walden II.*

If perfection is just around the corner, and we have the blueprint, the magic word, and a Hot Line to the Most High, who can prevail against us? For whoever is against us is therefore against both God and History and deserves whatever we dish out to him in the process of bringing peace on earth and general prosperity to the deserving—even to erstwhile enemies, if they learn to mind their manners. In our national anthem (which became officially that only in 1931), in the version of Francis Scott Key, one famous line runs: "Then conquer we must, *when* our cause it is just." But when millennialists—with their moral narcissism—sing it, they often

*And a tension old on these shores, if I read Hawthorne's story "Major Molyneux" aright.

change *when* to *for:* "Then conquer we must, *for* our cause it is just." Which is another way of saying that our cause is always just by definition. And if it is just, then nothing less will do than total solution, total destruction, unconditional surrender, and the righteous wrath of the *cherim* of the Old Testament that the Jew visited on the ungodly. So the American apostle of freedom is likely to echo Isaiah and exclaim:

> " . . . their blood shall be sprinkled upon my garments and I will stain
> all my raimant. For the day of vengeance is at hand."

So, to turn to the most famous hymn of the American latter-day *cherim,* on a peculiarly instructive and parabolic occasion: In 1899—notice the date—when a Civil War monument was being dedicated on Boston Common, Julia Ward Howe (escorted, I should add, by Joseph K. Wheeler, lately Lieutenant General CSA, and now Lieutenant General USA, and a hero of the Spanish-American War) received her most staggering ovation. When a famous singer, performing "The Battle Hymn of the Republic," came to the line: "As he died to make men holy, let us die to make men free," a hundred thousand patriots rose to their feet, sobbing, to sing the line together. A reporter from the Philadelphia *Press,* there to cover the august event, wrote: "If volunteers were needed for the Philippines [President] McKinley could have had us all right there." We cannot be sure that the reporter was an ironist. Perhaps he was just a good American, and really did regard the Philippine operetta as another holy crusade, and the suppression of Aguinaldo's brown-skinned dissidents as being on a moral par with the freeing of the American black-skinned slaves.

"America," Woodrow Wilson once declared, "is the only idealistic country in the world." But Wilson merely echoed what Reinhold Niebuhr would later call the illusions of our national infancy—the illusion of our innocence, virtue, and omnipotence—the feeling that the American is born into a permanent and air-conditioned Eden. This is the illusion that leads to crisis politics, a notion happily expressed by the banging meters of James Russell Lowell:

> Once to every man or nation
>   comes the moment to decide
> In the strife of Truth with Falsehood
>   for the good or evil side.

Choose the good and let the devil take the hindmost and God pick up the pieces. As Max Weber puts it:

> There is an abysmal contrast between conduct that follows the maxim of an ethic of ultimate ends—that is, in religious terms, "The Christian does rightly and leaves the result with the Lord"—and conduct that follows the maxim of an ethic of responsibility, in which case one has to give an account of the foreseeable results of his action.

Shakespeare, by the way, wrote several plays on this theme, most notably *King Lear.* Cordelia followed an ethic of ultimate ends—she loved Truth and couldn't tell a lie—and the girl sure played hell.

But Cordelia, perfect moral narcissist though she was, was capable of human warmth, possessed the tragic scale, and was somehow all of a piece. We Americans, though we are famous for our human warmth, can scarcely be said to be of tragic scale (we love success too much for that), and can scarcely be said to be all of a piece, for we tend to proclaim our righteousness most loudly at the very moment when the hand that isn't crossing our heart and body may well be in the cookie jar. And if somebody points out that one hand is indeed in the cookie jar, we are likely to claim that that's clearly what God intended—as a reward for our righteousness. As Eli Thayer, citizen of Connecticut, put it in the 1850s: "If a man does a good deed and makes money at the same time, it merely proves that his faculties are working in harmony."

To sum up my preamble, are we ready to take our second centennial as an occasion that may, possibly, teach us something? Are we ready to face the idea that we may not, after all, be the Chosen People? Are we ready even to consider the possibility that we are moral narcissists of great talent and are, as a consequence, somewhat unlovely and sometimes unlovable? Are we ready to learn from our past that moral definition is difficult and that there is such a thing as what Neibuhr calls the "irony of history"? For what was once our future has now become our past—and that is the deepest irony of all, and the irony hardest for the child-mind to grapple with.

Let us go back to Philadelphia in that Edenic moment in 1776 when all was to be made new. The Founding Fathers did make a new kind of nation—radically new. But it was radically new in both senses of the word *radical,* for when Jefferson wrote the Declaration, he looked not only to a violent break into the future but to a continuity with the past—with what was for him the root-past, Greece. The image of Athens hung over that room where he sat to pen the new radical charter of human liberty.

If Jefferson framed the idea of the new nation, it was Washington who, in the words of Justice Holmes, "carried the Revolution in his belly." It was the iron of Washington's character that made the nation possible; and, as Samuel Eliot Morison points out, Washington, whom we like to think of as a product of forest and Indian ambush, was more consciously the product of the Stoic philosophy of Rome, by which he, as a youth, set out, *deliberately,* to form his own character.

Washington and Jefferson were not alone. For a long time, the image of the Classical past hung over the new nation—even over the forests of Tennessee, where the boy Sam Houston read the *Iliad* by a Cherokee campfire, and over the plains of East Texas, where the man Sam Houston, on the campaign that led to San Jacinto, read Caesar's *Gallic Wars* in his tent at night. Certainly there was comedy when some tavern brawler fancied himself as Achilles or some ranting politico on the frontier hustings mistook himself for Cicero, but those things, too, in their comic way, reflect an overarching vision. When there is no vision, the people perish, and in that Edenic hour long ago, what would the vision of our future have been without the dynamism of our vision of the past?

Are we now free to envisage our future without a vision of the past? If, in the age of technology, a sense of the past cannot survive, then, as the historian J. H. Plumb grimly predicts in *The Death of the Past,* the role of history "as the interpreter of man's destiny will be taken by the social sciences." Which is to say that the idea of pondering the story of men as men, whether noble or vicious, will be replaced by the study of the statistics of nonideographic units of an infinite series, and computers will dictate how such units, which strangely enough do breathe and move and rejoice and suffer, can best be manipulated for their own good.

Now, Plumb does not mean that history is a book you can open at random, as if practicing Vergilian lots, to find the automatic answer to a problem. He is not thinking of the historian as a tipster at the race track. The deepest value of history keeps alive the sense that men have striven, suffered, achieved, and have been base or generous—have, in short, been men. In the simplest terms, can anyone look at the salt-dried fragment of the chest of an Egyptian soldier, dead three thousand years or more, with the stub of the lethal arrow yet fixed there, and not have a different sense of himself than he had had before? Or look at the little toy found in an Inca tomb, dated long before Pizarro, and not look with different eyes upon his own child playing on the nursery floor? Or read a page of Tacitus or Gibbon without being struck anew by the irony of good and evil interfused in our nature? It is hard enough, at best, to remember our humanity, but history helps us, at least a little.

There are, of course, those who say that we are indeed free to envisage our future without reference to the past. We have the techniques, they say, to conquer the evils of nature. Such people, however, now speak in somewhat more subdued tones than they did a few years ago, for now the voices of a number of other experts in technology are singing a different tune. Not to mention old-time dissidents such as Lewis Mumford, we now have the predictions of the scientists of the Club of Rome. Joseph Weuzenbaum, a professor of computer science at the Massachusetts Institute of Technology, affirms the need for a "science of limits." Daniel Callahan, director of the Institute of Society, Ethics, and the Life Sciences, sees a clear mandate to blunt the aggressive drive of technology if we are, literally, to survive. Robert Heilbroner, in *An Inquiry into the Human Prospect,* sees, in the face of the unlimited drive of technology, dwindling resources and political shortsightedness and irrelevance to be followed by a crackup and a neoprimitivism. René Dubos has recently published an essay called *Civilizing Technology* in which he, like C. P. Snow, in a speech at Independence, Missouri, insists on the possibility of famine and plague on an unprecedented scale, and still more recently John H. Knowles, president of the Rockefeller Foundation, and J. G. Harrar, the president emeritus, have voiced the same warnings.

Suppose, however, that such predictions are proved wrong, that we go on our merry way and that our technological resourcefulness is equal to the challenge. Even so, if we stop with the conquest of objective nature, we are likely to remain, in our future, little better than the armed barbarians that it sometimes seems we are. For what of our human nature? Are we free of the past, as we seek to conquer the evils we find in human nature? Some experts—most notably of late, B. F. Skinner, that apostle of total conditioning—maintain that we are free of the past, because man can be programmed by experts to be frictionless and happy units in the great sociotechnological apparatus, as Aldous Huxley, in a different tone of voice, predicted long ago in *Brave New World.*

The behaviorist has not yet, however, proved his case. And meanwhile the difficult task of civilizing our human nature remains—a task not rendered easier by the fact that, as we come more and more to see, man's fate is double, an outer and an inner fate, the world that the self is in, and the self that is a world. And more and more we see, painfully, that the two worlds are indissolubly linked and interpenetrating—mirror facing mirror, as it were—and more and more we see that one of the errors of the past, an error from which we must learn, has been to treat them as though each were in isolation.

Is the past, then, merely a nest of error, which we must analyze in order to avoid? Santayana, in *The Life of Reason,* said wittily that those who cannot remember the past are condemned to repeat it. By this token, history is a cautionary tale. You study the past to avoid repeating its errors. The tale of the past is indeed a tale of errors, and it would indeed be well if we could avoid repeating them. But what of mankind's apparently infinite talent for inventing new kinds of error? Can the past teach us not merely to avoid wrong decisions but to make right ones? Can history really be turned into philosophy, teaching by example? Does the past really harbor a secret that, if found out, will break the bank of the future?

That is the perennial dream: to discover in the past the laws that govern human events, just as the scientist, by studying nature, discovers the laws that permit us to predict and control nature. It is a dream that haunts the study of history, sociology, political science, economics. There is an early instance of it in Machiavelli, an instance clear and innocent in its outline. He set out to study the process by which power may be grasped and held, and to study the process merely as process—neutral, amoral, dehumanized, like a chemical process. He shocked the world, and quite unjustly his name became a synonym for unspeakable evil, in much the same way that Darwin, Marx, and Freud were to shock the later world— great men who, like Machiavelli, tried to see the inner logic of the past—the biological past, the historical past, the psychological past—to look on the nakedness of the past without prurience or shame.

There have been many since Machiavelli who have sought to define the laws of history and thus break the bank of the future— Vico, Marx, Henry Adams, Buckle, Spengler, Toynbee, and even Yeats in *A Vision,* with its crazy cones and gyres and glorious prose. But the bank of the future remains unbroken. Something goes wrong. Some explosively recalcitrant fact gets left out of the fine scheme, and this fact, like an unexploded grenade in a rubbish heap, is apt to cause trouble. For the future is always full of booby traps, and there is no indication that historians make the best prime ministers, secretaries of state, or even advisers to presidents, kings, and emperors. As James Russell Lowell points out, "with Guizot for an adviser, Louis Philippe, himself the eyewitness of two revolutions, became the easy victim of a third." Two great and successful governors, Caesar and Churchill, may be cited against this notion, but they were really governors who happened to write history, not historians who became governors. Machiavelli, the historical theorist of war, was opposed to the use of gunpowder, and he could not even handle a squadron of horses in peaceful maneuvers: he had to call an unlettered and pragmatic ruffian of a condottiere to unsnarl the mess. Machiavelli, the historical theorist of power, died poor and forgotten, and his hero Cesare Borgia, the man of unillusioned *virtù,* lost his chance at the papacy because of a fever that any poltroon might have had, and died in exile, in a nameless skirmish in Spain, where his body, stripped of armor, lay naked all night in a wooded ravine.

What, then, can we—historians, economists, sociologists—learn from the past? Are we, and those historians who think they can "look into the seeds of time and see which grain will grow and which will not," no better off than poor Macbeth, who thought that he, with the Weird Sisters to advise him, had broken the bank of the future, but who found that everything was, in the end, only a blood-drenched practical joke? Are we really prepared to say that we had just as soon have—as we too often lamentably do—a congressman, secretary of state, or president who is bone-ignorant of history? And if we are not prepared to go that far, then what do we expect that they should have learned from the past?

Arthur Schlesinger, Jr., a historian who has enjoyed the privilege of being privy to the making of great decisions—some of which went badly wrong—says that what men get from the study of the past is not a formula for making right decisions but what he calls historical insight—a sense of the climate in which decisions are made, or what we may call the medium in which action can be undertaken. A feeling for the medium—just as the writer must have a feeling for language, the sculptor for mass and form, the painter for color, etc. That feeling for the medium—it is the indefinable, untranslatable thing. Schlesinger illustrates his idea of insight by saying that after the Cuban missile crisis, Kennedy, to whom he attributes this gift of insight, remarked on the danger that since the Russians had backed down here, many people would assume that all you ever had to do was to get tough and raise the bet. In other words, the feel for the context was the key to the occasion, and Kennedy, on this occasion at least, had it—and he also knew that a merely automatic repetition of the policy as a formula, without reference to context, might well end in disaster.

On the matter of formula versus insight, we point out that in this debate about the uses of the past, the distinction is not a new one. Machiavelli, we have said, hoped to find the formula to break the bank of the future, and his personal failure stands as an image of the failure of his formula. But there was another Florentine named Francesco Guicciardini, a contemporary of Machiavelli, who, as a professional diplomat playing the ruthless game of power, had also thought long and deeply about the uses of the past. Not a scheme, not a formula, he says, can come out of the study of the past—but tact. For him, *il tatto*—tact—is all, and in his *Ricordi* we find, over and over again, the words "experience" and "discretion." The sense of the medium, insight, was what Guicciardini cultivated, and, with his tact, he grew old in honors.

To paraphrase Santayana, we can say that all that can save us from the tyranny of the past is insight into the past. Let us take a crying and perennial example of such a need for insight into our national past. We have lived, and live now, in a tension between the notion that American democracy is a vision that we must constantly try to realize in actuality, and the notion that American democracy has already received, by divine revelation, its embodiment in appropriate institutions—that is, the tension between the notion of democracy expressed in the Declaration of Independence and the notion that some citizens take to be embodied in the Constitution—the tension between the vision and the machine. With this tension in mind, we may muse back over our past—the long drift toward the Civil War and that war itself, the Draft Riots of 1863, the Homestead Strike, the Haymarket Riot, the Populist movement, the struggle for women's suffrage, the rise of the CIO in the 1930s, the Freedom Rides in Mississippi in the 1960s, and the more recent difficulties too numerous to list. Such musings might lead us to agree with what the poet Whittier said in the 1840s—and what blacks have said in the 1960s—that the history of the United States is the record of the attempt to make the "vision" of the Declaration come true in the "machine" of our institutions.

Even if we accept Whittier's insight, do we automatically find a right course of action when we are confronted with the next crisis? Is *every* strike to be supported? Is *every* riot to be condoned? How, exactly, is the machine to be made to conform to the vision? Every event has its context, and the context is always unique and in its uniqueness cannot be ignored. Even so, the "insight" would still provide the inestimable advantage of putting the context of the present event in the broader context of the past. This would give us a way of thinking about the problem, it would define the poles of the question, vision versus machine. Suppose, in the end, we should abandon Whittier's view, with its emphasis on "vision," and accept that of James Russell Lowell (later to be expressed more mordantly by Justice Holmes), that "Democracy is nothing more than an experiment in government . . . which must stand or fall on its own merits as others have done before it." Does this "insight" cancel out the other? No, it merely shifts the emphasis toward the "machine," which must not only conform to the "vision" but must actually "work." As we face any problem, both insights must be operative. They provide, in fact, a new polarity by which we may consider possible action.

We have been talking about the meaning of American history. But what about those of us who have little hand in making decisions of historical importance? Of what use are such "insights" as we have been talking about to us ordinary citizens? The answer is easy: all the use in the world. For we live in the world, and our understanding of it is of crucial importance to us. Only by trying to know our role in the world can we, in the end, come to know ourselves.

There is, however, another and more formidable objection to my line of thought. We live in a world that is defined more and more by science and technology. Is it not true that science is, in a sense, always seeking emancipation from the past, that it is ferociously committed to the future, that outmoded science is not science at all, and that all science except that of this morning is outmoded?

But is that future to which science is so ferociously committed an unconditioned future? And if it is conditioned, what conditions it but the past? That is, the world created by the past. Here Robert Oppenheimer suggests the root question: What historical situation made the rise of modern science possible at all? Why did the Greeks not develop it? They had, we are told, every specifically scientific requisite. But for modern science to develop, Oppenheimer hazards, a condition of general order was necessary, specifically in this case, an idea of progress having to do with the human situation in general, a special social and philosophical context for the technical prerequisites. If a culture not so prepared did make a technological discovery, what happened to it? Every schoolboy knows that the Chinese discovered gunpowder long ago, and every schoolboy has laughed at them for using it only for fireworks and not for cannon —an error that the Chinese have more lately and unlaughably compensated for. The Romans had a steam engine on the dock at

Alexandria, but they never built a second one: slave labor was too cheap. The Chinese had their gunpowder and the Romans had their steam engine—that is all very amusing; but in our time, do we not see fundamental tensions between our social system and certain technological possibilities? What about our economic structure and cybernetics? What about the bomb? What about the pill? What about the problem of leisure, if we do move out of the realm of necessity?

In these examples, we have been talking about applied science, about technology, but what about discovery in pure science? So obvious as to be scarcely worth mentioning are such famous cases as the conflicts between Galileo and the Inquisition, between Darwin and the Anglican bishops, and even more recently, that between the Soviet government and the Russian geneticists. But our modern free world of the West, we may counter, is beyond such foolishness. Perhaps it is—at the conscious level. But what of the unconscious level?

To take another instance, this one from the eighteenth century, when the Baron d'Holbach's revolutionary work on *The System of Nature* reached Germany from France, the response was tepid. "How hollow and empty did we feel," wrote Goethe, "in this melancholy, atheistical half-night, in which the earth vanished with all its images, the heaven with all its stars." In other words, the Germans, in their characteristic emotional and philosophical climate, were not ready for the French theory of mechanistic materialism—any more than the New England Transcendentalists were ready for science. They claimed, a half century later, to be the party of the future and thought themselves the masters of scientific culture; but they were, in fact, totally unconscious of their entrapment in a historical situation. Are we trapped in ours? And in what way? A study of its past might help us to answer these questions.

Some eminent thinkers maintain that science is now emancipated from social conditioning and that it is self-generating and self-propelling. Other eminent thinkers do not agree. But even if science is self-propelling, it does not automatically specify what uses shall be made of its findings, nor does it yet control the human responses to the world that it creates. We do not know our own relation to the science of our time or its relation to our total culture.

Is there no possible profit in our exploration of the question of what coherence may be observed between the scientific theories of a past age and its whole civilization? It is hard to see such relations in our own time, but if we can study them in the past, we have some help in understanding ourselves in our time. For example, in discussing the continuing and still largely unconscious effect of Newton on human sensibility even in the age of Einstein, C. C. Gillespie says, in *The Edge of Objectivity,* that this "is an element of culture, and to exist in a culture with no notion whence it comes" is to fail to be "aware and in that measure free."

Let us take an example of something that the study of the past might free us from. More and more, it filters through, even to so uninstructed a reader as this one, that the science of our time is becoming open-ended; that is, the machine model of the universe blew up a long time back, with the advent of quantum physics, and the old version of determinism blew up along with it. So "teleology," as Edmund Sinnott puts it, "far from being unscientific, is implicit in the very nature of organism," and more and more scientists refer to their science as only one method of snaring "reality," refer to artists as merely brother symbolists, and proclaim that the need for an expansion of understanding is fundamental.

Now here is the point: at the very same time, we see, in the world of technology, the depersonalizing process growing apace, with the constantly expanding destruction of the very concept of the responsible self, and we also see the consequences of this process in a general malaise and in frequent eruptions of violence in every sector of life, from slum to university campus. The trouble is that man feels himself devalued, alienated, powerless—in short, he feels that he has been made into a "thing." He lives, as Martin Buber has put it, in the realm of "It," rather than in the realm of "Thou." Might not a sense of the past indicate to us that modern technology is, instead of being "modern," very old-fashioned indeed—that it took off from old-fashioned science, from science based on the machine model, and has carried that model into the hearts of men, without ever revising its basic image in the light of subsequent developments in scientific thought? In other words, might not an understanding of the origins of various kinds of modern alienation be a step toward curing the disease?

To take a second example, of a somewhat different order, the study of the past might free us from our delusion that "progress"—which is shorthand for technology operating in the world—is automatic. For, in spite of our pride in progress as *our* achievement, as something that we have made, we have come, paradoxically, to abjure all pride and to trust "progress" as the thing that has made us, to bow abjectly before its power, which we take to be automatically beneficent.

But there is a paradox here. Sometimes we preen ourselves on *progress* as our special and wholly admirable achievement. Then, sometimes, when it is to our convenience, we regard progress as an objective, self-propelling power, which we then take to be automatically beneficent—or, if we need an alibi, maleficent. And it does become more and more apparent that we may need some alibis.

It is beyond all doubt that our science and technology are dazzling human achievements and that they will be still more dazzling, and it is beyond all doubt that the influence of the scientific mind extends to the solving of problems of a nonscientific nature. But one value of the past is to serve as a sort of measuring rod for our achievements—how great and how little. How much right have we to join Gibbon when, from the benefit of his rational and ironical distance, describing the capture of Jerusalem, he sneers at the ferocity of the Christian Crusaders splashing through blood to the Holy Sepulchre? What more appalling targets could he find for his irony than our own time, so blessed by "progress"—Buchenwald, Rotterdam, Hiroshima? And what would Jonathan Swift make of the filth of Harlem or Newark or Appalachia? Has Thomas Jefferson's nightmare of the great modern city come true—the city, which we once took as a mark of our highest achievement?

A look at the past reminds us of how great is the distance, and how short, over which we have come. The past makes us ask what we have done with our dazzling achievements—or what they have done with us. It makes us ask whether our very achievements are not ironical counterpoint and contrast to our fundamental failures. It makes us ask whether we are not the victims of our comforting dream of automatic and automatically benign progress. To put it another way, can science and technology alone—as some experts claim—civilize us? Or must we face the hard fact that somehow we must, after all, civilize ourselves?

Let us turn to another basic human interest—the arts, and specifically literature. Let us ask, first, why we read literature at all. Ultimately, we read it because it gives us an image of the human soul confronting its fate. But there is a double image. There is the image of the content, the character in a story—Hamlet, for instance—confronting his fate. Then there is the image that is the literary work itself, a work that, in all its complexity, is an image of how the writer confronts the image of fate that is the work's content. The play *Hamlet,* for example, taken in its entirety, embodies Shakespeare's feeling for human fate, and this feeling is to be distinguished from Hamlet's own feeling. These two kinds of image, in their very doubleness, have a powerful appeal for us, first, because we are all (though often unconsciously) inevitably concerned about our fate, and second, because our concern is itself twofold: we confront our fate and we confront ourselves in the act of confronting our fate. Literature, as Henri Bergson suggests, returns us to ourselves.

If this is so, why should not the literature that gives us images contemporary with our own facing up to contemporary problems be better than the literature of times and cultures different from our own? In other words, why bother with literature of the past? The answer is given in the question: because the literature of our own time is not different enough from ourselves. True, the literature of our own time is likely to be different, by and large, from the experience of any individual reader, and it is only because these differences exist that we turn to it at all. Without differences, any recognition of identity would be meaningless. For we need difference *and* identity, fused in the thing created by the imagination, to make us comprehend imaginatively our own nature and our own plight. As a child learns the self by learning other selves, so with us. The shifting arcades and perspectives of being and fate, the wilderness of mirrors, the ever unfolding and fluctuating ratio of identity and difference—we need these things in all their increasing complexity if we are to pursue the never-ending task of knowing the self.

Should we therefore abandon the reading of contemporary

works? No, for if it is true that we can know neither ourselves nor the literature of our time without some sense of the literature of the past, it is equally true that without some sense of the literature of the present—that is, of how our own experience relates to our literature—we cannot know the literature of the past. For instance, I have known more than one professor of Shakespeare whose self-complacent ignorance of modernity—of humanity, really—reduced all his learning to a dusty "about-ness." They knew all "about" Shakespeare, but that was all. They saw literature not as a vital and continuing process but merely as a list of names, dates, and sources.

A vital and continuing process—that would be one way, in fact, of describing a literary tradition. In this sense Petrarch, speaking of the proper relation of the new Italian literature to the old Latin literature, said that the resemblance of the new and the old should not be that of a portrait and the sitter, but of a son and the father. But Petrarch's description, though it tells a truth, is incomplete—incomplete because static. It omits one aspect of the relation of the writer to the past. The more he knows about the past, and the more he reveres the great creators of the past, the more he must struggle against them. He is like Jacob, who wrestled the angel all night in the place to be called Peniel and, though at the break of day he received the mystic wound in the thigh, would not let go of the mysterious stranger until he had exacted the blessing he craved and could say that he had "seen God face to face." In a recent and fascinating book called *The Anxiety of Influence,* Harold Bloom has described this struggle of a poet with the past as the dynamic of literary tradition. The self, by such a view, can be discovered only in the attempt to assert it against a powerful opponent from the past. Tradition, in the sense of formula, bars the future. In the sense of a dynamic, it unbars the future. And what may be said of the poet wrestling with his angel may also be said of us all, as we confront the literature of the past—or merely the past itself.

At this point I should say that two of the monumental writers of the American past, Hawthorne and Faulkner, have dealt specifically with this theme—not in regard to the past as literary tradition but as cultural tradition in the deepest and broadest sense. What makes Hawthorne vital for us today is precisely what he achieved by turning back to his past—his past as New England and his personal past. The matter here is both complex and instructive. As a man, he declared that he thanked God for every year that separated him from his ancestral New England past, but in wrestling with that necessary angel he arrived at a psychological understanding and an art that speaks to us profoundly a century and a half later and is part of our usable American past. Faulkner, in writing his tortuous and tortured myth of the South, has given not only us, but the world, a compelling image of man's painful and fructifying relation to the past.

But is the achievement of these American masters different, in the end, from that of all other masters looming behind the past? If literature—and in another mode, history—does anything for us, it stirs up in us a sense of existential yearning. The truths it presents come in the images of experience, and the images tease us out of thought toward truth as experience. The truth we want to come to is the truth of ourselves, of our common humanity, available in the projected self of art. We discover a numinous consciousness and for the first time may see both ourselves in the world and the world in us. This drama of the discovery of the self is timeless. Costume and décor do not matter. In it, the past becomes our present—no, it becomes our future. So far as we understand ourselves, that is, we may move freely into a future and need not be merely the victims of the next event in time that happens to come along. The dynamic understanding of the past gives us the possibility of a future.

And no country ever had a more dire need than ours for a dynamic understanding of its past and of the past in general. I cannot help, sometimes, connecting the appalling history textbooks my children studied with the appalling headlines I see in the morning paper. In these books I find embalmed every official lie, idiotic piety, and stereotypical attitude that characterizes our social and political life. Sometimes I have said so. Once not long ago, when my daughter was a little girl, I was hearing her history lesson. She must have noticed my mounting blood pressure, for she headed me off: "Oh, I know it's not the truth," she hastened to say, "it's just what we have to tell the teacher." What we have to tell the teacher, tell the subscriber, tell the electorate, tell the cash customer, tell ourselves—the lie about the past, the lie, not the truth, about the past, is exactly what prevents the new idea, the new political policy, the new economic program, the new poem, the new city, the new self—that lie, in short, is what prevents the future.

The "new self," I have said, and here I come back to the study of the past as a way of discovering the self. No period ever needed such a benefit more than this one, our "present," in which there are real symptoms of breakdown in our society, in which a stultifying flood of "communication" takes the place of community and communion, in which the words "identity crisis" and "alienation" are jargon among subliterate high-school dropouts high on pot and in the august pages of *Time* magazine.

But if we have this jargon, it still points to two basic needs. Everyone needs to know who he is—and needs to know his relation to society. In the Negro Revolution of the last decade we find in our society a poignant and violent dramatization of these needs. The Negro American wants to know his history—that is, he wants to know his identity—and so we have the black-history movement and the mythology of the Black Muslims. He wants others to recognize his history—that is, to accept him in a just relation to society. His plight is, of course, special. But it is also an analogue to the plight of all, and that, no doubt, was one reason for its wide appeal to the educated young white person in the 1960s.

For a long time philosophers had foreseen that plight. Long ago, Bertrand Russell saw the individual as more and more losing identity in the great power state and new industrial organizations. Santayana speculated that the old springs of poetry might dry up because of the constant presence of abstractions in the mind of modern man. Alfred North Whitehead pointed out the derangement of the time sense that had followed the accelerating changes of the Industrial Revolution—and this was long before the dizzying world of nuclear energy, cybernetics, and outer space had come into being. These things, of course, have enormously accelerated change, have created new anxieties, and have made it progressively difficult for the individual to locate himself in society and in time.

But what does the study of the past offer us here?

The most obvious answer—so obvious that it is rarely given—is that the past gives us a sense of time. In the simplest way, in the old-fashioned world, a person grew up flanked on one side by graybeards and on the other by babes. Time was not intellectually conceived; it was the very medium of existence, simple and unfracturable. In that fact were implicit the values that we now seek in the study of the past. This is a study that, in the fact that the past is both outside the present and encounterable in it and will be discernible in the future, instructs us in the nature of the life process. This study is one that, in the contrast between the fluid present and the determinate past, gives us a sense of freedom in our targeting toward the indeterminate future. In other words, in a primal way, in a gut way, the study of the past gives one a feeling for the structure of experience, for continuity, for establishing location on the shifting chart of being. And it might be argued that without this gut-feel for overarching time, as contrasted with fractured time, there can be no true sense of identity. As for the sense of community, it is clear that the placing of the individual in time automatically accomplishes much toward establishing his relation to others. He is, to begin with, established as a part of the general human story. By the same token, man, seeing himself in time as time-perceived-as-experience, was aware of himself in the context of nature, of nature-as-the-matrix-of-experience, and was aware of his brotherhood with other men in nature.

But within that great community are those lesser communities with which the individual may identify. If the young man dreaming of poetry feels cut off from the world about him, he can enter the society of Keats and Dante. He can see the continuity and variety of the human need that makes for poetry, and if the staggering achievements of the past fill him with despair, it is a noble despair, for they may also fill him with the conviction that the trying is worth the trying—for it affirms life. And so for all activities.

Even the revolutionary who would most violently repudiate the present inherited from the past turns to the past to find models of revolutionary heroism. After all, Karl Marx was a historian. The revolutionary, like all of us, must find his "ancestors," his secret community. The past is, in fact, the great pantheon where we can all find the bearers of the values by which we could live. It gives us the image of a community and of a role, an identity, within that community, the image of a self to be achieved.

And yet, in a way, it "gives" us nothing. We must *earn* what we get there. The past must be studied, worked at—in short, created. For the past, like the present, is fluid. History, the articulated past— all kinds, even our personal histories—is forever being rethought, refelt, rewritten, not merely as rigor or luck turns up new facts but as new patterns emerge, as new understandings develop, and as we experience new needs and new questions. There is no absolute, positive past available to us, no matter how rigorously we strive to determine it—as strive we must. Inevitably, the past, so far as we know it, is an inference, a creation, and this, without being paradoxical, can be said to be its chief value for us. In creating the image of the past, we create ourselves, and without that task of creating the past we might be said scarcely to exist. Without it, we sink to the level of a protoplasmic swarm.

The self is, of course, never finally created. It is a past, too, one that we must continually strive to articulate and to come to terms with. I once heard a woman, a very distinguished musical artist now verging into age, say that she looked forward to getting old, for then she could begin to understand her own life. The unexamined life, Socrates tells us in the *Apology,* is not worth living, and the past, the great general past and the personal past, gives us the paradigm and perspective by which we can inspect the life we live—that of our own age and of ourselves.

There is one more thing that the past is: the sovereign tonic for self-pity; and self-pity, as the obverse of our arrogance, is the endemic disease of our time and place. The classic symptom is a withdrawal from the world and from responsibility—in other words, a fit of the sulks. There are real reasons, as I have said, why it is difficult for us, particularly for the young, to find continuity and connection, and as a result we feel sorry for ourselves. But we also feel sorry for ourselves because the world is evil and we are too good and pure for it. We will retreat into personal purity—which being translated back into its root emotion is apt to mean that we are pretty sore because the evil world didn't promptly do us proper obeisance. Now let us grant that the world is evil—or rather, to make an important distinction, that it is full of evils. But if the past tells us anything, it is that gains against the powers of darkness are made in detail, one by one—inch by inch, as Thomas Jefferson said of gains in human freedom—and not by massive, absolute, apocalyptic bangs. When such bangs do come about, they are likely to create dire new evils even as they do away with the old ones.

But what, one may ask, if withdrawal is necessary to achieve the deepest personal vision—the extension of sensibility, the ecstasy of the vision of being that is the vision of the artist, saint, or philosopher. The answer is easy. If the past tells us anything, it tells us that even the vision must be earned. There is as little point in confusing ecstasy and withdrawal, as ecstasy and orgy. Orgy has its honorable place, and let us not knock it. But we should try to keep the categories clean. I think it highly improbable that Shakespeare confused a little fun in a back room of the Mermaid Tavern with the thrill he must have felt when a scene flashed up in his head like a match dropped in spilled gasoline. And somehow, even with the hints of the feasts that Plato gives us, I do not imagine Socrates finding his keenest delight in what I have been instructed to call a "group-grope."

If orgy and the earning of the vision sometimes seem to overlap, we must ask who among the partakers of orgy achieve the real vision. If Baudelaire and Rimbaud, in the search for poetry, might programmatically try, by drugs among other things, to derange the sensibility, to crack the shell of the accustomed and the logical, they were also workers, students of the art of poetry, technicians and thinkers of a high order. If *Kubla Khan* came to Coleridge in a static laudanum dream, it could come *only* to Coleridge the worker, the technician, and not to the prize inmate of some hospital for the deranged. If Hart Crane, in the innocence of the old Bohemia, downed his gin by the quart and hypnotized himself by playing a jazz record over and over, there was also the cold logic of hangover behind the poem, too. His good poems are not automatic writing. They are organized. Even great scientific discoveries have come in the visionary flash, in drama, even in nightmare, but as Pasteur puts it, vision comes only to *"l'esprit preparée."* Out of discipline, the artist, saint, scientist, and sage earn vision. And the same can be said of any of us who seeks as the highest achievement a vision of the significance of his own life, beyond all self-pity.

The past is the tonic for self-pity, first by putting us in relation to the community of those who have conquered it, but also in another way, in a fundamental, primal way, one by which it mobilizes our deepest energies: it tells us that we, too, shall soon be part of the past.

"Oh, gentlemen! The time of life is short," says Hotspur in Shakespeare's *Henry IV,* just before the battle in which he is to die. But the words come not as a wail but as a bugle blast, for he is about to add: "To spend that shortness basely were too long."

And there is also the nameless sergeant in Belleau Woods, back in World War I, who, as he rose to the charge on the German machine gun, shouted to his men: "Come on, you sons-of-bitches, do you want to live forever!"

What Hotspur says, what the sergeant says—their words are so simple, so vulnerable to all ironies. But even so, they echo the old heartening promise—the old energizing promise—the past makes to us. We, too, even in our flicker of time, can earn a place in the story.

How?

By creating the future. *That* is the promise the past makes to us.

WHY DO WE
READ FICTION?

*W*HY DO WE read fiction? The answer is simple. We read it because we like it. And we like it because fiction, as an image of life, stimulates and gratifies our interest in life. But whatever interests may be appealed to by fiction, the special and immediate interest that takes us to fiction is always our interest in a story.

A story is not merely an image of life, but life in motion—specifically, the presentation of individual characters moving through their particular experiences to some end that we may accept as meaningful. And the experience that is characteristically presented in a story is that of facing a problem, a conflict. To put it bluntly: no conflict, no story.

It is no wonder that conflict should be at the center of fiction, for conflict is at the center of life. But why should we, who have the

First published in *The Saturday Evening Post,* October 20, 1962.

constant and often painful experience of conflict in life and who yearn for inner peace and harmonious relation with the outer world, turn to fiction, which is the image of conflict? The fact is that our attitude toward conflict is ambivalent. If we do find a totally satisfactory adjustment in life, we tend to sink into the drowse of the accustomed. Only when our surroundings—or we ourselves— become problematic again do we wake up and feel that surge of energy which is life. And life more abundantly lived is what we seek.

So we, at the same time that we yearn for peace, yearn for the problematic. The adventurer, the sportsman, the gambler, the child playing hide-and-seek, the teen-age boys choosing up sides for a game of sandlot baseball, the old grad cheering in the stadium—we all, in fact, seek out or create problematic situations of greater or lesser intensity. Such situations give us a sense of heightened energy, of life. And fiction, too, gives us the fresh, uninhibited opportunity to vent the rich emotional charge—tears, laughter, tenderness, sympathy, hate, love, and irony—that is stored up in us and short-circuited in the drowse of the accustomed. Furthermore, this heightened awareness can be more fully relished now, because what in actuality would be the threat of the problematic is here tamed to mere imagination, and because some kind of resolution of the problem is, owing to the very nature of fiction, promised.

The story promises us a resolution, and we wait in suspense to learn how things will come out. We are in suspense to learn how things will come out. We are in suspense, not only about what will happen, but even more about what the event will mean. We are in suspense about the story in fiction because we are in suspense about another story far closer and more important to us—the story of our own life as we live it. We do not know how that story of our own life is going to come out. We do not know what it will mean. So, in that deepest suspense of life, which will be shadowed in the suspense we feel about the story in fiction, we turn to fiction for some slight hint about the story in the life we live. The relation of our life to the fictional life is what, in a fundamental sense, takes us to fiction.

Even when we read, as we say, to "escape," we seek to escape not *from* life but *to* life, to a life more satisfying than our own drab version. Fiction gives us an image of life—sometimes of a life we actually have and like to dwell on, but often and poignantly of one we have had and do not have now, or one we have never had and can never have. Or, perhaps most often, the ardent fisherman, when his rheumatism keeps him housebound, reads stories from *Field and Stream.* The baseball fan reads *You Know Me, Al,* by Ring Lardner. The little co-ed, worrying about her snub nose and her low mark in Sociology 2, dreams of being a debutante out of F. Scott Fitzgerald; and the thin-chested freshman, still troubled by acne, dreams of being a granite-jawed Neanderthal out of Mickey Spillane. When the Parthians in 53 B.C. beat Crassus, they found in the baggage of Roman officers some very juicy items called *Milesian Tales,* by a certain Aristides of Miletus; and I have a friend who in A.D. 1944 supplemented his income as a GI by reading aloud a juicy novel, *Forever Amber,* by a certain Kathleen Winsor, to buddies who found that the struggle over three-syllable words somewhat impaired their dedication to that improbable daydream.

And that is what, for all of us, fiction, in one sense, is—a daydream. It is, in other words, an imaginative enactment. In it we find, in imagination, not only the pleasure of recognizing the world we know and of reliving our past, but also the pleasure of entering worlds we do not know and of experimenting with experiences which we deeply crave but which the limitations of life, the fear of consequences, or the severity of our principles forbid to us. Fiction can give us this pleasure without any painful consequences, for there is no price tag on the magic world of imaginative enactment. But fiction does not give us only what we want; more importantly, it may give us things we hadn't even known we wanted.

In this sense, then, fiction painlessly makes up for the defects of reality. Long ago Francis Bacon said that poetry—which, in his meaning, would include our fiction—is "agreeable to the spirit of man" because it affords "a greater grandeur of things, a more perfect order, and a more beautiful variety" than can "anywhere be found in nature. . . ." More recently we find Freud putting it that the "meagre satisfactions" that man "can extract from reality leave him starving," and John Dewey saying that art "was born of need, lack, deprivation, incompleteness." But philosophers aside, we all know entirely too well how much we resemble poor Walter Mitty.

If fiction is—as it clearly is for some readers—merely a fantasy to redeem the liabilities of our private fate, it is flight from reality and therefore the enemy of growth, of the life process. But is it necessarily this? Let us look at the matter in another way.

The daydream which is fiction differs from the ordinary daydream in being publicly available. This fact leads to consequences. In the private daydream you remain yourself—though nobler, stronger, more fortunate, more beautiful than in life. But when the little freshman settles cozily with his thriller by Mickey Spillane, he finds that the granite-jawed hero is not named Slim Willett, after all—as poor Slim, with his thin chest, longs for it to be. And Slim's college instructor, settling down to *For Whom the Bell Tolls,* finds sadly that this other college instructor, who is the hero of the famous tale of sleeping bags, bridge demolition, tragic love and lonely valor, is named Robert Jordan.

In other words, to enter into that publicly available daydream which fiction is, you have to accept the fact that the name of the hero will never be your own; you will have to surrender something of your own identity to him, have to let it be absorbed in him. But since that kind of daydream is not exquisitely custom-cut to the exact measure of your secret longings, the identification can never be complete. In fact, only a very naïve reader tries to make it thrillingly complete. The more sophisticated reader plays a deep double game with himself; one part of him is identified with a character—or with several in turn—while another part holds aloof to respond, interpret, and judge. How often have we heard some sentimental old lady say of a book: "I just loved the heroine—I mean I just went through everything with her and I knew exactly how she felt. Then when she died I just cried." The sweet old lady, even if she isn't very sophisticated, is instinctively playing the double game too: she identifies herself with the heroine, but she survives the heroine's death to shed the delicious tears. So even the old lady knows how to make the most of what we shall call her role-taking. She knows that doubleness, in the very act of identification, is of the essence of role-taking: there is the taker of the role and there is the role taken. And fiction is, in imaginative enactment, a role-taking.

For some people—those who fancy themselves hardheaded and realistic—the business of role-taking is as reprehensible as indulgence in a daydream. But in trying to understand our appetite for fiction, we can see that the process of role-taking not only stems from but also affirms the life process. It is an essential part of growth.

Role-taking is, for instance, at the very center of children's play. This beginning of the child's long process of adaptation to others, for only by feeling himself into another person's skin can the child predict behavior; and the stakes in the game are high, for only thus does he learn whether to expect the kiss or the cuff. In this process of role-taking we find, too, the roots of many of the massive intellectual structures we later rear—most obviously psychology and ethics, for it is only by role-taking that the child comes to know, to know "inwardly" in the only way that finally counts, that other people really exist and are, in fact, persons with needs, hopes, fears, and even rights. So the role-taking of fiction, at the same time that it gratifies our deep need to extend and enrich our own experience, continues this long discipline in human sympathy. And this discipline in sympathy, through the imaginative enactment of role-taking, gratifies another need deep in us: our yearning to enter and feel at ease in the human community.

Play when we are children, and fiction when we are grown up, lead us, through role-taking, to an awareness of others. But all along the way, role-taking leads us, by the same token, to an awareness of ourselves; it leads us, in fact, to the creation of the self. For the individual is not born with a self. He is born as a mysterious bundle of possibilities which, bit by bit, in a long process of trial and error, he sorts out until he gets some sort of unifying self, the ringmaster self, the official self.

The official self emerges, but the soul, as Plato long ago put it, remains full of "ten thousand opposites occurring at the same time," and modern psychology has said nothing to contradict him. All our submerged selves, the old desires and possibilities, are lurking deep in us, sleepless and eager to have another go. There is knife-fighting in the inner dark. The fact that most of the time we are not aware of trouble does not mean that trouble is any the less present and significant; and fiction, most often in subtly disguised forms, liberatingly reenacts for us such inner conflict. We feel the pleasure of liberation even when we cannot specify the source of the pleasure.

Fiction brings up from their dark oubliettes our shadowy, deprived selves and gives them an airing in, as it were, the prison yard. They get a chance to participate, each according to his nature, in the life which fiction presents. When in Thackeray's *Vanity Fair* the girl Becky Sharp, leaving school for good, tosses her copy of Doctor Johnson's *Dictionary* out of the carriage, something in our own heart leaps gaily up, just as something rejoices at her later sexual and pecuniary adventures in Victorian society, and suffers, against all our sense of moral justice, when she comes a cropper. When Holden Caulfield, of Salinger's *Catcher in the Rye,* undertakes his gallant and absurd little crusade against the "phony" in our world, our own nigh-doused idealism flares up again, for the moment without embarrassment. When in Faulkner's *Light in August* Percy Grimm pulls the trigger of the black blunt-nosed automatic and puts that tight, pretty little pattern of slugs in the top of the over-turned table behind which Joe Christmas cowers, our trigger finger tenses, even while, at the same time, with a strange joy of release and justice satisfied, we feel those same slugs in our heart. When we read Dostoevski's *Crime and Punishment,* something in our nature participates in the bloody deed, and later, something else in us experiences, with the murderer Raskolnikov, the bliss of repentance and reconciliation.

For among our deprived selves we must confront the redeemed as well as the damned, the saintly as well as the wicked; and strangely enough, either confrontation may be both humbling and strengthening. In having some awareness of the complexity of self we are better prepared to deal with that self. As a matter of fact, our entering into the fictional process helps to redefine the dominant self, even, as it were, to re-create, on a sounder basis—sounder because better understood—the dominant self, the official "I." As Henri Bergson says, fiction "brings us back into our own presence"—the presence in which we must make our final terms with life and death.

The knowledge in such confrontations does not ordinarily come to us with intellectual labels. We don't say, "Gosh, I've got fifteen percent of sadism in me"—or thirteen percent of unsuspected human charity. No, the knowledge comes as enactment; and as imaginative enactment, to use our old phrase, it comes as knowledge. Even if it comes merely as a heightened sense of being, as the conflict in the story evokes the conflict in ourselves, evokes it with some hopeful sense of meaningful resolution, and with, therefore, an exhilarating sense of freedom.

Part of this sense of freedom derives, to repeat ourselves, from the mere fact that in imagination we are getting off scot-free with something which we, or society, would never permit in real life; from the fact that our paradoxical relation to experience presented in fiction—our involvement and noninvolvement at the same time—gives a glorious feeling of mastery over the game of life. But there is something more important that contributes to this sense of freedom, the expansion and release that knowledge always brings; and in fiction we are permitted to know in the deepest way, by imaginative participation, things which we would otherwise never know—including ourselves. We are free from the Garden curse: we may eat of the Tree of Knowledge, and no angel with flaming sword will necessarily appear.

But in the process of imaginative enactment we have, in another way, that sense of freedom that comes from knowledge. The image that fiction presents is purged of the distractions, confusions, and accidents of ordinary life. We can now gaze at the inner logic of things—of a personality, of the consequences of an act or a thought, of a social or historical situation, of a lived life. One of our deepest cravings is to find logic in experience, but in real life, how little of our experience comes to us in such a manageable form!

We have all observed how a person who has had a profound shock needs to tell the story of the event over and over again, every detail. By telling it he objectifies it, disentangling himself, as it were, from the more intolerable effects. This objectifying depends, partly at least, on the fact that the telling is a way of groping for the logic of the event, an attempt to make the experience intellectually manageable. If a child—or a man—who is in a state of blind outrage at his fate can come to understand that the fate which had seemed random and gratuitous is really the result of his own previous behavior or is part of the general pattern of life, his emotional response is modified by that intellectual comprehension. What is intellectually manageable is, then, more likely to be emotionally manageable.

This fiction is a "telling" in which we as readers participate and is, therefore, an image of the process by which experience is made manageable. In this process experience is foreshortened, is taken out of the ruck of time, is put into an ideal time where we can scrutinize it, is given an interpretation. In other words, fiction shows, as we have said, a logical—and psychological—structure which implies a meaning. By showing a logical structure, it relieves us, for the moment at least, of what we sometimes feel as the greatest and most mysterious threat of life—the threat of the imminent but "unknowable," of the urgent but "unsayable." In so far as a work of fiction is original and not merely a conventional repetition of the known and predictable, it is a movement through the "unknowable" toward the "knowable"—the imaginatively knowable. It says the "unsayable."

This leads us, as a sort of aside, to the notion that fiction sometimes seems to be, for the individual or for society, prophetic. Now looking back, we can clearly see how Melville, Dostoevski, James, Proust, Conrad, and Kafka tried to deal with some of the tensions and problems which have become characteristic of our time. In this sense they foretold our world—and even more importantly, forefelt it. They even forefelt us.

Or let us remember that F. Scott Fitzgerald and Hemingway did not merely report a period, they predicted it in that they sensed a new mode of behavior and feeling. Fiction, by seizing on certain elements in its time and imaginatively pursuing them with the unswerving logic of projected enactment, may prophesy the next age. We know this from looking back on fiction of the past. More urgently, we unconsciously turn to fiction of our own time to help us envisage the time to come and our relation to it.

But let us turn to more specific instances of that inner logic which fiction may reveal. In *An American Tragedy,* Dreiser shows us in what subtle and pitiful ways the materialism of America and the worship of what William James called the "bitch-goddess Success" can corrupt an ordinary young man and bring him to the death cell. In *Madame Bovary,* Flaubert shows us the logic by which Emma's yearning for color and meaning in life leads to the moment when she gulps the poison. In both novels we sense this logic most deeply because we, as we have seen, are involved, are accomplices. We, too, worship the bitch-goddess—as did Dreiser. We, too, have yearnings like Emma's, and we remember that Flaubert said that he himself was Emma Bovary.

We see the logic of the enacted process, and we also see the logic of the end. Not only do we have now, as readers, the freedom that leads to a knowledge of the springs of action; we have also the more difficult freedom that permits us to contemplate the consequences of action and the judgment that may be passed on it. For judgment, even punishment, is the end of the logic we perceive. In our own personal lives, as we well know from our endless secret monologues of extenuation and alibi, we long to escape from judgment; but here, where the price tag is only that of imaginative involvement, we can accept judgment. We are reconciled to the terrible necessity of judgment—upon our surrogate. In the story, it is our whipping boy and scapegoat that receives the punishment. We find a moral freedom in this fact that we recognize a principle of justice, with also perhaps some gratification of the paradoxical desire to suffer.

It may be objected here that we speak as though all stories were stories of crime and punishment. No, but all stories, from the gayest farce to the grimmest tragedy, are stories of action and consequence—which amounts to the same thing. All stories, as we have said, are based on conflict; and the resolution of the fictional conflict is, in its implications, a judgment too, a judgment of values. In the end some shift of values has taken place. Some new awareness has dawned, some new possibility of attitude has been envisaged. Or perhaps some old value is vindicated.

Not that the new value is necessarily "new" in a literal sense. The point, to come back to an old point, is that the reader has, by imaginative enactment, lived through the process by which the values become valuable. What might have been merely an abstraction has become vital, has been lived, and is, therefore, "new"— new because newly experienced. We can now rest in the value as experienced; we are reconciled in it; and that is what counts.

It is what counts, for in the successful piece of fiction, a comic novel by Peter de Vries or a gut-tearing work like Tolstoy's *War and Peace,* we feel, in the end, some sense of reconciliation with the world and with ourselves. And this process of moving through conflict to reconciliation is an echo of our own life process. The life process, as we know it from babyhood on, from our early relations with our parents on to our adult relation with the world, is a long process of conflict and reconciliation. This process of enriching and deepening experience is a pattern of oscillation—a pattern resembling that of the lovers' quarrel. When lovers quarrel, each asserts a special ego against that of the beloved and then in the moment of making up finds more keenly than before the joy of losing the self in the love of another. So in fiction we enter imaginatively a situation of difficulty and estrangement—a problematic situation that, as we have said earlier, sharpens our awareness of life—and moves through it to a reconciliation which seems fresh and gratifying.

Reconciliation—that is what we all, in some depth of being, want. All religion, all philosophy, all psychiatry, all ethics involve this human fact. And so does fiction. If fiction begins in daydream, if it relieves us from the burden of being ourselves, it ends, if it is good fiction and we are good readers, by returning us to the world and to ourselves. It reconciles us with reality, or helps us deal with reality.

Let us pause to take stock. Thus far what we have said sounds as though fiction were a combination of opium addiction, religious conversion without tears, a home course in philosophy, and the poor man's psychoanalysis. But it is not; it is fiction.

It is only itself, and that *itself* is not, in the end, a mere substitute for anything else. It is an art—an image of experience formed in accordance with its own laws of imaginative enactment, laws which, as we have seen, conform to our deep needs. It is an "illusion of life" projected through language, and the language is that of some individual man projecting his own feeling of life.

The story, in the fictional sense, is not something that exists of and by itself, out in the world like a stone or a tree. The materials of stories—certain events or characters, for example—may exist out in the world, but they are not fictionally meaningful to us until a human mind has shaped them. We are, in other words, like the princess in one of Hans Christian Andersen's tales; she refuses her suitor when she discovers that the bird with a ravishing song which he has offered as a token of love is only a real bird, after all. We, like the princess, want an artificial bird—an artificial bird with a real song. So we go to fiction because it is a *created* thing.

Because fiction is created by a man, it draws us, as human beings, by its human significance. To begin with, it is an utterance, in words. No words, no story. This seems a fact so obvious, and so trivial, as not to be worth the saying, but it is of fundamental importance in the appeal fiction has for us. We are creatures of words, and if we did not have words, we would have no inner life. Only because we have words can we envisage and think about experience. We find our human nature through words. So in one sense we may say that in so far as the language of the story enters into the expressive whole of the story, we find the deep satisfaction, conscious or unconscious, of a fulfillment of our very nature. It is important to remember this when we see the actual play made from fiction. When the medium changes from page to stage, the final impact changes. Not entirely, but significantly. A change in form is, ultimately, a change in meaning.

As an example of the relation of words, of style, to the expressive whole which is fiction, let us take Hemingway. We readily see how the stripped, laconic, monosyllabic style relates to the tight-lipped, stoical ethic, the cult of self-discipline, the physicality and the anti-intellectualism and the other such elements that enter into his characteristic view of the world. Imagine Henry James writing Hemingway's story *The Killers.* The complicated sentence structure of James, the deliberate and subtle rhythms, the careful parentheses—all these things express the delicate intellectual, social, and aesthetic discriminations with which James concerned himself. But what in the Lord's name would they have to do with the shocking blankness of the moment when the gangsters enter the lunchroom, in their tight-buttoned identical blue overcoats, with gloves on their hands so as to leave no fingerprints when they kill the Swede?

The style of a writer represents his stance toward experience, toward the subject of his story; and it is also the very flesh of our experience of the story, for it is the flesh of our experience as we read. Only through his use of words does the story come to us. As with language, so with the other aspects of a work of fiction. Everything there—the proportioning of plot, the relations among characters, the logic of motivation, the speed or retardation of the movement—is formed by a human mind into what it is, into what, if the fiction is successful, is an expressive whole, a speaking pattern, a form. And in recognizing and participating in this form, we find gratification, though often an unconscious one, as fundamental as any we have mentioned.

We get a hint of the fundamental nature of this gratification in the fact that among primitive peoples, decorative patterns are developed long before the first attempts to portray the objects of nature, even those things on which the life of the tribe depended. The pattern images a rhythm of life and intensifies the tribesman's sense of life.

Or we find a similar piece of evidence in psychological studies made of the response of children to comic books. "It is not the details of development," the researchers tell us, "but rather the general aura which the child finds fascinating." What the child wants is the formula of the accelerating buildup of tension followed by the glorious release when the righteous Superman appears just in the nick of time. What the child wants, then, is a certain "shape" of experience. Is his want, at base, different from our own?

At base, no. But if the child is satisfied by a nearly abstract pattern for the feelings of tension and release, we demand much more. We, too, in the build and shape of experience, catch the echo of the basic rhythm of our life. But we know that the world is infinitely more complicated than the child thinks. We, unlike the child, must scrutinize the details of development, the contents of life and of fiction. So the shaping of experience to satisfy us must add to the simplicity that satisfies the child something of the variety, roughness, difficulty, subtlety, and delight which belongs to the actual business of life and our response to it.

We want the factual richness of life absorbed into the pattern so that content and form are indistinguishable in one expressive flowering, in the process that John Dewey says takes "life and experience in all its uncertainties, mystery, doubt and half-knowledge and turns that experience upon itself to deepen and intensify its own qualities." Only then will it satisfy our deepest need—the need of feeling our life to be, in itself, significant.

SECTION

II

HAWTHORNE REVISITED:

SOME REMARKS ON

HELL-FIREDNESS

He [Hawthorne] says NO! in thunder; but the Devil himself cannot make him say *yes.* For all men who say *yes,* lie; and all men who say *no*—why, they are in the happy condition of judicious, unencumbered travellers in Europe; they cross the frontiers into Eternity with nothing but a carpetbag,—that is to say, the Ego.

—Herman Melville

THE RELATION OF Hawthorne to himself, to his own work, to the public world which he addressed, and, in the end, to the fame which he found in the world, was, in each case, a teasing, uneasy, and paradoxical one; and this fact provided him with his recurrent theme, his fundamental insight, and his obsession. He lived in the right ratio—right for the fueling of his genius—between an attachment to his region and a detached assessment of it; between attraction to the past and its repudiation; between attraction to the world and contempt for its gifts; between a powerful attraction to women and a sexual flinch; between a faith in life and a corrosive skepticism; between a capacity for affection and an innate coldness; between aesthetic passion and moral concern; between a fascinated attentiveness to the realistic texture, forms, and characteristics of nature and human nature, and a compulsive flight from that welter of life toward abstract ideas; and between, most crucially of all, a

First published in *The Sewanee Review,* Winter 1973, as "Hawthorne Revisited."

deep knowledge of himself and an ignorance of himself instinctively cultivated in a fear of the darker potentialities of self.

The drama of such subjective tensions is played out objectively in the work. Hawthorne is the first American writer of fiction in whose work we can sense the inner relation of life to fiction; we may say, in fact, that Hawthorne discovered American literature in its inwardness, and that, in one sense, this role was as important as the work itself. Thus we may think of Hawthorne as a "culture hero"—the man discovering and enacting a role that changes the possibilities of a society, a role involving the deep sensibility by which experience may be newly grasped and values framed.

Hawthorne was born in Salem, Massachusetts, on July 4, 1804, of a family that had been prominent in the early days of the colony. The early "Hathornes" (Nathaniel was the first of the family to add the *w*) were, it seems, of that type of "black, masterful men," as D. H. Lawrence calls them in *Studies in Classic American Literature,* who, in a "black revulsion" from the Old World, came over a "black sea." The founder of the family, William Hathorne, who arrived in 1630, "the bearded, sable-cloaked, and steeple-crowned progenitor" whom Hawthorne describes in the preamble to *The Scarlet Letter,* won fame as a soldier and judge, and as Mayor Hathorne appears in Hawthorne's sketch "Main Street," ordering a certain Quaker, Anne Coleman, to be bound to the tail of a cart and given ten stripes in Salem, ten in Boston, and ten in Dedham, and then driven off into the forest. By 1804, however, the renown and prosperity of the family were in sad eclipse, and when four years later Hawthorne's father, a young sea captain, died at Surinam, his widow and three children were left dependent upon her relatives.

Certainly this contrast between the great past and the meager present had something to do with the boy's cast of mind. We hear of the self-aggrandizing fantasies which he told his sisters as tales to amuse them. And such tales were the first manifestations of the nostalgic appeal of a lost glory and a lost certainty of mission, the sense of a curse intertwined with the glory of the past, the proud alienation from the people who now occupied the big houses with less legitimate claim than a "Hathorne," the angry, compensatory ambition which, in itself, might be mystically accursed and which, therefore, should be denied in a ferocious, programmatic modesty.

Hawthorne's isolation drew something not only from the fact of the family's collapse but from the way the other members of the family responded to it. The mother, a very young woman, withdrew into a grim and lifelong ritual of widowhood, isolating herself even in the isolation of the family. We do not know the precise relationship between Hawthorne and his mother—"whose grief," he reports, "outlasted even its vitality, and grew to be merely a torpid habit, and was saddest then"—but we do know that it was charged in a way which Hawthorne himself did not even suspect until his sudden and overmastering emotion at her death released him, as Mark Van Doren has suggested, for the supreme effort of composing *The Scarlet Letter,* the most moving and deeply human of his works.

At Bowdoin College, in the backwoods of Maine, not at fashionable Harvard, Hawthorne was "an idle student," as he was to say of himself, "negligent of college rules and the Procrustean details of academic life, rather choosing to nurse my own fancies than to dig into Greek roots." He belonged to the Athenaean literary society, which was "progressive" and "infected" with Jacksonian democracy, and there, too, he found his devoted friends, loyal Democrats too—Jonathan Cilley, Franklin Pierce, and Horatio Bridge. Longfellow was then in Bowdoin with precocious fame as scholar and poet, but Hawthorne's preference for Cilley and Pierce, who were to become politicians, and for Bridge, who was to be a naval officer, conforms to a pattern in his character and life; he yearned, as he himself was to put it, to be "a man in society," to learn "the deep, warm secret" by which other people seemed to live but which somehow eluded him. That secret was one possessed by active men, the kind of men he was to prefer to associate with, or, more commonly, to observe.

As for his attitude toward himself, he once wrote his sister Louisa: "I have thought much upon the subject, and have finally come to the conclusion that I shall never make a distinguished figure in the world, and all I hope or wish is to plod along with the multitude." As though mere averageness could impart the "deep, warm secret, the life within the life." If this letter to Louisa is straightforward and serious, there is in other letters of the period, as some biographers have pointed out, an element of irony, banter, and perverseness that would seem to screen the depth in which he fought out this issue—and other issues—with himself. And Cilley wrote of him: "I love Hawthorne; I admire him; but I do not know him. He lives in a mysterious world of thought and imagination which he never permits me to enter."

We have some evidence that in that "mysterious world" Hawthorne was facing the threat of his own ambition. Among other glimpses, we have that afforded by the title character of Hawthorne's first novel, *Fanshawe,* a college story written shortly after he left Bowdoin, published anonymously, at the author's expense, in 1828, and then withdrawn; Fanshawe, the author writes,

> had hitherto deemed himself unconnected with the world, unconcerned in its feelings, and uninfluenced by it in any of his pursuits. In this respect he probably deceived himself. If his inmost heart could have been laid open, there would have been discovered that dream of undying fame, which, dream as it is, is more powerful than a thousand realities.

With such a "dream" Hawthorne, immediately after college, locked himself up in a southwest room on the third floor of a house on Herbert Street, in Salem. This was the famous "dismal chamber" under the eaves, where he isolated himself to discover his materials, his style, and his destiny.

In *Mosses from an Old Manse,* in a sketch called "A Select Party," appears a young man in poor attire who turns out to be "the Master Genius for whom our country is looking anxiously into the mist of time." The Genius, it develops,

> dwells as yet unhonored among men, unrecognized by those who have known him from his cradle; the noble countenance which should be distinguished by a halo diffused around it passes daily amid the throng of people toiling and troubling themselves about the trifles of a moment, and none pay reverence to the worker of immortality.

And here is as good a statement as any of the life Hawthorne led in the thirteen years in Salem, passing "unhonored" and "unrecognized." He read widely, by one account every book in the library of the Salem Athenaeum—where he wouldn't go himself but sent his sister Elizabeth to fetch his reading matter. Isolated even from his mother and two sisters, even at meals sometimes, he worked day after day, going out late, often after dark, for an hour, whatever the weather, coming back to sup on a pint bowl of chocolate full of crumbled bread. In the summer he always took a trip, in New England, looking at the country and at all those strange folk who had the "deep, warm secret," putting down in his notebooks the fruit of his scrupulous observation just as though he would be able to write of such characters. And over the years, in a mood "half savage, half despairing," as Bridge puts it, he kept on writing. He was soaked, of course, in Latin, English, and French literature, and made a special study of the novel, but we know that he especially soaked himself in the history of New England, in Felt's *Annals of Salem* and Cotton Mather's *Magnalia Christi Americana,* in which, as he put it, "true events and real personages move before the reader with the dreamy aspect which they wore in Cotton Mather's singular mind"—and were to wear in his own singular mind.

After five years of grinding discipline, Hawthorne was ready to give up his aspirations, but in 1830, a sketch, "The Hollow of Three Hills," was published in the Salem *Gazette,* and a little later "The Gentle Boy" was accepted by Samuel Griswold Goodrich, the publisher of the *Token,* one of the popular annuals of the period, those handsomely got-up little collections of romantic, sentimental, moralistic, and humorous tales, essays, and engravings. This was a start. But even if for the next several years Hawthorne's work regularly appeared there (over such pen names as Ashley A. Boyce, Oberon, M. Aubépine, and "The Author of 'The Gentle Boy' "), money remained a serious problem for the now not so young author, and, worse, with his increasing sense of being estranged from normal experience, he began to feel himself a failure as a man.

But in 1837 the turn came. His Bowdoin friend Horatio Bridge secretly underwrote, to the amount of $250, the publication of a collection of his pieces, *Twice-Told Tales.* Longfellow wrote a fatuously uncomprehending but laudatory review of it in the influential *North American Review,* and the fame began.

· · ·

What had Hawthorne actually achieved during the dozen years of his apprenticeship? Let us look at several pieces of the period, beginning with a fumbling example of his art, "Alice Doane's Appeal." Though Hawthorne never thought well enough of this to put it in a collection, it is, in its very crudity, instructive, for it shows how Hawthorne, even in the early years, was reaching toward his subject and his insight. Here are the elements of incest, patricide, witchcraft, the haunted mind and the secret guilt, murder, the rising of the dead; all the elements from the Gothic romances are present, but they are already domesticated, put into seventeenth-century New England.

Here Hawthorne is already aiming at a "thickness" of effect and meaning in his work, with reference at many levels—at the ethical, the personal and psychological, the social, the historical. He wants the story to exist, as it were, as a tissue of interrelated meanings— the "meanings" somehow to be a reflex of their interrelations, in the interfusion of the "actual circumstance of life" and what in "The Hollow of Three Hills," another early piece, he called "dreams and madmen's reveries." But he would have said that truth can lie in such dreams and reveries and would have known that the dreamer and the madman was himself.

As much as Poe, Hawthorne was a pioneer in that kind of hallucinatory fiction which is characteristic of modernity. But he was also pioneering his own fiction, laying hand to themes and methods which allowed him to achieve the mastery of such stories as "The Gentle Boy" (1828), "Roger Malvin's Burial" (1830), "My Kinsman, Major Molineux" (1832), and "Young Goodman Brown" (1835). These pieces, too, belong to Hawthorne's young manhood, and in them it is easy to see what prompted him to write, in 1851, in the letter dedicating *The Snow Image* to Bridge:

> In youth, men are apt to write more easily than they really know or feel; and the remainder of life may be art idly spent in realizing and convincing themselves of the wisdom which they uttered long ago. The truth that was only in the fancy then may have since become substance in the mind and heart.

Here Hawthorne is saying that unconsciously—literally, out of the unconscious—a writer may find the meaning and the method which later, consciously, he may explore and develop; that is, in writing, a man may be discovering, among other things, himself. To have intuited this truth was one of Hawthorne's most brilliant achievements. But the truth, once intuited, was one that he could rarely bring himself to contemplate for long, and that gives us another of the deep paradoxes in his life and work. The work that reveals may also be used to conceal.

"The Gentle Boy" is one of the first tales in which Hawthorne's special power appears. Let us examine it as a precursor of *The Scarlet Letter.* It has the same deep grounding in the past, it presents the same outrage to humanity which Hawthorne considered implicit in Puritan society, and we can easily find here the qualities which make Austin Warren say that Hawthorne's "pictures are ancestral and prophetic"; and we can find, too, the same ambivalence toward the past which Hawthorne expressed in "Main Street": "Let us thank God for having given us such ancestors; and let each successive generation thank Him, not less fervently for being one step further from them in the march of ages." But at first glance the story seems to be a piece of straight realism, an episode from actual history, treated at the level of actuality without the tangential reference to "dreams" and "reveries." This literal singleness of vision is, in a way, deceptive, for there is another kind of depth which connects it with the more symbolic stories.

We may approach this notion by asking how ideas of good and bad are deployed in the story. Casually regarded, the story would seem to present the inhuman Puritan rigor, of the sort we find in "The Maypole of Merry Mount" and *The Scarlet Letter,* set over against a gentle and humane Quakerism. We remember, however, that even in the historical introduction Hawthorne indicates a balancing of the "bad" between Puritans and Quakers. Let us look at the first sentence: "In the course of the year 1656, several of the people called Quakers, led, as they professed, by the inward movement of the spirit, made their appearance in New England." We cannot miss the irony in the phrase "as they professed" and so must consider what is the real content of "the inward movement of the spirit." Hawthorne then proceeds to say of the Quakers that their "enthusiasm, heightened almost to madness by the treatment which they received, produced actions contrary to the rules of decency, as well as of rational religion"—and there, though there may also be irony directed against the Puritans in the phrase "rational religion," the criticism of the Quakers is manifest. Furthermore, when Hawthorne mentions the execution of the father of the "Boy" and his fellow Quaker, he says that the Puritan government had "indulged" the victims, and his irony is double-edged, one edge being set against the motivations—we might say the combination of masochism and arrogance—in the victims themselves. We may recall, too, how Hawthorne says of the Quakers that the "revengeful feelings were not less deep because they were inactive" or refers to Catharine's "unbridled fanaticism" and her "fierce and vindictive nature." As Hawthorne says elsewhere, the human being is better rendered by the wishes of the heart than by actions.

There is another criticism of the Quakers important in the story. Their fanaticism violates the "duties of the present life," that "deep, warm secret, the life within the life"; and this violation would be an example of the "unpardonable sin" which Hawthorne defines in his journal as "a want of love and reverence for the Human Soul," and which appears often in his work. In other words, though the Puritan rigor commits the same violation in a more obvious, objective, and brutal fashion, the Quaker, for all his professions, is no better. He, too, commits what we may call the sin of abstraction, of setting a scheme, a principle, against the human warmth.

This is not to say that life can be lived without abstractions, principles, schemes, theologies; but it is to say that in the polarity which Hawthorne here explores—that between abstractions, however high and noble in their intent, and the "deep, warm secret"— lies the potentiality of the most heartrending tragedy. And so we have the ironic pattern of this story: the two abstractions, Puritanism and Quakerism, though seeming to be contrasted, one on the side of rigor and arrogance, the other on the side of love and humility, in reality conspire to destroy the Gentle Boy with his fund of "unappropriated love"—love that such a world does not know how to appropriate.

Certainly the boy carrying this "unappropriated love" is set in contrast to the unloving world, but we must wonder, in the context of the ironies of the story, how absolute is even this contrast. One answer would seem to lie in the sentence concerning Ilbrahim:

"The disordered imaginations of both his father and mother had perhaps propagated a certain unhealthiness in the mind of the boy"—that is, his own taste for suffering, and the sense of suffering as a kind of inverted vengeance. This instinct would lead him, by a strand of hidden logic, to his friendship with another outcast, the cripple, and thus to the beating and his death. This irony can be paired with the more absolute irony in the fact that Catharine returns to her son and the "warm secret" only in the moment when she is ready to curse God for having "crushed my very heart in His Hand."

To sum up, the whole story, even according to this limited account, suggests appalling depths, both psychologically and philosophically, and it is hard to realize that for generations it was regarded as one of the author's more edifying and consoling productions. Hawthorne himself remarked of it that here he had been "led deeper into the universal heart than art has been able to follow." We can wonder if he ever knew exactly how deep.[1]

The story ends with a return to the historical perspective. The persecution of the Quakers is abated. Even Catharine has become, in the settlement, an object of acceptance and pity. The story, if left at this level, offers some notion of historical progress. But for the moment let us consider the qualifying phrases attached to the acceptance and pity which Catharine receives:

> When the course of years had made the features of the unobtrusive mourner familiar in the settlement, she became a subject of not deep, but general interest; a being on whom the otherwise superfluous sympathies of all might be bestowed. Everyone spoke to her with that degree of pity which it is pleasant to experience.

They were even ready to bury her "with decent sadness and tears that were not painful." We shall find this same irony at the end of *The Scarlet Letter* in the qualified victory which Hester achieves.

To generalize, we may say that in the acceptance which Catharine receives we do not find a change of heart, merely a change in

[1] For an elaborate psychoanalytic reading of the story, see Frederick C. Crews, *The Sins of the Fathers*.

behavior, which people may now adopt as an emotional indulgence, like the tears that are "not painful"; the change in behavior is caused merely by the fact that the issues which had originally provoked the violence have now changed, and that the violence remains, ready to be discharged elsewhere. We cannot, however, take this ironic view of history as one which Hawthorne dogmatically held; it, too, must be subjected to skeptical scrutiny, irony subjected to the test of irony, as we shall see in "My Kinsman, Major Molineux," which, in its view of history, is especially related to *The Scarlet Letter.*

In this connection, as an aside, we may guess that in Hawthorne's emotional involvement with the violence of the New England past is some feeling that in that violence there was at least a confronting of reality, which was lacking in the doctrines of Transcendentalists, Brook Farmers, and Unitarians, and in Emerson, along with the current horde of reformers. If there was violence and cruelty in that older society, there was also, in that very fact, a sense of reality and grim meaningfulness, something that paradoxically appealed to the Hawthorne who could not find the "warm secret," and who, by the same token, could write, in an early journal, of the contemporary world: "The fight with the world, this struggle of a man among men—the agony of the universal effort to wrench the means of a living from a host of greedy competitors—all this seems to be like a dream to me." But the past was not a dream. It had, literally, happened. And blood, for fundamental convictions, had been shed there—and by men who had, as demonstrated by that fact, a sense of "reality."

In "The Gentle Boy" there is a narrative of literal events, with an analysis of the quite literal characters. The author reasons inductively from this to certain general notions about human nature. But in "My Kinsman, Major Molineux," though the narrative has a literal dimension (Robin, a real lad, comes to the real city of Boston, and so on), certain elements, as we shall see, are inexplicable at a merely literal level; and this suggests that the literal elements are projections of a character's desires and dreams. We are dealing here with the interpenetration of the subjective and objective worlds, and the story is a "fable" rather than a "history." This difference, and the method by which psychological and moral "truths" are embodied rather than presented discursively, carries us closer to the center of Hawthorne's special genius.

"My Kinsman, Major Molineux" is obviously concerned with an initiation, Robin's struggle toward maturity. He comes to the city expecting to be protected by his father's cousin, but after certain mysterious and disturbing adventures, finds himself thrown on his own resources, given the option of remaining in the city to rise in the world, if he can, by his own exertions and merits. The story ends with the option open. Into this simple scheme flow and intermingle the various kinds of meaning.

One kind of interpretation which, according to a number of critics, is involved is what we may somewhat loosely term the Freudian. Critics who take this approach to the story say, characteristically, that the overt content does not account for its great force, that we must look for the elements that play upon the unconscious of the reader (however consciously the author may or may not have worked such elements into the story). By this reading, the story presents a young man in typical rebellion—and, as is typical, a largely unconscious rebellion—against the repressive figure of the father, with more or less emphasis on an implicit Oedipal conflict; and this theme is, as is sometimes reductively insisted, of central importance in Hawthorne's work.

To summarize this reading, we begin by pointing out that more than the literal father is involved; various persons take a paternal role. First, there is the kinsman in town, who represents not only help and protection, but authority. The vigorous lad, though wanting help, also characteristically wants freedom and unconsciously postpones as long as possible the finding of the kinsman. For example, he "forgets," in a typically Freudian fashion, to ask the ferryman the way to Molineux's house. When he does accost a stranger, he is rebuffed with what appears to be irrational violence, and the scene provokes, from the barber's helpers who see it, the first outburst of that inimical laughter that will accompany Robin's progress.

Here, if the story is to make sense, we must ask the meaning of the man's rebuff of Robin. The man is "in years," habitually strikes his staff down with a peremptory perpendicular thrust, and regularly utters "two successive hems" of a "sepulchral" intonation; furthermore, when for no good reason he threatens Robin with the stocks, he says, "I have authority, I have—hem-hem—authority." So the old man is another image of the father. In the tavern (where Robin is drawn as much by the smell of food as by desire for directions and where he promises himself he will sit some day, that is, when he is "grown up"), he again encounters a threatening figure in the man with the bulging forehead, and when he mentions to the tavernmaster his kinsman's name, the previously obsequious fellow threatens him as though he were a lad running away from indenture; Robin is, in fact, in his half-avowed desires, a runaway bondservant—that is, a "son"—and in one sense, Robin "dreams" the threat.

For a time now Robin makes no further effort to get directions, this with some shadow of justification after the rebuffs; but when we reach the mean streets, we begin to sense more completely that the rebuffs provide him with an alibi for acting on his secret desires. Here he certainly could not expect to find the house of Molineux, and when he encounters the pretty trollop with the red petticoat, the inviting eye, and the absurdly improbable story of this being the house of the rich Major, and the Major asleep upstairs, it begins to emerge that what Robin is really seeking is sexual freedom. But, dismissing the merely literal level, is it so absurdly improbable that the trollop should say that this is the Major's house? For the Major is a "father," and is not this the "dream" version, the "projection," of the son's fascinated and envious feelings about the father's sexual world? And by this token, the inviting prostitute, the father's mistress, is the projection of the son's secret Oedipal desires—desires which he knows are guilty, for at some sound the woman suddenly releases his hand and disappears. Then suddenly there appears the watch, threatening him with the stocks, and his sense of guilt is thus embodied in another father figure, armed with his significant iron-shod stave.

After the nightmare scene of the street deserted by all except the wandering bands of men with outlandish attire and strange gibberish, Robin again encounters the man with the bulging forehead from the tavern, who had seemed to have some strange knowledge of him. His face now painted half black and half red "as if two individual devils, a fiend of fire and a fiend of darkness, had united themselves," the man greets him with another threat, but then, in a mysterious complicity, tells him to wait there and he will see his kinsman pass.

Now follows the scene of Robin's peering into the church window, where moonlight strikes the Bible, and Robin, in his guiltiness, is aware of the graves in the churchyard and his own loneliness—his sense of loss, in other words, of the old protection. Then, longing for that protection, he tries to imagine how his father and the family would have spent "that evening of ambiguity," in religious devotions and family affections; and in his distress at now being forever excluded from that circle—that is, at having to grow up—he cries out: "Am I here, or there?" Is he, in other words, grown up or not?

Waking from a confused dream, Robin sees another man and addresses him in a "lamentable cry" (no longer the brash and demanding adolescent, but the lost child), and the stranger speaks to him in a kind voice as "my good lad," in the role of a father to whom, now, Robin can tell his story. Then Robin hears the sound of the mob, which he at first takes to be "some prodigious merrymaking"—which in a sense it is, for there appears the Major, in the midst of the howling mob, on a cart, in "tarred-and-feathered dignity," his ruin the mark of the lad's secretly desired victory over the "father." But Robin is at first ambivalently struck by "pity and terror," before he bursts into the loudest laughter of all the throng, the throng which appears "as a dream broken forth from some feverish brain." The laughter is the mark of his release from the long inner struggle. Meanwhile, among all the figures of the evening who now reappear, there is the trollop in the red petticoat twitching his arm, to confirm, as it were, his victory.

But it is not yet quite a victory. After the street is empty of the throng, Robin, shaken and exhausted, wants to leave the city and asks the kindly gentleman the way to the ferry and, shall we say, the safety of home. Then the gentleman, the kindly father who no longer uses authority, gives him the option of remaining in the world and trying to rise without help—that is, to become an adult.

This summary has omitted certain relevant details. For instance, we may take the inimical laughter that follows Robin everywhere as not only an echo of his own guilt, but also as an echo of his fear and shame at the absurd temerity of his attempt to become a man. Again, the angry man who finally appears painted like a devil is to be the destroyer of the father, a devil to be feared as a mark of guilt but also the evil one who will do the lad's secretly wished work for him. And another corroborative detail appears in the oak cudgel, a phallic symbol, the natural woodsman's weapon with the threat of which the lad, in his callow arrogance, thinks to conquer all the complex difficulties of the city—that is, the adult world.

Assuming that some such account as this is acceptable as one line of the story, we may well ask what it stacks up to, what it, in itself, means. Is it merely descriptive, diagnostic, or does Hawthorne take some evaluative attitude toward this process inherent in life? The answer lies, it would seem, in an extension of the ambivalence of feeling in Robin himself. The process of repudiating the father—of growing up—is necessary; but in the very moment of victory, there is "pity and terror"—human pity, we are tempted to say, for the inevitable victim and terror for the self who, as human, is bound to undergo, in time, the same fate. In the life process, which in one perspective can be viewed as a "senseless uproar" and "frenzied merriment,"[2] there is, if we regard the victim as an individual, the trampling "on an old man's heart." To put it another way, remembering that "pity and terror" is the formulation sacred to tragedy, Hawthorne is seeing the natural life process as, in one perspective, tragic: pain is inevitably involved, and in the victim there is tragic dignity, like that of a "dead potentate, mighty no more but majestic in his agony"—even if the "majesty" is simply the illusion that is carried over from the nursery.

[2]We notice that the first old man whom Robin accosts, and whom we have here taken in the role of the authoritative father, now participates in the mirth at the Major's expense. Is there a contradiction between the role of father and this lack of sympathy with the dethronement of another "father," Molineux? Presumably not, for the victim is always isolated in his personal story, with all the rest of the world, including those who have suffered and will suffer, caught up in the wild and heartless celebration of the process. In any case, a role—say the role of the old man—is not fixed, is not an identity. As the wise and kindly father whom Robin last encounters says to him: "May not a man have several faces, Robin, as well as two complexions?"

This Freudian "meaning" is, as we have said, only one of the several which flow into the story, and it clearly does not account for all the elements in it. The Freudian approach deals with a natural process, presumably, but the process occurs in a social, moral, and philosophical context and, in fact, has come to exist only in such contexts. So we may look at the story in, for example, the light of its "moral" theme. Robin is initiated into adulthood, but the full initiation involves the confrontation with evil, not merely the Freudian guilts but evil as a force operative in the world and in the heart.

The boy came into the city armed with his club and his "shrewdness," but this is a world where neither force nor ordinary common sense avails. He is, as one critic, Daniel Hoffman, has put it (in *Form and Fable in American Fiction*), a kind of parody of the smart Yankee—Brother Jonathan, the peddlers of folk anecdote, Jack Downing, Sam Slick—and, we may add, of the hero posited by Emerson's essay "Self-Reliance." To quote Hoffman, Robin is "the Great American Boob, the naif whose odyssey leads him, all uncomprehending, into the dark center of experience." In his callow arrogance, and in his stupid trust in cudgel and shrewdness, Robin has not even been able to recognize the image of the Devil in the man with the painted face, and in the end, in his "mental inebriety," by his joining, by his shout ("the loudest there"), with the nightmare procession, he surrenders himself, for the moment in any case, to that horrid ringleader who had fixed his glance full upon him as he rode past. When he is left shaken and confused, ready to go home, the option the wise stranger leaves with him is the fundamental *moral* option: to go home that is, to flee into a dream of innocence, which would really be ignorance and cowardice—or to stay in the city and, in experience and moral awareness, to try to deal with the hard terms of actuality.

In the historical setting we find another line of meaning that flows into the story, a meaning identified by Queenie Leavis. The setting presents, in embryo, the story of revolution—the American Revolution. The kinsman is not only a "father," but also a royal governor, or at least a representative of such power. So in the historical theme we find a parallel to the Freudian and moral themes. The first feature of Hawthorne's treatment to strike us is the strange inversion of the officially patriotic view which occurs elsewhere in his work. Here the leader of the patriots is, in one aspect, the Devil, the patriots themselves are a dehumanized mob, a nightmare crew, and Molineux, politically the representative of oppression, appears "majestic still in his agony." In the interpretation of the historical process of revolution, we have a parallel with Hawthorne's attitude toward the "revolution" of achieving maturity: both involve a tragic paradox, there are human costs in the process, and both processes, like that of moral initiation, involve the problem of evil.

We must not take it, however, that the story necessarily implies that revolution, any more than the growing up of a lad, is wrong or bad. As a matter of fact, a strong case has been made, again by Daniel Hoffman, that the riotous and violent "merrymaking" is to be taken symbolically as a kind of Saturnalia, and the painted ring-leader as a Lord of Misrule; and this would imply that after the debauch, necessary to the rebirth of society, order will be restored and the roots of continuity rediscovered. If this idea is acceptable, it provides merely another ambiguity of the "night of ambiguities." It would in no wise cancel the import of the story that the part of wisdom is to recognize the paradoxical aspects of reality and to confront the tragic tension at its core. And we may take the story, too, as a rebuke to the easy chauvinism, the democratic mystique, the doctrine of manifest destiny, the belief in automatic progress, and the moral complacency parading as philosophy which characterized much American life of his time—and, it must be added, of our time, too.

Let us look at one last element in the story. Several critics have emphasized the importance of the inimical laughter which pursues Robin until the moment when he finally joins in that "tremendous ridicule." We have seen how, in one dimension, the laughter can be taken as an echo, self-directed, of Robin's fear, guilt, and shame; how, in another, it embodies the depersonalized cruelty of the natural and historical process; and how, in another, it expresses the purgation of the Saturnalia.

But as it aimlessly echoes through the complex arches and vaultings of the story, its most pervasive and profound effect, the effect to be emphasized here, is to establish a counterpoint of tonality for the meaning of the story. Anthony Trollope, writing in praise of

The Scarlet Letter, makes a remark that, at first glance, seems peculiar; he says that in the novel is "a touch of burlesque—not as to the suffering of the sufferers, but as to the great question whether it signifies much in what way we suffer. . . . Hawthorne seems to ridicule the very woes which he expends himself in depicting." And in *The House of the Seven Gables,* Hawthorne refers to the "tragic power of laughter." Of "My Kinsman, Major Molineux," we may even say, not too fancifully, that in the "tremendous ridicule" we hear the story laughing at itself, laughing so boisterously at the tragic awareness of life that the Man in the Moon, at his distance, or with his irony, finds all frolicsome. But this would be only one last ambiguity. For the tragic awareness would, in our human perspective, remain.

In considering the various themes that are involved in "My Kinsman, Major Molineux," we must, in the end, insist on the interpenetration of all the themes. After all, the story is quite solidly set in history and in the consciousness of Robin, and all the meanings are merely functions of his literal story. In other words, we are not dealing with the standard type of allegory but with a pervasive and massive symbolism, the basic symbol being the story itself, which, in its literalism, absorbs and fuses the various kinds of import. It is well to remember that in "The Antique Ring," when the storyteller is asked what thought he would embody in the ring, we have the answer: "You know that I can never separate the idea from the symbol in which it manifests itself."[3]

Hawthorne's earlier dip into Brook Farm (1841) had merely confirmed the bias of his genius, and his stay in Concord, to which he moved in 1843, was clearly a sojourn amid the alien corn. Of the high-minded community he recorded: "Never was a poor little country village infested with such a variety of queer, strangely dressed, oddly behaved mortals, most of whom took upon them-

---

[3] This notion is like the doctrine of symbolism of Coleridge, and other Romantics, who take the true symbol (as distinguished from the items of allegory) as "participating" in the "reality" which it represents. In this early story Hawthorne managed to create a fiction in which the symbol and the reality interfuse. In this connection, see, too, Paul Tillich's analysis of the symbolism of the Cross, in *Christ and Culture.* Hawthorne's notion of allegory is certainly not to be confused with Emerson's doctrine of correspondences.

selves to be important agents of the world's destiny, yet were simply bores of the first water." And even for Emerson, "that everlasting rejector of all that is, and seeker for he knows not what," Hawthorne remarked that earlier he could have demanded "of this prophet the master word that would solve me the riddle of the universe, but now, being happy, I felt as if there were no questions to be put, and therefore admired Emerson as a poet of deep beauty and austere tenderness, but sought nothing from him as a philosopher."

Hawthorne and Emerson could not, in fact, manage conversation together; Emerson put in his journal that Hawthorne's fiction was "not good for anything"; and Henry James, with remarkable precision of imagery, was to explain this lack of comprehension by saying that "Emerson, as a spiritual sun-worshipper, could have attached but a moderate value to Hawthorne's cat-like faculty of seeing in the dark." James added, by way of further explanation, that for Emerson the idea of sin was the "soul's mumps and measles"—a disease of childhood. It should be clear what Hawthorne would make of this.

Within two years Hawthorne had left Concord for the different kind of loneliness of Salem, where, in his natal spot, in the routine of his post as surveyor of customs, he could meditate his masterpiece. When in 1849 he lost his political appointment, he was ready to begin the actual writing. A few weeks later his mother died, and there followed the emotional upheaval which, he said, he himself could not understand. Some years later, looking back on this period of the composition of *The Scarlet Letter,* Hawthorne said that he was "in a very nervous state then, having gone through diversity of direction, while writing it. I think I have never overcome my adamant in any other instance."[4]

---

[4]This is a significant reference to the allegorical tale in *The Snow Image,* "The Man of Adamant." Richard Digby, a Puritan romantic obsessed with spiritual pride and suffering apparently from a disease by which calcium was deposited in his heart, withdraws into a sepulchral cave and refuses to be enticed forth by human love or any interpretation of religion different from his own; a century later his calcified form, "a repulsive personage," is found seated in the cave. To interpret Hawthorne's remark, then, we should say that before the death of his mother he had suffered from some stony inhibition of his emotional life, from which the shock of her death released him for his fullest expression. But it is not to be suggested that the death of the mother accounts for the conception of *The Scarlet Letter* or for the beginning of work on it. The death simply made certain forces available to the labor.

When Hawthorne read this new book to his wife, it "sent her to bed with a grievous headache"—as well it might, for there must have been a considerable shock to find revealed here a man who, in the years of marriage, she had never realized existed and whom she had been unable to sense behind the cool façade of the tales. The book was, as he dolorously put it, fearing that it would never be generally acceptable, "positively a hell-fired story, into which I found it almost impossible to throw a cheering light."

Why did Sophia Hawthorne take to her bed with a "grievous headache"? Why did Emerson, when asked what he thought of the novel, murmur, "Ghastly, ghastly"? Why did Julian Hawthorne declare, upon rereading the work, long after Hawthorne's death, that he found it impossible to reconcile the father he had known with the author of the fiction? And why did the author himself refer to it, in a different tonality, we may be sure, as "hell-fired"? The answer to these questions would bring us close to the significance of the novel, but the only way to approach an answer is through the novel itself.

The Scarlet Letter is another example of Hawthorne's inclination to treat violent materials in the long perspective of the past. In this work Hawthorne not only takes his materials from the past, in which the violence may be regarded at arm's length, but omits what might have been the most violently emotional phase of the story— the account of the growth of passion, the temptation, and the fall. Indeed, he does not even begin with the story itself, but with the introductory discussion of the custom house, which serves as a screen between the reader and the possible intensity of action, as a distancing device. Then, when he does enter the story proper, he opens with the first stage of the long train of consequences, the moment when Hester steps forth from the jail to face public shame. Even this is introduced by a kind of prologue, which puts the event in the perspective of meaning as contrasted with a direct shock to the emotions: the scene of the throng of men in "sad-colored garments" contrasted with the wild rose bush blooming at the very door of the jail, "in token that the deep heart of Nature could pity and be kind." So we have here in this contrast the first indication of the thematic tension, which represents an intellectualizing of emotion.

The same contrast is to be developed, more deeply and ironically, in the fact that the women waiting at the jail, who, as women, should "naturally" exhibit some sympathy and understanding for Hester's plight, are more savage than the men in their condemnation: that is, there is a contrast between their natural role and their social role. To continue, when Hester does appear, the scarlet *A* on her bosom presents a variation on the same thematic line; for, embroidered in gold thread with a "gorgeous luxuriance of fancy," it is—"naturally," shall we say?—an object of beauty, while socially considered it is a badge of infamy.

This set of contrasts, we shall see as the story develops, will lead us to another and deeper paradox, in that the act which is a "sin" is also presented as the source of deepened understanding and development. This, however, is to run ahead of ourselves, and for the moment what we see is that the woman who, we have learned from the crowd, is a creature to be reviled steps forth, surprisingly enough, in a beauty and pride which make "a halo of the misfortune and ignominy." The point here is simply to observe how freighted with meaning are the details of the narrative and how coherently these suggestions will be developed.

If we look at the first three chapters, we find a marvelously compact and exciting introductory section; for *The Scarlet Letter* is, in point of fact, the first American novel to be truly "composed," in the sense that we shall find Henry James using the term; that is, the first novel to consider form as, in itself, an expression of emotion and meaning. In connection with the structure of the novel, we must note that in this first scene Hester stands on the scaffold. This fact is of the deepest significance, for the scaffold is crucial to the whole conception. With this opening scene, the great scene of Dimmesdale's midnight vigil on it (in Chapter 12, at the middle of the novel), and the denouement and Dimmesdale's death on it at the end, the scaffold becomes the seminal image of the novel, the locus of both agony and vision.

Now, at the beginning, Hester, standing on the scaffold, experiences, in a flash of memory, the "entire track along which she had been treading since her happy infancy"—aware, however vaguely,

of a pattern in her fate. Across the crowd she suddenly sees the old
man who is her husband, and who, as though an incarnation of her
past, seems to be summoned by her thoughts of it. His identity is
not yet divulged to us, but from the sinister tone of his questioning
of a bystander, we get what exposition we need, getting it as an
action thrusting forward (as the old man, referring to Hester's
unknown partner in guilt, threatens, "He will be known"), not as
mere exposition. Then, as the apex of this "triangular" scene, we
first see Dimmesdale, placed high with the great and powerful of
the state who judge and administer judgment: poor Dimmesdale,
whose sermon to Hester now, with all its doubleness of motivation
and of meaning, is a dynamic development of, and a guide to, his
private drama.

Chapter 4, with the scene between Hester and Chillingworth,
may be taken as the last phase of the first movement of the novel.
Here Chillingworth defines for himself, and for us, his role, and
forces Hester into her decision to keep silent about his identity, a
decision which gives the key to the future action. The novel is now
in train: we have a masterful piece of exposition, the characters
established in their archetypal stances, with a maximum of economy
in presenting the past and a maximum of suspense in the thrust
toward the future.

After the essentially dramatic exposition of the first four chapters,
there is a second movement, this of generalized narrative rather
than scene, analytical rather than dramatic. Here we have a description of the kind of life Hester works out for herself in the "charmed
circle" of her moral isolation and, as a corollary, a further presentation of her character. Why has she remained in Boston to be a "type
of shame"? Because here she has encountered reality; "her sin, her
ignominy, were the roots which she had struck in the soil." But
there was another motive, although she "hid the secret from herself." Dimmesdale is here, with whom "she deemed herself connected in a union . . . that would bring them together before the
bar of final judgment, and make that their marriage altar, for a joint
futurity of endless retribution." So in the very idea of "endless
retribution" with her lover there enters an element of sexual gratification, torment as ecstasy, a thing totally removed from the idea
of true penitence; it was an idea that "the tempter of souls" thrust

upon her, and then "laughed at the passionate and desperate joy with which she seized, and then strove to cast it from her."

Meanwhile, Hester lives by doing sewing and performing acts of charity, even for those who revile her in the moment of accepting it. She was a "martyr," but she "forbore to pray for her enemies lest, in spite of her forgiving aspiration, the words of blessing should stubbornly twist themselves into a curse." She felt, too, that the letter had "endowed her with a new sense," that it "gave her a sympathetic knowledge of the hidden sin in other hearts." In regard to this she was torn between the temptation to believe that all "purity" was a "lie," and the impulse to "believe that no fellow mortal was guilty like herself." (But she will, at the end, develop another option in which she will rest: that of using the knowledge coming from "sin" as a means to assist and comfort others.)

The only society possible to her is little Pearl. She dresses the child gorgeously, the richness of color being an expression of that part of her own nature otherwise suppressed. The child, often presented as little more than an allegory, is a kind of elf, outside the ordinary world, a child of "nature" who says to Hester, "I have no Heavenly Father." There comes a time when the authorities are about to remove Pearl from Hester's care, and only the arguments advanced by Dimmesdale prevent this, a fact which confirms Chillingworth in his suspicions of the minister's guilt.

In the second movement of the novel, too, the course of the relation of Dimmesdale and Chillingworth is traced. Dimmesdale is living in anguish. Tormented by his guilt and by his weakness in not bringing himself to confess it, he can still self-deceivingly argue that there are men who, though guilty, retain "a zeal for God's glory and man's welfare," and therefore "shrink from displaying themselves black and filthy in the view of men," because by such a course "no evil of the past can be redeemed by better service." He keeps a scourge in his closet and pitilessly brings blood to his own shoulders, all the while laughing bitterly. But all his acts of penance are fruitless; there is, he says, "penance" but not "penitence," only a "mockery of penitence." In other words, as in Hester's thought of union in the torture of "endless retribution," there is, in Dimmesdale's pangs of penance, a kind of sexual gratification.

Even as he suffers, Dimmesdale "has achieved a brilliant popularity in his sacred office," having "won it indeed by his sorrows," for, in a kind of parallel to Hester's notion that she could intuit the guilt in the hearts of others, Dimmesdale's "burden" is what makes "his sympathies so intimate with the sinful brotherhood of mankind" that his pain issues in "gushes of sad, persuasive eloquence."

As a result of his torment, Dimmesdale's health fails, and the learned stranger Chillingworth moves into the same house with him, ostensibly to save him for the greater glory of God and of New England. Chillingworth is there, of course, out of his desire for vengeance, which now amounts to a mania, a mania intertwined with his intellectual passion for anatomizing the soul and body of the sufferer. Dimmesdale, out of the morbidity of his sensibility, is aware of an inimical agency but cannot identify it.

With Chapter 12, the second movement of the novel ends, the long section of generalized narration and analysis being concluded by the night scene in which Dimmesdale, forecasting the climactic scene at the end of the novel, mounts the scaffold. Now, "in this vain show of expiation," Dimmesdale is "overcome with a great horror of mind, as if the universe were gazing at a scarlet token on his naked breast," where in fact there had long been "the gnawing and poisonous tooth of bodily pain." In his agony Dimmesdale shrieks, and then, being sure that his voice has summoned the whole town to see his shame, he exclaims, with an echo of the Biblical account of the crucifixion, "It is done!" The town does not rouse itself to witness Dimmesdale's agony (as it will in the end), but there is the ghostlike appearance of the old governor at his window and at another the head of his sister, the witch, and then, in the street, unaware of him, the Reverend Mr. Wilson, who has been praying by the deathbed of old Winthrop, the former governor.

It is the passing of Mr. Wilson that stirs up the wild self-torturing humor in Dimmesdale that is to appear again after the forest scene with Hester; and this "grisly sense of the humorous" summons up his vision of what the morning will reveal:

The neighbourhood would begin to rouse itself. The earliest riser, coming forth in the dim twilight, would perceive a vaguely defined figure aloft on the place of shame; and, half crazed betwixt alarm and curiosity, would go, knocking from door to door, summoning all the people to behold the ghost—as he needs must think it—of some defunct transgressor. A dusky tumult would flap its wings from one house to another. Then—the morning light still waking stronger— old patriarchs would rise up in great haste, each in his flannel gown, and matronly dames, without pausing to put off their night-gear. The whole tribe of decorous personages, who had never heretofore been seen with a single hair of their heads awry, would start into public view, with the disorder of a nightmare in their aspects. Old Governor Bellingham would come grimly forth, with his King James's ruff fastened askew; and Mistress Hibbins, with some twigs of the forest clinging to her skirts, and looking sourer than ever, as having hardly got a wink of sleep after her night ride; and good Father Wilson, too, after spending half the night at a death-bed, and liking ill to be disturbed, thus early, out of his dreams about the glorified saints. Hither, likewise, would come the elders and deacons of Mr. Dimmesdale's church, and the young virgins who so idolized their minister, and had made a shrine for him in their white bosoms; which, now, by the by, in their hurry and confusion, they would scantly have given themselves time to cover with their kerchiefs. All people, in a word, would come stumbling over their thresholds, and turning up their amazed and horror-stricken visages around the scaffold.

At this Dimmesdale, "to his own infinite alarm," burst out into wild laughter, and this laughter, as by the logic of dream, evokes the "light, airy, childish" laughter of Pearl, the "good" witch (unlike the sister of Governor Bellingham), the child who is of nature, who has "no Heavenly Father." And there is Hester, who, with Pearl, ascends the scaffold to stand by his side. Then the red meteor flames in the sky, and in that red glare appears Chillingworth, who has come, he says, to lead Dimmesdale home.

The scaffold scene not only brings to focus, there at the middle of the novel, all the forces that, in their complexity and ambiguity, are at work, but also provides a new thrust of plot. For the scene impels Hester to seek out her husband to persuade him to have mercy on his victim. Chillingworth refuses, but he offers an insight into himself and his private story. He is, he says, now a "fiend," and he demands: "Who made me so?" To which, Hester, shuddering at a new sense of guilt, replies: "It was myself." But even the "fiend" can see the pity of their situation: "Peradventure, hadst thou met earlier with a better love than mine, this evil had not been. I pity thee for the good that has been wasted in thy nature."

But when Hester says that she pities him for the same reason and makes a last plea that, to save his own soul, he release Dimmesdale, he can only reply that "it has all been a dark necessity." And in one of the most important thematic statements of the novel, he continues: "Ye that have wronged me are not sinful, save in a kind of typical illusion; neither am I fiendlike who have snatched a fiend's office from his hand. It is our fate. Let the black flower blossom as it may!"

The refusal of Chillingworth to relinquish Dimmesdale justifies Hester, she feels, in breaking her promise not to divulge his identity, and so prepares for the end of the third movement of the novel in the forest scene (Chapter 17), in which the strong and vital Hester attempts to save Dimmesdale by persuading him to flee from America and seek a new life, and which comes to a climax when she snatches the *A* from her bosom and casts it away.

This scene, in the beautiful interpenetration of elements in the structure of the work, not only provides a forward thrust for action (it prepares for the end), but interprets the past. We had never seen, or been told anything about, the relation of the lovers before the opening of the novel, but now, in this "natural" forest scene, we understand how Hester, in her "natural" strength and vitality, is the "seducer" of Dimmesdale, and we understand that it must have been this way, however unconsciously, in the beginning of their story before the novel opens. We understand more precisely than before another element of both structure and meaning: the tension, in life and in man, between "nature" and "idea," the doom of man's essential division of flesh and spirit.

Other elements are to emerge in the fourth movement. In the forest scene itself we notice the reaction of little Pearl, who will not cross the brook to her mother and Dimmesdale until the *A* is restored to its place—to declare Hester's identity (and, for that matter, Dimmesdale's too). The forest scene throws a special light on the split between flesh and spirit. It would seem that man, in seeking the freedom of nature (discarding the *A* and preparing to

flee), loses his identity, that is, his moral history. But, at the same
time, in the ambiguity of experience, we see that the most immediate consequence of this decision to discard the mark of guilt and to
flee to make a new life (by discarding penance without having
achieved penitence) is the great burst of "natural" energy for the
nearly moribund Dimmesdale.

Associated with this energy as he rushes homeward is a kind of
diabolic humor, like that observed on the midnight scaffold, which
now amounts to a parody of Dimmesdale's gift of intuitive sympathy for the sinful hearts of others and which now expresses itself in
a desire to entrap others in their own corruption—to whisper a
wicked joke in the ear of a young girl or an atheistical argument
into that of a poor widow who has nothing left but her Christian
faith. Dimmesdale experiences, in other words, a sudden release of
his suppressed sexual energy (brilliantly analyzed by Frederick
Crews in his study of Hawthorne), which had been spent in penance and which now comes out in an anarchic denial of all "purity";
but he is still so much the man of faith that he can think of his new
energy only in terms of the joy of Christian conversion—"risen up
all made anew, and with new powers to glorify Him that hath been
merciful." (And this little passage may be put in balance with the
last words of Dimmesdale in the climactic scene of the novel.) This
is a parody of conversion, and as such the carrier of a double irony.
First, Dimmesdale does not realize the nature of the "joy," not
even when it eventuates in the anarchic obscenities. Second,
Dimmesdale does not realize that he, being the "religionist" he is,
cannot escape into the guiltlessness of pure nature. He is doomed
to penitence—doomed, as it were, to be saved. This is his "dark
necessity."

Another consequence flows from the forest scene. As the new
"joy" of Dimmesdale bursts forth into the obscene comedy on the
way homeward, so, once in his chamber, it bursts forth in the
composition of the election day sermon that he will give before his
flight into "guiltlessness." As he sits in his chamber, and sees his
old Bible there, he thinks of himself as he had once been; and he
"eyes that former self with scornful, pitying, but half-envious curiosity." Even as he repudiates that old pious self, his pen is racing
ahead as though beyond his control. What if this eloquence, which

soon all auditors will consider divinely inspired, springs from the same energy that had been bursting out in the anarchic obscenities? Hawthorne would certainly not regard this as a simple irony undercutting the validity and spirituality of the sermon. There is an irony, to be sure, but an irony involving the very doubleness of human nature.

The fifth, and last, movement of the novel begins with a public gathering, which architecturally balances the scene outside the jail at the beginning of the story. Hester and Pearl are now in the crowd waiting for the great procession to the church where Dimmesdale will give his sermon. Here Hester encounters the captain of the Bristol ship that is to take her, Pearl, and her lover away (the captain, let us note, is "outside" society and its values, a creature of the wild ocean like a creature of the unredeemed forest, where the Devil lurks and witches foregather); but from him, the agent of freedom, she gets the news, not of freedom and guiltlessness, but of pursuing guilt in the person of Chillingworth, who has found out the secret of their intended flight and taken passage on the same ship.

A second shock awaits Hester when she sees Dimmesdale in the procession, suddenly seeming far beyond her among the great, his mind "far and deep in its own region" and his eyes not sparing even a glance for her. Her spirit sinks with "the idea that all must have been delusion." And upon her thoughts, to compound this distress, there breaks Mistress Hibbins, the witch, speaking of the Black Man in the forest and how Dimmesdale had signed a bond there with him.

At the time of the sermon, with symbolic appropriateness, Hester is outside the church, standing by the scaffold of the pillory, with the sense in her "that her whole orb of life . . . was connected with this spot, as the one point that gave it unity"—as it gives the novel unity. As she stands there, she cannot hear the actual words of the sermon, only the flow of the minister's peculiarly musical and expressive voice, with an "essential character of plaintiveness." The fact that she cannot hear the words has symbolic significance, of course, for, in a sense, she and her lover do not speak the same language. They belong to different dimensions of life that scarcely intersect—only in their "love." His obsessed spirituality, which is his "necessary" story, is not for her. So what she hears is not a message from his dimension, but the "whisper, or the shriek, as it might be conceived, of suffering humanity." And it is the same secret voice of "suffering humanity," not the message, that provokes the "rapture of the congregation—though, ironically enough, they think they are moved by the message which foretells a high and glorious destiny" for the settlers in New England, that "newly gathered people of the Lord."

When, after the sermon, Dimmesdale summons Hester and Pearl to the scaffold with him for the climactic scene of the confession, several features should be remarked. First, the role of Chillingworth, we now see, is not to uncover the sinner, but to prevent the confession, for in the confession his victim "escapes" him. Second, in Dimmesdale's penitent confession there is, in the very ecstasy of self-abasement, a kind of egotism; he is, he proclaims, the "one sinner of the world." Third, as a corollary of this egotism, when Hester, from the depth of her feeling, cries out for assurance that they will meet in the immortal life, Dimmesdale replies that the "law" has been broken and it may be vain to hope for a "pure reunion." He does add that God is merciful, but with this reference to mercy, his egotism totally reasserts itself, and the mercy now referred to is to be directed at Dimmesdale alone. If God had not mercifully given Dimmesdale the "burning torture" on his breast, the company of the "dark, terrible old man," and death in "triumphant ignominy," then he "had been lost forever."

Poor Hester is utterly forgotten. In fact, we should add that if the confession is an "escape" from Chillingworth, it is also, in a deeper fashion, an "escape" from Hester—from nature, from flesh, from passion, from sexuality, from, in the end, woman, who is the unclean one, the temptress. So, even in the heroic moment, there is the deepest of all ambiguities.

It is easy to see how, if a reader ignores all the characters except Dimmesdale, if he does not attend very closely to what Dimmesdale does and says, and if he accepts Dimmesdale's values as Hawthorne's, he can take *The Scarlet Letter* as *merely* a story of conscience and redemption. But, clearly, Sophia with her "grievous headache," Emerson with his "Ghastly, ghastly," and Hawthorne with his "hell-fired" saw more. Each in his own way saw the tragic tensions, the pitiful instances of waste, the irremediable askewness of life which the story, taken as a whole, delineates.

Taken as a whole: that is the point. Even in Dimmesdale's story there are ambiguities. How much, for instance, is there of spiritual aspiration, and how much of fear of nature, fear of his own nature, sexual incertitude, and narcissism? But whatever Dimmesdale may actually be taken to be, he is only part of the pattern of the novel. Chillingworth, for instance, is a thematic and psychological counterpoint to him; and even, in the novel, a structural counterpoint, for the relation of each to Hester gives one principle of the action, and one principle of balance to the action. Psychologically and thematically, their roles are even more significant. Both are men "outside" of nature, Chillingworth with his passion for study (to be directed, of course, to the good of mankind) and Dimmesdale with his aspiration to spirituality (so as to be a model for the redemption of mankind). When Chillingworth comes to the vital Hester he is already old, twisted, withered, and all but impotent, and if Dimmesdale discovers passion with her, there is inevitably the self-loathing we find expressed in the fact that part of his penance is to stare at his own face in a mirror. If Chillingworth, out of envy of what he takes to be the successful lover, and in his outraged vanity, devotes himself to the torture of Dimmesdale, then we find, as a parallel, Dimmesdale's obsessively gratifying process of self-torture. In the end, the two men are more important to each other than Hester is to either; theirs is the truest "marriage"—and a marriage of two perfect egotists.

Hester's story is one of penance, it is clear. She accepts her role as the outcast, the revulsion of society and the insults from even those unfortunates whom she succors, but she does this out of pride rather than humility. She has, in fact, stayed here for reasons having nothing to do with penance, to be near Dimmesdale and, perhaps more importantly, to fulfill some obscure sense of what Hawthorne calls the "unity" of her life and what we might call her identity. Further, her isolation has freed her mind to speculate about the nature of society, and to decide that society is not fixed by God in immutable law but is subject to change. This is not penance; and certainly not penitence.

Hawthorne says, indeed, that Hester had in her the making of a harsh prophetess who might attempt to create the future. It is this strain of coldness and harshness developed in her adversity, in her "battle" with the world, which he deplores, even as he admires her courage. This point is reinforced in the last scaffold scene. When Pearl, as though aroused by the "great scene of grief," comes out of the "spell" to kiss at last her father's lips, Hawthorne says that her tears "were the pledge that she would grow up in human joy and sorrow, nor forever do battle with the world, but be a woman in it"—unlike her mother.

The scaffold scene, then, would say that Hester has been forced to do battle with the world and that part of her tragedy lies in the consequent hardening of her womanliness; only in the meeting with Dimmesdale in the forest, where love is again "aroused," does her natural womanliness return: "Such was the sympathy of Nature—that wild, heathen nature of the forest, never subjugated by human law, nor illumined by higher truth."[5]

Hester, strong, vital, beautiful, is indeed the wonderful "natural" creature, one of those dark, passionate temptresses that Hawthorne put into fiction and, apparently, flinched from in life; but even so, another source of her tragedy lies in the fact that she cannot be merely "natural." Here we must consider that the men she has accepted are not men we would reasonably expect as her sexual partners. We can argue that accident and social conditions may well have played a part here, and this is true; but *dramatically* regarded, what we have is the natural woman yearning, as it were, toward a condition beyond her "naturalness." Dramatically, psychologically, and thematically regarded, it is not an accident that Hester takes up with the old and twisted Chillingworth, and when she deserts him, it is for the pale, beautiful Dimmesdale and his pathologically sensitive conscience and narcissistic spirituality, instead of for some strapping officer of militia who would wear his religion more lightly, could gratify her appetites more single-mindedly, and could sleep better o' nights. From the very start there has been an askewness in her fate, an askewness that Chillingworth recognizes when he says, "hadst thou met earlier with a better love

[5]This scene has strong parallels with the scene in Melville's *Billy Budd* where the chaplain meditates on the "innocence" of the "barbarian" boy.

than mine, this evil had not been." But what he does not recognize is the possibility that there may also be a reason why "naturalness" yearns beyond "nature."

The last chapter is balanced, as a kind of epilogue, against the first, which, as we have said, serves as a prologue. The climactic scaffold scene must, then, be regarded in the context of this conclusion. The meaning of Dimmesdale's confession is, in this epilogue, subjected to debate, and the mere fact qualifies the interpretation of the whole story. There is, too, considerable complexity in the way the story of Chillingworth is worked out. Deprived of the terrible meaning of his own life, he withers away, but in the very withering he provides means for Pearl to achieve her life. As heiress to his fortune, she goes to Europe, marries a nobleman, and, as we are given to understand, fulfills the prediction that she would not "do battle with the world, but be a woman in it." This may be taken as a happy normality coming out of the distorted lives—but if so, then with what illogicality, and after what waste! Pearl's happiness can scarcely be taken to discount the grief of all the others.

As for Hester, can the final meaning of her life be taken to discount the grief? She returns from Europe to resume her life in the withdrawn cottage and resumes, by her own choice, the scarlet letter—for only thus could she feel that her own life had found meaning. Now as she distributes comfort and counsel to women suffering from "wounded, wasted, wronged, misplaced, or erring and sinful passion," she assures them that a "brighter period" would come when the relation of man and woman would be "on a surer ground of mutual happiness." This, we must observe, is at the farthest remove from penitence, for the message that Hester, by implication, gives the suffering women is not that they are "sinners" in need of redemption, but that they are victims of a social order that violates nature.

How seriously are we, the readers, to take this prediction that would give to the novel, at least in a qualified way, a "happy ending"? Not very seriously, for, by a last strange irony, Hester, whose identity and vision have been made possible only by her "sin," can say that the prophetess of the new dispensation must be a woman "lofty, pure, and beautiful," and wise too, but, unlike

Hester herself, not wise through a "dusky grief." This would be a world freed of all guilt, a world of natural joy. It is her dream, but scarcely the world Hawthorne envisaged.

In this connection, it may be recalled that just as *The Scarlet Letter* was often misread as a cautionary tale of sin and conscience, it could also be misread as a tract in which Hester is primarily a martyr for the liberation of women—and of men, too—from a sexually repressive society. Such was the interpretation in a transcendentalist discussion of the novel by a certain George Bailey Loring, a young physician, writing in Theodore Parker's *Massachusetts Quarterly Review*—transcendentalist in so far as the doctrine of "self-reliance" and the validity of "intuition" were taken to imply sexual release from the sanctions of both church and state.

This element of conflict between the individual and society is clearly present in *The Scarlet Letter,* and it is reasonable to suppose that the influence of the Transcendentalists may have sharpened it in Hawthorne's mind. But Hawthorne's concern with the rigors of Puritan society, as with the complex tensions of sexual encounters, long preceded the initial meeting of earnest seekers in George Ripley's study that is usually understood to have officially ushered in the movement.

The meaning of *The Scarlet Letter* is far more tangled and profound than Dr. Loring ever imagined, and bears no simple relation to transcendental reformism. The concern of Hawthorne here, as in his work in general, lies in the tension between the demands of spirit and those of nature. Indeed, the Transcendentalists had insisted upon this issue, but Hawthorne's view, profoundly ironical as it was in seeing the tension between the two realms as the very irremediable essence of life, in its tragedy and glory and even comedy, was far different from anything that ever crossed a transcendental mind.

Even nature, which, in the novel, is thematically set against the sanctions of society, cannot be taken simply. The forest is a haunt of evil as well as of good, and the wishes of the heart may be wicked as well as benign. In the tale "The Holocaust," for example, when all the marks of evil and vanity have been consigned to the flames, the world is not purged; there remains the human heart. In that world of ambiguities, there is, inevitably, a terrible illogic. Good and bad may be intertwined; good may be wasted; accident, not justice, rules. Man is doomed to live in a world where nature is denied and human nature distorted, and—most shatteringly of all —in a world where love and hate may be "the same thing at bottom," and even vice or virtue may represent nothing more than what Chillingworth calls "a typical illusion." But men must live by the logic of their illusions, as best they can—Dimmesdale by his, Hester by hers, and Chillingworth by his. That is their last and darkest "necessity." What compensation is possible in such a world comes from the human capacity for achieving scale and grandeur even in illusion—one might say by insisting on the coherence of the illusion—and from the capacity for giving pity. And here we must remind ourselves that Hawthorne found it "almost impossible to throw a cheering light" on the book.

So much for the hell-firedness of *The Scarlet Letter.*

MARK TWAIN

*E*VERYBODY KNOWS THAT a profound incoherence marked the life of Samuel Clemens, whose very existence was one long double take and who lived with a double that he had summoned into existence in order, himself, to exist at all. His feelings on any subject, but especially on the subject of himself, were violently divided; his humor was the cry of despair of a man incapable of feeling himself worthy of love. In his last coma, out of the old obsession and a self-knowledge that had never, however, proved deep enough to be redemptive, he spoke of a dual personality and of Dr. Jekyll and Mr. Hyde.

We know, too, that there was an especially bitter division of feeling in relation to the backward region of Clemens' birth and the great world of thriving modernity that he went out so successfully into, and between the past and the present—or rather, the future. When the little band of Confederate irregulars to which Sam Clemens belonged dissolved without firing even one shot in anger, Sam

First published in *The Southern Review,* Summer 1972.

simply cut himself off from his Southern heritage, his father's ill-grounded pride in high Virginia lineage, and the aura of glory about the mahogany sideboard brought from Kentucky. He resigned, in a sense, from history, which he indifferently left in the hands of Confederate or Yankee heroes, and headed West, where the future was all. Later he was to regard Sir Walter Scott as the source of the Southern disease whose contagion he had thus fled and was, in *A Connecticut Yankee at King Arthur's Court,* to equate chivalry with the barbarous irrationality that the rational Yankee tries to redeem. But though the young Sam did repudiate the historical past, he did not, or could not, repudiate the personal past, and for his *doppelgänger* Mark Twain, the story of that past became the chief stock-in-trade.

What is equally significant is the complex of feelings that went into the telling of that tale. Twain knew the hard facts of his world. He knew that Hannibal, Missouri, had its full quota of degradation and despair. He knew that the glittering majesty of the steamboat was not much more than a cross between a floating brothel richly afflicted with venereal disease and a gambling hell full of stacked decks and loaded dice. Indeed, in cold print both Hannibal and the South were to get their realistic due, and in 1876, writing to one of the erstwhile boys of Hannibal, Twain chides his old companion's nostalgic yearnings:

> As for the past, there is but one good thing about it, . . . that it is past. . . . I can see by your manner of speech, that for more than twenty years you have stood dead still in the midst of the dreaminess, the romance, the heroics, of sweet but happy sixteen. Man, do you know that this is simply mental and moral masturbation? It belongs eminently to the period usually devoted to *physical* masturbation, and should be left there and outgrown.

In the wilderness of paradox and ambivalence in which he lived, Twain, during the first days of his happy marriage, enjoying a mansion and a solid bank account, could yet write to another companion:

> The old life has swept before me like a panorama; the old days have trooped by in their glory again; the old faces have looked out of the

mists of the past; old footsteps have sounded in my listening ears; old hands have clasped mine; and the songs I loved ages and ages ago have come wailing down the centuries.

In all the new splendor and bliss of mutual love, Twain discovered the poetry of the old life and, in fact, certain restrictions of the new that, before many years had passed, would make him look back on the time when he had been a demigod in the pilothouse watching the stars reflected in the mysterious river and declare nostalgically that the pilot was "the only unfettered and entirely independent human being that lived upon the earth." And make him, in a letter to the widow of another boyhood companion, declare: "I should greatly like to relive my youth . . . and be as we were, and make holiday until fifteen, then all drown together."

But Sam Clemens did not drown. He went out into the world and became Mark Twain, with his head chock-full of memories of Hannibal, his ears ringing with the language of that village, and his heart torn in a tumult of conflicting feelings.

In spite of such doublenesses and incoherences in life, there is an extraordinary coherence in the work of the *doppelgänger* of Sam Clemens, the most obvious example being the use of the personal incoherence to provide the dramatic tension of creation. This internal coherence of motivation suggests also a coherence of relation among the individual works, a dynamic of growth by which everything, good and bad, could be absorbed into the masterworks and by which all subsequent works appear as exfoliations and refinements. In turn, the internal coherence is suggested by the key image of Twain's work, that of the journey. For if Twain were a wanderer who, with no address ever definitely fixed, founded our "national literature," the key image we refer to here is not a record of his surroundings back and forth over two continents but of the journey into the darkest of all continents—the self. In *A Connecticut Yankee,* the explorer gets as close to the heart of darkness as he ever could—or dared—get, and all subsequent works represent merely additional notes and elaborations of detail of that shocking experience.

. . .

It may be useful to remind ourselves what discoveries in earlier works led to the creation of the big fulfilling books, *Adventures of Huckleberry Finn* and *A Connecticut Yankee.*

In *Innocents Abroad* (1869) Twain discovered what kind of book he could write. First, he came upon the image of the journey, obviously a simple objective journey but not quite so obviously a journey in which the main character is ruefully or outrageously puzzled by the lunacies of the world through which he travels. Second, the book represents a double vision—in this early instance, rather simple and schematic, a travel book that is at the same time a parody of travel books. Third, Mark Twain–actor playing the role of Mark Twain on the lecture platform is here transformed into Mark Twain–author writing a book in which Mark Twain is the main character. Fourth, the book represents Twain's discovery of the rich new middle class of the Gilded Age in America, the class into which he was to marry, by whose standards he would live, whose tyrannies he would fret against, and whose values he would loathe, here for the first time experiencing an ambivalence that was to become more bitter and significant. Fifth, Twain here struck upon a method that was to stand him in good stead. He learned how to make the method of the lecture platform into a book. He once said that his characteristic lecture (derived from the oral anecdote of frontier humor, full of turns and booby traps) was like a plank with a line of square holes into which he could put plugs appropriate for a particular moment or a particular audience, and this structure persisted, for better and worse, through later work, though, with increasing sophistication, often played against the developmental structure of fictional action and theme.

Mark Twain's second book, *Roughing It* (1872), also took a journey for its "plank," but where the narrator of *Innocents Abroad* had been static, simply the "lecturer" transferred from platform to book, now the narrator is in motion, is undergoing step by step the "education of the West," is being forced to submit his romantic illusions to the shock of reality. When the book ends he is a new man, and Twain has discovered his version of the great American theme of initiation that is to be central for his finest work. But there is another important development. On board the *Quaker City* the narrator had merely faced, in his traveling companions, individual examples of a world, selected more or less at random, but now in *Roughing It* he must create a world. This movement toward fiction is more importantly marked, however, in the fact that the narrator himself is more of a creation, and we have now observed the first step in the process by which the author will find fictional identification with Huck or Hank.

In his first novel, *The Gilded Age* (1874), which was to give the epoch its name, Twain again, though less explicitly, used both the image of a journey and the plank-and-plug technique. Both the image and the technique were, however, of a sort to compound rather than correct the hazards of a collaboration—and this was, of course, a collaboration—with Charles Dudley Warner, who, as one of the breed of novelists battening on the new middle class, was supposed to provide the fictional know-how for the inexperienced Twain. Though scarcely more than a huddle of improvisations, *The Gilded Age* did its own part in preparing the way for Twain's greatness. Here, for the first time, he created a fully rounded fictional character. Colonel Beriah Sellers—*"the* new American character," as William Dean Howells called him—was a gaudy combination of promoter and bunkum artist, dreamer and con man, idealist and cynic, ballyhoo expert and vote-broker; and, in the Reconstruction world, an expert in bribery, the old Confederate learning the way of new Yankeedom and collaborating with a good Unionist to get rich at the public expense while ostensibly trying to elevate the black freedman: "Yes, sir, make his soul immortal but don't touch the nigger as he is."

Beyond Colonel Sellers, however, and perhaps of more significance, Twain here pictured for the first time the little towns and lost villages of back-country America. Now they are done with grim realism; but in the same novel, for the first time in print, Twain was also exploring the world of luxury, greed, self-deception, pharisaism, and cold hypocrisy, the contempt for which was to force him to take refuge in the dream version of rural America that was to find its image in mythical Hannibal. The ambivalence about both the world of rich modernity and that of the old back country had already (though not in literature) been emerging, for instance, as we have seen, in the very first days of his happy marriage into the world of wealth.

With "Old Times on the Mississippi," which he undertook for the *Atlantic* in 1874, Twain developed the poetry of old America —the Edenic dream, the vision of a redemptive simplicity that haunts the tenderfoot going West, the apprentice pilot on the texas deck, and Huck on his raft, a poetry antithetical to the grim realism that had begun with *The Gilded Age* and was to continue as one pole of later work. Specifically, with "Old Times" we enter the world of Hannibal and the river in which Tom Sawyer and Huck Finn were to come to immortal life. But at a thematic level, both "Old Times on the Mississippi" and *Life on the Mississippi* are more deeply prophetic of *The Adventures of Tom Sawyer* and *Adventures of Huckleberry Finn*. As the tenderfoot in *Roughing It* learns the West, so the landlubber learns the river, and here, as before, the story of initiation concerns the correction of illusion by the confrontation of reality. Here the illusion is explicit only in its aesthetic dimension: to the uninitiated observer the river is a beautiful spectacle, but to the old pilot it is a "wonderful book." Though a "dead language to the uneducated passenger [who] . . . saw nothing but all manner of pretty pictures," the same objects "to the trained eye were not pictures at all but the grimmest and most dead-earnest of reading matter." In other words, Twain is dealing with an image (and a narrative) of innocence and experience, a theme that was to prove deeply central in both *Tom Sawyer* and *Huckleberry Finn*, considered either individually or in contrast to each other. For with *Tom Sawyer* (1876) we have, as Twain declared, "simply a hymn, put into prose to give it a worldly air"—that is, we have the Edenic dream of innocence which the mystic journey of Huck will put to various tests.

In the complexity of his inspiration, *Tom Sawyer* goes back, as we have suggested, to the first days of Twain's marriage when an early draft of what was later to be Tom's courtship of Betty Thatcher, known as the "Boy's Manuscript," was (as a matter of fact) composed. And in its early form, something of the same impulse carried over into *Huckleberry Finn*, which was begun while Twain was reading proofs on *Tom Sawyer* and which he then regarded as a companion volume. But this new book did not get beyond the ramming of the raft by the steamboat before he laid it aside. Over the years he added to it, but it was not until the stimulus of writing *Life on the Mississippi* (1883) that he was able to push it through. The book was published in 1885, after an overwhelming advertising campaign and a series of lecture-readings by the author himself. The results of the advertising campaign were gratifying even to the avarice of Mark Twain, although reviewers were inclined to find the book crude, irreverent, and even vicious.

Let us rehearse the simple facts of the story. With the treasure that he now shares with Tom as a result of earlier adventures, Huck has been adopted into the respectable world of St. Petersburg under the tutelage of Widow Douglas and Miss Watson. He misses his old freedom, but begins to accept the new regime of spelling, soap, and prayers. His father reappears to claim Huck, but when in a drunken rage the old man threatens his life, Huck escapes to the island after making it seem that he has been murdered by a robber. Here he is joined by Nigger Jim, the slave of Miss Watson who, in spite of her piety, is being tempted to sell him downriver. Huck, disguised as a girl, makes a scouting expedition to shore and finds that the island is not safe from slave-catchers, and he and Jim take to the river. Huck is troubled by his conscience at thus depriving Miss Watson of her property, but follows his natural instinct. The plan to escape to freedom in a Northern state fails when they miss Cairo, Illinois, in a fog. Then the raft is sunk by a steamboat and the two, barely escaping with their lives, are separated.

Huck is taken in by the Grangerford family, aristocratic planters, and enjoys their hospitality until a slaughterous outbreak of their bloody feud with the Shepherdsons puts him on his own again. He manages to rejoin Jim, and the growth of his human understanding of the slave constitutes the psychological action, which concludes when Huck decides that if saving Jim may get him damned, he'll just have to go to hell.

Meanwhile, the pair pass through various adventures that exhibit the irrationalities of society and the cruelties possible to human nature. The life on the river comes to an end when the vagabond "King" and "Duke," the rogues whom they have befriended, betray Jim for a share in a presumptive reward and Jim is held captive on the downriver plantation of the Phelps family, kin of Tom Sawyer. When Huck goes to the plantation with the idea of rescuing Jim, he is taken for Tom, who is expected on a visit. To save Jim, he accepts the role, and when the real Tom appears, Tom accepts the role of Sid, another boy in the family connection. Tom institutes one of his elaborate adventures to rescue Jim, with Huck participating in the nonsense to placate Tom. After Jim's rescue, during which Tom gets shot in the leg, Jim stays with him and is recaptured; but all comes out happily, for as is now explained, Miss Watson on her deathbed had long since freed Jim, and Tom had withheld this information merely to enjoy a romantic adventure. Huck is now taken in by the Phelps family to be civilized, but he is thinking of escape to the Indian country.

The story, or rather Twain's treatment of the story, has provoked a vast body of criticism and various interpretations. The most simple view is to regard *Huckleberry Finn* as merely a companion piece to *Tom Sawyer*—more of the same tale of what it was like to be a boy in mythical Hannibal. As far as it goes, this view is valid. But it does not accommodate certain features of the book that are undeniably there.

The book is, indeed, a series of boyish adventures, but these adventures take place in an adult world, and the journey on the raft is, as the critic Bernard DeVoto has put it, a "faring forth with inexhaustible delight through the variety of America." The "faring forth" gives, "objectively and inwardly, a panorama of American life, comic and serious, or with the comic and serious intertwined, all levels, all types of that life."

We must remember, however, that here we refer to the objective world of the novel and to the "inwardness" of that world. But what of the "inwardness" of the observers of that adult world? With this question we engage the central issue of the novel, for whenever the boyish world of Huck and Jim touches the adult world—the "shore" world—something significantly impinges upon the "river" idyll. If the basic fact of the novel is that it is a journey, we must think not only of the things seen on the journey but also of who sees them and the effect of the seeing. The journey, in fact, has begun with inward motives of great urgency; both Huck and Jim are more than footloose wanderers—they are escaping from their respective forms of bondage, forms imposed by society. To flee they give themselves to the river; and it is not illogical to agree with the poet T. S. Eliot and the critic Lionel Trilling that the river may be taken to have a central role. As Eliot implies when he says that the river has no clear point of beginning and fades out into its delta toward the sea, the river seems to be an image of a timeless force different from the fixed order of the dry land, an image of freedom and regeneration; or as Trilling puts it, the river is a god to which Huck can turn for renewal.

In any case, the river provides not only a principle of structural continuity but also a principle of thematic continuity. The experience on the river, with its special tone of being, is set against that on land. Huck says: "It was kind of solemn, drifting down the big, still river—looking up at the stars, and we didn't ever feel like talking loud, and it warn't often we laughed." Not only does the river teach a feeling of awe before the universe, but also a kind of human relationship at odds with the vanity, selfishness, competitiveness, and hypocrisy of society: "What you want, above all things, on a raft is for everybody to be satisfied, and feel right and kind toward the others."

But society—in which people are not "satisfied"—pursues the fugitives even on the river; the steamboat runs down the raft. When Huck and Jim escape by diving deep into the bosom of the river beneath the murderous paddle wheel, this event—like the dive that Frederick Henry, in *A Farewell to Arms,* takes into the Tagliamento River to escape the Italian battle-police and the insanity of the world of institutions—is a baptism that frees them, now fully, into the new life.

If we are to understand the significance of Huck's baptism, we must understand Huck himself, for Huck is the carrier of the meaning of the novel. The focal significance of Huck is emphasized by the fact that as early as 1875, Twain, in considering a sequel to *Tom Sawyer,* said to Howells (who had urged him to make Tom grow up in another book) that Tom "would not be a good character for it." He was, he said, considering a novel that would take a boy of twelve "through life," and added that the tale would have to be told "autobiographically—like *Gil Blas.* " If the wanderings of the new picaroon are to be "through life," we expect the wanderer to learn something about life, and if, as Twain declared, the tale must be told as autobiography (it would be "fatal" otherwise, he said to

Howells), the reason must be that the personality of the learner is crucially important.

In other words, Twain needed a hero who would be sensitive enough to ask the right questions of his adventures in growing up, and intelligent enough to demand the right answers. Furthermore, if Twain was to make the process of learning dramatically central to the tale, he could not well trust it to a third-person narrator, as in *Tom Sawyer*. The hero would have to tell his own tale with all its inwardness, and in his own telling, in the language itself, exhibit both his own nature and the meaning of his experience.

In Huck's language—"a magnificent expression," as DeVoto puts it, "of the folk mind"—Twain found a miraculous solution. It is no less miraculous for springing from a well-defined tradition, or rather, from two traditions. The first, of course, was that of the frontier humorists, from Augustus Baldwin Longstreet, Davy Crockett, and the anonymous writers of the Crockett almanacs on to George Washington Harris and his *Sut Lovingood,* a tradition that had fed the humor of lecturers and journalists like Artemus Ward and the early Mark Twain. The second was that of the early writers of the local-color school, such as James Russell Lowell, Harriet Beecher Stowe, and Bret Harte. But the use of dialect by writers had become more and more cumbersome and mechanical; it set up a screen between the language and the meaning. Furthermore, the dialect itself was a mark of condescension. The writer and the reader, proud of superior literacy, looked down on the dialect and the speaker.

What Twain needed was a language based on colloquial usage and carrying that flavor, but flexible and natural, with none of the mechanical burden of dialect writing. At the same time, even if the speaker were of inferior literacy, his language had to be expressive enough to report subtleties of feeling and thought. In achieving this, Twain established a new relation between American experience as *content* and language as a direct *expression*—not merely a *medium of expression*—of that experience. The language, furthermore, implied a certain kind of fiction, a fiction that claimed a certain relation to the experience it treated. That Mark Twain was aware of this situation is indicated at the very beginning of the novel: "You didn't know about me without you have read a book by the name of *The Adventures of Tom Sawyer;* but that ain't no matter. The book was made by Mr. Mark Twain, and he told the truth, mainly." Here Huck asserts himself as the literal subject about which Mr. Mark Twain had written in *Tom Sawyer;* but now he himself is to tell his own tale. He is, then, freestanding in his natural habitat outside of both "Mr. Mark Twain's" book and his own, insisting on a special veracity about experience. Actually, Huck Finn is only another fictional dramatization, but a dramatization validated by the language that springs directly from the world treated. The invention of this language, with all its implications, gave a new dimension to our literature. As Hemingway says in *The Green Hills of Africa* (a book which directly descends from Mark Twain's travel books), "All modern American literature comes from one book by Mark Twain called *Huckleberry Finn.*"

Huck's language itself is a dramatization of Huck. On one hand, it reaches back into the origins of Huck as the son of the whiskey-sodden Pap sleeping it off with the hogs; it was a language Pap could speak. It is indicative of the world of common, or even debased, life from which Huck moves to his awakening; but as we have said, it is a language capable of poetry, as in this famous description of dawn on the river:

> Not a sound anywhere—perfectly still—just like the whole world was asleep, only sometimes the bull-frogs a-cluttering, maybe. The first thing to see, looking away over the water, was a kind of dull line—that was the woods on t'other side—you couldn't make nothing else out; then a pale place in the sky; then more paleness, spreading around; then the river softened up, away off, and warn't black any more, but gray; you could see little dark spots drifting along, ever so far away—trading scows and such things; and long black streaks—rafts; sometimes you could hear a sweep screaking; or jumbled up voices, it was so still, and sounds come so far; and by-and-by you could see a streak on the water which you know by the look of the streak that there's a snag there in a swift current which breaks on it and makes that streak look that way; and you see the mist curl up off of the water, and the east reddens up, and the river, and you make out a log cabin in the edge of the woods, away on the bank on t'other side of the river, being a wood-yard, likely, and piled up by them cheats so you can throw a dog through it anywheres; then

the nice breeze springs up, and comes fanning you from over there, so cool and fresh, and sweet to smell, on account of the woods and the flowers; but sometimes not that way, because they've left dead fish laying around, gars, and such, and they do get pretty rank; and next you've got the full day, and everything smiling in the sun, and the song-birds just going it!

The first thing we notice here is what Leo Marx has called a "powerful pastoral impulse." But Huck's poetry represents more than that. It is a dramatic poetry, a poetry concerned with the human condition, and this is presumably what Howells meant when he said, in 1901, that the book was "more poetic than picaresque, and of a deeper psychology." It is the interfusion of the style with the "deeper psychology" that makes *Huck Finn* truly revolutionary and that made the discovery of Huck's personal style the base, subsequently, of Twain's own style and of the style of many writers to come. Howells called Twain the Lincoln of our literature, and we may interpret this by saying that as Lincoln freed the slave, Twain freed the writer.

In the light of the general implications of Huck's style, let us return to what it signifies about him. When we find a language capable of poetic force, we must remember that it is spoken by a speaker, and a speaker capable of poetic thought and feeling. The language derives from Pap's world, but it indicates a most un-Paplike sensibility, and this sensibility, even in its simplest poetic utterances, prepares us for Huck's moral awakening as, bit by bit, he becomes aware of the way the world really wags. The language of Huck is, then, an index to the nature of his personal story—his growing up.

Tom Sawyer, it is true, is also the story of growing up, but there is a crucial difference between the two versions. Huck's growing up is by the process of a radical criticism of society, while Tom's is by a process of achieving acceptance in society. Tom's career is really a triumph of conventionality, and though Tom is shown as the "bad" boy, we know that he is not "really bad." He is simply a good healthy boy making the normal experiments with life, and we know, from our height of indulgent condescension, that in the end all will be well.

And all is well. Tom is accepted into the world of civilized and rational St. Petersburg. Even Huck, as an adjunct to Tom, is accepted as worthy to be "civilized," and this, in the light of his deplorable beginnings and generally unwashed condition, is a good American success story, cheering to parents and comforting to patriots.

Huckleberry Finn is a companion piece to *Tom Sawyer,* but a companion piece in reverse, a mirror image; it is the American *un-success* story, the story that had been embodied in Leatherstocking, proclaimed by Thoreau, and was again to be embodied in Ike McCaslin of Faulkner's *The Bear,* the drama of the innocent outside of society. Tom's story ends once he has been reclaimed by society, but Huck's real story does not even begin until he has successfully penetrated the world of respectability and, in the well-meaning clutches of the Widow and Miss Watson, begins to chafe under their ministrations. Here Mark Twain indicates the thematic complexity of Huck's rebellion by two additional facts. It is not the mere tyranny of prayers, spelling, manners, and soap that drives Huck forth; Tom and Pap also play significant roles in this story.

Tom, in a sense, dominates not only his gang but Huck, too. He is an organizer and has a flair for leadership, but the secret of his power is his imagination: medieval chivalry, brigandage, piracy, treasure hunts, glorious rescues, and wild adventures drawn from his reading fill his head and must be enacted—with Tom, of course, in the major role. Against this world of fantasy and exaggeration, for which he has the name of "stretchers" or plain lies, Huck brings the criticism of fact, and when he can't keep his mouth shut, Tom calls him a "numbskull." Huck rejects this "dream" escape from civilization:

> So then I judged that all that stuff was only just one of Tom Sawyer's lies. I reckoned he believed in the A-rabs and the elephants, but as for me, I think different. It had all the marks of a Sunday-school.

In repudiating romantic adventure and criticizing the romantic view of life, Huck is simply doing what Mark Twain had done in *Roughing It* and was to do in *Life on the Mississippi,* with its criticism of his own nostalgic memories and the Southern legend, and more specifically (and more lethally) in *A Connecticut Yankee.* It is not merely that the romantic lies offend Huck's realistic sense. They offend his moral sense, too; for it is behind the façade of such lies, rationalized and justified by them, that society operates, and we notice that he concludes the remark on Tom's fantasy by saying, "It had all the marks of a Sunday-school"—Sunday school, and religion in general, being the most effective façade behind which society may carry on its secular operations. The equating of Tom's romantic lies with the lies of Sunday school tells us that Tom, in his romantic fantasies, is merely using his "stretchers" to escape from society's "stretchers"—lies as a cure for lies. And the repudiation of Tom's lies prepares us for the bitter unmasking of society's lies that is to occur on the journey downriver.

We have said that Huck has sensitivity and a poetic sense; so we must ask how this squares with his repudiation of Tom's imagination. Tom's brand of imagination is basically self-indulgent—even self-aggrandizing—in its social dimension; for instance, it makes Tom the leader, and more broadly considered, it justifies the injustices of society. But Huck's imagination, as we learn on the journey, has two distinct differences from this brand. First, it is a way of dealing with natural fact, of relating to fact, as in the night scene on the raft or the description of dawn; the poetry here derives from a scrupulously *accurate* rendering of natural fact. Second, it is a way of discovering and dealing with moral fact, a poetry that, as we have said, is concerned with the human condition and as such is the root of his growth; and this distinction comes clear in the end when Tom, on the Phelps plantation, is willing to put Jim through the rigamarole of the rescue just to satisfy his romantic imagination, when he could easily free him by reporting the facts of Miss Watson's deathbed manumission.[1] To sum up, the repudiation of Tom's imagination is of deeper significance than the flight from the Widow's soap and Miss Watson's "pecking."

[1]The English critic V. S. Pritchett, in an essay in the *New Statesman and Nation* (August 2, 1941), says that "Huck never imagines anything except fear," and contrasts him with Tom, who might grow up "to build a civilization" because "he is imaginative." Huck, he continues, "is low-down plain ornery, because of the way he was brought up with 'Pap.' " That is, he is a natural "bum." It would seem that the critic is, simply, wrong. If his view is correct, what of the series of moral criticisms that Huck brings to bear on society?

Pap's role in preparing for Huck's flight is more complex than Tom's. When he reappears, he seems at first a means of escape from civilization—from prayers, spelling, manners, and soap into the freedom of nature. Certainly Pap has little contact with civilization at this level, and for one moment he does seem to be the free "outsider." But he is an "outsider" only in so far as he is *rejected;* he is the offal of civilization, a superfluous and peculiarly filthy part and parcel of civilization. His outsideness means no regeneration, for in his own filthiness he carries all the filth of civilization, as is clearly illustrated by his railing against the free Negro and his talk about the government and his vote. Pap is an outsider only by vice and misfortune—in contrast to the outsider by philosophy, which is what Huck is in the process of becoming. Pap, Tom, and the Widow, that apparently ill-assorted crew, all represent aspects of bondage and aspects of civilization from which Huck flees.

Huck, moreover, is fleeing from Pap to save his quite literal life, for whether or not Pap is the "natural" man, he is a most unnatural father bent on carving up his son with a clasp knife. This literal fact symbolically underscores the significance of the journey. The escape from Pap is symbolically, as Kenneth Lynn puts it in *Mark Twain and Southwestern Humor,* a murder. Literally, Huck has had a gun on Pap all night, clearly prepared to pull the trigger if he goes on another rampage; and later, when to fool Pap about his flight he kills a pig and sprinkles the blood about the shack, the pig is a surrogate for Pap, who sleeps with the pigs—who is, therefore, a pig. But the blood is to indicate that Huck himself has been murdered, and so we have, symbolically, not only a murder but a suicide; Huck "murders" the piglike past and himself "dies" into a new life—a theme restated by the later baptism in the river.

This episode has, in fact, an additional dimension; to grow up implies the effort of seeking individuation from society and from the father—that is, from the bond of the group and from the bond of blood. So Huck, now free from both society and his father, goes forth to find the terms on which his own life may be possible. We have here a journey undertaken, at the conscious level, as a flight, but signifying, at the unconscious level, a quest; and this doubleness is precisely what we find in the psychological pattern of adolescence.

To speak of the journey as a quest, as the stages in the movement toward freedom, we refer to the fact that Huck, episode by episode, is divesting himself of illusions. Illusion, in other words, means bondage: Tom's lies, the lies of Sunday school, all the lies that society tells to justify its values and extenuate its conduct, are the bonds. For Huck the discovery of reality, as opposed to illusion, will mean freedom. And here we may note that the pattern of the movement from illusion to reality follows that of *Roughing It* and of *Life on the Mississippi.* The main action of *Huckleberry Finn,* in fact, may be taken as the movement toward reality after the Edenic illusion of *Tom Sawyer*—i.e., Mark Twain's revision of his own idyllic dream of boyhood and Hannibal after his return to that world preparatory to writing *Life on the Mississippi.* And the contrast between illusion and reality is, of course, central to Twain's work in its most serious manifestations; it is at the root of his humor, as well.

To return to the theme of the quest, Huck's voyage toward spiritual freedom is counterpointed structurally by Jim's search for quite literal freedom. This contrapuntal relationship is complex, but the most obvious element is that many of the lies of society have to do with the enslavement of Jim. Miss Watson, though a praying woman, will sell him downriver. The woman who receives Huck in his disguise as Sarah Mary Williams will be kind to him and protect him, but when it comes to catching Jim for the reward, she innocently asks, "Does three hundred dollars lay round every day for people to pick up?" And in Pap's drunken tirade about the "free nigger" with his fine clothes and gold watch and chain, we see a deeper motivation than greed, the need of even the lowest to feel superior to someone.

Not that all of the evils of society have to do directly with Jim. There are the men on the river who would let a raft with a dying man drift on because they are afraid of smallpox. There are the Grangerfords with their bloody code of honor, and Colonel Sherburn's cold-blooded gunning down of Boggs. There is the mob that under the guise of administering justice would gratify its sadism and envy by lynching Sherburn, but will turn coward before him and then, right afterwards, go to the circus; and the mob that, justly, takes care of the rascally King and Duke, but in doing so becomes, for Huck, the image of human cruelty. Even so, all the lies, as we have observed, are forms of bondage, and the dynamic image for this theme is the slave; and this dominant image implies the idea that all lies are one lie, that all evil springs from the same secret root.

This idea of the fusion of evil with evil leads to a fundamental lesson that Huck learns in his continuing scrutiny of society: as one evil may fuse with another, so good may fuse with evil, and neither good nor evil commonly appears in an isolable form. Society is a mixture and the human being is, too. The woman who would catch Jim for three hundred dollars is a kind woman. The men on the river (chasing runaway slaves, in fact) who are afraid of smallpox do have a human conscience, at least enough of one to make them pay two twenty-dollar gold pieces as conscience money. The Grangerfords, even with their blood-drenched honor, are kind, hospitable, dignified, totally courageous, and even chivalric in their admiration of the courage of the Shepherdsons. Sherburn, too, is a man of intelligence and courage.[2]

The discovery of the interfusion of evil with good marks a step toward Huck's growing up, but he has reached another stage when he learns that the locus of the problem of evil is his own soul. And

[2]The treatment of Colonel Sherburn, and especially of the Grangerfords, illustrates how Twain, the artist, lifts himself above the specific views and prejudices of Clemens, the man. Clemens, shall we say, abhors Sir Walter Scott and the Scott-infected South with its chivalric pretensions, but Twain, in spite of the brutal gunning of Boggs, recognizes the basic courage in Sherburn when he stands off the mob. As for the Grangerfords, Huck is enchanted by them, even by "The Battle of Prague" played on the tinny little piano by the Grangerford girls. Here it must be remembered that Huck is the index of response for the novel, and even if a little fun is being had at Huck's innocence, we cannot basically discount his response. The Grangerfords are indeed full of absurdity—even bloody absurdity—but they play out their drama with generosity, warmth, courage, and flair. They are, to say the least, outside the "genteel tradition" from which Huck—and Twain, the artist—are fleeing. Another aspect of the Grangerford interlude, the love passage between the Shepherdson Romeo and the Grangerford Juliet, is very important: a little later we have the absurdity of the balcony scene of Shakespeare's play presented by the King and the Duke, and this counterpoints the absurd but real—and in the end, tragic—parody of Shakespeare already given. The relation between the absurd and the serious is very complex: irony within irony. By the way, it is of some significance that Huck is drawn into the Shepherdson-Grangerford love story, and this counterpoints, with differences, the way he is drawn into the romantic charades of Tom Sawyer.

here the relationship with Jim is crucial; for it is this relationship that provides a specific focus for the general questions raised by the scrutiny of society. Coming down the river, Huck has more and more freed himself from the definition of Jim that society would prescribe: an inferior creature justly regarded as property. Huck even comes to "humble" himself before a "nigger" and apologize to him. The climax of this process comes in the famous Chapter XXXI when Huck's "conscience" dictates that he write to Miss Watson and turn Jim over to her. Having written the letter, he feels cleansed, "reformed," saved from the danger of hellfire. But the human reality of Jim on the raft, of Jim's affection for him, undoes all Huck's good intentions, and in a moment of magnificently unconscious irony, he bursts out, "All right, then, I'll go to hell," and tears up the letter.

Here, of course, Twain is concerned with the inherited doctrine of conscience as "revelation," in contrast with the notion of conscience as merely the voice of the particular society in which a person has been born. For him conscience was, as he put it in his *Notebook,* "a mere machine, like my heart—but moral, not physical . . . merely a *thing;* the creature of *training;* it is whatever one's mother and Bible and comrades and laws and system of government and habitat and heredities have made it." In such a question, Twain, constantly and pathologically tormented by guilt and conscience, might well find the dynamic emotional center of his work. One escape from his suffering was in the idea of determinism; if he could regard man as "merely a machine, moved wholly by outside influences," then he was guiltless; and if conscience could be regarded (as a corollary) as "a mere machine . . . merely a thing," then its anguishing remarks were meaningless.

In Huck, then, Twain is exploring another possibility of alleviating his torments of conscience, a way which would also relieve him from the grip of an iron determinism. Against the conscience of revelation Huck would set not the relief of determinism, but the idea of what we may call a "free consciousness" forged by the unillusioned scrutiny of experience. Huck wants to look at the world directly, with his own eyes, and this desire and talent is the reward for being outside society, having no stake in it. When on the Phelps plantation, in the plot with Tom to rescue Jim, Huck objects to some of Tom's romantic irrelevancies, Tom says: "Huck, you don't ever seem to want to do anything regular; you want to be starting something fresh all the time." Huck is, in short, a moral pragmatist; he wants to derive his values "fresh," to quarry them out of experience, to create his own moral consciousness.

In his creation of Huck, Twain, in a revolutionary and literally radical way, is undercutting impartially both conventional society and religion, and the tradition of antinomianism in America. Twain was simply against all notions of revelation, and to him the "higher law," the idea that one with God is a majority, and an encyclical all looked alike; any quarrels among Mrs. Grundy, Henry David Thoreau, Theodore Parker, the Pope of Rome, and a certified case of paranoia were, according to Twain's theory, strictly intramural.

Huck is an antinomian, to be sure, but his antinomianism is of a root-and-branch variety, and one mark of it is in emotional attitude: he is as much against the arrogance of an antinomian who would take his conscience as absolute as against that of any established order. Huck's free consciousness comes not from any version of revelation, but from a long and humble scrutiny of experience; humility is the mark of Huck's mind. Furthermore, if Twain recognizes that conscience is conditioned, is a historical accident, he would recognize the corollary that more things than society may do the conditioning and that the appeal to "conscience," the "higher law," or to revelation from on high may simply be an expression of the antinomian's deep psychic needs, not necessarily wholesome or holy.

Huck is, in short, an antinomian of an educable "consciousness," not of the absolute "conscience." As an antinomian, he is much closer to the naturalist William James than to the idealist Emerson; he would recognize, even in the moment when he violates "conscience" and follows the dictates of "consciousness," putting his soul in jeopardy of hellfire, that a crucial decision is always a gamble (the awareness that there is no absolute standard by which a choice is to be judged). Furthermore, if the consciousness has been educated to the freedom of choice, the process has also been an education in humility—not only humility but charity—and this aspect of Huck's development comes into focus (there are many other aspects of it) when he learns to recognize and accept the love of a creature for whom he had had only the white man's contempt, however amiable, and whose company he had originally accepted only because of an animal loneliness. And here we may recall that if Jim comes to Huck originally in the moment of loneliness, it is significant that when Huck goes to seek Jim after his reported capture, the description of the Phelps plantation is centered on the impression of loneliness: ". . . then I knowed for certain I wished I was dead—for that the distant wail and hum of a spinning wheel is the lonesomest sound in the whole world."

The forging of Huck's free consciousness has, indeed, many aspects. With the flight from society, with the symbolic patricide, the symbolic suicide, and the symbolic baptism, Huck has lost his old self. He must seek a new self; and so we see emerging the psychological pattern in which, with every new venture back to shore—that is, to society—Huck takes on a new role, has a new personal history to tell, a new "self" to try on for size. In every instance, there is, of course, a good practical reason for this role-playing, but beyond such reasons the act represents a seeking for identity; such an identity will, presumably, allow him to achieve freedom in contact with society (and role-playing is, we should remind ourselves, characteristic of the process of growing up). Huck is not, in other words, seeking to exist outside society—to be merely an outcast, like Pap; for we must remind ourselves that at the beginning of the journey and at the Phelps farm he can suffer loneliness. What Huck is seeking, then, is simply a new kind of society, a kind prefigured by the harmony and mutual respect necessary on a raft. But Huck is also seeking a new kind of father, and here is where Jim assumes another dimension of significance; Jim is the "father" who can give love, even when the son, Huck, is undeserving and ungrateful. The role of Jim finds its clearest definition and confirmation in Chapter XXXI when Huck thinks back upon the relationship, but it has a subsidiary confirmation in the fact that Jim on the raft is the father deprived of his blood children (whom he intends to buy once he has his own freedom) who now needs to find a "son" to spend his love on.

To sum up: Though on the negative side the novel recounts the discovery of the "lies" in society and even in the "conscience," it recounts, on the positive side, the discovery of a redemptive vision for *both society and the individual.* It is a vision of freedom to be achieved by fidelity to experience, humility, love, charity, and pity for suffering, even for the suffering of those who, like the King and the Duke, are justly punished. This is not to say that such a vision is explicitly stated. It is implied, bit by bit, as Huck drifts down the river; it is, we might say, the great lesson inculcated by the symbolic river—the lesson that men can never learn on shore.

But what is the relation between this vision and the world of reality on shore?

In the last section of the novel, Huck does come back to shore, and the crucial nature of the return is signaled by the question that Mrs. Phelps asks him when he tells his lie about the blowing up of a cylinder head on the steamboat that never existed:

> "Good gracious! anybody hurt?"
> "No'm. Killed a nigger."

So with his answer Huck has fallen back into society and society's view that a "nigger" is not human, is not "anybody"—this in the very moment when he has come ashore to rescue Jim.

This moment signals, too, the issue that has provoked the most searching critical debate about the novel. According to one side of the debate, the last section undercuts all the meaning developed in the main body of the novel, and the working out of the end is, as Hemingway puts it, "just cheating."

Here we see the repetition of the old situation in which Huck had been reared, the "good" people, now Silas Phelps and Aunt Sally, holding Jim for a reward; but this fact, which earlier, on the raft, would have been recognized as one of the "lies" of society, is now quite casually accepted. Even the rescuing of Jim is presented to the reader not in terms of Huck's values as earned on the river—even though he is still the narrator—but in terms of Tom's, as a comic game. Huck's role now is simply to underscore the comic point of this game, by giving the same realistic criticisms of Tom's romantic fancies that we have known from long back.

These "land-changes" that the novel undergoes imply other,

more important ones. Huck is no longer the central character, the focus of action and meaning, but now merely the narrator; and indeed he has regressed to the stage of limited awareness exhibited in *Tom Sawyer.* Associated with this regression is a change in the role of Jim: Huck no longer recognizes him as the surrogate father (whose love had been the crucial factor in his own redemptive awakening), and now simply regards him as a thing (a chattel slave is, legally, a "thing"); and so the reader is presumed to accept him as that, a counter to be manipulated in the plot and a minstrel-show comic.

All of the changes that we have listed are associated with a basic change of tone. We are back in the world of *Tom Sawyer,* with a condescending and amused interest in the pranks and fancies of boyhood; and even the rescue of Jim becomes merely a lark, a charade, not to be taken seriously, for at the end we learn that Jim was free all the time, and presumably we are to accept as a charming stunt the fact that Tom has withheld this information in order to have his "adventure."

The third section simply does not hang together, and our first impulse is to ask what brought Twain to this pass. Clearly, during the process of writing the book, he was feeling his way into it, "discovering" it, and when he got to the end of the second section, he did not know where to go. Henry Nash Smith, in "Sound Heart and a Deformed Conscience" (a chapter in his *Mark Twain: the Development of a Writer*), holds that Twain finally took refuge in the tradition of backwoods humor. It is true that the novel has been, from the start, a "hybrid"—"a comic story in which the protagonists have acquired something like a tragic depth"—and so there was a certain logic in choosing the comic resolution, which would, by returning to the tone of the beginning, establish a structural symmetry and which would solve the main plot problem by getting Jim legally freed. In one sense, the trouble was that Twain, in the river journey, had wrought better than he knew and differently from his original intention, and the "tragic depths" he had opened up were not now to be easily papered over. Twain was, apparently, aware that he hadn't been quite able to paper things over, and so at the end does try to fuse the serious elements of the novel with the comic. First, he gives a flicker of the old role of Jim in having him stay with the wounded Tom, in that act reconverting him from "thing" to man and echoing Jim's old role in relation to Huck. Second, Twain tacks on the last few sentences—to which we must return.

From the foregoing account, it would seem that the last section is, indeed, "cheating." But, on the other side of the debate, we find, for example, the critic Lionel Trilling and the poet T. S. Eliot. Trilling follows much the same line of thought as Smith in commenting on the "formal aptness" that returns us at the end to the world of Tom Sawyer, but finds this grounding of the arch much more satisfying than does Smith, seeming to feel that the problem of the "tragic depths" is thus exorcised. T. S. Eliot goes further, and in addition to recognizing a formal aptness in that the "mood of the end should bring us back to that of the beginning," argues that since the river, with its symbolic function of a life force, has "no beginning and no end," it is "impossible for Huck as for the River to have a beginning or end—a *career.*" The novel, that is, can have no form more significant than the mere closure in tonal repetition. If this is not the right end, what, Eliot asks, "would have been right?" And he adds that no book ever written "ends more certainly with the right words"—the statement of Huck that he can't stand to be adopted and "sivilized" as Aunt Sally now threatens to do: "I been there before." He is about ready to cut out for the "territory."

Let us, however, explore what might be involved in a "right" ending for the novel. Clearly, such an ending would have to take into account the main impulse of meaning through the second section; it would, in other words, have to accommodate the new Huck. This does not imply that the story should have a happy ending—i.e., Huck in a society embodying the values of the vision on the river. Such an ideal society never existed, nor is ever likely to exist; as Bertrand Russell has remarked, the essence of an ideal is that it is *not* real. But there are different degrees in which a society may vary from the ideal; there are more acceptable and less acceptable compromises, and the new vision gained by Huck would certainly preclude the easy acceptance of the old values exemplified on the Phelps plantation and by the whole action of the third section. The compromise here simply isn't good enough. We want *both* the "formal satisfaction" of returning the arch of narrative to the firm grounding in the original world of Tom Sawyer (that is, in the "real" world) and a "thematic satisfaction."

Here we must emphasize that the novel is not, ultimately, about a literal Huck (though he is literal enough, God knows) and the possibility of a final perfection in the literal world. Imagine, for example, an ending in which land-society, like that on the raft, would become a utopia, with all tensions resolved between man and man, man and society, and man and nature. Such an ending would be totally irrelevant to the novel we now have. What the present novel is about is, rather, the eternal dialectic between the real and the ideal. It is, more specifically, about the never-ending effort in life to define the values of self-perfection in freedom. But if the distinction made earlier between "conscience" and "consciousness" be followed to its logical conclusion, the freedom would be one in which man, even in repudiating the "lies" of society, would not deny the necessity of the human community and would assume that the "dream" of such a "freedom" would somehow mitigate the "slavery" of the real world.

Or should the novel be taken to deny the necessity of community? Does it suggest that the human community is not only beyond redemption in the ideal, but beyond hope in the slow, grinding amelioration perhaps possible in the real process of history, and that, therefore, the only integrity to be found is in the absolute antinomianism of "flight"—literal or symbolic—to the "territory"? But even if Huck must take flight from society, is the flight negative or positive in its motivation? Does Huck—or will Huck—flee merely in protest against the real world, or in the expectation that in the "territory" he will find the ideal community? The original flight from Pap and Miss Watson was, of course, negative—simply "flight from." What about the possibility now envisaged in the end? Even if one professes to be uncertain about Huck's expectations, there can be no uncertainty about Twain's. He knew all too well what Huck, however far West he went, would find—a land soon to be swept by buffalo-skinners, railroad builders, blue-coated cavalry, Robber Barons, cold-deck artists, miners, whores, schoolteachers, cowhands, bankers, sheep raisers, "bar-critters," and a million blood brothers of Old Pap and a million blood sisters of

Miss Watson. Or, to treat the flight West as symbolic rather than literal, Twain knew that there is no escaping the real world—not even by dreaming of Hannibal or the Mississippi in moonlight, viewed from the texas deck.

Considering all this, we might take Huck as the embodiment of the incorrigible idealism of man's nature, pathetic in its hopeful self-deception and admirable in its eternal gallantry, forever young, a kind of Peter Pan in patched britches with a corncob pipe stuck in the side of his mouth, with a penchant for philosophical speculation, a streak of poetry in his nature, and with no capacity for growing up.

But thus far we have been scanting one very important element that bears on interpretation—the function of Jim. His reduction, in the third section, from the role of father seems to be more than what we have been taking it to be—merely one of the sad aspects of the land-world. To go back, we remember that he had assumed that role after the symbolic patricide performed by Huck, and that the role was central to the development of Huck on the journey downriver. But once he and Huck are ashore, the relationship ends; Huck loses the symbolic father. But—and we must emphasize this fact—he also loses the literal father, for now Jim tells him that Old Pap is, literally, dead. So, to translate, Huck is "grown up." He has entered the world, he must face life without a father, symbolic or literal, the "good" father of the dream on the river or the "bad" father of the reality on shore.

In this perspective of meaning *Huckleberry Finn* is, in addition to whatever else it may be, a story of growing up, of initiation—very similar, for instance, to Hawthorne's "My Kinsman, Major Molineux" and Katherine Anne Porter's "Old Mortality." Jim's report of the death of Pap clinches the fact that Huck must now go it alone and, in doing so, face the grim necessity of re-living and re-learning, over and over, all the old lessons. The world has not changed, there will be no utopia, after all. Perhaps, however, Huck has changed enough to deal, in the end, with the world—and with himself. Or has he changed enough? If he lights out for the territory, will that mean that he has grown up? Or that he has not? Is the deep meaning of the famous last sentence so clear, after all? It often seems clear—but—

And here we may recall that the two great stories by Hawthorne and Katherine Anne Porter are open-ended—are stories of the dialectic of life.

There are, indeed, incoherences in *Huckleberry Finn.* But the book survives everything. It survives not merely because it is a seminal invention of a language for American fiction, nor because Huck's search for a freedom of "consciousness" dramatizes the new philosophical spirit which was to find formulation with William James; nor because it is a veracious and compelling picture of life in a time and place, or because Huck is vividly alive as of that time and place; nor because, in the shadow of the Civil War and the bitter aftermath, it embodies a deep skepticism about the millennial dream of America, or because it hymns youthful hope and gallantry in the face of the old desperate odds of the world. All these things, and more, are there, but the book survives ultimately because all is absorbed into a powerful, mythic image.

That mythic image, like all great myths, is full of internal tensions and paradoxes, and it involves various dimensions—the relation of the real and the ideal, the nature of maturity, the fate of the lone individual in society. In its fullness, the myth is not absorbed formally into the novel. It bursts out of the novel, stands behind the novel, overshadows the novel, undercuts the novel. Perhaps what coherence we can expect is not to be sought in the novel itself, in formal structure, plot, theme, and so on. Perhaps it resides in the attitude of the author, who, as novelist facing the myth he has evoked, finally throws up his hands and takes refuge, cynically if you will, in the tradition of backwoods humor, repudiating all sophisticated demands and norms. He throws up his hands, however, not merely because he cannot solve a novelistic problem (which is true), but because the nature of the "truth" in the myth cannot be confronted except by irony—perhaps an irony bordering upon desperation—an irony that finds a desperately appropriate expression in the refuge in a reductive, primitive form that makes a kind of virtue of the inability to control the great, dark, and towering genie long since and unwittingly released from the bottle.

And so we may find in the ending of *Huckleberry Finn* a strange parallel to Twain's manner on the lecture platform, as described by an early reviewer. According to that report, he would gaze out of his "immovable" face, over "the convulsed faces of his audience, as much as to say, 'Why are you laughing?' " Now, at the end of *Huckleberry Finn,* having released the dark genie from the bottle, he turns his "immovable" face on us, his audience, and pretends there is no genie towering above us and that he has simply been getting on with his avowed business of being the "funny man."

But with this very act, he has taken another step toward the dire time when he will "never be quite sane at night."

In *The Prince and the Pauper,* a children's book laid in Tudor England, Mark Twain had, in 1881, taken his first excursion into historical fiction. This work, which interrupted the composition of *Huckleberry Finn,* was nothing more than a piece of sentimental junk cynically devised to captivate his own children, clergymen of literary inclinations, nervous parents, and genteel reviewers, but it broke ground for *A Connecticut Yankee.* That work, however, was on the direct line of Mark Twain's inspiration; it was connected with the grinding issues of his nature, and it drew deeply on earlier work. Laid in the sixth century, in Arthurian England, it put the new American mind in contrast with feudal Europe, the remains of which the "Innocents" of the *Quaker City,* and their chronicler, had had to face on their tour. But *A Connecticut Yankee* also harks back to the contrast between the "feudal" South and the "modern" North that looms so large in *Life on the Mississippi;* it embodies not only the spirit of social criticism found in *Huckleberry Finn,* but something of Huck's pragmatic mind that always wanted to start things "fresh"; and in a paradoxical way, after it celebrates the new Yankee order of industry, big business, and finance capitalism, it also returns to the Edenic vision of Hannibal and the river found in *Tom Sawyer* and *Huckleberry Finn.*

Most deeply, however, *A Connecticut Yankee* draws on the social and personal contexts of the moment in which it was composed. At this time Mark Twain was totally bemused by one James W. Paige, the inventor of a typesetting machine which Twain was trying to organize a company to manufacture, and by which he dreamed of becoming a financial titan. Behind Hank Morgan, the Yankee, stands Paige. And, we may add, stands Twain himself, for if Hank (a superintendent in the Colt Arms Company) is an inventor (he claims that he can "invent, contrive, create" anything), he quickly becomes the "Boss"—a titan of business such as Twain dreamed of becoming.

The medieval values that Hank confronts were not confined to Arthurian Britain. For one thing, there was also present-day England, for whatever remnants had remained of an Anglophilia once cherished by Twain were now totally demolished by Matthew Arnold, who, after a visit to America, had declared, in "Civilization in the United States," that the idea of "distinction" in this country could not survive the "glorification of 'the average man' and the addiction to the 'funny man.'" In his outraged patriotism and outraged *amour propre,* Twain, a "funny man," tended to merge the England of Arthur with that of Victoria.

In addition, the Romantic movement had discovered—or created—the Middle Ages, and made them current in nineteenth-century thought and art. Tennyson's *Idylls of the King* ranked in the esteem of the pious only a little lower than the New Testament, and James Russell Lowell's "The Vision of Sir Launfall" was a close contender for the popularity prize with the Book of Common Prayer. The poetry of William Morris and the painting of the Pre-Raphaelites, with Ruskin's Gothic aestheticism and the related social theories that pitted medieval spirituality and happy craftsmanship against the age of the machine, had great vogue in the United States, a vogue that found its finest bloom in Henry Adams and Charles Eliot Norton, who wistfully pointed out to his students at Harvard that there were in America no French cathedrals.

This cult of medievalism had a strongly marked class element; usually it was cultivated by persons of aristocratic background or pretensions, often with an overlay of sentimental Catholicism. It was also associated with wealth, but with inherited wealth as contrasted with that, usually greater, of the new kind of capitalist; for inherited wealth, untainted by immediate contact with the crude world of business, was "genteel." It was only natural, then, that a poem like Sidney Lanier's "Symphony" and the early novels attacking business should use the aristocratic feudal virtues as the thongs with which to scourge the businessman. So when Hank guns down Malory's knights in armor with his six-shooters, he is also gunning down Tennyson, Ruskin, Lowell, Lanier, *et al. A Connecticut Yankee* is, in fact, the first fictional glorification of the businessman.

But Hank is arrayed not only against Sir Sagramar le Desirious and Alfred Lord Tennyson and their ilk, but also against the spectral legions of Lee, abetted by the ghost of Sir Walter Scott. It was highly appropriate that Twain should have given a first public reading of *A Connecticut Yankee* (an early version) to an audience in which sat General William Tecumseh Sherman, for if anybody was equipped to understand Hank's kind of warfare, it was the gentleman who, as first president of the Louisiana State University, had remarked to a Southern friend that "In all history no nation of mere agriculturalists had ever made successful war against a nation of mechanics," and who, a little later, was to lift the last gauzy film of chivalric nonsense to expose the stark nakedness of war.

If the anachronistically slaveholding society of Britain is an image of the Old South and if Hank's military masterpiece, the Battle of the Sand Belt, in which, after the explosion of Hank's mines, the air is filled with the ghastly drizzle of the atomized remains of men and horses, is an image of the Civil War (the first "modern" war), then Hank's program for Britain is a fable of the Reconstruction of the South and the pacification of that undeveloped country. Furthermore, in being a fable of that colonial project, this is also a fable of colonialism in general and of the great modern period of colonialism in particular, which was now well under way from the Ganges to the Congo; thus to Hank, Britain is simply something to develop in economic terms—with, of course, as a paternalistic benefit to the natives, the by-product of a rational modern society. In this context *A Connecticut Yankee* is to be set alongside Conrad's *Nostromo* and *The Heart of Darkness* and the works of Kipling.

There is, however, another and more inclusive context in which to regard it. More and more in our century we have seen a special variety of millennialism—the variety in which bliss (in the form of a "rational" society) is distributed at gunpoint or inculcated in concentration camps. So in this context, *A Connecticut Yankee* is to be set alongside historical accounts of Fascist Italy, Nazi Germany, or Communist Russia. This novel was prophetic.

The germ of *A Connecticut Yankee* was, however, much more simple than may have just been suggested. An entry from 1884 in Mark Twain's notebook read:

> Dream of being a knight errant in armor in the middle ages. Have the notions and habits of thought of the present day mixed with the necessities of that. No pockets in the armor. No way to manage certain requirements of nature. Can't scratch. Cold in the head—can't blow—can't get a handkerchief, can't use iron sleeve. Iron gets red hot in the sun—leaks in the rain, gets white with frost and freezes me solid in winter. Suffer from lice and fleas. Make disagreeable clatter when I enter church. Can't dress or undress myself. Always getting struck by lightning. Fall down, can't get up. See Morte d'Arthur.

What Twain began with was burlesque, merely the torpedoing of highfalutin' pretensions. But within a year after the first entry, there is a note for a battle scene "between a modern army with gatling guns (automatic) 600 shots a minute . . . torpedos, balloons, 100-ton cannon, iron-clad fleet & Prince de Joinville's Middle Age Crusaders." Thus we have what we may take as the poles of Mark Twain's inspiration for the book, on the one hand the satirical burlesque and on the other the sadistic and massive violence motivated by a mysterious hatred of the past.

The body of the work has to do with Hank's operations from the moment when he decides that he is "just another Robinson Crusoe," and has to "invent, contrive, create, reorganize things." The narrative proceeds in a two-edged fashion: there is the satirical exposure of the inhuman and stultifying life in Arthur's kingdom, with the mission for modernization and humanitarian improvement, but there is also the development of Hank's scheme for his economic and political aggrandizement, his way of becoming the "Boss." By and large, it seems that the humanitarian and selfish interests coincide; what is good for Hank is good for the people of Britain, and this would imply a simple fable of progress, with the reading that technology in a laissez-faire order automatically confers the good life on all. There is no hint, certainly, that Twain is writing in a period of titanic struggle between labor and capital, a struggle consequent upon the advent of big technology. In the new order in Britain there are no labor problems. The boys whom Hank had secretly recruited and instructed in technology are completely loyal to him, and as his Janissaries, will fight for him in the great Armageddon to come, enraptured by their own godlike proficiency; if they represent "labor," they have no parallel in the nineteenth-century America of the Homestead strike and the Haymarket riot.

In the fable there are, indeed, many lags and incoherences that, upon the slightest analysis, are visible. Twain had not systematically thought through the issues in his world, or his own attitudes, and he did not grasp, or did not wish to grasp, the implications of his own tale. During the course of composition he had written—in a letter of either cynical deception or confusion of mind—that he had no intention of degrading any of the "great and beautiful characters" found in Malory, and that Arthur would keep his "sweetness and purity," but this scarcely squares with the finished product. Again, though the narrative, once finished, shows no hint of the tensions in the world of the new capitalism, Twain most inconsistently could, when the socialist Dan Beard illustrated the first edition and made the fable apply to contemporary persons and abuses,[3] enthusiastically exclaim, "What luck it was to find you!" And though Twain, now reading Carlyle's *French Revolution,* could proclaim himself a "Sansculotte," he was at the same time dreaming of his elevation to the angelic choir of Vanderbilt, Rockefeller, and other Bosses. And most telling of all, though *A Connecticut Yankee* was rapturously received, even by such discerning readers as Howells, as a great document of the democratic faith, and though Twain himself, sometimes at least, took it as such, Hank is not ethically superior to Jay Gould or Diamond Jim Brady in many of his manipulations. What Hank turns out to be is merely the "Boss," more of a boss than even Boss Tweed ever was, something like a cross between a Carnegie and a commissar.

[3]For instance, one illustration shows two examples of the standard allegorical female figure of Justice blindfolded, one for the sixth century and one for the nineteenth, the former holding up scales in which a hammer tagged "Labor" is outweighed by a crown tagged "Title," and the latter with a scales in which a hammer is outweighed by a fat bag tagged $1,000,000.

There are various other logical confusions in *A Connecticut Yankee,* but one is fundamental. If the original idea of the book had been a celebration of nineteenth-century technology, something happened to that happy inspiration, and in the end progress appears a delusion, Hank's modernization winds up in a bloody farce, and Hank himself can think of the people whom he had undertaken to liberate as merely "human muck." In the end Hank hates life, and all he can do is to look nostalgically back on the beauty of pre-modern Britain as what he calls his "Lost World," and on the love of his lost wife Sandy, just as Twain could look back on his vision of boyhood Hannibal.

What emerges here is not only the deep tension in Twain, but that in the period. There was in America a tension concerning the Edenic vision, a tension between two aspects of it: some men had hoped to achieve it in a natural world—as had Jefferson—but some had hoped to achieve it by the conquest of nature. The tension, in its objective terms, was, then, between an agrarian and an industrial order; but in subjective terms the tension existed, too, and in a deep, complex way it conditioned the American sensibility from *Snow-Bound* through *A Connecticut Yankee* and Henry Adams' idea of the Virgin versus the dynamo, on through the poetry of T. S. Eliot and John Crowe Ransom, to the debased Rousseauism of a hippie commune.

The notion of the Edenic vision reminds us of *Huckleberry Finn,* for thematically *A Connecticut Yankee* is a development of that work—and the parallel in the very names of the heroes suggests the relation: *Huck/Hank.* Huck journeys through the barbarous South, Hank through barbarous Britain, both mythic journeys into a land where mania and brutality are masked by pretensions of chivalry, humanity, and Christianity. After each encounter with a shocking fact of the land-world, Huck returns to his private Eden on the river and in the end contemplates flight to an Edenic West. In other words, Huck belongs to the world of Jefferson's dream, in which man finds harmony with man in an overarching harmony of man in nature. Hank, however, is of sterner stuff. When he encounters a shocking fact he undertakes to change it—to conquer both nature and human nature in order to create a rational society.

Both Huck and Hank come to a desperate collision with reality,

Huck on the Phelps farm and Hank at the Battle of the Sand Belt; but the end of the project of regeneration through technology and know-how is more blankly horrible than life on the Phelps farm, with not even a façade of humor but only the manic glee of the victors exalted by their expertise of destruction. The "human muck" has refused the rule of reason—and the prophet of reason has done little more than provide magnificently lethal instruments by which man may vent his mania.

When the book was finished, Twain wrote to Howells: "Well, my book is written—let it go. But if it were only to write over again there wouldn't be so many things left out. They burn in me. . . . They would require a library—and a pen warmed up in hell." But the pen had already been warmed enough to declare that dark forces were afoot in history and in the human soul to betray all aspiration, and with this we find, at the visceral level of fable, the same view of history later to be learnedly, abstractly, and pitilessly proclaimed by Henry Adams and dramatized in (to date) two world wars.

As for Mark Twain himself, the shadows were soon to gather. The metaphysical despair of *A Connecticut Yankee* was shortly to be compounded by personal disasters, bankruptcy (from which, with an irony worthy of his own invention, he was to be rescued by one H. H. Rogers, of the Standard Oil trust, one of the more ruthless of the Barons), the death of Livy (by which was added to grief his guilt of having robbed her of the Christian faith), the deaths of the adored Suzy and of a second daughter, Jean, the deaths of friends, and what seems to have been a struggle against madness. His fame continued; he walked up and down Fifth Avenue in his eye-catching white suit that advertised his identity; he consorted with the rich and great, and once Andrew Carnegie even addressed him in a letter as "Saint Mark"; he played billiards to the point of exhaustion; he received an honorary degree from Oxford, which mollified the Anglophobia that had been enshrined in *A Connecticut Yankee;* he railed at the degeneracy of the age and the abuses of wealth and power and at American imperialism in the Philippines and at Belgian imperialism in the Congo, and greeted Gorky, on his visit to the United States, as an apostle of Russian democracy. But nothing really helped much, as he was never, as he put it, "quite sane at night."

Nothing helped much, that is, except writing. He kept on wielding his pen "warmed up in hell," with flashes of genius, as in *Pudd'nhead Wilson* (1894), *The Man that Corrupted Hadleyburg* (1899), and *The Mysterious Stranger* (published posthumously), in work that obsessively rehearsed, in various disguises, his own story and his own anguish. He took refuge in a massive autobiography, in which chronology is replaced by association as a principle of continuity and as a method for mastering his own experience and plumbing his own nature; he was trying to achieve truth by thus recording a voice to speak from the grave.

But perhaps there was no truth to be achieved. Perhaps there was only illusion, after all, as he put it in the unfinished story called "The Great Dark" and in a letter to Sue Crane, his sister-in-law:

> I dreamed that I was born and grew up and was a pilot on the Mississippi and a miner and a journalist in Nevada and a pilgrim in the *Quaker City,* and had a wife and children and went to live in a villa at Florence—and this dream goes on and on and sometimes seems so real that I almost believe it is real. But there is no way to tell, for if one applied tests they would be part of the dream, too, and so would simply aid the deceit. I wish I knew whether it is a dream or real.

"THE GREAT MIRAGE":

CONRAD AND

NOSTROMO

*E*ARLY IN 1903, from Pent Farm, which he had rented from Ford Madox Ford, Joseph Conrad wrote to John Galsworthy: "Only with my head full of a story, I have not been able to write a single word—except the title, which shall be, I think: *Nostromo.*" On July 8 of the same year, he wrote to R. B. Cunninghame Graham: "I am dying over that cursed *Nostromo* thing. All my memories of Central America seem to slip away. I just had a glimpse 25 years ago,—a short glance. That is not enough *pour batir un roman dessus.*" Then on September 1 of 1904, in a letter to Galsworthy, came the cry of triumph: "Finished! Finished! on the 30th in Hope's house in Stanford in Essex." Three days later, in a letter to William Rothenstein, the note of triumph has faded away:

First published in *The Sewanee Review,* Summer 1951, as "Nostromo." Included as the Introduction to the 1951 Modern Library edition of *Nostromo,* and in *Selected Essays,* 1958.

What the book is like, I don't know. I don't suppose it'll damage me: but I know that it is open to much intelligent criticism. For the other sort I don't care. Personally, I am not satisfied. It is something—but not *the* thing I tried for. There is no exultation, none of that temporary sense of achievement which is so soothing. Even the mere feeling of relief at having done with it is wanting. The strain has been too great, has lasted too long.

And the same day he wrote to Edward Garnett: "Nostromo is finished; a fact upon which my friends may congratulate me as upon a recovery from a dangerous illness."

It was not *the* book that Conrad had tried for. Let us grant that much, for who has ever written *the* book he tried for? But it remains Conrad's supreme effort. He had, as he was to say later in *A Personal Record*, "like the prophet of old 'wrestled with the Lord' for my creation, for the headlands of the coast, for the darkness of the Placid Gulf, the light on the snows, the clouds on the sky, and for the breath of life that had to be blown into the shapes of men and women, of Latin and Saxon, of Jew and Gentile." Here, in *A Personal Record*, the tone of fatigue and frustration has gone: the memory of the heroic struggle remains. And in 1920, in the Preface to *The Secret Agent*, which had been composed years before, just after *Nostromo*, Conrad refers to *Nostromo* as "an intense creative effort on what I suppose will remain my largest canvas."

In many ways *Nostromo* is more fully the fruit of a creative effort than is any other of his stories. It is not a story of those parts of the world that he had known best, the Malay Peninsula and the China seas—the parts where some critics, bemused by Conrad's exoticism and their own notion of his alienation from the modern world, would locate his best work. Rather, it is a story of a part of the world that Conrad had never laid eyes on, the west coast of South America. In general his fiction had depended, by his own account in the Preface to *Within the Tides,* on the conditions of his active life, even though more on "contacts, and very slight contacts at that, than on actual experiences." In the Author's Note to *Nostromo* we discover what "contact" had suggested Nostromo's story and how different the germ in real life is from the imaginative fulfillment. But the story of the stolen silver, suggested by the thievery of a cynical ruffian, and the figure of the magnificent capataz, suggested by old Dominic, padrone of the *Tremolino* in the days of Conrad's youth, and the severe charm of Antonia, suggested by Conrad's first love back in Poland, and even the skeptic Decoud, suggested perhaps by some deep, inner voice of Conrad himself, account for little of the finished novel. And they give us nothing of the land, remote and magisterial and vivid, that Conrad evoked in that supreme effort of his imagination.

For it was imagination and not recollection on which he had now to depend. Long before, in 1875 and 1876, when on the *Saint-Antoine* (running guns for a revolution), Conrad had been ashore for a few hours at ports on the Gulf of Mexico, but of the coast that might have given him a model for his Occidental Province and its people he knew nothing. There were books and hearsay to help, the odds and ends of information. But in the end, the land, its people, and its history had to be dreamed up, evoked out of the primal fecund darkness that always lies below our imagination.

The tempo of the book re-enacts for us the process of its creation; the stately vistas and massive involutions of the early chapters while the mists part, as it were, from the land; the nervous concentration of force and complication of event when the individual passions sublimate themselves in historical process; the moment of pause and poise when history has become anecdote and the creative conquest seems to have been complete; then, last, the personal story of Nostromo, before Linda's final, unappeasable cry—"Never! Gian' Battista!"—rings out over the dark Gulf, the part that is really a violent *coda* to the book, the product of the "volcanic overflow" with which, Conrad tells us, he finished his twenty months of agonized concentration. The land and all in it was dreamed up, but it is one of the most solid and significant dreams that we know, more solid and significant than most of our actualities. It is, in my view, the masterwork of that *"puissant rêveur,"* as Gustav Kahn once called Conrad.

Nostromo has not, however, been universally acclaimed. Some readers with whom it is dangerous to disagree have not found it to their taste. For example, Joseph Warren Beach harbors objections to the technique, as does Albert Guerard, Jr., who finds the first part an "uncontrolled elaboration of historical detail," and here and elsewhere misses a detached narrator; Morton Zabel speaks of the "dramatic impenetrability"; even F. R. Leavis, who has done a perceptive and laudatory essay on the novel and finds it Conrad's masterpiece, ends his remarks by saying that the "reverberation of *Nostromo* has something hollow about it," and that "with the color and life there is a suggestion of a certain emptiness." My purpose is not to answer these objections, though some answers will be implied if I do manage to carry out my purpose, the purpose of saying what kind of book *Nostromo* is and what it means.

We can begin with the proposition that *Nostromo* is central for Conrad's work. When *Nostromo* appeared in 1904, Conrad had already published eight books, and this work included *The Nigger of the "Narcissus"* and *Lord Jim* and the famous novelettes "Heart of Darkness" and "Amy Foster." Already the world of Conrad's imagination had exhibited its characteristic persons and issues. Already we can find the themes of isolation and alienation, of fidelity and human solidarity, of moral infection and redemption, of the paradox of action and idea, of the "true lie," of the problem of history. The characteristic themes and situations and persons had emerged, but had emerged piecemeal, though in *Lord Jim* and "Heart of Darkness" Conrad had begun to move toward the massive synthesis and complex interfusion which was to engage him in *Nostromo*. As the earlier fiction seems to move toward *Nostromo*, so the later fiction seems to represent, by and large, specializations and elaborations of elements that had been in suspension in that work.

To take some examples, Dr. Monygham is an older and more twisted Lord Jim, the man who had failed the test, not like Jim by abandoning his post and breaking the code of the sea, but by betraying friends under the torture of a South American dictator. His personal story, like the story of Jim, is the attempt to restore himself to the human community and to himself, though he, unlike Jim, survives the attempt. Mitchell and Don Pépé belong to the tribe of Captain MacWhirr of "Typhoon," those men who by lack of imagination (and Conrad took imagination to be a great gift and a great curse) never see all that life may contain "of perfidy, of violence, and of terror," and who, perhaps for that very reason, may cling simply and nobly to duty and fidelity.

Gould himself is a kind of cousin of Kurtz of "Heart of Darkness," though Gould is doomed to his isolation, not like Kurtz by avarice, vanity, and violence, by refusing his mission as a light-bringer, by repudiating the idea, but by accepting his mission as light-bringer and bearer of the idea. He accepts his mission, but ironically enough, he falls a victim to the impersonal logic of "material interests" and in the end is the slave of his silver, not by avarice, not by vanity, certainly not vanity in any simple sense, but because he has lost love to the enormous abstraction of his historical role. As Kurtz betrays his Intended to the Heart of Darkness, so Gould betrays his wife to what he takes to be the Heart of Light.

As for Emilia Gould, she is the victim of her husband's mission. Over against the abstractions, she sets up the human community, the sense of human solidarity in understanding and warmth and kindness outside the historical process. It is to her that the dying Nostromo makes his confession. It is she who compels the devotion of the bitter Dr. Monygham. Around her the other characters gather to warm their hands, as it were, at her flame. All but Charles Gould, bemused by his silver and his mission. Her role corresponds, in a way, to the role of Tekla in *Under Western Eyes,* who had been led into revolutionary activity by her sympathy for suffering, had been disillusioned by the character of the revolutionary prophet and tyrannical "feminist" whom she serves and by the abstractions he utters, and finds her fulfillment only when she can devote herself to the broken, dying, guilt-tortured Razumov. As Conrad puts it: "There was nothing in that task to become disillusioned about." But without that flicker of sardonic irony, he says of Mrs. Gould: "It had come into her mind that for life to be large and full, it must contain the care of the past and of the future in every passing moment of the present."

Somehow related to both Charles Gould and Emilia Gould stands the old Garibaldino, Giorgio Viola. He, like Emilia Gould, believes in the human bond, in a brotherhood of liberty, and has risked his life in the hope of bringing the day of liberty nearer to men; but like the idealism of Charles Gould, his idealism is tainted with abstraction. Tainted, but not destroyed, and some warmth remains in his nobility of purpose and his Roman rigor. Viola leans toward Nostromo, would take him as a son, and perhaps we find a symbolic force in this. For Nostromo is the natural man, the son of the people with the pride of the people, contemptuous of the "*hombres finos,*" with their soft hands inexpert on tiller or rifle, half magnificent unconscious animal and half the confused, conscious, tempted man,* who is virtuous merely by vanity, for until the combination of opportunity and rancor strikes him he wants nothing but "reputation," that full awareness of his identity ideally projected in the minds and on the tongues of men. As he says to Charles Gould, who wants to reward him for his heroism: "My name is known. . . . What more can you do for me?" This is the man whom old Viola would draw into his orbit by uniting him with Linda, the daughter who carried something of the Garibaldino's depth and fidelity. But Nostromo, who has lived by his vanity, though his vanity idealized, turns to the other daughter, Giselle, the "bad" daughter, and dies by consequence. Nostromo has natural grandeur; but natural grandeur unredeemed by principle, by idea, is not enough.

Without too much wrenching we may take Nostromo's significance as a parallel to that of Captain Brierly in *Lord Jim.* Brierly is the "natural" hero, his achievements all the product of luck and sound nerves and vanity; his suicide results when, seeing Jim on trial for cowardice, he realizes that the natural heroism is not enough and cannot find more in himself to sustain him. We may even say that Nostromo, too, commits a kind of suicide: he has destroyed the self by which he had lived. When, after the theft of the silver, he returns to the port but does not resume his work, he asks Captain Mitchell, "How can I look my cargadores in the face after losing a lighter?" And Mitchell replies that it had merely been a fatality, that it could not have been helped. "*Si, si!*" Nostromo replies and turns away. It all now seems fated to Nostromo, fated

---

*We may take as the key passage about Nostromo the moment at the end of Chapter VII of Part III, when Nostromo, having swum from the Isabels after the burying of the silver, goes to sleep in a "lair" of grass and then wakes: "He stood knee-deep among the whispering undulations of the green blades, with the lost air of a man just born into the world. Handsome, robust, and supple, he threw back his head, flung his arms open, and stretched himself with a slow twist of the waist and a leisurely growling yawn of white teeth, as natural and free from evil in the moment of waking as a magnificent and unconscious wild beast. Then, in the suddenly steadied glance fixed upon nothing from under a forced frown, appeared the man."

because he had had nothing to depend on to prevent his succumbing and therefore cannot see how things could have been otherwise. But the whole passage bears a kind of double meaning: Nostromo's smile that wrenched Captain Mitchell's heart, and the "*Si, si!*" as he averts his head. He has lost what he had lived by.

Last, we turn to Decoud, the skeptic. He is one of the isolated men, not isolated by foreign blood and speech like the poor, gabbling hero of "Amy Foster," or by a crime like Kurtz or Lord Jim, or by his conception of his role or mission like Gould or Viola, or by personal history like Flora de Barral and Captain Anthony of *Chance* with their "mystic wound" that alienates them from each other.

Decoud's isolation is more like the isolation of Heyst of *Victory;* it is intellectual; that is, whatever its origin may be, even though in such a mystic wound as that of Flora, it presents itself to its victim, and to us, in terms of reason and argument, as a philosophy. But Decoud's philosophy is not the philosophy of Heyst. Heyst fancies himself as the absolute observer, who shrinks from all involvement in life except such involvement as his detached kindness permits. Decoud is a connoisseur of sensation, a *boulevardier,* a dilettante of experience, who "recognized no other virtue than intelligence, and had erected passions into duties." He has only tolerant amusement, tinged with scorn, for the Goulds, for "the sentimentalism of people that will never do anything for the sake of their passionate desire, unless it comes to them clothed in the fair robes of an idea."

But for Decoud, as the story develops, even his own skepticism becomes the subject of skepticism. With self-irony he observes how his passion for Antonia casts him in the role of the father of a revolution and the herald of Progress, and later in the role of heroic adventurer when he finds himself on the dark Gulf in the lighter with Nostromo and the load of silver. And referring to Charles Gould, whose sentimentalism he has just remarked on, he can say that such men "live on illusions which somehow or other help them to get a firm hold of the substance." Where Heyst comes to conversion with the last words, "Ah, Davidson, woe to the man whose heart has not learned while young to hope, to love—and to put its trust in life!" Decoud comes to his end with no vision beyond that which skepticism can achieve by preying upon skepticism, the objective recognition of the pragmatic efficacy of faith despite the fact that faith is an "illusion." What this signifies, however, in the total pattern of the novel we shall come to later.

So much for the main characters of *Nostromo* and their relation to the Conradian family of characters. But we cannot speak of the characters as such, for Conrad, in one sense, had little concern for character independently considered. He is no Dickens or Shakespeare, with relish for the mere variety and richness of personality. Rather, for him a character lives in terms of its typical involvement with situation and theme: the fable, the fable as symbol for exfoliating theme, is his central fact. Therefore, in placing the characters of *Nostromo* we have necessarily touched on the situations and themes. But let us linger a moment longer on this topic.

Conrad writes in *A Personal Record:* "Those who read me know my conviction that the world, the temporal world, rests on a few very simple ideas, so simple that they must be as old as the hills. It rests notably, among others, on the idea of Fidelity." Or again in his tribute to the Merchant Service in 1918, an essay called "Well Done": "For the great mass of mankind the only saving grace that is needed is steady fidelity to what is nearest to hand and heart in the short moment of each human effort." Fidelity and the sense of the job, the discipline of occupation which becomes a moral discipline with its own objective laws, this, for example, is what saves Marlow in "Heart of Darkness" as it had saved the Roman legionaries, those "handy men," when they had ventured into the dark heart of Britain.

Fidelity and the job sense make for the human community, the solidarity in which Conrad finds his final values, "the solidarity of all mankind in simple ideas and sincere emotions." It is through the realization of this community that man cures himself of that "feeling of life-emptiness" which had afflicted the young hero of *The Shadow-Line* before he came to his great test.

The characteristic story for Conrad becomes, then, the relation of man to the human communion. The story may be one of three types: the story of the MacWhirr or the Don Pépé or the Captain Mitchell, the man who lacks imagination and cannot see the "true horror behind the appalling face of things," and who can cling to fidelity and the job; the story of the Kurtz or Decoud, the sinner against human solidarity and the human mission; the story of the redemption, of Lord Jim, Heyst, Dr. Monygham, Flora de Barral, Captain Anthony, Razumov.

The first type of story scarcely engages Conrad. He admires the men of natural virtue, their simplicity, their dogged extroverted sense of obligation and self-respect. But his attitude toward them is ambivalent: they are men ''thus fortunate—or thus disdained by destiny or by the sea.'' They live in a moral limbo of unawareness. They may not be damned like Kurtz or Decoud and achieve that strange, perverse exultation of horror or grim satisfaction by recognizing their own doom, or be saved like Dr. Monygham or Flora de Barral. We may almost say that their significance is in their being, not in their doing, that they have, properly speaking, no ''story''; they are the static image of the condition which men who are real and who have real ''stories'' may achieve by accepting the logic of experience, but which, when earned, has a dynamic value the innocent never know. The man who has been saved may reach the moment of fulfillment when he can spontaneously meet the demands of fidelity, but his spontaneity must have been earned, and only by the fact of its having been earned is it, at last, significant. Therefore, it is the last type of story that engages Conrad most fully, the effort of the alienated, whatever the cause of his alienation, crime or weakness or accident or the ''mystic wound,'' to enter again the human communion. And the crisis of this story comes when the hero recognizes the terms on which he may be saved, the moment, to take Morton Zabel's phrase, of the ''terror of the awakening.''

In this general connection some critics have been troubled by, or at least have commented on, the fact that Conrad's prefaces and essays, and even his autobiographical writings and letters, seem ambiguous, contradictory, false, or blandly misleading in relation to the fiction. His comments on Fidelity, such as that above from *A Personal Record*, and his remarks on human solidarity seem so far away from the dark inwardness of his work, this inwardness taken either as the story of his heroes or as the nature of his creative process. When we read parts of *A Personal Record*, for example, we see the image of the false Conrad conjured up by reviewers long ago, the image that William McFee complained about: ''a two-fisted shipmaster" telling us simply how brave men behave. And we realize how far this image is from the Conrad who suffered from gout, malaria, rheumatism, neuralgia, dyspepsia, insomnia, and nerves; who, after the Congo experience and its moral shock, says of himself, "I lay on my back in dismal lodgings and expected to go out like a burnt-out candle any moment. That was nerves . . ."; who suffered "moments of cruel blankness"; who on one occasion, years later, had two doctors attending him, each unaware of the other, and who at the same time emptied all medicine into the slop; who advised an aspiring writer that "you must search the darkest corners of your heart," and told the successful and simple-souled Galsworthy, a sort of MacWhirr of literature, "the fact is you want more scepticism at the very fountain of your work. Scepticism, the tonic of minds, the tonic of life, the agent of truth—the way of art and salvation"; and who said of his own work, "For me, writing— the only possible writing—is just simply the conversion of nervous force into phrases."

But should we be troubled by this discrepancy between the two Conrads, the Conrad who praised the simple ideas and sincere emotions and the Conrad of the neurotic illnesses and the dark inwardness? No, we should not, but in saying that we should not, I mean a little more than what has been offered elsewhere as a resolution of the discrepancy, the notion that the introverted and lonely Conrad, with a sizable baggage of guilts and fears, yearned, even as he mixed some contempt with his yearning, for the simplicity and certainty of the extroverted MacWhirrs of the world. I mean, in addition to this, a corollary of what has been said above about the story of awakening and redemption being the story that engaged Conrad most fully.

Perhaps the corollary can be stated in this fashion: If the central process that engaged Conrad is the process of the earned redemption, that process can only be rendered as "story," and any generalization about it would falsify the process. Instinctively or consciously, Conrad was willing to give the terms of the process, the poles of the situation, as it were, but not an abstract summary. The abstract summary would give no sense of the truth found within, in what, according to the Preface to *The Nigger of the "Narcissus,"* is "that lonely region of stress and strife."

There is another discrepancy, or apparent discrepancy, that we must confront in any serious consideration of Conrad—that between his professions of skepticism and his professions of faith. Already I have quoted his corrosive remark to Galsworthy, but that remark is not as radical as what he says in a letter to R. B. Cunninghame Graham:

> The attitude of cold unconcern is the only reasonable one. Of course, reason is hateful—but why? Because it demonstrates (to those who have courage) that we, living, are out of life—utterly out of it. The mysteries of a universe made of drops of fire and clods of mud do not concern us in the least. The fate of humanity condemned ultimately to perish from cold is not worth troubling about. . . .

Here, clearly enough, we see the trauma inflicted by nineteenth-century science, a "mystic wound" that Conrad suffered from in company with Hardy, Tennyson, Housman, Stevenson, and most men since their date.

Cold unconcern, an "attitude of perfect indifference," is, as he says in the letter to Galsworthy, "the part of creative power." But this is the same Conrad who speaks of Fidelity and the human communion, and who makes Kurtz cry out in the last horror and Heyst come to his vision of meaning in life. And this is the same Conrad who makes Marlow of "Heart of Darkness" say that what redeems is the "idea only," and makes the devoted Miss Haldin of *Under Western Eyes* say of her dead heroic brother, "Our dear one once told me to remember that men serve always something greater than themselves—the idea."

It is not some, but all, men who must serve the "idea." The lowest and the most vile creature must, in some way, idealize his existence in order to exist, and must find sanctions outside himself. This notion appears over and over in Conrad's fiction. For instance, there is the villainous Ricardo of *Victory,* one of the three almost allegorical manifestations of evil. "As is often the case with lawless natures, Ricardo's faith in any given individual was of a simple, unquestioning character. For a man must have some support in life." Or when Ricardo thinks of the tale of how Heyst had supposedly betrayed Morrison:

For Ricardo was sincere in his indignation before the elementary principle of loyalty to a chum violated in cold blood, slowly, in a patient duplicity of years. There are standards in villainy as in virtue, and the act as he pictured it to himself acquired an additional horror from the slow pace of that treachery so atrocious and so tame.

Then there is the villain Brown of *Lord Jim.* When, after Jim has allowed him to escape, he falls upon the unsuspecting men of Dain Waris, the act is not a "vulgar massacre":

Notice that even in this awful outbreak there is a superiority as of a man who carries right—the abstract thing—within the envelope of his common desires. It was not a vulgar and treacherous massacre; it was a lesson, a retribution. . . .

Even bloodthirstiness or villainy must appeal beyond itself to the "idea." The central passage of *Lord Jim,* Stein's speech about the "destructive element," is the basic text for this theme of Conrad:

A man that is born falls into a dream like a man who falls into the sea. If he tries to climb out into the air as inexperienced people endeavor to do, he drowns—*nicht wahr?* . . . No! I tell you! The way is to the destructive element submit yourself, and with the exertions of your hands and feet in the water make the deep, deep sea keep you up.

I take this, in the context of the action, to read as follows: It is man's fate to be born into the "dream"—the fate of all men. By the dream Conrad here means nothing more or less than man's necessity to justify himself by the "idea," to idealize himself and his actions into moral significance of some order, to find sanctions. But why is the dream like the sea, a "destructive element"? Because man, in one sense, is purely a creature of nature, an animal of black egotism and savage impulses. He should, to follow the metaphor, walk on the dry land of "nature," the real, naturalistic world, and not be dropped into the waters he is so ill equipped to survive in. Those men who take the purely "natural" view, who try to climb out of the sea, who deny the dream and man's necessity to submit to the idea, who refuse to create values that are, quite literally, "super-natural" and therefore human, are destroyed by the dream. They drown in it, and their agony is the agony of their frustrated humanity. Their failure is the failure to understand what is specifically human. They are the Kurtzes, the Browns, in so far as they are villains, but they are also all those isolated ones who are isolated because they have feared to take the full risk of humanity. To conclude the reading of the passage, man, as a natural creature, is not born to swim in the dream, with gills and fins, but if he submits in his own imperfect, "natural" way, he can learn to swim and keep himself up, however painfully, in the destructive element. To surrender to the incorrigible and ironical necessity of the "idea," that is man's fate and his only triumph.

Conrad's skepticism is ultimately but a "reasonable" recognition of the fact that man is a natural creature who can rest on no revealed values and can look forward to neither individual immortality nor racial survival. But reason, in this sense, is the denial of life and energy, for against all reason man insists, as man, on creating and trying to live by certain values. These values are, to use Conrad's word, "illusions," but the last wisdom is for man to realize that though his values are illusions, the illusion is necessary, is infinitely precious, is the mark of his human achievement, and is, in the end, his only truth.

From this notion springs the motif of the "true lie," as we may term it, which appears several times in Conrad's fiction. For a first example, we may think of the end of "Heart of Darkness," when Marlow returns from the Congo to his interview with Kurtz's Intended, whose forehead, in the darkening room, "remained illumined by the unextinguishable light of belief and love." She demands to know her beloved's last words, and Marlow, confronted by her belief and love, manages to say: "The last word he pronounced was—your name." He is not able to tell her the literal truth, the words—"The horror! The horror!"—that Kurtz had uttered with his failing breath. If he had done so, "it would have been too dark—too dark altogether . . ." He has, literally, lied, but his lie is a true lie in that it affirms the "idea," the "illusion," belief and love.

Again, in *Under Western Eyes,* Miss Haldin speaks of bringing

Razumov, supposedly the friend of her dead brother, to speak to the bereaved mother: "It would be a mercy if mamma could be soothed. You know what she imagines. Some explanation perhaps may be found, or—or even made up, perhaps. It would be no sin."

And even in *Nostromo* the lie that is true, that is no sin, reappears. The incorruptible capataz, dying, is on the verge of telling Mrs. Gould the secret of the stolen treasure, but she will not hear him. When she issues from the room, Dr. Monygham, with the "light of his temperamental enmity to Nostromo" shining in his eyes, demands to know if his long-nourished suspicion of the "incorruptible" Nostromo is correct. He longs to know, to soothe the old wound of his own corruptibility. "He told me nothing," Mrs. Gould says, steadily, and with her charitable lie affirms forever the ideal image of the dead capataz.

Skepticism is the reasonable view of the illusion, but skepticism, the attitude of the intelligence that would be self-sufficient, cannot survive, ironically enough, except by the presence of illusion. The fate of the skeptic Decoud, the "imaginative materialist," who had undertaken to be the natural man in that he had erected passions into duties, is the key parable, among many parables in Conrad, of the meaning of skepticism. Decoud had thought himself outside the human commitments, outside the influence of the "idea," the worshiper of reason, which told him that the only reality is sensation. In so far as his skepticism is "natural," he recognizes the skepticism of Nostromo, the natural man who, "like me, has come casually here to be drawn into the events for which his scepticism as well as mine seems to entertain a sort of passive contempt."

But Decoud's worship of nature and reason is not enough. As soon as he finds himself outside the human orbit, alone with sea and sky, he cannot live. Even skepticism demands belief to feed on; the opposite pole of the essential situation must be present for skepticism to survive.

> Solitude from mere outward condition of existence becomes very swiftly a state of soul in which the affectation of irony and scepticism have no place. . . . After three days of waiting for the sight of some human face, Decoud caught himself entertaining a doubt of his own individuality. It had emerged into the world of cloud and water, of

natural forces and forms of nature. In our activity alone do we find
the sustaining illusion of an independent existence as against the
whole scheme of things of which we form a helpless part.

Decoud has reached the ultimate stage of skepticism: his skepticism has dissolved his identity into nature. But even at this moment
of his spiritual, and physical, death, he experiences the "first moral
sentiment of his manhood," the vague awareness of "a misdirected
life." Now both intelligence and passion are "swallowed up easily
in this great unbroken solitude of waiting without faith." In this
"sadness of a sceptical mind," he beholds "the universe as a succession of incomprehensible images." His act of shooting himself and
letting his body fall into the sea is merely the literal repetition of
an already accomplished fate: he is "swallowed up in the immense
indifference of things."

How are we to reconcile the moral of the story of Decoud, or
of Heyst, with Conrad's statements of a radical skepticism—or with
even a radical pessimism, the notion of man as a savage animal
driven by a black ego? Can we say, as F. R. Leavis says, that "*Nostromo* was written by a Decoud who wasn't a complacent dilettante,
but was positively drawn towards those capable of 'investing their
activities with spiritual value'—Monygham, Giorgio Viola, Señor
Avellanos, Charles Gould"? Or can we say, as Albert Guerard, Jr.,
says, that against man's heart of darkness we can "throw up only
the barrier of semi-military ethics; courage, order, tradition and
unquestioned discipline; and as a last resort, the stoic's human
awareness of his own plight, a pessimism '*plus sombre que la nuit*'"?
Both these statements are, in one sense, true. They do describe the
bias of Conrad's temperament as I read it, but they do not describe,
to my satisfaction at least, the work that Conrad produced out of
that temperament. We must sometimes force ourselves to remember that the act of creation is not simply a projection of temperament, but a criticism and purging of temperament.

If Conrad repudiates the Decouds of the world, even as they
speak with, as Leavis says, his "personal *timbre*," he also has for the
MacWhirrs of the world, the creatures of "semi-military ethics," a
very ambivalent attitude, and some of the scorn of a man who
knows at least a little of the cost of awareness and the difficulty of

virtue. In other words, his work itself is at center dramatic: it is about the cost of awareness and the difficulty of virtue, and his characteristic story is the story of struggle and, sometimes, of redemption. Skepticism, he wrote to Galsworthy, is "the tonic of minds, the tonic of life, the agent of truth—the way of art and salvation." This is, I suppose, a parallel to Hardy's famous statement: ". . . if way to the Better there be, it exacts a full look at the Worst. . . ." It is a way of saying that truth is not easy, but it is also a way of saying that truth, and even salvation, may be possible. Must we choose between the Decouds and the MacWhirrs? There is also Stein; and Emilia Gould, who thought: "Our daily work must be done to the glory of the dead, and for the good of those who come after."

Let us turn, at long last, to *Nostromo,* the novel. In this book Conrad endeavored to create a great, massive, multiphase symbol that would render his total vision of the world, his sense of individual destiny, his sense of man's place in nature, his sense of history and society.

First, *Nostromo* is a complex of personal stories, intimately interfused, a chromatic scale of attitudes, a study in the definition and necessity of "illusion" as Conrad freighted that word. Each character lives by his necessary idealization, up the scale from the "natural" man Nostromo, whose only idealization is that primitive one of his vanity, to Emilia Gould, who, more than any other, has purged the self and entered the human community.

The personal stories are related not only in the contact of person and person in plot and as carriers of variations of the theme of illusion, but also in reference to the social and historical theme. That is, each character is also a carrier of an attitude toward, a point of view about, society; and each is an actor in a crucial historical moment. This historical moment is presumably intended to embody the main issues of Conrad's time: capitalism, imperialism, revolution, social justice. Many of the personal illusions bear quite directly on these topics: Viola's libertarianism, with its dignity and leonine self-sufficiency and, even, contempt for the mob; Charles Gould's obsession in his mission; Avellanos' liberalism and Antonia's patriotic piety; Holroyd's concern with a "pure form of Christianity" which serves as a mask and justification for his imperi-

alistic thirst for power; even the posturing and strutting "Caesa-
rism" of Pedrito Montero, whose imagination had been inflamed
by reading third-rate historical novels.

All readers of Conrad know the classic picture of imperialism at
its brutal worst in "Heart of Darkness," the degradation and insanity of the process, and remember the passage spoken by Marlow:

> "The conquest of the earth, which mostly means the taking it away
> from those who have a different complexion or slightly flatter noses
> than ourselves, is not a pretty thing when you look into it too much.
> What redeems it is the idea only."

In "Heart of Darkness" we see the process absolutely devoid of
"idea," with lust, sadism, and greed rampant. In *Nostromo* we see
the imperialistic process in another perspective, as the bringer of
order and law to a lawless land, of prosperity to a land of grinding
poverty. At least, that is the perspective in which Charles Gould
sees himself and his mine:

> "What is wanted here is law, good faith, order, security. Anyone can
> declaim about these things, but I pin my faith to material interests.
> Only let the material interests once get a firm footing, and they are
> bound to impose the conditions on which alone they can continue
> to exist. That's how your money-making is justified here in the face
> of lawlessness and disorder. It is justified because the security which
> it demands must be shared with an oppressed people."

This passage and Gould's conception of his own role may be
taken as the central fact of the social and historical theme of *Nostromo.* But how does Conrad intend us to regard this passage?
Albert Guerard, Jr., in his careful and brilliant study of Conrad, says
that the mine "corrupts Sulaco, bringing civil war rather than progress." That strikes me as far too simple. There has been a civil war,
but the forces of "progress"—i.e., the San Tomé mine and the
capitalistic order—have won. And we must admit that the society
at the end of the book is preferable to that at the beginning.

Charles Gould's statement, and his victory, are, however, hedged
about with all sorts of ironies. For one thing—and how cunning is

this stroke!—there is Decoud's narrative, the letter written to his sister in the midst of the violence, that appears at the very center of the book; and the voice of the skeptic tells us how history is fulfilled. For another thing—and this stroke is even more cunning—old Captain Mitchell, faithful-hearted and stupid, the courageous dolt, is the narrator of what he pleases to call the "historical events." His is the first human voice we have heard, in Chapter II of Part I, after the mists part to exhibit the great panorama of the mountains, campo, city, and gulf; and in Chapter X of Part III, just after Nostromo has made his decision to ride to Cayta and save the Concession and the new state, the voice of Captain Mitchell resumes. He is speaking long afterward, to some nameless distinguished visitor, and now all the violence and passion and the great anonymous forces of history come under the unconscious irony of his droning anecdotes. We can say of Captain Mitchell what Conrad says of Pedrito Montero, inflamed by his bad novels read in a Parisian garret: his mind is "wrapped . . . in the futilities of historical anecdote." Captain Mitchell's view is, we may say, the "official view": "Progress" has triumphed, the world has achieved itself, there is nothing left but to enjoy the fruits of the famous victory. Thus the very personalities of the narrators function as commentary (in a triumph of technical virtuosity) as their voices are interpolated into Conrad's high and impersonal discourse.

But we do not have to depend merely on this subtle commentary. Toward the end of the book, at a moment of pause when all seems to be achieved on a sort of Fiddler's Green at the end of history, a party has gathered in the garden of the Casa Gould. They discuss in a desultory way the possibility of a new revolution, and the existence of secret societies in which Nostromo, despite his secret treasure and growing wealth, is a great force. Emilia Gould demands: "Will there never be any peace?" And Dr. Monygham replies:

"There is no peace and no rest in the development of material interests. They have their law and their justice. But it is founded on expediency, and is inhuman; it is without rectitude, and without the continuity and force that can be found only in a moral principle. Mrs. Gould, the time approaches when all that the Gould Concession stands for shall weigh as heavily upon the people as the barbarism, cruelty, and misrule of a few years back."

The material interests have fulfilled their historical mission, or are in the process of fulfilling it. Even Charles Gould, long before, in defining his mission to bring order through the capitalistic development, had not seen that order as the end, only as a phase. He had said: "A better justice will come afterwards. That's our ray of hope." And in this connection we may recall in *Under Western Eyes* how, after hearing the old teacher of languages give his disillusioned view of revolution, Miss Haldin can still say: "I would take liberty from any hand as a hungry man would snatch at a piece of bread. The true progress must begin after." In other words, the empire-builder and hard-bitten realist Gould and the idealistic girl join to see beyond the era of material interests and the era of revolution the time of "true progress" and the "better justice." Somewhere, beyond, there will be, according to Miss Haldin's version, the period of concord:

> I believe that the future will be merciful to us all. Revolutionist and reactionary, victim and executioner, betrayer and betrayed, they shall all be pitied together when the light breaks on our black sky at last. Pitied and forgotten; for without that there can be no union and no love.

Emilia Gould, trapped in her "merciless nightmare" in the "Treasure House of the World," leans over the dying capataz and hears him say, "But there is something accursed in wealth." Then he begins to tell her where the treasure is hidden. But she bursts out: "Let it be lost for ever."

If in this moment of vision, Emilia Gould and (in a sense that we shall come to) Conrad himself repudiate the material interests as merely a step toward justice, what are we to make of revolution? We may remember that Conrad most anxiously meditated the epigraphs of his various books, and that the epigraph of *Nostromo* is the line from Shakespeare: "So foul a sky clears not without a storm." It is innocent to think that this refers merely to the "storm" which is the action of the novel, the revolution that has established the order of material interests in Sulaco. If the sky has cleared at the end of that episode, even now in the new peace we see, as Dr. Monygham sees, the blacker and more terrible thunderheads piling up on the far horizon.

"Heart of Darkness" and *Nostromo* are, in one sense, an analysis and unmasking of capitalism as it manifested itself in the imperialistic adventure. Necessarily this involves the topic of revolution. The end of *Nostromo* leaves the sky again foul, and in the years immediately after finishing that novel Conrad turns to two studies of revolution, *The Secret Agent,* begun in 1905 and published in 1907, and *Under Western Eyes,* begun in 1908 and published in 1911. These books are in their way an analysis and unmasking of revolution to correspond to the already accomplished analysis and unmasking of capitalism and imperialism. In the world of revolution we find the same complex of egotism, vanity, violence, and even noble illusion. As the old teacher of languages in *Under Western Eyes* puts it:

> A violent revolution falls into the hands of the narrow-minded fanatics and of tyrannical hypocrites at first. Afterwards comes the turn of all the pretentious intellectual failures of the time. Such are the chiefs and the leaders. You will notice that I have left out the mere rogues. The scrupulous and the just, the noble, humane, and devoted natures; the unselfish and the intelligent may begin a movement—but it passes away from them. They are not the leaders of a revolution. They are its victims: the victims of disgust, of disenchantment—often of remorse. Hopes grotesquely betrayed, ideal caricatured—that is the definition of revolutionary success. There have been in every revolution hearts broken by such successes.

We could take this, in appropriate paraphrase, as a summary of the situation at the end of *Nostromo.* There is the same irony of success. There has been the same contamination of the vision in the very effort to realize the vision. As Emilia Gould reflects: "There was something inherent in the necessities of successful action which carried with it the moral degradation of the idea."

Man, however, is committed to action. The Heysts, who repudiate action, find their own kind of damnation. Wisdom, then, is the recognition of man's condition, the condition of the creature made without gills or fins but dropped into the sea, the necessity of living with the ever renewing dilemma of idea as opposed to nature, morality to action, "utopianism" to "secular logic" (to take Razumov's terms from *Under Western Eyes*), justice to material interests. Man must make his life somehow in the dialectical process of these terms, and in so far as he is to achieve redemption he must do so through an awareness of his condition that identifies him with the general human communion, not in abstraction, not in mere doctrine, but immediately. The victory is never won, the redemption must be continually re-earned. And as for history, there is no Fiddler's Green, at least not near and soon. History is a process fraught with risks, and the moral regeneration of society depends not upon shifts in mechanism but upon the moral regeneration of men. But nothing is to be hoped for, even in the most modest way, if men lose the vision of the time of concord, when "the light breaks on our black sky at last." That Platonic vision is what makes life possible in its ruck and confusion, if we are to take Conrad's word from the essay called "Books":

> I would require from him [the artist] many acts of faith of which the first would be the cherishing of an undying hope; and hope, it will not be contested, implies all the piety of effort and renunciation. It is the God-sent form of trust in the magic force and inspiration belonging to the life of this earth. We are inclined to forget that the way of excellence is in the intellectual, as distinguished from emotional, humility. What one feels so hopelessly barren in declared pessimism is just its arrogance. It seems as if the discovery made by many men at various times that there is much evil in the world were a source of proud and unholy joy unto some of the modern writers. That frame of mind is not the proper one in which to approach seriously the art of fiction. It gives an author—goodness only knows why—an elated sense of his own superiority. And there is nothing more dangerous than such an elation to that absolute loyalty towards his own feelings and sensations an author should keep hold of in his most exalted moments of creation.
>
> To be hopeful in an artistic sense it is not necessary to think that the world is good. It is enough to believe that there is no impossibility of its being made so.

Nothing, however, is easy or certain. Man is precariously balanced in his humanity between the black inward abyss of himself and the black outward abyss of nature. What Conrad meant by and felt about man's perilous balance must already be clear, if I can make it clear at all. But now I shall speak of *Nostromo* as an image of this.

The setting of the story, the isolation of Sulaco, is in itself significant. The serrated wall of the Cordillera, hieratic and snow-capped, behind the Campo, the Azuera and the Golfo Placido define a little world that comes to us as complete—as a microcosm, we may say, of the greater world and its history. Man is lost in this overwhelming scene. The story of the two gringos, spectral and alive, on the peninsula of Azuera is, of course, a fable of greed and of the terrifying logic of material interests unredeemed. But it is also a fable, here at the threshold of *Nostromo,* of man lost in the blankness of nature. At the center of the book, to resume the same theme, we find the story of Decoud, who loses his identity into the "world of cloud and water, of natural forces and forms of nature." When he commits suicide, he falls into the "immense indifference of things." Then at the very end of the novel, in the last paragraph, Dr. Monygham, in the police-galley, hears the wild, faithful cry uttered by Linda, the name of Nostromo: "Never! Gian' Battista!"

> It was another of Nostromo's successes, the greatest, the most enviable, the most sinister of all. In that true cry of love and grief that seemed to ring aloud from Punta Mala to Azuera and away to the bright line of the horizon, overhung by a big white cloud shining like a mass of solid silver, the genius of the magnificent capataz de cargadores dominated the dark gulf containing his conquests of treasure and love.

This, too, is a fable: the passionate cry in the night that is a kind of triumph in the face of the immense indifference of things. It is a fable with a moral not unlike that of the second of Yeats's "Two Songs from a Play":

> Whatever flames upon the night
> Man's own resinous heart has fed.

Or to take another fable, one from Conrad's essay on Henry James:

> When the last aqueduct shall have crumbled to pieces, the last airship fallen to the ground, the last blade of grass have died upon a dying earth, man, indomitable by his training in resistance to misery and pain, shall set this undiminished light of his eyes against the feeble glow of the sun. . . .
>
> For my own part, from a short and cursory acquaintance with my kind, I am inclined to think that the last utterance will formulate, strange as it may appear, some hope now to us utterly inconceivable.

I have tried to define my reading of Conrad's work in general and of *Nostromo* in particular. In these matters there is not, and should not be, an ultimate "reading," a final word and orthodoxy of interpretation. In so far as a work is vital, there will continually be a development, an extrapolation of significance. But at any one moment each of us must take the risk of his sensibility and his logic in making a reading. I have taken this risk, and part of the risk is the repudiation, or at least criticism, of competing interpretations.

There is one view, not uncommonly encountered, that Conrad did not intend his fiction to have "meaning." We encounter, for example, the comment of Edward Crankshaw: "Bothering about what Conrad meant in 'Heart of Darkness' is as irrelevant as bothering about what Mozart meant in the Haffner Symphony." Conrad himself gives some support to this view in his skeptical bias, in his emphasis on the merely spectacular value of life, and in not a few of his remarks on his literary intentions, particularly in the famous one: "My task which I am trying to achieve is, by the power of the written word, to make you hear, to make you feel—it is, before all, to make you *see.*"

All of this seems to me, however, to mean nothing more than that Conrad was an artist, that he wanted, in other words, to arrive at his meanings immediately, through the sensuous renderings of passionate experience, and not merely to define meanings in abstraction, as didacticism or moralizing. Conrad made no split between literature and life. If anything, he insisted on the deepest inward relationship. As he put it about the writer in the essay "Books": "It is in the impartial practice of life, if anywhere, that the promise of perfection for his art can be found, rather than in the absurd formulas trying to prescribe this or that particular method of technique or conception."

Over and over again, Conrad implies what he says in the Author's Note to *Chance:* "But every subject in the region of intellect and emotion must have a morality of its own if it is treated at all sincerely; and even the most artful writer will give himself (and his morality) away in about every third sentence." And even to the famous sentence about his intention being, before all, to make us "*see,*" we find an addition: "That—and no more, and it is everything." To seeing in its fullest sense, to "our sympathetic imagination," as Conrad says in "Autocracy and War," we must look "for the ultimate triumph of concord and justice."

If in *A Personal Record* Conrad declares himself an "imperfect Esthete," in the same sentence he admits that he is "no better philosopher." Leavis goes so far as to affirm that Conrad cannot be said to have a philosophy: "He is not one of those writers who clear up their fundamental attitudes for themselves in such a way that we may reasonably, in talking of them, use that portentous term." In discussing this remark, as I am about to do, I run the risk of making Conrad's work seem too schematic and of implying that he somehow sat down and worked out a philosophy which he then projected, with allegorical precision, into fiction. I mean nothing of the sort, but I do mean to say that in my judgment Leavis takes Conrad's work as too much a casual matter of temperament. For I think that even if Conrad is as "imperfect" a philosopher as he is an esthete, he is still, in the fullest sense of the term, a philosophical novelist.

The philosophical novelist, or poet, is one for whom the documentation of the world is constantly striving to rise to the level of generalization about values, for whom the image strives to rise to symbol, for whom images always fall into a dialectical configuration, for whom the urgency of experience, no matter how vividly and strongly experience may enchant, is the urgency to know the meaning of experience. This is not to say that the philosophical novelist is schematic and deductive. It is to say quite the contrary, that he is willing to go naked into the pit, again and again, to make the same old struggle for his truth. But we cannot better Conrad's own statement for the philosophical novelist, the kind of novelist he undertook, quite consciously, to be: "Even before the most seductive reveries I have remained mindful of that sobriety of interior life, that asceticism of sentiment, in which alone the naked form of truth, such as one conceives it, can be rendered without shame."

For him the very act of composition was a way of knowing, a way of exploration. In one sense this is bound to be true of all composition, but the matter of degree and self-consciousness is important in our present distinction, even crucial. We know a little of how *Nostromo* came to be, how it rose out of a feeling of blankness, how its composition was, in sober fact, an exploration and a growth, how the "great mirage," as Edward Garnett called it, took shape until it could float before us, vivid and severe, one of the few mastering visions of our historical moment and our human lot.

ERNEST HEMINGWAY

*I*N MAY, 1929, in *Scribner's Magazine,* the first installment of *A Farewell to Arms* appeared. The novel was completed in the issue of October, and was published in book form the same year. Ernest Hemingway was already regarded, by a limited literary public, as a writer of extraordinary freshness and power, as one of the makers, indeed, of a new American fiction. *A Farewell to Arms* more than justified the early enthusiasm of the connoisseurs for Hemingway, and extended his reputation from them to the public at large. Its great importance was at once acknowledged, and its reputation has survived through the changing fashions and interests of many years.

What was the immediate cause of its appeal? It told a truth about the first world war, and a truth about the generation who had fought it and whose lives, because of the war, had been wrenched

First published as "Hemingway" in *The Kenyon Review,* Winter 1947. Included as the Introduction to the Modern Standard Authors edition of *A Farewell to Arms,* Charles Scribner's Sons, 1949, and in *Selected Essays,* 1958.

from the expected pattern and the old values. Other writers had told or were to tell similar truths about this war. John Dos Passos in *Three Soldiers,* E. E. Cummings in *The Enormous Room,* William Faulkner in *Soldiers' Pay,* Maxwell Anderson and Laurence Stallings in *What Price Glory?* All these writers had presented the pathos and endurance and gallantry of the individual caught and mangled in the great anonymous mechanism of a modern war fought for reasons that the individual could not understand, found insufficient to justify the event, or believed to be no reasons at all. And *A Farewell to Arms* was not the first book to record the plight of the men and women who, because of the war, had been unable to come to terms with life in the old way. Hemingway himself in *The Sun Also Rises,* 1926, had given the picture of the dislocated life of young English and American expatriates in the bars of Paris, the "lost generation," as Gertrude Stein defined them. But before that, F. Scott Fitzgerald, who had been no nearer to the war than an officers' training camp, had written of the lost generation. For the young people about whom Fitzgerald wrote, even when they were not veterans and even when their love stories were enacted in parked cars, fraternity houses, and country clubs and not in the cafés and hotels of Paris, were like Hemingway's expatriates under the shadow of the war and were groping to find some satisfaction in a world from which the old values had been withdrawn. Hemingway's expatriates had turned their backs on the glitter of the Great Boom of the 1920s, and Fitzgerald's young men were usually drawn to the romance of wealth and indulgence, but this difference is superficial. If Hemingway's young men begin by repudiating the Great Boom, Fitzgerald's young men end with disappointment in what even success has to offer. "All the sad young men" of Fitzgerald—to take the title of one of his collections of stories—and the "lost generation" of Hemingway are seekers for landmarks and bearings in a terrain for which the maps have been mislaid.

A Farewell to Arms, which appeared ten years after the first world war and on the eve of the collapse of the Great Boom, seemed to sum up and bring to focus an inner meaning of the decade being finished. It worked thus, not because it disclosed the end results that the life of the decade was producing—the discontents and disasters that were beginning to be noticed even by unreflective people—but because it cut back to the beginning of the process, to the moment that had held within itself the explanation of the subsequent process.

Those who had grown up in the war or in its shadow could look back nostalgically, as it were, to the lost moment of innocence of motive and purity of emotion. If those things had been tarnished or manhandled by the later business of living, they had, at least, existed, and on a grand scale. If they had been tarnished or manhandled, it was not through the fault of the individual who looked back to see the image of the old simple and heroic self in Frederick or Catherine, but through the impersonal grindings of the great machine of the universe. *A Farewell to Arms* served, in a way, as the great romantic alibi for a generation, and for those who aped and emulated that generation. It showed how cynicism or disillusionment, failure of spirit or the worship of material success, debauchery or despair, might have been grounded in heroism, simplicity, and fidelity that had met unmerited defeat. The early tragedy could cast a kind of flattering and extenuating afterglow over what had come later. The battlefields of *A Farewell to Arms* explained the bars of *The Sun Also Rises*—and explained the young Krebs, of the story "Soldier's Home," who came back home to a Middle Western town to accept his own slow disintegration.

This is not said in disparagement of *A Farewell to Arms.* It is, after all, a compliment to the hypnotic force of the book. For the hypnotic force of the book was felt from the first, and it is not unusual for such a book to be relished by its first readers for superficial reasons and not for the essential virtues that may engage those who come to it later.

In accounting for the immediate appeal of *A Farewell to Arms,* the history of the author himself is of some importance. In so far as the reader knew about Ernest Hemingway in 1929, he knew about a young man who seemed to typify in his own experience the central experience of his generation. Behind the story of *A Farewell to Arms* and his other books there was the shadow of his own story that could stamp his fiction with the authenticity of a document and, for the more impressionable, with the value of a revelation. He could give an ethic and a technique for living, even in the face of defeat or frustration, and yet his own story was the story that we have always loved: the American success story.

He was born in Oak Park, Illinois, in the Middle West—that region which it was fashionable to condemn (after Mencken and Sinclair Lewis) as romanceless, but which became endowed, paradoxically enough, with the romance of the American average. His father was a physician. There were two boys and four girls in the family. In the summers the family lived in northern Michigan, where there were Indians, and where lake, streams, and forests gave boyhood pursuits their appropriate setting. In the winters he went to school in Oak Park. He played football in high school, ran away from home, returned and, in 1917, graduated. After graduation he was for a short time a reporter on the *Kansas City Star,* but the war was on and he went to Italy as a volunteer ambulance driver. He was wounded and decorated, and after his recovery served in the Italian army as a soldier. For a time after the war he was a foreign correspondent for the *Toronto Star,* in the Near East.

In the years after the war Hemingway set about learning, quite consciously and with rigorous self-discipline, the craft and art of writing. During most of his apprenticeship he lived in Paris, one of the great number of expatriates who were drawn to the artistic capital of the world to learn to be writers, painters, sculptors, or dancers, or simply to enjoy on a low monetary exchange the freedom of life away from American or British conventions. "Young America," writes Ford Madox Ford, "from the limitless prairies leapt, released, on Paris. They stampeded with the madness of colts when you let down the slip-rails between dried pasture and green. The noise of their advancing drowned all sounds. Their innumerable forms hid the very trees on the boulevards. Their perpetual motion made you dizzy." And of Hemingway himself: "He was presented to me by Ezra [Pound] and Bill Bird and had rather the aspect of an Eton-Oxford, huskyish young captain of a midland regiment of His Britannic Majesty. . . . Into that animated din would drift Hemingway, balancing on the point of his toes, feinting at my head with hands as large as hams and relating sinister stories of Paris landlords. He told them with singularly choice words in a slow voice."[1]

[1] Introduction to the Modern Library edition of *A Farewell to Arms.*

The originality and force of Hemingway's early stories, published in little magazines and in limited editions in France, were recognized from the first by many who made their acquaintance. The seeds of his later work were in those stories of *In Our Time,* concerned chiefly with scenes of inland American life and a boy's growing awareness of that life in contrast to vivid flashes of the disorder and brutality of the war years and the immediate postwar years in Europe. There are both contrast and continuity between the two elements of *In Our Time.* There is the contrast between the lyric rendering of one aspect of the boyhood world and the realistic rendering of the world of war, but there is also a continuity, because in the boyhood world there are recurring intimations of the blackness into which experience can lead even in the peaceful setting of Michigan.

With the publication of *The Sun Also Rises,* in 1926, Hemingway's work reached a wider audience, and at the same time defined more clearly the line his genius was to follow and his role as one of the spokesmen for a generation. But *A Farewell to Arms* gave him his first substantial popular success and established his reputation. It was a brilliant and compelling novel; it provided the great alibi; it crowned the success story of the American boy from the Middle West, who had hunted and fished, played football in high school, been a newspaper reporter, gone to war and been wounded and decorated, wandered exotic lands as a foreign correspondent, lived the free life of the Latin Quarter of Paris, and, at the age of thirty, written a best seller—athlete, sportsman, correspondent, soldier, adventurer, and author.

It would be possible and even profitable to discuss *A Farewell to Arms* in isolation from Hemingway's other work. But Hemingway is a peculiarly personal writer, and for all the apparent objectivity and self-suppression in his method as a writer, his work, to an uncommon degree, forms a continuous whole. One part explains and interprets another part. It is true that there have been changes between early and late work, that there has been an increasing self-consciousness, that attitudes and methods that in the beginning were instinctive and simple have become calculated and elaborated. But the best way to understand one of his books is, nevertheless, to compare it with both earlier and later pieces and seek to discern motives and methods that underlie all of his work.

Perhaps the simplest way into the whole question is to consider what kind of world Hemingway writes about. A writer may write about his special world merely because he happens to know that world, but he may also write about that special world because it best dramatizes for him the issues and questions that are his fundamental concerns—because, in other words, that special world has a kind of symbolic significance for him. There is often—if we discount mere literary fashion and imitation—an inner and necessary reason for the writer's choice of his characters and situations. What situations and characters does Hemingway write about?

They are usually violent. There is the hard-drinking and sexually promiscuous world of *The Sun Also Rises;* the chaotic and brutal world of war, as in *A Farewell to Arms, For Whom the Bell Tolls,* many of the inserted sketches of *In Our Time,* the play *The Fifth Column,* and some of the stories; the world of sport, as in "Fifty Grand," "My Old Man," "The Undefeated," "The Snows of Kilimanjaro"; the world of crime, as in "The Killers," "The Gambler, the Nun, and the Radio," and *To Have and Have Not.* Even when the situation of a story does not fall into one of these categories, it usually involves a desperate risk, and behind it is the shadow of ruin, physical or spiritual. As for the typical characters, they are usually tough men, experienced in the hard worlds they inhabit, and not obviously given to emotional display or sensitive shrinking—men like Rinaldi or Frederick Henry of *A Farewell to Arms,* Robert Jordan of *For Whom the Bell Tolls,* Harry Morgan of *To Have and Have Not,* the big-game hunter of "The Snows of Kilimanjaro," the old bullfighter of "The Undefeated," or the pugilist of "Fifty Grand." Or if the typical character is not of this seasoned order, he is a very young man, or boy, first entering the violent world and learning his first adjustment to it.

We have said that the shadow of ruin is behind the typical Hemingway situation. The typical character faces defeat or death. But out of defeat or death the character usually manages to salvage something. And here we discover Hemingway's special interest in such situations and characters. His heroes are not squealers, welchers, compromisers, or cowards, and when they confront defeat they realize that the stance they take, the stoic endurance, the stiff upper lip mean a kind of victory. If they are to be defeated, they are defeated upon their own terms; some of them have even courted their defeat; and certainly they have maintained, even in the practical defeat, an ideal of themselves—some definition of how a man should behave, formulated or unformulated—by which they have lived. They represent some notion of a code, some notion of honor, that makes a man a man, and that distinguishes him from people who merely follow their random impulses and who are, by consequence, "messy."

In case after case, we can illustrate this "principle of sportsmanship," as Edmund Wilson has called it, at the center of a story or novel. Robert Jordan, in *For Whom the Bell Tolls,* is somehow happy as he lies, wounded, behind the machine gun that is to cover the escape of his friends and his sweetheart from Franco's Fascists. The old bullfighter, in "The Undefeated," continues his incompetent fight even under the jeers and hoots of the crowd, until the bull is dead and he himself is mortally hurt. Francis Macomber, the rich young sportsman who goes lion-hunting in "The Short, Happy Life of Francis Macomber," and who has funked it and bolted before a wounded lion, at last learns the lesson that the code of the hunter demands that he go into the bush after an animal he has wounded. Brett, the heroine of *The Sun Also Rises,* gives up Romero, the young bullfighter with whom she is in love, because she knows she will ruin him, and her tight-lipped remark to Jake, the newspaperman who is the narrator of the novel, might almost serve as the motto of Hemingway's work: "You know it makes one feel rather good deciding not to be a bitch."

It is the discipline of the code that makes man human, a sense of style or good form. This applies not only in isolated, dramatic cases such as those listed above, but is a more pervasive thing that can give meaning, partially at least, to the confusions of living. The discipline of the soldier, the form of the athlete, the gameness of the sportsman, the technique of an artist can give some sense of the human order, and can achieve a moral significance. And here we see how Hemingway's concern with war and sport crosses his concern with literary style. If a writer can get the kind of style at which Hemingway, in *Green Hills of Africa,* professes to aim, then "noth-

ing else matters. It is more important than anything else he can do."
It is more important because, ultimately, it is a moral achievement.
And no doubt for this reason, as well as for the reason of Henry
James's concern with cruxes of a moral code, he is, as he says in
Green Hills of Africa, an admirer of the work of Henry James, the
devoted stylist.

But to return to the subject of Hemingway's world: the code and
the discipline are important because they can give meaning to life
that otherwise seems to have no meaning or justification. In other
words, in a world without supernatural sanctions, in the God-abandoned world of modernity, man can realize an ideal meaning only
in so far as he can define and maintain the code. The effort to do
so, however limited and imperfect it may be, is the characteristically
human effort and provides the tragic or pitiful human story. Hemingway's attitude on this point is much like that of Robert Louis
Stevenson in "Pulvis et Umbra":

> Poor soul, here for so little, cast among so many hardships, filled
> with desires so incommensurate and so inconsistent, savagely sur-
> rounded, savagely descended, irremediably condemned to prey
> upon his fellow lives: who should have blamed him had he been of
> a piece with his destiny and a being merely barbarous? And we look
> and behold him instead, filled with imperfect virtues . . . an ideal of
> decency, to which he would rise if it were possible; a limit of shame,
> below which, if it be possible, he will not stoop. . . . Man is indeed
> marked for failure in his effort to do right. But where the best
> consistently miscarry, how tenfold more remarkable that all should
> continue to strive; and surely we should find it both touching and
> inspiriting, that in a field from which success is banished, our race
> should not cease to labor. . . . It matters not where we look, under
> what climate we observe him, in what stage of society, in what depth
> of ignorance, burthened with what erroneous morality; by campfires
> in Assiniboia, the snow powdering his shoulders, the wind plucking
> his blanket, as he sits, passing the ceremonial calumet and uttering
> his grave opinions like a Roman senator; on ships at sea, a man
> inured to hardship and vile pleasures, his brightest hope a fiddle in
> a tavern and a bedizened trull who sells herself to rob him, and he
> for all that, simple, innocent, cheerful, kindly like a child, constant
> to toil, brave to drown, for others; . . . in the brothel, the discard

of society, living mainly on strong drink, fed with affronts, a fool, a thief, the comrade of thieves, and even here keeping the point of honor and the touch of pity, often repaying the world's scorn with service, often standing firm upon a scruple, and at a certain cost, rejecting riches:—everywhere some virtue cherished or affected, everywhere some decency of thought or carriage, everywhere the ensign of man's ineffectual goodness! . . . under every circumstance of failure, without hope, without help, without thanks, still obscurely fighting the lost fight of virtue, still clinging, in the brothel or on the scaffold, to some rag of honor, the poor jewel of their souls! They may seek to escape, and yet they cannot; it is not alone their privilege and glory, but their doom; they are condemned to some nobility. . . .

Hemingway's code is more rigorous than Stevenson's and perhaps he finds fewer devoted to it, but, like Stevenson, he can find his characteristic hero and characteristic story among the discards of society, and, like Stevenson, is aware of the touching irony of that fact. But for the moment the important thing in the parallel is that, for Stevenson, the world in which this drama of pitiful aspiration and stoic endurance is played out is apparently a violent and meaningless world—"our rotary island loaded with predatory life and more drenched with blood . . . than ever mutinied ship, scuds through space."

Neither Hemingway nor Stevenson invented this world. It had already appeared in literature before their time, and that is a way of saying that this cheerless vision had already begun to trouble men. It is the world we find pictured (and denied) in Tennyson's "In Memoriam"—the world in which human conduct is a product of "dying Nature's earth and lime." It is the world pictured (and not denied) in Hardy and Housman, a world that seems to be presided over by blind Doomsters (if by anybody), as Hardy put it in his poem "Hap," or made by some brute and blackguard (if by anybody), as Housman put it in his poem "The Chestnut Casts Its Flambeaux." It is the world of Zola or Dreiser or Conrad or Faulkner. It is the world of, to use Bertrand Russell's phrase, "secular hurryings through space." It is the God-abandoned world, the world of Nature-as-all. We know where the literary men got this picture. They got it from the scientists of the nineteenth century. This is Hemingway's world, too, the world with nothing at center.

Over against this particular version of the naturalistic view of the world, there was, of course, an argument for Divine Intelligence and a Divine purpose, an argument that based itself on the beautiful system of nature, on natural law. The closely knit order of the natural world, so the argument ran, implies a Divine Intelligence. But if one calls Hemingway's attention to the fact that the natural world is a world of order, his reply is on record in a story called "A Natural History of the Dead." There he quotes from the traveler Mungo Park, who, naked and starving in an African desert, observed a beautiful little moss-flower and meditated thus:

> Can the Being who planted, watered, and brought to perfection, in this obscure part of the world, a thing which appears of so small importance, look with unconcern upon the situation and suffering of creatures formed after his own image? Surely not. Reflections like these would not allow me to despair: I started up and, disregarding both hunger and fatigue, travelled forward, assured that relief was at hand; and I was not disappointed.

And Hemingway continues:

> With a disposition to wonder and adore in like manner, as Bishop Stanley says [the author of *A Familiar History of Birds*], can any branch of Natural History be studied without increasing that faith, love and hope which we also, everyone of us, need in our journey through the wilderness of life? Let us therefore see what inspiration we may derive from the dead.

Then Hemingway presents the picture of a modern battlefield, where the bloated and decaying bodies give a perfect example of the natural order of chemistry—but scarcely an argument for faith, hope, and love. That picture is his answer to the argument that the order of nature implies meaning in the world.

In one of the stories, "A Clean, Well-Lighted Place," we find the best description of what underlies Hemingway's world of violent action. In the early stages of the story we see an old man sitting late in a Spanish café. Two waiters are speaking of him.

"Last week he tried to commit suicide," one waiter said.
"Why?"
"He was in despair."
"What about?"
"Nothing."
"How do you know it was nothing?"
"He has plenty of money."

The despair beyond plenty of money—or beyond all the other gifts of the world: its nature becomes a little clearer at the end of the story when the older of the two waiters is left alone, reluctant too to leave the clean, well-lighted place:

> Turning off the electric light he continued the conversation with himself. It is the light of course but it is necessary that the place be clean and pleasant. You do not want music. Certainly you do not want music. Nor can you stand before a bar with dignity although that is all that is provided for these hours. What did he fear? It was not fear or dread. It was a nothing that he knew too well. It was all a nothing and a man was nothing too. It was only that and light was all it needed and a certain cleanness and order. Some lived in it and never felt it but he knew it all was nada y pues nada y nada y pues nada. Our nada who art in nada, nada be thy name thy kingdom nada thy will be nada in nada as it is in nada. Give us this nada our daily nada and nada us our nada as we nada our nadas and nada us not into nada but deliver us from nada; pues nada. Hail nothing full of nothing, nothing is with thee. He smiled and stood before a bar with a shining steam pressure coffee machine.
> "What's yours?" asked the barman.
> "Nada."

At the end the old waiter is ready to go home:

> Now, without thinking further, he would go home to his room. He would lie in bed and finally, with daylight, he would go to sleep. After all, he said to himself, it is probably only insomnia. Many must have it.

And the sleepless man—the man obsessed by death, by the meaninglessness of the world, by nothingness, by nada—is one of the recurring symbols in the work of Hemingway. In this phase Hemingway is a religious writer. The despair beyond plenty of money, the despair that makes a sleeplessness beyond insomnia, is the despair felt by a man who hungers for the sense of order and assurance that men seem to find in religious faith, but who cannot find grounds for his faith.

Another recurring symbol is the violent man. But the sleepless man and the violent man are not contradictory; they are complementary symbols. They represent phases of the same question, the same hungering for meaning in the world. The sleepless man is the man brooding upon nada, upon chaos, upon Nature-as-all. (For Nature-as-all equals moral chaos; even its bulls and lions and kudu are not admired by Hemingway as creatures of conscious self-discipline; their courage has a meaning only in so far as it symbolizes human courage.) The violent man is the man taking an action appropriate to the realization of the fact of nada. He is, in other words, engaged in the effort to discover human values in a naturalistic world.

Before we proceed with this line of discussion, it might be asked, "Why does Hemingway feel that the quest necessarily involves violence?" Now, at one level, the answer to this question would involve the whole matter of the bias toward violence in modern literature. But let us take it in its more immediate reference. The typical Hemingway hero is the man aware, or in the process of becoming aware, of nada. Death is the great nada. Therefore, whatever code or creed the hero gets must, to be good, stick even in the face of death. It has to be good in the bull ring or on the battlefield and not merely in the study or lecture room. In fact, Hemingway is anti-intellectual, and has a great contempt for any type of solution arrived at without the testings of immediate experience.

So aside from the question of a dramatic sense that would favor violence, and aside from the mere matter of personal temperament (for Hemingway describes himself on more than one occasion as obsessed by death), the presentation of violence is appropriate in his work because death is the great nada. In taking violent risks, man confronts in dramatic terms the issue of nada that is implicit in all of Hemingway's world.

But to return to our general line of discussion. There are two aspects to this violence that is involved in the quest of the Hemingway hero, two aspects that seem to represent an ambivalent attitude toward nature.

First, there is the conscious sinking into nature, as we may call it. On this line of reasoning we would find something like this: if there is at center only nada, then the only sure compensation in life, the only reality, is gratification of appetite, the relish of sensation.

Continually in the stories and novels, one finds such sentences as this from *Green Hills of Africa:* ". . . drinking this, the first one of the day, the finest one there is, and looking at the thick bush we passed in the dark, feeling the cool wind of the night and smelling the good smell of Africa, I was altogether happy." What is constantly interesting in such sentences is the fact that happiness, a notion that we traditionally connect with a complicated state of being, with notions of virtue, of achievement, etc., is here equated with a set of merely agreeable sensations. For instance, in "Cross-Country Snow," one of the boys, George, says to the other, Nick, who in story after story is a sort of shadow of Hemingway himself, "Maybe we'll never go skiing again, Nick." And Nick replies, "We've got to. It isn't worth while if you can't." The sensations of skiing are the end of life. Or in another story, "Big Two-Hearted River: Part II," a story that is full of the sensation-as-happiness theme, we find this remark about Nick, who has been wading in a trout stream: "Nick climbed out onto the meadow and stood, water running down his trousers and out of his shoes, his shoes squelchy. He went over and sat on the logs. He did not want to rush his sensations any." The careful relish of sensation—that is what counts, always.

This intense awareness of the world of the senses is, of course, one of the things that made the early work of Hemingway seem, upon its first impact, so fresh and pure. Physical nature is nowhere rendered with greater vividness than in his work, and probably his only competitors in this department of literature are William Faulkner, among the modern, and Henry David Thoreau, among the older American writers. The meadows, forests, lakes, and trout streams of America, and the arid, sculpturesque mountains of Spain, appear with astonishing immediacy, and immediacy not dependent upon descriptive flourishes. But not only the appearance of land-scape is important; a great deal of the freshness comes from the discrimination of sensation, the coldness of water in the "squelchy" shoes after wading, the tangy smell of dry sagebrush, the "cleanly" smell of grease and oil on a field piece.[2] Hemingway's appreciation of the aesthetic qualities of the physical world is important, but a peculiar poignancy is implicit in the rendering of those qualities; the beauty of the physical world is a background for the human predicament, and the very relishing of the beauty is merely a kind of desperate and momentary compensation possible in the midst of the predicament.

This careful relishing of the world of the senses comes to a climax in drinking and sex. Drink is the "giant-killer," the weapon against man's thought of nada. And so is sex, for that matter, though when sexual attraction achieves the status of love, the process is one that attempts to achieve a meaning rather than to forget meaningless-ness in the world. In terms of drinking and sex, the typical Heming-way hero is a man of monel-metal stomach and Homeric prowess in the arts of love. And the typical situation is love, with some drinking, against the background of nada—of civilization gone to pot, of war, or of death—as we get it in all of the novels in one form or another, and in many of the stories.

It is important to remember, however, that the sinking into na-ture, even at the level of drinking and mere sexuality, is a self-conscious act. It is not the random gratification of appetite. We see this quite clearly in *The Sun Also Rises* in the contrast between Cohn, who is merely a random dabbler in the world of sensation, who is merely trying to amuse himself, and the initiates like Jake and Brett, who are aware of the nada at the center of things and whose dissipations, therefore, have a philosophical significance. The initi-ate in Hemingway's world raises the gratification of appetite to the level of a cult and a discipline.

The cult of sensation, as we have already indicated, passes over very readily into the cult of true love, for the typical love story is presented primarily in terms of the cult of sensation. (*A Farewell to*

[2]Commented on by Ford Madox Ford in his introduction to the Modern Library edition of *A Farewell to Arms.*

Arms, as we shall see when we come to a detailed study of that novel, is closely concerned with this transition.) Even in the cult of true love it is the moment that counts, and the individual. There is never any past or future to the love stories, and the lovers are always isolated, not moving within the framework of obligations of an ordinary human society. The notion of the cult—a secret cult composed of those who have been initiated into the secret of nada—is constantly played up.

In *A Farewell to Arms,* for instance, Catherine and Frederick are two against the world, a world that is, literally as well as figuratively, an alien world. The peculiar relationship between Frederick and the priest takes on a new significance if viewed in terms of the secret cult. We shall come to this topic later, but for the moment we can say that the priest is a priest of Divine Love, the subject about which he and Frederick converse in the hospital, and that Frederick himself is a kind of priest, one of the initiate in the end, of the cult of profane love. This same pattern of two against the world, with an understanding confidant or interpreter, reappears in *For Whom the Bell Tolls*—with Pilar, the gipsy woman who understands "love," substituting for the priest of *A Farewell to Arms.*

The initiates of the cult of love are those who are aware of nada, but their effort, as members of the cult, is to find a meaning to put in place of the nada. That is, there is an attempt to make the relationship of love take on a religious significance in so far as it can give meaning to life. This general topic is not new with the work of Hemingway. It is one of the literary themes of the nineteenth century—and has, as a matter of fact, a longer history than that.

If the cult of love arises from and states itself in the language of the cult of sensation, it is an extension of the sinking-into-nature aspect of the typical Hemingway violence; but in so far as it involves a discipline and a search for a "faith," it leads us to the second aspect of the typical violence.

The violence, although in its first aspect it represents a sinking into nature, at the same time, in its second aspect, represents a conquest of nature, and of nada in man. It represents such a conquest not because of the fact of violence, but because the violence appears in terms of a discipline, a style, and a code. It is, as we have already seen, in terms of a self-imposed discipline that the heroes make one gallant, though limited, effort to redeem the incoherence of the world: they attempt to impose some form upon the disorder of their lives, the technique of the bullfighter or sportsman, the discipline of the soldier, the fidelity of the lover, or even the code of the gangster, which, though brutal and apparently dehumanizing, has its own ethic. (Ole Anderson, in "The Killers," is willing to take his medicine without whining, and even recognizes some necessity and justice in his plight. Or the dying Mexican, in "The Gambler, the Nun, and the Radio," refuses to squeal despite the detective's argument: "One can, with honor, denounce one's assailant.")

If it is said that Frederick in *A Farewell to Arms* does not, when he deserts, exhibit the discipline of the soldier, the answer is simple: his obligation has been constantly presented as an obligation to the men in his immediate command, and he and the men in his command have never recognized an obligation to the total war—they recognize no meaning in the war and are bound together only by a squad sense and by their immediate respect for each other; when Frederick is separated from his men his obligation is gone. His true obligation then becomes the fidelity to Catherine.

The discipline, the form, is never quite capable of subduing the world, but fidelity to it is part of the gallantry of defeat. By fidelity to it the hero manages to keep one small place "clean" and "well-lighted," and manages to retain, or achieve for one last moment, his dignity. There should be, as the old Spanish waiter reflects, a "clean, well-lighted place" where one could keep one's dignity at the late hour.

We have said earlier that the typical Hemingway character is tough and, apparently, insensitive. But only apparently, for the fidelity to a code, to the discipline, may be the index to a sensitivity that allows the characters to see, at moments, their true plight. At times, and usually at times of stress, it is the tough man in the Hemingway world, the disciplined man, who is actually aware of pathos or tragedy. The individual toughness (which may be taken to be the private discipline demanded by the world) may find itself in conflict with the natural human reactions; but the Hemingway hero, though he may be aware of the claims of the natural reaction, the spontaneous human emotion, cannot surrender to it because he knows that the only way to hold on to the definition of himself, to "honor" or "dignity," is to maintain the discipline, the code. For example, when pity appears in the Hemingway world—as in "The Pursuit Race"—it does not appear in its maximum but in its minimum manifestation.

What this means in terms of style and method is the use of understatement. This understatement, stemming from the contrast between the sensitivity and the superimposed discipline, is a constant aspect of the work, an aspect that was caught in a cartoon in *The New Yorker.* The cartoon showed a brawny, muscle-knotted forearm and a hairy hand that clutched a rose. It was entitled "The Soul of Ernest Hemingway." Just as there is a margin of victory in the defeat of the Hemingway characters, so there is a little margin of sensitivity in their brutal and apparently insensitive world. Hence we have the ironical circumstance—a central circumstance in creating the pervasive irony of Hemingway's work—that the revelation of the values characteristic of his work arises from the most unpromising people and the most unpromising situations— the little streak of poetry or pathos in "The Pursuit Race," "The Killers," "My Old Man," "A Clean, Well-Lighted Place," or "The Undefeated." We have a perfect example of it in the last-named story. After the defeat of the old bullfighter, who is lying wounded on an operating table, Zurito, the picador, is about to cut off the old fellow's pigtail, the mark of his profession. But when the wounded man starts up, despite his pain, and says, "You couldn't do a thing like that," Zurito says, "I was joking." Zurito becomes aware that, after all, the old bullfighter is, in a way, undefeated, and deserves to die with his coleta on.

This locating of the poetic, the pathetic, or the tragic in the unpromising person or situation is not unique with Hemingway. It is something with which we are acquainted in a great deal of our literature since the Romantic Movement. In such literature, the sensibility is played down, and an antiromantic surface sheathes the work; the point is in the contrast. The impulse that led Hemingway to the simple character is akin to the one that drew Wordsworth to the same choice. Wordsworth felt that his unsophisticated peasants were more honest in their responses than the cultivated man, and were therefore more poetic. Instead of Wordsworth's peasant we have in Hemingway's work the bullfighter, the soldier, the revolutionist, the sportsman, and the gangster; instead of Wordsworth's children we have the young men like Nick, the person just on the verge of being initiated into the world. There are, of course, differences between the approach of Wordsworth and that of Hemingway, but there is little difference on the point of marginal sensibility. In one sense, both are anti-intellectual, and in such poems as "Resolution and Independence" or "Michael" one finds even closer ties.

I have just indicated a similarity between Wordsworth and Hemingway on the grounds of a romantic anti-intellectualism. But with Hemingway it is far more profound and radical than with Wordsworth. All we have to do to see the difference is to put Wordsworth's Preface to the *Lyrical Ballads* over against any number of passages from Hemingway. The intellectualism of the eighteenth century had merely put a veil of stereotyped language over the world and a veil of snobbism over a large area of human experience. That is Wordsworth's indictment. But Hemingway's indictment of the intellectualism of the past is that it wound up in the mire and blood of 1914 to 1918; that it was a pack of lies leading to death. We can put over against the Preface of Wordsworth, a passage from *A Farewell to Arms*:

> I was always embarrassed by the words sacred, glorious, and sacrifice and the expression in vain. We had heard them, sometimes standing in the rain almost out of earshot, so that only the shouted words came through, and had read them, on proclamations that were slapped up by billposters over other proclamations, now for a long time, and I had seen nothing sacred, and the things that were glorious had no glory and the sacrifices were like the stockyards at Chicago if nothing was done with the meat except to bury it. There were many words that you could not stand to hear and finally only the names of places had dignity. . . . Abstract words such as glory, honor, courage, or hallow were obscene beside the concrete names of villages, the numbers of roads, the names of rivers, the numbers of regiments and the dates.

I do not mean to say that the general revolution in style, and the revolt against the particular intellectualism of the nineteenth century, was a result of the first world war. As a matter of fact, that revolt was going on long before the war, but for Hemingway, and for many others, the war gave the situation a peculiar depth and urgency.

Perhaps we might scale the matter thus: Wordsworth was a revolutionist—he truly had a new view of the world—but his revolutionary view left great tracts of the world untouched; the Church of England, for instance. Arnold and Tennyson, a generation or so later, though not revolutionists themselves, are much more profoundly stirred by the revolutionary situation than ever Wordsworth was; that is, the area of the world involved in the debate was for them greater. Institutions are called into question in a more fundamental way. But they managed to hang on to their English God and their English institutions. With Hardy, the area of disturbance has grown greater, and what can be salvaged is much less. He, like the earlier Victorians, had a strong sense of community to sustain him in the face of the universe that was for him, as not finally for Arnold and Tennyson, unfriendly, or at least neutral and Godless. But his was a secret community, different from that of social institutions. It was a human communion that, as a matter of fact, was constantly being violated by institutions. Their violation of it is, in fact, a constant source of subject matter and a constant spring of irony. Nevertheless, Hardy could refer to himself as a meliorist. He could not keep company with Wordsworth or Tennyson or Arnold; and when Hardy, having been elected an Honorary Fellow of Magdalene College, Cambridge, was to be formally admitted, the Master, Doctor Donaldson (as we know from A. C. Benson's *Diary*), was much afraid that Hardy might dislike the religious service. The occasion, however, went off very well, even though Hardy, after impressing the Master with his knowledge of ecclesiastical music, did remark, "Of course it's only a sentiment to me now." Hardy listened to a sermon by the Archdeacon of Zanzibar, who declared that God was "a God of *desire*—who both hated and loved—not a mild or impersonal force." But even though Hardy could not accept the God of the Bishop of Zanzibar, he still had faith in the constructive power of the secret community.

Now, in Hemingway we see something very like Hardy's secret community, but one much smaller, one whose definition has become much more specialized. Its members are those who know the code. They recognize each other, they know the password and the secret grip, but they are few in number, and each is set off against the world like a wounded lion ringed round by waiting hyenas (*Green Hills of Africa* gives us the hyena symbol—the animal whose death is comic because it is all hideously "appetite": wounded, it eats its own intestines). Furthermore, this secret community is not constructive; Hemingway is no meliorist. In fact, there are hints that somewhere in the back of his mind, and in behind his work, there is a kind of Spenglerian view of history: our civilization is running down. We get this most explicitly in *Green Hills of Africa:*

A continent ages quickly once we come. The natives live in harmony with it. But the foreigner destroys, cuts down the trees, drains the water, so that the water supply is altered and in a short time the soil, once the sod is turned under, is cropped out and, next, it starts to blow away as it has blown away in every old country and as I had seen it start to blow in Canada. The earth gets tired of being exploited. A country wears out quickly unless man puts back in it all his residue and that of all his beasts. When he quits using beasts and uses machines, the earth defeats him quickly. The machine can't reproduce, nor does it fertilize the soil, and it eats what he cannot raise. A country was made to be as we found it. We are the intruders and after we are dead we may have ruined it but it will still be there and we don't know what the next changes are. I suppose they all end up like Mongolia.

I would come back to Africa but not to make a living from it. . . . But I would come back to where it pleased me to live; to really live. Not just let my life pass. Our people went to America because that was the place for them to go then. It had been a good country and we had made a bloody mess of it and I would go, now, somewhere else as we had always had the right to go somewhere else and as we had always gone. You could always come back. Let the others come to America who did not know that they had come too late. Our people had seen it at its best and fought for it when it was well worth fighting for. Now I would go somewhere else.

This is the most explicit statement, but the view is implicit in case after case. The general human community, the general human project, has gone to pot. There is only the little secret community of, paradoxically enough, individualists who have resigned from the general community, and who are strong enough to live without any of the illusions, lies, and big words of the herd. At least, this is the case up to the novel *To Have and Have Not,* which appeared in 1937. In that novel and in *For Whom the Bell Tolls,* Hemingway attempts to bring his individualistic hero back to society, to give him a common stake with the fate of other men.

But to return to the matter of Wordsworth and Hemingway. What in Wordsworth is merely simple or innocent is in Hemingway violent: the gangster or bullfighter replaces the leech-gatherer or the child. Hemingway's world is a more disordered world, and the sensibility of his characters is more ironically in contrast with their world. The most immediate consideration here is the playing down of the sensibility as such, the sheathing of it in the code of toughness. Gertrude Stein's tribute is here relevant: "Hemingway is the shyest and proudest and sweetest-smelling storyteller of my reading." But this shyness manifests itself in the irony. In this, of course, Hemingway's irony corresponds to the Byronic irony. But the relation to Byron is even more fundamental. The pity is valid only when it is wrung from the man who has been seasoned by experience. Therefore a premium is placed on the fact of violent experience. The "dumb ox" character, commented on by Wyndham Lewis, represents the Wordsworthian peasant; the character with the code of the tough guy, the initiate, the man cultivating honor, gallantry, and recklessness, represents the Byronic aristocrat.

The failures of Hemingway, like his successes, are rooted in this situation. The successes occur in those instances where Hemingway accepts the essential limitations of his premises—that is, when there is an equilibrium between the dramatization and the characteristic Hemingway "point," when the system of ironies and understatements is coherent. On the other hand, the failures occur when we feel that Hemingway has not respected the limitations of his premises—that is, when the dramatization seems to be "rigged" and the violence, therefore, merely theatrical. The characteristic irony, or understatement, in such cases, seems to be too self-conscious. For example, let us glance at Hemingway's most spectacular failure, *To Have and Have Not.* The point of the novel is based on the contrast between the smuggler and the rich owners of the yachts along the quay. But the irony is essentially an irony without any center of reference. It is superficial, for, as Philip Rahv indicates, the only difference between the smuggler and the rich is that the rich were successful in their buccaneering. The revelation that comes to the smuggler dying in his launch—"a man alone ain't got no . . . chance"—is a meaningless revelation, for it has no reference to the actual dramatization. It is, finally, a failure in intellectual analysis of the situation.

There is, I believe, a good chance that *For Whom the Bell Tolls* will not turn out to be Hemingway's best novel (an honor I should reserve for *A Farewell to Arms*) primarily because in this most ambitious of the novels Hemingway does not accept the limitations of his premises. I do not mean to imply that it is on a level with *To Have and Have Not.* There is a subtler irony in the later novel. I have pointed out that the irony in *To Have and Have Not* is that of the contrast between the smuggler and the rich in the yachts along the pier; that is, it is a simple irony, in direct line with the ostensible surface direction of the story. But the irony in *For Whom the Bell Tolls* runs counter to the ostensible surface direction of the story. As surface, we have a conflict between the forces of light and the forces of darkness, freedom versus fascism, etc. Hero and heroine are clearly and completely and romantically aligned on the side of light. We are prepared to see the Fascist atrocities and the general human kindness of the Loyalists. It happens to work out the other way. The scene of horror is the massacre by the Loyalists, not by the Fascists. Again, in the attack on El Sordo's hill by the Fascists, we are introduced to a young Fascist lieutenant, whose bosom friend is killed in the attack. We are suddenly given this little human glimpse—against the grain of the surface. But this incident, we discover later, is preparation for the very end of the novel. We leave the hero lying wounded, preparing to cover the retreat of his friends. The man who is over the sights of the machine gun as the book ends is the Fascist lieutenant, whom we have been made to know as a man, not as a monster. This general ironical conditioning of the overt story line is reflected also in the attitude of Anselmo, who kills but cannot believe in killing. In other words, the irony here is much more functional, and more complicated, than that of *To Have and Have Not;* the irony affirms that the human values may transcend the party lines.

Much has been said to the effect that *To Have and Have Not* and *For Whom the Bell Tolls* represent a basic change of point of view, an enlargement of what I have called the secret community. Now, no doubt that is the intention behind both books, but the temper of both books, the good one and the bad one, is the old temper, the cast of characters is the old cast, and the assumptions lying far below the explicit intention are the old assumptions.

The monotony and self-imitation, into which Hemingway's work sometimes falls, are again an effect of a failure in dramatization. Hemingway, apparently, can dramatize his "point" in only one basic situation and with only one set of characters. He has, as we have seen, only two key characters, with certain variations from them by way of contrast or counterpoint. His best women characters, by the way, are those who most nearly approximate the men; that is, they embody the masculine virtues and point of view characteristic of Hemingway's work.

But the monotony is not merely a monotony deriving from the characters as types; it derives, rather, from the limitations of the author's sensibility, which seems to come alive in only one issue. A more flexible sensibility, one capable of making nicer discriminations, might discover great variety in such key characters and situations. But Hemingway's successes are due, in part at least, to the close co-ordination that he sometimes achieves between the character and the situation, and the sensibility as it reflects itself in the style.

The style characteristically is simple, even to the point of monotony. The characteristic sentence is simple, or compound; and if compound, there is no implied subtlety in the co-ordination of the clauses. The paragraph structure is, characteristically, based on simple sequence. There is an obvious relation between this style and the characters and situations with which the author is concerned—a relation of dramatic decorum. (There are, on the other hand, examples, especially in the novels, of other, more fluent, lyrical effects, but even here this fluency is founded on the conjunction *and;* it is a rhythmical and not a logical fluency. And the lyrical quality is simply a manifestation of that marginal sensibility, as can be demonstrated by an analysis of the occasions on which it appears.)

But there is a more fundamental aspect of the question, an aspect that involves not the sensibility of the characters but the sensibility of the author. The short, simple rhythms, the succession of co-ordinate clauses, the general lack of subordination—all suggest a dislocated and ununified world. The figures who live in this world live a sort of hand-to-mouth existence perceptually, and conceptually they hardly live at all. Subordination implies some exercise of discrimination—the sifting of reality through the intellect. But in Hemingway we see a romantic anti-intellectualism.

In Wordsworth, too, we see this strain of anti-intellectualism. He, too, wishes to clear away the distorting sophistications of the intellect, and to keep his eye on the object. The formulations of the intellect create the "veil of familiarity" that he would clear away. His mode, too, was to take unpromising material and reveal in it the lyric potentiality. He, too, was interested in the margin of sensibility. He, too, wished to respect the facts, and could have understood Hemingway's rejection of the big abstract words in favor of "the concrete names of villages, the numbers of roads, the names of rivers, the numbers of regiments and the dates."

The passage from *A Farewell to Arms* from which the above quotation comes is, of course, the passage most commonly used to explain the attitude behind Hemingway's style. But we can put with it other passages of a similar import, and best of all a sentence from the story "Soldier's Home." Krebs, the boy who has been through the war and who comes back home to find himself cut off from life, had "acquired the nausea in regard to experience that is the result of untruth or exaggeration." He is a casualty not of bullet or bayonet, but of the big, abstract words. Hemingway's style is, in a way, an attempt to provide an antidote for that "nausea."

A Farewell to Arms is a love story. It is a compelling story at the merely personal level, but it is much more compelling and significant when we see the figures of the lovers silhouetted against the flame-streaked blackness of war, of a collapsing world, of nada. For there is a story behind the love story. That story is the quest for meaning and certitude in a world that seems to offer nothing of the sort. It is, in a sense, a religious book; if it does not offer a religious solution, it is nevertheless conditioned by the religious problem.

The very first scene of the book, though seemingly casual, is important if we are to understand the deeper motivations of the story. It is the scene at the officers' mess where the captain baits the priest. "Priest every night five against one," the captain explains to Frederick. But Frederick, we see in this and later scenes, takes no part in the baiting. There is a bond between him and the priest, a bond that they both recognize. This becomes clear when, after the officers have advised Frederick where he should go on his leave to find the best girls, the priest turns to him and says that he would like to have him go to Abruzzi, his own province:

> "There is good hunting. You would like the people and though it is cold it is clear and dry. You could stay with my family. My father is a famous hunter."
> "Come on," said the captain. "We go whorehouse before it shuts."
> "Goodnight," I said to the priest.
> "Goodnight," he said.

In this preliminary contrast between the officers, who invite the hero to go to the brothel, and the priest, who invites him to go to the cold, clear, dry country, we have in its simplest form the issue of the novel.

Frederick does go with the officers that night, and on his leave he does go to the cities, "to the smoke of cafés and nights when the room whirled and you needed to look at the wall to make it stop, nights in bed, drunk, when you knew that that was all there was, and the strange excitement of waking and not knowing who it was with you, and the world all unreal in the dark and so exciting that you must resume again unknowing and not caring in the night, sure that this was all and all and all and not caring." Frederick, at the opening of the novel, lives in the world of random and meaningless appetite, knowing that it is all and all and all, or thinking that he knows that. But behind that there is a dissatisfaction and disgust.

Upon his return from his leave, sitting in the officers' mess, he tries to tell the priest how he is sorry that he had not gone to the clear, cold, dry country—the priest's home, which takes on the shadowy symbolic significance of another kind of life, another view of the world. The priest had always known that other country.

> He had always known what I did not know and what, when I learned it, I was always able to forget. But I did not know that then, although I learned it later.

What Frederick learns later is the story behind the love story of the book.

But this theme is not merely stated at the opening of the novel and then absorbed into the action. It appears later, at crucial points, to define the line of meaning in the action. When, for example, Frederick is wounded, the priest visits him in the hospital. Their conversation makes even plainer the religious background of the novel. The priest has said that he would like to go back after the war to the Abruzzi. He continues:

> "It does not matter. But there in my country it is understood that a man may love God. It is not a dirty joke."
> "I understand."
> He looked at me and smiled.
> "You understand but you do not love God."
> "No."
> "You do not love Him at all?" he asked.
> "I am afraid of him in the night sometimes."
> "You should love Him."
> "I don't love much."
> "Yes," he said. "You do. What you tell me about in the nights. That is not love. That is only passion and lust. When you love you wish to do things for. You wish to sacrifice for. You wish to serve."
> "I don't love."
> "You will. I know you will. Then you will be happy."

We have here two important items. First, there is the definition of Frederick as the sleepless man, the man haunted by nada. Second, at this stage in the novel, the end of Book I, the true meaning of the love story with Catherine has not yet been defined. It is still at the level of appetite. The priest's role is to indicate the next stage of the story, the discovery of the true nature of love, the "wish to do things for." And he accomplishes this by indicating a parallel between secular love and Divine Love, a parallel which implies Frederick's quest for meaning and certitude. And to emphasize further this idea, Frederick, after the priest leaves, muses on the high, clean country of the Abruzzi, the priest's home that has already been endowed with the symbolic significance of the religious view of the world.

In the middle of Book II (Chapter xviii), in which the love story begins to take on the significance that the priest had predicted, the point is indicated by a bit of dialogue between the lovers.

> "Couldn't we be married privately some way? Then if anything happened to me or if you had a child."
> "There's no way to be married except by church or state. We are married privately. You see, darling, it would mean everything to me if I had any religion. But I haven't any religion."
> "You gave me the Saint Anthony."
> "That was for luck. Some one gave it to me."
> "Then nothing worries you?"
> "Only being sent away from you. You're my religion. You're all I've got."

Again, toward the end of Book IV (Chapter xxxv), just before Frederick and Catherine make their escape into Switzerland, Frederick is talking with a friend, the old Count Greffi, who has just said that he thought H. G. Wells's novel *Mr. Britling Sees It Through* a very good study of the English middle-class soul. But Frederick twists the word *soul* into another meaning.

> "I don't know about the soul."
> "Poor boy. We none of us know about the soul. Are you *Croyant*?"
> "At night."

Later in the same conversation the Count returns to the topic:

"And if you ever become devout pray for me if I am dead. I am asking several of my friends to do that. I had expected to become devout myself but it has not come." I thought he smiled sadly but I could not tell. He was so old and his face was very wrinkled, so that a smile used so many lines that all gradations were lost.

"I might become very devout," I said. "Anyway, I will pray for you."

"I had always expected to become devout. All my family died very devout. But somehow it does not come."

"It's too early."

"Maybe it is too late. Perhaps I have outlived my religious feeling."

"My own comes only at night."

"Then too you are in love. Do not forget that is a religious feeling."

So here we find, again, Frederick defined as the sleepless man, and the relation established between secular love and Divine Love.

In the end, with the death of Catherine, Frederick discovers that the attempt to find a substitute for universal meaning in the limited meaning of the personal relationship is doomed to failure. It is doomed because it is liable to all the accidents of a world in which human beings are like the ants running back and forth on a log burning in a campfire and in which death is, as Catherine says just before her own death, "just a dirty trick." But this is not to deny the value of the effort, or to deny the value of the discipline, the code, the stoic endurance, the things that make it true—or half true—that "nothing ever happens to the brave."

This question of the characteristic discipline takes us back to the beginning of the book, and to the context from which Frederick's effort arises. We have already mentioned the contrast between the officers of the mess and the priest. It is a contrast between the man who is aware of the issue of meaning in life and those who are unaware of it, who give themselves over to the mere flow of accident, the contrast between the disciplined and the undisciplined. But the contrast is not merely between the priest and the officers. Frederick's friend, the surgeon Rinaldi, is another who is on the same "side" of the contrast as the priest. He may go to the brothel with his brother officers, he may even bait the priest a little, but his personal relationship with Frederick indicates his affiliations; he is one of the initiate. Furthermore, he has the discipline of his profession, and, as we have seen, in the Hemingway world, the discipline that seems to be merely technical, the style of the artist or the form of the athlete or bullfighter, may be an index to a moral value. "Already," Rinaldi says, "I am only happy when I am working." (Already the seeking of pleasure in sensation is inadequate for Rinaldi.) This point appears more sharply in the remarks about the doctor who first attends to Frederick's wounded leg. He is incompetent and does not wish to take the responsibility for a decision.

> Before he came back three doctors came into the room. I have noticed that doctors who fail in the practice of medicine have a tendency to seek one another's company and aid in consultation. A doctor who cannot take out your appendix properly will recommend to you a doctor who will be unable to remove your tonsils with success. These were three such doctors.

In contrast with them there is Doctor Valentini, who is competent, who is willing to take responsibility, and who, as a kind of mark of his role, speaks the same lingo, with the same bantering, ironical tone, as Rinaldi—the tone that is the mark of the initiate.

So we have the world of the novel divided into two groups, the initiate and the uninitiate, the aware and the unaware, the disciplined and the undisciplined. In the first group are Frederick, Catherine, Rinaldi, Valentini, Count Greffi, the old man who cut the paper silhouettes "for pleasure," and Passini, Manera, and the other ambulance men in Frederick's command. In the second group are the officers of the mess, the incompetent doctors, the "legitimate hero" Ettore, and the "patriots"—all the people who do not know what is really at stake, who are deluded by the big words, who do not have the discipline. They are the messy people, the people who surrender to the flow and illusion of things. It is this second group who provide the context of the novel, and more especially the context from which Frederick moves toward his final complete awareness.

The final awareness means, as we have said, that the individual is thrown back upon his private discipline and his private capacity to endure. The hero cuts himself off from the herd, the confused world, which symbolically appears as the routed army at Caporetto. And, as Malcolm Cowley has pointed out,[3] the plunge into the flooded Tagliamento, when Frederick escapes from the battle police, has the significance of a rite. By this "baptism" Frederick is reborn into another world; he comes out into the world of the man alone, no longer supported by and involved in society.

> Anger was washed away in the river along with my obligation. Although that ceased when the carabiniere put his hands on my collar. I would like to have had the uniform off although I did not care much about the outward forms. I had taken off the stars, but that was for convenience. It was no point of honor. I was not against them. I was through. I wished them all the luck. There were the good ones, and the brave ones, and the calm ones and the sensible ones, and they deserved it. But it was not my show any more and I wished this bloody train would get to Maestre and I would eat and stop thinking.

So Frederick, by a decision, does what the boy[4] Nick does as the result of the accident of a wound. He makes a "separate peace." And from the waters of the flooded Tagliamento arises the Hem-

[3]Introduction to the *Portable Hemingway,* the Viking Press. In this general connection one may consider the strategic advantage that Hemingway has in that it is the Italian army from which his hero deserts. If his hero had, for instance, deserted from the American army, the American reader's resistance to accepting the act would have been much greater—the reader's own immediate loyalties, etc., would have been betrayed by Frederick's act. And by the same token the resistance to the symbolic meaning of the act—the resigning from society—would have been much greater. The reader is led to accept the act because the desertion is from a "foreign" army. The point is indicated in a passage of dialogue between Frederick and Catherine. Frederick complains that he doesn't want them to have to live in secret and on the run like criminals.

"I feel like a criminal. I've deserted from the army."

"Darling, *please* be sensible. It's not deserting from the army. It's only the Italian army."

It may be objected that since Hemingway himself saw service on the Italian front, it is only natural that his story should be laid there and that by consequence the fact has no symbolic significance and no significance as fictional strategy. But the fact that circumstances of personal history dictated the setting of the story does not prevent the author from seizing on and using the advantages inherent in the situation.

[4]*In Our Time,* Chapter vi.

ingway hero in his purest form, with human history and obligation washed away, ready to enact the last phase of his appropriate drama, and learn from his inevitable defeat the lesson of lonely fortitude.

This is not the time to attempt to give a final appraisal of Hemingway's work as a whole or even of this particular novel—if there is ever a time for a "final" appraisal. But we may touch on some of the objections which have been brought against his work.

First, there is the objection that his work is immoral or dirty or disgusting. This objection appeared in various quarters against *A Farewell to Arms* at the time of its first publication. For instance, Robert Herrick wrote that if suppression were to be justified at all, it would be justified in this case. He said that the book had no significance, was merely a "lustful indulgence," and smelled of the "boudoir," and summarized his view by calling it "garbage."[5] That objection has, for the most part, died out, but its echoes can still be occasionally heard, and now and then at rare intervals some bigot or high-minded but uninstructed moralist will object to the inclusion of *A Farewell to Arms* in a college course.

The answer to this moralistic objection is fundamentally an answer to the charge that the book has no meaning. The answer would seek to establish the fact that the book does deal seriously with a moral and philosophical issue, which, for better or worse, does exist in the modern world in substantially the terms presented by Hemingway. This means that the book, even if it does not end with a solution that is generally acceptable, still embodies a moral effort and is another document of the human effort to achieve ideal values. As for the bad effect it may have on some readers, the best answer is perhaps to be found in a quotation from Thomas Hardy, who is now sanctified but whose most famous novels, *Tess of the D'Urbervilles* and *Jude the Obscure,* once suffered the attacks of the dogmatic moralists, and one of whose books was burned by a bishop:

> Of the effects of such sincere presentation on weak minds, when the courses of the characters are not exemplary and the rewards and punishments ill adjusted to deserts, it is not our duty to consider too

5 "What Is Dirt?" *Bookman,* November, 1929.

closely. A novel which does moral injury to a dozen imbeciles, and has bracing results upon intellects of normal vigor, can justify its existence; and probably a novel was never written by the purest-minded author for which there could not be found some moral invalid or other whom it was capable of harming.[6]

Second, there is the objection that Hemingway's work, especially of the period before *To Have and Have Not,* has no social relevance, that it is off the mainstream of modern life, and that it has no concern with the economic structure of society. Critics who hold this general view regard Hemingway, like Joseph Conrad and perhaps like Henry James, as an exotic. There are several possible lines of retort to this objection. One line is well stated in the following passage by David Daiches if we substitute the name of Hemingway for Conrad:

> Thus it is no reproach to Conrad that he does not concern himself at all with the economic and social background underlying human relationships in modern civilization, for he never sets out to study those relationships. The Marxists cannot accuse him of cowardice or falsification, because in this case the charge is not relevant [though it might be relevant to *To Have and Have Not* or to *For Whom the Bell Tolls*]. That, from the point of view of the man with a theory, there are accidents in history, no one can deny. And if a writer chooses to discuss those accidents rather than the events which follow the main stream of historical causation, the economic, or other, determinist can only shrug his shoulder and maintain that these events are less instructive to the students than are the major events which he chooses to study; but he cannot accuse the writer of falsehood or distortion.[7]

That much is granted by one of the ablest critics of the group who would find Hemingway an exotic. But a second line of retort would fix on the word *instructive* in the foregoing passage, and would ask what kind of instruction, if any, is to be expected of fiction, as fiction. Is the kind of instruction expected of fiction in direct compe-

[6]"The Profitable Reading of Fiction," in *Life and Art, Essays, Notes and Letters.*
[7]For a contrary view of the work of Conrad, see "The Great Mirage," page 137.

tition, at the same level, with the kind of instruction offered in Political Science I or Economics II? If that is the case, then out with Shakespeare and Keats and in with Upton Sinclair.

Perhaps *instruction* is not a relevant word, after all, for this case. This is a very thorny and debatable question, but it can be ventured that what good fiction gives us is the stimulation of a powerful image of human nature trying to fulfill itself, and not instruction in an abstract sense. The economic man and political man are important aspects of human nature and may well constitute part of the *materials* of fiction. Neither the economic nor the political man is the complete man; other concerns may still be important enough to engage the attention of a writer—such concerns as love, death, courage, the point of honor, and the moral scruple. A man has to live with other men in terms not only of economic and political arrangements but also of moral arrangements; and he has to live with himself, he has to define himself. It can truly be said that these concerns are all interrelated in fact, but it might be dangerously dogmatic to insist that a writer should not bring one aspect into sharp, dramatic focus.

And it might be dangerously dogmatic to insist that Hemingway's ideas are not relevant to modern life. The mere fact that they exist and have stirred a great many people is a testimony to their relevance. Or to introduce a variation on that theme, it might be dogmatic to object to his work on the ground that he has few basic ideas. The history of literature seems to show that good artists may have very few *basic* ideas. They may have many ideas, but the ideas do not lead a life of democratic give-and-take, of genial camaraderie. No, there are usually one or two basic, obsessive ones. Like Savonarola, the artist may well say: *"Le mie cose erano poche e grandi."* And the ideas of the artist are grand simply because they are intensely felt, intensely realized—not because they are, by objective standards, by public, statistical standards, "important." No, that kind of public, statistical importance may be a condition of their being grand but is not of the special essence of their grandeur. (Perhaps not even the condition—perhaps the grandeur inheres in the fact that the artistic work shows us a parable of meaning—how idea is felt and how passion becomes idea through order.)

An artist may need few basic ideas, but in assessing his work we must introduce another criterion in addition to that of intensity. We must introduce the criterion of area. An artist's basic ideas do not operate in splendid isolation; to a greater or lesser degree, they prove themselves by their conquest of other ideas. Or again differently, the focus is a focus of experience, and the area of experience involved gives us another criterion of condition, the criterion of area. Perhaps an example would be helpful here. We have said that Hemingway is concerned with the scruple of honor, that this is a basic idea in his work. But we find that he applies this idea to a relatively small area of experience. In fact, we never see a story in which the issue involves the problem of definition of the scruple, nor do we ever see a story in which honor calls for a slow, grinding, day-to-day conquest of nagging difficulties. In other words, the idea is submitted to the test of a relatively small area of experience, to experience of a hand-picked sort, and to characters of a limited range.

But within that range, within the area in which he finds congenial material and in which competing ideas do not intrude themselves too strongly, Hemingway's expressive capacity is very powerful and the degree of intensity is very great. He is concerned not to report variety of human nature or human situation, or to analyze the forces operating in society, but to communicate a certain feeling about, a certain attitude toward, a special issue. That is, he is essentially a lyric rather than a dramatic writer, and for the lyric writer virtue depends upon the intensity with which the personal vision is rendered rather than upon the creation of a variety of characters whose visions are in conflict among themselves. And though Hemingway has not given—and never intended to give—a documented diagnosis of our age, he has given us one of the most compelling symbols of a personal response to our age.

WILLIAM FAULKNER

*A*T THE AGE of fifty-three, William Faulkner has written nineteen books which for range of effect, philosophical weight, originality of style, variety of characterization, humor, and tragic intensity are without equal in our time and country. Let us grant, even so, that there are grave defects in Faulkner's work. Sometimes the tragic intensity becomes mere sensationalism, the technical virtuosity mere complication, the philosophical weight mere confusion of mind. Let us grant that much, for Faulkner is a very uneven writer. The unevenness is, in a way, an index to his vitality, his willingness to take risks, to try for new effects, to make new explorations of material and method. And it is, sometimes at least, an index to a very important fact about Faulkner's work. The fact is that he writes of two Souths: he reports one South and he creates another. On one hand he is a perfectly straight realistic writer, and on the other he is a symbolist.

First published in *The New Republic,* August 12 and August 26, 1946, as "Cowley's Faulkner," Parts I and II. Included in *Selected Essays,* 1958.

Let us speak first of that realistic South, the South which we can recognize by its physical appearance and its people. In this realistic way we can recognize that county which Faulkner calls Yoknapatawpha County, the county in which most of his stories occur and most of his people live. Jefferson, the county seat of Yoknapatawpha County, is already the most famous county seat in the nation, and is as solidly recognizable as anybody's home town. There is Miss Emily's house, the big squarish frame house, once white, decorated with cupolas and spires and scrolled balconies, in the heavily lightsome style of the seventies, once on the most select street but now surrounded by garages and cotton gins, lifting its stubborn and coquettish decay above the cotton wagons and gasoline pumps. There is Uncle Gavin's law office. There is the cedar-bemused cemetery. There is the jail where a hundred years ago, or near, the jailer's daughter, a young girl, scratched her name with a diamond on a windowpane. There are the neat small new one-story houses designed in Florida and California, set with matching garages in their neat plots of clipped grass and tedious flower beds. Then beyond that town where we recognize every item, the country stretches away, the plantation houses, the cotton fields, the back country of Frenchman's Bend, where Snopeses and Varners live, the Beat Four section, where the Gowrie clan holds the land and brawls and makes whiskey in the brush.

We know everything about Yoknapatawpha County. Its 2,400 square miles lie between the hills of north Mississippi and the rich black bottom lands. No land in all fiction lives more vividly in its physical presence than this county of Faulkner's imagination—the pine-winey afternoons, the nights with a thin sickle of moon like the heel print of a boot in wet sand, the tremendous reach of the big river in flood, yellow and sleepy in the afternoon, and the little piddling creeks, that run backward one day and forward the next and come busting down on a man full of dead mules and hen houses, the ruined plantation which was Popeye's hangout, the swamps and fields and dusty roads, the last remnants of the great original forests, "green with gloom" in summer, "if anything actually dimmer than they had been in November's gray dissolution, where even at noon the sun fell only in windless dappling upon earth which never completely dried." A little later I shall speak of what the physical world means to Faulkner, but for the moment I wish only to insist on its vividness, its recognizability.

This county has a population of 15,611 persons, who spill in and out of Faulkner's books with the startling casualness of life, not explaining themselves or asking to be explained, offering their being with no apology, as though we, the readers, were the intruders on their domain. They compose a society with characters as various as the Bundrens of *As I Lay Dying*; the Snopeses of *The Hamlet* and several stories; the Gowries of *Intruder in the Dust*; Ike McCaslin of "The Bear" and "Delta Autumn"; Percy Grimm, the gun-mad Nazi prototype of *Light in August*; Temple Drake, the dubious little heroine of *Sanctuary*; the Compsons, the ruined great family; Christmas, the tortured and self-torturing mulatto of *Light in August*; Dilsey, the old Negro woman, heroic and enduring, who stands at the center of *The Sound and the Fury*; Wash, the no-good poor-white; and Sutpen, the violent bearer of the great design which the Civil War had brought to nothing, in *Absalom, Absalom!*; and the tall convict of *The Wild Palms*. No land in all fiction is more painstakingly analyzed from the sociological point of view. The descendants of the old families, the descendants of bushwhackers and carpetbaggers, the swamp rats, the Negro cooks and farm hands, the bootleggers and gangsters, tenant farmers, college boys, county-seat lawyers, country storekeepers, peddlers—all are here in their fullness of life and their complicated interrelations. The marks of class, occupation, and history are fully rendered, and we know completely their speech, food, dress, houses, manners, and attitudes.

Faulkner not only gives us the land and the people as we can see them today; he gives us glimpses of their history. His stories go back to the time when the Indians occupied Yoknapatawpha County and held slaves, and the first Compson came with a small, light-waisted, strong-hocked mare that could do two furlongs in under a half-minute, and won all the races from Ikkemotubbe's young braves until Ikkemotubbe swapped him a square mile of that land for the little mare. We know how Sartorises, the aristocrats, and Sutpens, nameless, driven, rancorous, ambitious men, seized the land, created a society, fought a war to defend that society, lost the war, and watched their world change and the Snopeses arise.

The past is dramatized in situation after situation, in its full complication. It is a recognizable past, not a romanticized past, though we find many characters in Faulkner who are themselves romantics about that past, Quentin of *The Sound and the Fury* or Hightower of *Light in August.*

The land, the people, and their history—they come to us at a realistic level, at the level of recognition. This realistic, recognizable world is one of the two Souths about which Faulkner writes. As a realist he knows this world; it is the world he lives in and carries on his daily business in. To represent this world with full fidelity is in itself a great achievement, and I would not underrate it. But this achievement is not Faulkner's claim to our particular attention. That claim is the world he creates out of the materials of the world he presents. Yoknapatawpha County, its people and its history, is also a parable—as Malcolm Cowley has called it, a legend.

We can approach the significance of this legend by thinking of the land and its history as a fate or doom—words that are often on Faulkner's page. From the land itself, from its rich soil yearning to produce, and from history, from an error or sin committed long ago and compounded a thousand times over, the doom comes. That is, the present is to be understood, and fully felt, only in terms of the past.

The men who seized the land from the Indians were determined to found an enduring and stable order. They brought to this project imagination and rectitude and strength and integrity and cunning and endurance, but their project—or their great "design," to use Sutpen's word from *Absalom, Absalom!*—was doomed from the first. It was "accurst"—to use one of Faulkner's favorite words—by chattel slavery. There is a paradox here. The fact of slavery itself was not a single, willed act. It was a natural historical growth. But it was an evil, and all its human and humane mitigations and all its historical necessity could not quiet the bad conscience it engendered. The Civil War began the fulfillment of the doom. The war was fought with courage and fortitude and strength but with divided conscience. Not that the enemy was the bearer of light—the enemy was little better than a blind instrument of doom or fate. After the Civil War the attempt to rebuild according to the old plan and for the old values was defeated by a combination of forces: the carpetbaggers, the carriers of Yankee exploitation—or better, a symbol of it, for the real exploiters never left their offices fifteen hundred miles away—and the Snopeses, a new exploiting indigenous class descended from the bushwhackers and landless whites.

Meanwhile, most of the descendants of the old order are in various ways incompetent. For one thing, in so far as they carry over into the new world the code of behavior prescribed by the old world, some sense of honor and honesty, they are at a disadvantage in dealing with the Snopeses, who have no code, who are pure pragmatists. But often the descendant of the old order clings to the letter of his tradition and forgets the spirit. George Marion O'Donnell, in one of the first perceptive essays ever published on Faulkner, pointed out the story "There Was a Queen" as an example of this. The heroine, in order to get possession of certain obscene and insulting letters written her by a Snopes, gives herself to a detective who has blackmailed her. That is, to protect her reputation, she is willing to perform the act which will render the reputation a mere sham.

We find something of the same situation with the whining Mrs. Compson, the mother in *The Sound and the Fury,* who with her self-pity and insistence on her "tradition" surrenders all the decency which the tradition would have prescribed, the honor and courage. Or the exponents of the tradition may lose all contact with reality and escape into a dream world of alcohol or rhetoric or madness or sexual dissipation. Or they fall in love with defeat and death, like Quentin Compson, who commits suicide at Harvard. Or they lose nerve and become cowardly drifters. Or, worst of all, they try to come to terms with reality by adopting Snopesism, like the last Jason of *The Sound and the Fury,* whose portrait is one of the most terrifying in all literature—the paranoidal self-deceiver, who plays the cotton market and when he loses, screams about those "kikes" in New York who rob him, who himself robs the daughter of his sister Caddy over the years and in the end makes her into the desperate and doomed creature she becomes, who under the guise of responsibility for his family—the ailing mother, the idiot brother, the wild niece—tortures them all with an unflagging sadistic pleasure.

The point to insist on here is that you do not characteristically have noble examples of antique virtue beset by little and corrupt men. There are a few such examples of the antique virtue—old Ike McCaslin, for example, whom we shall come to later—but the ordinary situation is to find the descendant of the old order contributing, actively or passively, to his own ruin and degradation. He is not merely a victim, and he frequently misunderstands his own tradition.

Over against these people there stand, as we have said, the forces of "modernism," embodied in various forms. There are, of course, the Snopeses, the pure exploiters, descendants of barn-burners and bushwhackers, of people outside of society, belonging to no side, living in a kind of limbo, not even having the privilege of damnation, reaching their apotheosis in Flem Snopes, who becomes a bank president in Jefferson. But there is also Popeye, the gangster of *Sanctuary,* with eyes like "rubber knobs," a creature with "that vicious depthless quality of stamped tin," the man who "made money and had nothing he could do with it, spend it for, since he knew that alcohol would kill him like poison, who had no friends and had never known a woman." Popeye is a kind of dehumanized robot, a mere mechanism, an abstraction, and as such he is a symbol for what Faulkner thinks of as modernism, for the society of finance capitalism.

It is sometimes said that Faulkner's theme is the disintegration of the Southern traditional life. For instance, Malcolm Cowley, in his fine introduction to the *Portable Faulkner,* says that the violence of Faulkner's work is "an example of the Freudian method turned backward, being full of sexual nightmares that are in reality social symbols. It is somehow connected in the author's mind with what he regards as the rape and corruption of the South." And Maxwell Geismar, whose lack of comprehension of Faulkner strikes me as monumental, interprets Faulkner's work as merely Southern apologetics, as "the extreme hallucinations" of a "cultural psychosis."

It is true that Faulkner deals almost exclusively with the Southern scene, it is true that the conflict between past and present is a constant concern for him, it is true that the Civil War is always behind his work as a kind of backdrop, and it is true, or at least I think it is true, that in Faulkner's work there is the implication that

Northern arms were the cutting edge of modernism. But granting all this, I should put the emphasis not in terms of South and North, but in terms of issues common to our modern world.

The Faulkner legend is not merely a legend of the South but of a general plight and problem. The modern world is in moral confusion. It does suffer from a lack of discipline, of sanction, of community of values, of a sense of mission. We don't have to go to Faulkner to find that out—or to find that it is a world in which self-interest, workableness, success provide the standards of conduct. It was a Yankee who first referred to the bitch-goddess Success. It is a world in which the individual has lost his relation to society, the world of the power state in which man is a cipher. It is a world in which man is the victim of abstraction and mechanism, or at least, at moments, feels himself to be. It can look back nostalgically upon various worlds of the past, Dante's world of the Catholic synthesis, Shakespeare's world of Renaissance energy, or the world of our grandfathers who lived before Shiloh and Gettysburg, and feel loss of traditional values and despair in its own aimlessness and fragmentation. And of those older worlds, so it seems now, was a world in which, as one of Faulkner's characters puts it, men "had the gift of living once or dying once instead of being diffused and scattered creatures drawn blindly from a grab bag and assembled"—a world in which men were, "integer for integer," more simple and complete.

At this point we must pause to consider an objection. Someone will say, and quite properly, that there never was a golden age in which man was simple and complete. Let us grant that. But we must grant that even with that realistic reservation, man's conception of his own role and position has changed from time to time. It is unhistorical to reduce history to some dead level, and the mere fact that man in the modern world is worried about his role and position is in itself significant.

Again, it may be objected, and quite properly, that any old order that had satisfied human needs would have survived; that it is sentimental to hold that an old order is killed from the outside by certain wicked people or forces. But when this objection is applied to Faulkner it is based on a misreading of his work. The old order, he clearly indicates, did *not* satisfy human needs, did *not* afford justice, and therefore was "accurst" and held the seeds of its own ruin. But the point is this: the old order, even with its bad conscience and confusion of mind, even as it failed to live up to its ideal, cherished the concept of justice. Even in terms of the curse, the old order as opposed to the new order (in so far as the new order is equated with Snopesism) allowed the traditional man to define himself as human by setting up codes, ideas of virtue, however mistaken; by affirming obligations, however arbitrary; by accepting the risks of humanity. But Snopesism has abolished the concept, the very possibility of entertaining the idea of virtue. It is not a question of one idea and interpretation. It is simply that no idea of virtue is conceivable in the world in which practical success is the criterion.

Within the traditional world there had been a notion of truth, even if man in the flow of things could not readily define or realize his truth. Take, for instance, a passage from "The Bear."

> *'All right,' he said. 'Listen,' and read again, but only one stanza this time and closed the book and laid it on the table. 'She cannot fade, though thou has not thy bliss,' McCaslin said: 'Forever wilt thou love, and she be fair.'*
>
> *'He's talking about a girl,' he said.*
>
> *'He had to talk about something,' McCaslin said. Then he said, 'He was talking about truth. Truth is one. It doesn't change. It covers all things which touch the heart—honor and pride and pity and justice and courage and love. Do you see now?'*

The important thing, then, is the presence of the concept of truth—that covers all things which touch the heart and define the effort of man to rise above the mechanical process of life.

When it is said, as it is sometimes said, that Faulkner is "backward-looking," the answer lies, I think, in the notion expressed above. The "truth" is neither of the past nor of the future. Or rather, it is of both. The constant ethical center of Faulkner's work is to be found in the glorification of human effort and human endurance, which are not confined to any one time. It is true that Faulkner's work contains a savage attack on modernity, but the values he admires *are* found in our time. The point is that they are found most often in people who are outside the stream of the dominant world, the "loud world," as it is called in *The Sound and the Fury.* Faulkner's world is full of "good" people—Byron Bunch, Lucas Beauchamp, Dilsey, Ike McCaslin, Uncle Gavin, Benbow, the justice of the peace in *The Hamlet,* Ratliff of the same book, Hightower of *Light in August*—we could make an impressive list, probably a longer list from Faulkner than from any other modern writer. "There are good men everywhere, at all times," Ike McCaslin says in "Delta Autumn."

It is not ultimately important whether the traditional order (Southern or other) as depicted by Faulkner fits exactly the picture which critical historical method provides. Let it be granted that Faulkner does simplify the matter. What remains important is that his picture of the traditional order has a symbolic function in contrast to the modern world which he gives us. It is a way of embodying his values—his "truth."

In speaking of the relation of the past to the present, I have mentioned the curse laid upon the present, the Southern present at least, by slavery. But also, as I have said, Faulkner is not concerned ultimately with the South, but with a general philosophical view. Slavery merely happens to be the particular Southern curse. To arrive at his broader philosophical view, we can best start with his notions of Nature.

For one thing, one of the most impressive features of Faulkner's work is the vivid realization of the natural background. It is accurately observed, as accurately as in Thoreau, but observation provides only the stuff from which Faulkner's characteristic effects are gained. It is the atmosphere that counts, the infusion of feeling, the symbolic weight. Nature provides a backdrop—of lyric beauty, as in the cow episode of *The Hamlet;* of homely charm, as in the trial scene after the spotted horses episode of the same book; of sinister, brooding force, as in the river episodes from *The Wild Palms*—a backdrop for the human action and passion.

Nature is, however, more than a backdrop. There is an interrelation between man and nature, something not too unlike the Wordsworthian communion. At least, at moments, there is the communion, the interrelation. The indestructible beauty is there, beyond man's frailty. "God created man," Ike McCaslin says in "Delta Autumn," "and He created the world for him to live in and I reckon He created the kind of world He would have wanted to live in if He had been a man."

Ideally, if man were like God, as Ike McCaslin puts it, man's attitude toward nature would be one of pure contemplation, pure participation in nature's great forms and appearances, pure communion. The appropriate attitude for this communion is love, for with Ike McCaslin, who is as much Faulkner's spokesman as any other character, the moment of love is equated with godhood. But since man "wasn't quite God himself," since he lives in the world of flesh, he must be a hunter, user, and violator. To return to McCaslin's words: God "put them both here: man and the game he would follow and kill, foreknowing it. I believe He said, 'So be it.' I reckon He even foreknew the end. But He said, 'I will give him his chance. I will give him warning and foreknowledge too, along with the desire to follow and the power to slay. The woods and the fields he ravages and the game he devastates will be the consequence and signature of his crime and guilt, and his punishment.' "

There is, then, a contamination implicit in the human condition—a kind of Original Sin, as it were—the sin of use, exploitation, violation. So slavery is but one of the many and constant forms of that Original Sin. But it is possible—and necessary if man is to strive to be human—to achieve some measure of redemption through love. For instance, in "The Bear," the great legendary beast which is pursued from year to year to the death is also an object of love and veneration, and the symbol of virtue; and the deer hunt of "Delta Autumn" is for old Ike McCaslin a ritual of renewal. Those who have learned the right relationship to nature—"the pride and humility" which Ike as a boy learns from the half-Negro, half-Indian Sam Fathers (he learns it appropriately from an outcast)— are set over against those who do not have it. In "The Bear," General Compson speaks up to Cass McCaslin to defend the wish of the boy Ike McCaslin to stay an extra week in the woods:

> "You've got one foot straddled into a farm and the other foot straddled into a bank; you aint even got a good hand-hold where this boy was already an old man long before you damned Sartorises and Edmondses invented farms and banks to keep yourselves from having to find out what this boy was born knowing and fearing too

maybe but without being afraid, that could go ten miles on a compass because he wanted to look at a bear none of us had ever got near enough to put a bullet in and looked at the bear and came the ten miles back on the compass in the dark; maybe by God that's the why and the wherefore of farms and banks."

The Sartorises and Edmondses, according to General Compson, have in their farms and banks something of the contamination, they have cut themselves off from the fundamental truth which young Ike already senses. But the real contamination is that of the pure exploiters, the apostles of abstractionism, those who have the wrong attitude toward nature and therefore toward other men.

We have a nice fable of this in the opening of *Sanctuary,* in the contrast between Benbow, the traditional man, and Popeye, the symbol of modernism. While the threat of Popeye keeps Benbow crouching by the spring, he hears a Carolina wren sing, and even under these circumstances tries to recall the local name for it. And he says to Popeye: "And of course you dont know the name of it. I dont suppose you'd know a bird at all, without it was singing in a cage in a hotel lounge, or cost four dollars on a plate." Popeye, as we may remember, spits in the spring (he hates nature and must foul it), is afraid to go through the woods ("Through all them trees?" he demands when Benbow points out the short cut), and when an owl whisks past them in the twilight, he claws at Benbow's coat with almost hysterical fear. "It's just an owl," Benbow explains. "It's nothing but an owl."

The pure exploiters are, however, caught in a paradox. Though they may gain ownership and use of a thing, they never really have it. Like Popeye, they are impotent. For instance, Flem Snopes, the central character and villain of *The Hamlet,* who brings the exploiter's mentality to the quiet country of Frenchman's Bend, finally marries Eula Varner, a kind of fertility goddess or earth goddess; but his ownership is meaningless, for she never refers to him as anything but "that man"—she does not even have a name for him—and he had got her only after she had given herself willingly to one of the hot-blooded boys of the neighborhood. In fact, nothing can, in one sense, be "owned." Ike McCaslin, in "The Bear," says of the land which had come down to him:

'It was never Father's and Uncle Buddy's to bequeath to me to repudiate because it was never Grandfather's to bequeath them to bequeath me to repudiate because it was never old Ikkemotubbe's to sell to Grandfather for bequeathment and repudiation. Because it was never Ikkemotubbe's fathers' fathers' to bequeath Ik-kemotubbe to sell to Grandfather or any man because on the instant when Ikkemotubbe discovered, realized, that he could sell it for money, on that instant it ceased ever to have been his forever, father to father to father, and the man who bought it bought nothing.'

In other words, reality cannot be bought. It can only be had by love.

The right attitude toward nature and man is love. And love is the opposite of the lust for power over nature or over other men, for God gave the earth to man, we read in "The Bear," not "to hold for himself and his descendants inviolable title forever, generation after generation, to the oblongs and squares of the earth, but to hold the earth mutual and intact in the communal anonymity of brotherhood, and all the fee He [God] asked was pity and humility and sufferance and endurance and the sweat of his face for bread." It is the failure of this pity that curses the earth and brings on the doom. For the rape of nature and the rape of man are always avenged. Mere exploitation without love is always avenged because the attitude which commits the crime in itself leads to its own punishment, so that man finally punishes himself. It is along this line of reasoning that we can read the last page of "Delta Autumn":

This land which man has deswamped and denuded and derivered in two generations so that white men can own plantations and commute every night to Memphis and black men own plantations and ride in jim crow cars to Chicago to live in millionaires' mansions on Lakeshore Drive, where white men rent farms and live like niggers and niggers crop on shares and live like animals, where cotton is planted and grows man-tall in the very cracks of the sidewalks, and usury and mortgage and bankruptcy and measureless wealth, Chinese and African and Aryan and Jew, all breed and spawn together until no man has time to say which one is which nor cares. . . . No wonder the ruined woods I used to know dont cry for retribution! he thought: The people who have destroyed it will accomplish its revenge.

Despite the emphasis on the right relation to nature, and the communion with nature, the attitude toward nature in Faulkner's work does not involve a sinking into nature. In Faulkner's mythology man has "suzerainty over the earth," he is not of the earth, and it is the human virtues that count—"pity and humility and endurance." If we take even the extreme case of the idiot Snopes and his fixation on the cow in *The Hamlet* (a scene whose function in the total order of the book is to show that even the idiot pervert is superior to Flem), a scene in which the human being appears as close as possible to the "natural" level, we find that the scene is the most lyrical in Faulkner's work: even the idiot is human and not animal, for only human desires, not animal desires, must clothe themselves in poetry. I think that George Marion O'Donnell is right in pointing to the humanism-naturalism opposition in Faulkner's work, and over and over again we find that the point of some story or novel has to do with the human effort to break out of the mechanical round of experience at the merely "natural" level—"not just to eat and evacuate and sleep warm," as Charlotte Rittenmeyer says in *The Wild Palms,* "so we can get up and eat and evacuate in order to sleep warm again," or not just to raise cotton to buy niggers to raise cotton to buy niggers, as it is put in another place. Even when a character seems to be caught in the iron ring of some compulsion, of some mechanical process, the effort may be discernible. And in Quentin's attempt in *The Sound and the Fury* to persuade his sister Caddy, who is pregnant by one of the town boys of Jefferson, to confess that she has committed incest with him, we find among other things the idea that "the horror" of the crime and the "clean flame" of guilt would be preferable to the meaninglessness of the "loud world." More is at stake in Quentin's attitude than the snobbery of a Compson, which would prefer incest to the notion that his sister has had to do with one of the underbred town boys.

And that leads us to the question of class and race. There is a current misconception on this point, the notion that Faulkner's Snopesism is a piece of snobbery. It is true that the Snopeses are poor whites, descendants of bushwhackers (those who had no side in the Civil War but tried to make a good thing out of it), but any careful reader should realize that a Snopes is not to be equated with a poor white. For instance, the book most fully about the poor white, *As I Lay Dying,* is charged with sympathy and poetry. There are a hundred touches like that in Cash's soliloquy about the phonograph:

> I reckon it's a good thing we ain't got ere a one of them. I reckon I wouldn't never get no work done a-tall for listening to it. I don't know if a little music ain't about the nicest thing a fellow can have. Seems like when he comes in tired of a night, it ain't nothing could rest him like having a little music played and him resting.

Or like the long section devoted to Addie Bundren, a section full of eloquence like that of this paragraph:

> And then he died. He did not know he was dead. I would lie by him in the dark, hearing the dark land talking of God's love and His beauty and His sin; hearing the dark voicelessness in which the words are the deeds, and the other words that are not deeds, that are just the gaps in peoples' lacks, coming down like the cries of geese out of the wild darkness in the old terrible nights, fumbling at the deeds like orphans to whom are pointed out in a crowd two faces and told, That is your father, your mother.

The whole of *As I Lay Dying* is based on the heroic effort of the Bundren family to fulfill the promise to the dead mother to take her body to Jefferson; and the fact that Anse Bundren, after the effort is completed, immediately gets him a new wife, "the duck-shaped woman," does not negate the heroism of the effort or the poetry in which it is clothed. We are told by one critic that "what should have been the drama of the Bundrens thus becomes in the end a sort of brutal farce," and that we are "unable to feel the tragedy because the author has refused to accept the Bundrens, as he did accept the Compsons, as tragic." Rather, I should say, the Bundrens come off a little better than the latter-day Compsons, the whining, self-deluding mother, the promiscuous Caddy, the ineffectual Quentin, and the rest, including the vile Jason. The Bundrens at least are capable of the heroic effort. What the conclusion indicates is that even such a fellow as Anse Bundren, in the grip of an idea, in terms of promise or code, can rise above his ordinary level; Anse falls back at the end, but only after the prop of the obligation has been removed. And we can recall that Wash Jones has been capable of some kind of obscure dream, as his attachment to Sutpen indicates, and that in the end, in his murder of Sutpen, he achieves dignity and manhood.

The final evidence that the Snopeses are not to be equated with "poor white" comes in *The Hamlet*. The point of the book is the assault made by the Snopes family on a community of plain, hard-working small farmers. And if the corruption of Snopesism does penetrate into the community, there is no one here, not even Flem Snopes, who can be compared to Jason of *The Sound and the Fury*, the Compson who has embraced Snopesism.

As for the poor white, there has been a grave misconception in some quarters concerning the Negro in Faulkner's work. In one of Faulkner's books it is said that every white child is born crucified on a black cross, and remarks like this have led to the notion that Faulkner "hates" Negroes—or at least all Negroes except the favored black servitors. For instance, we find Maxwell Geismar exclaiming what a "strange inversion" it is to take the Negro, who is the "tragic consequence," and to exhibit him as the "evil cause" of the failure of the old order in the South. But all this is to misread the text. It is slavery, not the Negro, which is defined quite flatly as the curse, and the Negro is the black cross in so far as he is the embodiment of the curse, the reminder of the guilt, the incarnation of the problem. The black cross is, then, the weight of the white man's guilt, the white man who now sells salves and potions to "bleach the pigment and straighten the hair of Negroes that they might resemble the very race which for two hundred years had held them in bondage and from which for another hundred years not even a bloody civil war would have set them completely free." The curse is still operative, as the crime is still compounded.

The actual role of the Negro in Faulkner's fiction is consistently one of pathos or heroism. There is Dilsey, under whose name in the Compson genealogy Faulkner writes, "They endured," and whose role in *The Sound and the Fury* is to be the very ethical center of the book, the vessel of virtue and compassion. Then there is the Negro in "Red Leaves," the slave held by Indians who is hunted down to be killed at the funeral of the chief. When he is overtaken, one of the Indians says to him, "You ran well. Do not be ashamed," and when he walks among the Indians, he is "the tallest there, his high, close, mud-caked head looming above them all." And old Sam Fathers is the fountain of the wisdom which Ike McCaslin, Faulkner's philosopher, finally gains, and the repository of the virtues central for Faulkner—"an old man, son of a Negro slave and an Indian king, inheritor on the one hand of the long chronicle of a people who had learned humility through suffering and learned pride through the endurance which survived the suffering, and on the other side the chronicle of a people even longer in the land than the first, yet who now existed there only in the solitary brotherhood of an old and childless Negro's alien blood and the wild and invincible spirit of an old bear." Even Christmas in *Light in August* is a mixture of pathos and heroism. With his mixed blood, he is the lost, suffering, enduring creature, and even the murder he commits at the end is a fumbling attempt to define his manhood, an attempt to break out of the iron ring of mechanism, for the woman whom he kills has become a figure of the horror of the human which has surrendered human attributes.

Or for a general statement let us take a passage from "The Bear":

'Because they will endure. They are better than we are. Stronger than we are. Their vices are vices aped from white men or that white men and bondage have taught them: improvidence and intemperance and evasion—not laziness: evasion: of what white men had set them to, not for their aggrandisement or even comfort but his own—" and McCaslin.

'All right. Go on: Promiscuity. Violence. Instability and lack of control. Inability to distinguish between mine and thine—' and he

'How distinguish, when for two hundred years mine did not even exist for them?' and McCaslin

'All right. Go on. And their virtues—' and he

'Yes. Their own. Endurance—' and McCaslin

'So have mules:' and he

'—and pity and tolerance and forbearance and fidelity and love of children—' and McCaslin

'So have dogs:' and he

'—whether their own or not or black or not. And more: what they got not only from white people but not even despite white people because they had it already from the old free fathers a longer time free than us because we have never been free—'

It is in *Intruder in the Dust,* however, that his views of the Negro are most explicit and best dramatized. Lucas Beauchamp, the stiff-necked and high-nosed old Negro man, is accused on good evidence of having shot a white man in the back, and is lodged in the Jefferson jail with a threat of lynching. The lynching is averted and Lucas's innocence established by a boy and an old lady. But what is important about the book is twofold: First, there is the role of Lucas as hero, the focus of dignity and integrity. Second, there is the quite explicit and full body of statement, which comes to us through the lips of Gavin, the lawyer-uncle of the boy who saves Lucas. To quote Gavin:

'. . . the postulate that Sambo is a human being living in a free country and hence must be free. That's what we are really defending [against the North]: the privilege of setting him free ourselves: which we will have to do for the reason that nobody else can since going on a century ago now the North tried it and have been admitting for seventy-five years now that they failed. So it will have to be us. Soon now this sort of thing [the lynching] wont even threaten anymore. It shouldn't now. It should never have. Yet it did last Saturday and it probably will again, perhaps once more, perhaps twice more. But then no more, it will be finished; the shame will still be there of course but then the whole chronicle of man's immortality is in the suffering he has endured, his struggle toward the stars in the stepping-stones of his expiations. Someday Lucas Beauchamp can shoot a white man in the back with the same impunity to lynchrope or gasoline as a white man; in time he will vote anywhen and anywhere a white man can and send his children to the same school anywhere the white man's children go and travel anywhere the white man travels as the white man does it. But it won't be next Tuesday. . . .'

This is not the whole passage, or even the burden of the whole passage, but it merits our lingering. The motive behind the notion of "defending" against the North is not merely resentment at easy

Phariseeism. It is something else, two other things in fact. First, the realization that legislation in itself never solves a really fundamental question. Legislation can only reflect a solution already arrived at. Second, the problem is finally one of understanding and, in a sense, conversion: conversion and, as the passage puts it, expiation. That is, the real problem is a spiritual and moral one. The story of *Intruder in the Dust* is, in a sense, the education of the boy, and the thing he learns is a lesson in humanity. This can be brought to focus on two parallel episodes. He sees Lucas on the street one day, and Lucas walks past him without recognition. Later he realizes that Lucas had been grieving for his dead wife. Again, in the cemetery where the body of a Gowrie had been exhumed, he sees old Stub Gowrie, the father of the man Lucas had presumably killed, and realizes that this head of the brawling, mean, lawless Gowrie clan is grieving, too. The recognition of grief, the common human bond, that is his education.

That is the central fact in Faulkner's work, the recognition of the common human bond, a profound respect for the human. There are, in one way, no villains in his work, except those who deny the human bond. Even some of the Snopes family are, after all, human: the son of the barn-burner in the story "Barn-Burning," or Mink in *The Hamlet*. The point about the Gowries in *Intruder in the Dust* is the same: the Gowries seem to be the enemy, the pure villains, but in the end there is the pure grief on old Stub's face, and he is human, after all.

If respect for the human is the central fact of Faulkner's work, what makes that fact significant is that he realizes and dramatizes the difficulty of respecting the human. Everything is against it, the savage egotism, the blank appetite, stupidity and arrogance, even virtues sometimes, the misreading of our history and tradition, our education, our twisted loyalties. That is the great drama, however, the constant story. His hatred of "modernism"—and we must quote the word to give it his special meaning—arises because he sees it as the enemy of the human, as abstraction, as mechanism, as irresponsible power, as the cipher on the ledger or the curve on a graph.

And the reference to modernism brings us back to the question of the past and the present. But what of the future? Does Faulkner come to a dead end, setting up traditional virtues against the blank present, and let the matter stand there? No, he does not. But he holds out no easy solutions for man's "struggle toward the stars in the stepping-stones of his expiations." He does, however, give a sense of the future, though as a future of struggle in working out that truth referred to in "The Bear." We can remember that old Ike McCaslin, at the end of "Delta Autumn," gives General Compson's hunting horn to the mulatto girl who has been deserted by his young kinsman, saying, "We will have to wait." And *The Sound and the Fury,* which is Faulkner's *Waste Land,* ends with Easter and the promise of resurrection.

SECTION

III

MELVILLE
THE POET

F. O. MATTHIESSEN has undertaken to give in twenty-two pages[1] a cross section of the rather large body of the poetry of Herman Melville. If he had intended to give merely a little gathering of his poet's best blossoms, his task would have been relatively easy. But he has also undertaken, as he says in his brief but instructive preface, to "take advantage of all the various interests attaching to any part of Melville's work." So some items appear because they present the basic symbols which are found in the prose or because they "serve to light up facets of Melville's mind as it developed in the years after his great creative period."

In one sense all one can do is to say that Mr. Matthiessen, with the space permitted by the series to which this book belongs ("The Poets of the Year"), has carried out his plan with the taste

First published in *The Kenyon Review*, Spring 1946. Included in *Selected Essays*, 1958.
[1]*Selected Poems of Herman Melville.*

and discernment which could have been predicted by any reader of his discussion of Melville's poetry in the *American Renaissance.* But I shall take this occasion to offer a few remarks supplementary to the preface and to point out other poems and passages in Melville's work which I hope Mr. Matthiessen admires or finds interesting but which could have no place in his arbitrarily limited collection.

First, I wish to comment on Melville's style. It is ordinarily said that he did not master the craft of verse. Few of his poems are finished. Fine lines, exciting images, and bursts of eloquence often appear, but they appear side by side with limping lines, inexpressive images, and passages of bombast. In a way, he is a poet of shreds and patches. I do not wish to deny the statement that he did not master his craft, but I do feel that it needs some special interpretation.

If, for example, we examine the poems under the title "Fruit of Travel Long Ago," in the *Timoleon* volume of 1891, we see that the verse here is fluent and competent. In his belated poetic apprenticeship, he was capable of writing verse which is respectable by the conventional standards of the time. But the effects which he could achieve within this verse did not satisfy him. Let us look at the poem called "In a Bye-Canal." The first section gives us verse that is conventionally competent:

> A swoon of noon, a trance of tide,
> The hushed siesta brooding wide
>   Like calms far off Peru;
> No floating wayfarer in sight,
> Dumb noon, and haunted like the night
>   When Jael the wiled one slew.
> A languid impulse from the car
> Plied by my indolent gondolier
> Tinkles against a palace hoar,
>   And hark, response I hear!
> A lattice clicks; and lo, I see
> Between the slats, mute summoning me,
> What loveliest eyes of scintillation,
> What basilisk glance of conjuration!

But the next eight lines are very different. The metrical pattern is sorely tried and wrenched.

> Fronted I have, part taken the span
> Of portent in nature and peril in man.
> I have swum—I have been
> 'Twixt the whale's black fluke and the white shark's
>   fin;
> The enemy's desert have wandered in,
> And there have turned, have turned and scanned,
> Following me how noiselessly,
> Envy and Slander, lepers hand in hand.

Then the poem returns to its normal movement and tone:

> All this. But at the latticed eye—
> "Hey, Gondolier, you sleep, my man;
> Wake up!" And shooting by, we ran;
> The while I mused, This surely now,
> Confutes the Naturalists, allow!
> Sirens, true sirens verily be,
> Sirens, waylayers in the sea.
> Well, wooed by these same deadly misses,
> Is it shame to run?
> No! Flee them did divine Ulysses,
> Brave, wise, and Venus' son.

The poem breaks up. The central section simply does not go with the rest. It is as though we have here a statement of the poet's conviction that the verse which belonged to the world of respectability could not accommodate the rendering of the experience undergone " 'Twixt the whale's black fluke and the white shark's fin."[2] Perhaps the violences, the distortions, the wrenchings in the versification of some of the poems are to be interpreted as the result not of mere ineptitude but of a conscious effort to develop a ner-

[2]Can this be an echo of the "wolf's black jaw" and the "dull ass' hoof" in Ben Jonson's "An Ode to Himself" (*Underwoods*)? In both Jonson and Melville, the content is the same: the affirmation of independence in the face of a bad and envious age.

vous, dramatic, masculine style. (In this connection, the effort at a familiar style in *John Marr and Other Sailors,* especially in "Jack Roy," is interesting.) That Melville was conscious of the relation of the mechanics of style to fundamental intentions is ably argued by William Ellery Sedgwick in *Herman Melville: The Tragedy of Mind* in connection with the verse of *Clarel.* Mr. Sedgwick argues that the choice of short, four-beat lines, usually rhyming in couplets, a form the very opposite to what would have been expected, was dictated by a desire to confirm himself in his new perspective. "The form of *Clarel* was prop or support to his new state of consciousness, in which his spontaneous ego or self-consciousness no longer played an all-commanding role." I would merely extend the application of the principle beyond *Clarel,* without arguing, as Mr. Sedgwick argues in the case of *Clarel,* that Melville did develop a satisfactory solution for his problem.

If we return to "In a Bye-Canal," we may observe that the poem is broken not only by a shift in rhythm but also by a shift in tone. The temper of the poem is very mixed. For instance, the lines

> Dumb noon, and haunted like the night
> When Jael the wiled one slew

introduce a peculiarly weighted, serious reference into the casual first section which concludes with the playful *scintillation-conjuration* rhyme. Then we have the grand section of the whale and the shark. Then the realistic admonition to the gondolier. Then the conclusion, with its classical allusion, at the level of *vers de société.* Probably no one would argue that the disparate elements in this poem have been assimilated, as they have, for example, in Marvell's "To His Coy Mistress." But I think that one may be well entitled to argue that the confusions of temper in this poem are not merely the result of ineptitude but are the result of an attempt to create a poetry of some vibrancy, range of reference, and richness of tone.

In another form we find the same effort much more successfully realized in "Jack Roy" in the difference between the two following stanzas:

> Sang Larry o' the Cannakin, smuggler o' the wine,
> At mess between guns, lad in jovial recline:

"In Limbo our Jack he would chirrup up a cheer,
The martinet there find a chaffing mutineer;
From a thousand fathoms down under hatches o'
    your Hades
He'd ascend in love-ditty, kissing fingers to your
    ladies!"
Never relishing the knave, though allowing for the
    menial,
Nor overmuch the king, Jack, nor prodigally genial.
Ashore on liberty, he flashed in escapade,
Vaulting over life in its levelness of grade,
Like the dolphin off Africa in rainbow a-sweeping—
Arch iridescent shot from seas languid sleeping.

Or we find the same fusion of disparate elements in "The March into Virginia," one of Melville's best poems:

Did all the lets and bars appear
To every just or larger end,
Whence should come the trust and cheer?
Youth must its ignorant impulse lend—
Age finds place in the rear.
All wars are boyish, and are fought by boys,
The champions and enthusiasts of the state:

No berrying party, pleasure-wooed,
No picnic party in the May,
Ever went less loath than they
Into that leafy neighborhood.
In Bacchic glee they file toward Fate,
Moloch's uninitiate;

But some who this blithe mood present,
As on in lightsome files they fare,
Shall die experienced ere three days are spent—
Perish, enlightened by the volleyed glare;[3]
Or shame survive, and, like to adamant,
The throe of Second Manassas share.

[3]Melville's double use of the word *enlightened* here is interesting and effective. The poem "Shiloh, a Requiem" echoes the metaphorical sense of the word in the line, "What like a bullet can undeceive?"

On a smaller scale, Melville's effort to get range and depth into his poetry is illustrated by the occasional boldness of his comparisons. For example, in "The Portent," the beard of John Brown protruding from the hangman's cap is like the trail of a comet or meteor presaging doom.

> Hidden in the cap
> Is the anguish none can draw;
> So your future veils its face,
> Shenandoah!
> But the streaming beard is shown
> (Weird John Brown),[4]
> The meteor of the war.

Or in one of the early poems, "In a Church of Padua," we find the confessional compared to a diving-bell:

> Dread diving-bell! In thee inurned
> What hollows the priest must sound,
> Descending into consciences
> Where more is hid than found.

It must be admitted that Melville did not learn his craft. But the point is that the craft he did not learn was not the same craft which some of his more highly advertised contemporaries did learn with such glibness of tongue and complacency of spirit. Even behind some of Melville's failures we can catch the shadow of the poem which might have been. And if his poetry is, on the whole, a poetry of shreds and patches, many of the patches are of a massy and kingly fabric—no product of the local cotton mills.

But to turn to another line of thought: Both Mr. Matthiessen and Mr. Sedgwick have been aware of the importance of the short poems in relation to Melville's general development. Mr. Sedgwick does give a fairly detailed analysis of the relation of *Battle-Pieces* to *Clarel*. "Even in the *Battle-Pieces*," he says, "we feel the reservations of this (religious) consciousness set against the easy and partial affirmations of patriotism and partisan conflict." And

---

[4]The depth and precision of the word *weird* is worthy of notice.

he quotes, as Mr. Matthiessen has quoted in the preface to the present collection and in the *American Renaissance,* an extremely significant sentence from the prose essay which Melville appended to the *Battle-Pieces:* "Let us pray that the terrible historic tragedy of our time may not have been enacted without instructing our whole beloved country through pity and terror." And Mr. Sedgwick refers to one of the paradoxes of "The Conflict of Convictions," that the victory of the Civil War may betray the cause for which the North was fighting:

> Power unanointed may come—
> Dominion (unsought by the free)
> And the Iron Dome
> Stronger for stress and strain,
> Fling her huge shadow athwart the main;
> But the Founders' dream shall flee. . . .

But even in this poem there are other ideas which relate to Melville's concern with the fundamental ironical dualities of existence: will against necessity, action against ideas, youth against age, the changelessness of man's heart against the concept of moral progress, the bad doer against the good deed, the bad result against the good act, ignorance against fate, etc. These ideas appear again and again, as in "The March into Virginia":

> Did all the lets and bars appear
> To every just or larger end,
> Whence should come the trust and cheer?
> Youth must the ignorant impulse lend—
> Age finds place in the rear.
> All wars are boyish, and are fought by boys,
> The champions and enthusiasts of the state.

Or in "On the Slain Collegians":

> Youth is the time when hearts are large,
> And stirring wars
> Appeal to the spirit which appeals in turn
> To the blade it draws.

If woman incite, and duty show
(Though made the mask of Cain),
Or whether it be Truth's sacred cause,
Who can aloof remain
That shares youth's ardour, uncooled by the snow
Of wisdom or sordid gain?

Youth, action, will, ignorance—all appear in heroic and dynamic form as manifestations of what Mr. Sedgwick has called Melville's "radical Protestantism," the spirit which had informed *Moby Dick*. But in these poems the commitment is nicely balanced, and even as we find the praise of the dynamic and heroic we find them cast against the backdrop of age, idea, necessity, wisdom, fate. Duty may be made the "mask of Cain" and "lavish hearts" are but, as the poem on the Collegians puts it, "swept by the winds of their place and time." All bear their "fated" parts. All move toward death or toward the moment of wisdom when they will stand, as "The March into Virginia" puts it, "enlightened by the volleyed glare."

Man may wish to act for Truth and Right, but the problem of definitions is a difficult one and solution may be achieved only in terms of his own exercise of will and his appetite for action. That is, his "truth" and the Truth may be very different things in the end. "On the Slain Collegians" sums the matter up:

What could they else—North or South?
Each went forth with blessings given
By priests and mothers in the name of Heaven;
    And honour in both was chief.
Warred one for Right, and one for Wrong?
So be it; but they both were young—
Each grape to his cluster clung,
All their elegies are sung.

Or there is "The College Colonel," the young officer who returns from the war, a crutch by his saddle, to receive the welcome of the crowd and especially, as "Boy," the salute of age. But to him comes "alloy."

It is not that a leg is lost
It is not that an arm is maimed.
It is not that the fever has racked—
Self he has long disclaimed.
But all through the Seven Days' Fight,
And deep in the Wilderness grim,
And in the field-hospital tent,
And Petersburg crater, and dim
Lean brooding in Libby, there came—
Ah heaven!—what *truth* to him.

The official truth and the official celebration are equally meaningless to him who has been "enlightened by the volleyed glare"— who has known pity and terror.

The event, the act, is never simple. Duty may be made the mask of Cain. In "The Conflict of Convictions," it is asked:

Dashed aims, at which Christ's martyrs pale,
Shall Mammon's slaves fulfill?

And in the same poem, in the passage which Mr. Sedgwick quotes, Melville conjectures that the Iron Dome, stronger for stress and strain, may fling its huge, imperial shadow across the main; but at the expense of the "Founders' dream." But other dire effects of the convulsion, even if it involves Right, may be possible. Hate on one side and Phariseeism on the other may breed a greater wrong than the one corrected by the conflict. The "gulfs" may bare "their slimed foundations," as it is phrased in the same poem in an image which is repeated in "America." The allegorical female figure, America, is shown sleeping:

But in that sleep contortion showed
The terror of the vision there—
A silent vision unavowed,
Revealing earth's foundations bare,
And Gorgon in her hiding place.
It was a thing of fear to see
So foul a dream upon so fair a face,
And the dreamer lying in that starry shroud.

Even if the victory is attained, there is no cause for innocent rejoicing. As, in "The College Colonel," the hero looks beyond the cheering crowd to his "truth," so in "Commemorative of a Naval Victory," the hero must look beyond his "festal fame":

> But seldom the laurel wreath is seen
> Unmixed with pensive pansies dark;
> There's a light and shadow on every man
> Who at last attains his lifted mark—
> Nursing through night the ethereal spark.
> Elate he never can be;
> He feels that spirits which glad had hailed his worth,
> Sleep in oblivion.—The shark
> Glides white through the phosphorous sea.

There is more involved here than the sadness over the loss of comrades. The shark comes as too violent and extravagant an image for that. The white shark belongs to the world of the "slimed foundations" which are exposed by the convulsion. It is between the whale's black fluke and the white shark's fin that wisdom is learned. He is the Maldive shark, which appears in the poem by that name, the "Gorgonian head" (the "Gorgon in her hiding place" appears too in the bared foundations of earth glimpsed in the dream of "America"), the "pale ravener of horrible meat," the Fate symbol.

We may ask what resolution of these dualities and dubieties may be found in Melville's work. For there is an effort at a resolution. The effort manifests itself in three different terms: nature, history, and religion.

In reference to the first term, we find the simple treatment of "Shiloh":

> Foemen at morn, but friends at eve—
> Fame or country least their care:
> (What like a bullet can undeceive!)
> But now they lie low,
> While over them the swallows skim
> And all is hushed at Shiloh.

Mortal passion and mortal definition dissolve in the natural process, as in "Malvern Hill":

> We elms of Malvern Hill
> Remember everything;
> But sap the twig will fill:
> Wag the world how it will,
> Leaves must be green in Spring.

The focal image at the end of "A Requiem for Soldiers Lost in Ocean Transports" repeats the same effect:

> Nor heed they now the lone bird's flight
> Round the lone spar where mid-sea surges pour.

There is, however, a step beyond this elegiac calm of the great natural process which absorbs the human effort and agony. There is also the historical process. It is possible, as Melville puts it in "The Conflict of Convictions," that the "throes of ages" may rear the "final empire and the happier world." The Negro woman in "Formerly a Slave" looks

> Far down the depth of thousand years,
> And marks the revel shine;
> Her dusky face is lit with sober light,
> Sibylline, yet benign.

In "America," the last poem of *Battle-Pieces,* the contorted expression on the face of the sleeping woman as she dreams the foul dream of earth's bared foundations, is replaced, when she rises, by a "clear calm look."

> . . . It spake of pain,
> But such a purifier from stain—
> Sharp pangs that never come again—
> And triumph repressed by knowledge meet,
> And youth matured for age's seat—
> Law on her brow and empire in her eyes.
> So she, with graver air and lifted flag;

> While the shadow, chased by light,
> Fled along the far-drawn height,
> And left her on the crag.

"Secession, like Slavery, is against Destiny," Melville wrote in the prose Supplement to *Battle-Pieces.* For to him, if history was fate (the "foulest crime" was inherited and was fixed by geographical accident upon its perpetrators), it might also prove to be redemption. In *Mardi,* in a passage which Mr. Sedgwick quotes in reference to the slaves of Vivenza, Melville exclaims: "Time—all-healing Time—Time, great philanthropist! Time must befriend these thralls." Melville, like Hardy, whom he resembles in so many respects and with whose war poems his own war poems share so much in tone and attitude, proclaimed that he was neither an optimist nor a pessimist, and in some of his own work we find a kind of guarded meliorism, like Hardy's, which manifests itself in the terms of destiny, fate, time, that is, in the historical process.

The historical process, however, does not appear always as this mechanism of meliorism. Sometimes the resolution it offers is of another sort, a sort similar to the elegiac calm of the natural process: the act is always poised on the verge of history, the passion, even at the moment of greatest intensity, is always about to become legend, the moral issue is always about to disappear into time and leave only the human figures, shadowy now, fixed in attitudes of the struggle. In "Battle of Stone River, Tennessee," we find the stanzas which best express this.

> With Tewksbury and Barnet heath,
> In days to come the field shall blend,
> The story dim and date obscure;
> In legend all shall end.
> Even now, involved in forest shade
> A Druid-dream the strife appears,
> The fray of yesterday assumes
> The haziness of years.
>   In North and South still beats the vein
>   Of Yorkist and Lancastrian.

But Rosecrans in the cedarn glade
And, deep in denser cypress gloom,
Dark Breckinridge, shall fade away
Or thinly loom.
The pale throngs who in forest cowed
Before the spell of battle's pause,
Forefelt the stillness that shall dwell
On them and their wars.
    North and South shall join the train
    Of Yorkist and Lancastrian.

In "The March into Virginia" the young men laughing and chatting on the road to Manassas are "Moloch's uninitiate" who "file toward Fate."

All they feel is this: 'tis glory,
A rapture sharp, though transitory
Yet lasting in belaurelled story.

The glory of the act ends in legend, in the perspective of history, which is fate. Human action enters the realm where it is, to take a line from "The Coming Storm,"

Steeped in fable, steeped in fate.

Nature and history proved the chief terms of resolution in *Battle-Pieces*. Only rarely appears the third term, religion, and then in a conventional form. For instance, there is "The Swamp-Angel," which deals with the bombardment of Charleston:

Who weeps for the woeful City
Let him weep for our guilty kind;
Who joys at her wild despairing—
Christ, the Forgiver, convert his mind.

It is actually in the terms of nature and history that the attitude which characterizes *Clarel* first begins to make itself felt. Mr. Sedgwick has defined Melville's attitude as the result of a "religious conversion to life." In it he renounced the quest for the "uncreated

good," the individualistic idealism of *Moby Dick,* the "radical Protestantism." Mr. Sedgwick continues: "Behind *Clarel* lies the recognition that for ripeness, there must be receptivity; that from the
point of view of the total consciousness it is not more blessed to give
than to receive. One receives in order to be received into life and
fulfilled by life. . . . Melville's act was toward humanity, not away
from it. He renounced all the prerogatives of individuality in order
to enter into the destiny which binds all human beings in one great
spiritual and emotional organism. He abdicated his independence
so as to be incorporated into the mystical body of humanity." There
is the affirmation at the end of *Clarel:*

> But through such strange illusions have they passed
> Who in life's pilgrimage have baffled striven—
> Even death may prove unreal at the last,
> And stoics be astounded into heaven.
>
> Then keep thy heart, though yet but ill-resigned—
> Clarel, thy heart, the issues there but mind;
> That like the crocus budding through the snow—
> That like a swimmer rising from the deep—
> That like a burning secret which doth go
> Even from the bosom that would hoard and keep;
> Emerge thou mayst from the last whelming sea,
> And prove that death but routs life into victory.

Or we find the same attitude expressed by the comforting spirit
which appears at the end of "The Lake":

> She ceased and nearer slid, and hung
> In dewy guise; then softlier sung:
> "Since light and shade are equal set,
> And all revolves, nor more ye know;
> Ah, why should tears the pale cheek fret
> For aught that waneth here below.
> Let go, let go!"
>
> With that, her warm lips thrilled me through,
> She kissed me while her chaplet cold
> Its rootlets brushed against my brow

With all their humid clinging mould.
She vanished, leaving fragrant breath
And warmth and chill of wedded life and death.

And when, in the light of these poems we look back upon "The Maldive Shark" we see its deeper significance. As the pilot fish may find a haven in the serrated teeth of the shark, so man, if he learns the last wisdom, may find an "asylum in the jaws of the Fates."

This end product of Melville's experience has, in the passage which I have already quoted from Mr. Sedgwick, been amply defined. What I wish to emphasize is the fact that there is an astonishing continuity between the early poems, especially *Battle-Pieces,* and *Clarel.* Under the terms of nature and history, the religious attitude of *Clarel* and "The Lake" is already being defined.

JOHN GREENLEAF WHITTIER:

POETRY

AS EXPERIENCE

*T*HE FIRST WHITTIER, Thomas, arrived in Massachusetts in 1638. He was a man of moral force, as is attested by the fact that a generation before the family had any connection with Quakers, he took grave risks in protesting against their persecution.[1] Despite his espousal of a dangerously unpopular cause, he still had influence in his little world, and was a holder of office. He was, too, a physical giant, and at the age of sixty-eight, still vigorous enough to hew the oak timbers for a new house, the solid two-story structure in Haverhill where, on December 17, 1807, the poet was to be born.

At Haverhill, John Whittier, the great-grandson of old Thomas and the father of John Greenleaf, worked a farm of 185 indifferent acres and saw to it that his sons did their share. John Greenleaf loved the land but loathed the work on it. For one thing, he was

First published in *The Sewanee Review,* Winter 1971, as "Whittier."
[1]The family did not become Quakers until 1694, when Joseph Whittier, a son of old Thomas, married a granddaughter of one of the Quakers his father had defended.

frail and at the age of seventeen suffered an injury from overexertion; for another thing, he early had a passion for study. His verses began early, too, and one of them sets forth the intellectual ambition that was to dominate his youth:

> And must I always swing the flail,
> And help to fill the milking pail?
> I wish to go away to school,
> I do not wish to be a fool.

In light of these verses, Whittier's boyhood circumstances, and his admiration for Burns, certain critics have been tempted to think of Whittier, as more than one European critic has thought of Robert Frost, as a "peasant poet." Nothing could be more wide of the mark. The error arises from a confusion to which our contemporary urban, plutocratic society is peculiarly prone: a poor (or even any) farmer is, obviously, a peasant. The Whittiers were farmers, certainly; and if they were not, in relation to time and place, exactly poor, they were not rich. But to think of them as peasants is to fail to realize that what makes a peasant is a psychological rather than an economic fact. The peasant is a member of a fairly rigid and stable subculture that he accepts, fatalistically or pridefully, as the only world in which he can fulfill himself. But when Jefferson thought of his independent farmer, he was not thinking of a peasant: he was thinking of a type central to a whole society. And when the poet Whittier looked backward on the family past he saw the "founding fathers" of a whole new world—a whole society—and if anything characterized his early manhood, it was an almost pathological ambition to take his "rightful" place in that whole society.

The presence, however significant, of folk elements in Whittier's work does not make him a peasant poet any more than the presence of such elements in Faulkner's work makes him a peasant novelist. Indeed, to think of Whittier as a peasant poet is as absurd as to think of Lincoln as a "peasant president." And certainly it is absurd to regard Whittier as a brother to those peasant poets of the eighteenth century in England, such as Mary Collier, the "Poetical Washerwoman," and Stephen Duck, the "Thresher Poet," or John Clare of the nineteenth century, who, when he was patronized in a great house, was set down to his meal with the servants. In one sense, all is a matter of role, and it is hard to imagine Whittier, however full of Quaker meekness, gratefully accepting the role of a guest in the scullery. If he loved Burns, we must remember that when the American quoted "a man's a man for a' that," he held the Declaration of Independence in mind as a gloss.

The house of the Quaker farmer at Haverhill had books, and after absorbing them, the son reached out for others, for Milton, who was to become a personal rather than a poetic model, and such un-Quakerish works as the stage plays of Shakespeare.[2] Already, by the age of fourteen, Whittier had heard a Scot, "a pawky auld carle," singing songs of Robert Burns at the kitchen hearth of the Whittiers, and in the same year, the schoolmaster, Joshua Coffin, sat in the same spot and read from a volume of Burns, which he then lent to the young listener. "This was about the first poetry I had ever read," Whittier was to say, "with the exception of that of the Bible (of which I had been a close student) and it had a lasting influence upon me. I began to make rhymes myself, and to imagine stories and adventures." It was thus by Burns, and Burns through the voice of the "pawky auld carle," that Whittier's eyes, according to a later account in the poem "Burns," were opened to the land and life around him as the substance of poetry:

> I matched with Scotland's heathery hills
> The sweetbrier and the clover;
> With Ayr and Doon, my native rills,
> Their wood-hymns chanting over.

But it was not only to nature that Burns opened the boy's eyes. He was already steeped in the legends and folklore of his region,

---

[2]There was no Shakespeare in the little library at the Whittier farmhouse. But even if that library was limited, it was not that of a stupid or illiterate family. Here were, naturally, the Bible, the works of William Penn and other Quakers, and of John Bunyan; various accounts of shipwreck and exotic travel; the multivolume set of Charles Rollin's *The Ancient History of Egyptians, Carthaginians,* etc., translated from the French; Lindley Murray's *English Reader . . . Selected from the Best Writers;* and Sir Walter Scott's *The Pirate.* At an early age Whittier could tell the whole story of the Bible from Genesis to Revelations, and had vast amounts of it by heart. See John A. Pollard, *John Greenleaf Whittier: Friend of Man,* pp. 589–91.

which he had absorbed as naturally as the air he breathed, but Burns interpreted what the boy had naturally absorbed and showed that it was the stuff of poetry. So Whittier, as early as Hawthorne, and earlier than Longfellow, was to turn to the past of New England for subject matter, and by 1831, in a poem called "New England," was expressing his ambition to be the poet of his region. His first volume, a mixture of eleven poems and seven prose pieces, published in 1831 in Hartford, was called *Legends of New England*. [3]

To return to Whittier's literary beginnings, Milton and Burns were not the only models he proposed to himself. There was the flood of contemporary trash, American and English, from writers like Felicia Hemans, Lydia Sigourney, N. P. Willis, the elder Dana, Lydia Maria Child, Bernard Barton, and John Pierpont. The marks of their incorrigible gabble remained on Whittier's sensibility more indelibly than those made by the work of even the idolized Burns; and it is highly probable that Whittier, in spite of the fact that he was to deplore "the imbecility of our poetry," could not nicely distinguish the poetic level of Burns from that of, say, Lydia Sigourney, the "sweet singer of Hartford," who was his friend. He could write, too, of Longfellow's "A Psalm of Life": "These nine simple verses are worth more than all the dreams of Shelley, Keats, and Wordsworth. They are alive and vigorous with the spirit of the day in which we live—the moral steam enginery of an age of action." Whenever "moral steam enginery" came in the door, whatever taste Whittier did happen to have went precipitously out the window. "Strictly speaking," as Hawthorne put it, "Whittier did not care much for literature."[4] And, if a letter written late in life is to be believed, he cared less for poetry than prose: "I regard good prose writing as really better than rhyme."

[3]Later Whittier was to try to buy up and destroy all copies, but he did reprint an "Extract" in his collected edition. The "Extract" begins: "How has New England's romance fled," and this line tells the whole story of the difference between Whittier's or Longfellow's sense of the past and Hawthorne's. They were drawn merely by the picturesque and anecdotal, Hawthorne by a psychological and moral interest.

[4]As good a proof of this as any is the fact that Whittier found Hawthorne merely a pleasant teller of tales. It is not too hard to believe that Whittier would have instinctively flinched from the inwardness and shadows of Hawthorne's work. In fact, he may have lived only by such a refusal to regard inwardness and shadows.

But, in addition to all the other poets good and bad that Whittier read, there was, inevitably, Byron. In fact, it was under the aegis of Byron that Whittier, with a poem called "The Exile's Departure," written when he was eighteen, first found his way into print. His elder sister Mary had secretly sent the poem, with only the signature "W," to the *Free Press,* the newspaper at Newburyport. There, on June 8, 1826, it was published—not only published but accompanied by the hope of the editor that "W" would continue to favor him with pieces equally "beautiful."

This editor was William Lloyd Garrison, then only twenty-one, destined to become the most intransigent and famous of the abolitionists. He was also to have a lasting effect on the shape of Whittier's life, but the most immediate effect came when Garrison, having discovered the identity of "W," drove fourteen miles to the Whittier farm, burst in upon the family, and lectured John Whittier on his duty to give the son "every facility for the development of his remarkable genius." To this oratory of a beardless youth, old John Whittier replied: "Sir, poetry will not give him bread."

Nevertheless, the father did allow his son to enroll, one year and some fifty poems later, as a freshman—that is, as a freshman in high school—in the Haverhill Academy, just then established. For two sessions, broken by a stint at schoolmastering, Whittier managed to support himself at the Academy, and this was the end of his formal education. By this time his poetry, which issued in a swelling stream, had appeared in distant places like Boston, Hartford, and Philadelphia, and was being widely reprinted by newspaper editors. Whittier was something of a local celebrity, had friends and admirers (whose efforts to raise money for continuing his education at college came to nothing), and was inflamed with ambition and the ignorant confidence that the world was his for the reaching out. He could write that he felt "a consciousness of slumbering powers."

Whittier had already had some experience in the office of the local newspaper, and it was to be through journalism that he entered the great world and became a writer—a pattern very common in America in the nineteenth century but, for various reasons, now rare. Whittier, anxious to take a hand in the "moral steam enginery" of the age, aspired to the editorship of the *National Philan-*

thropist of Boston, the first prohibition paper in the country, which Garrison had been editing. Alcohol had not proved a worthy challenge to Garrison's mettle, and now he was resigning from the *Philanthropist* to establish, in Bennington, Vermont, the *Journal of the Times,* which was to take as its twin targets slavery and war. Though Garrison sponsored Whittier as his successor in the crusade for prohibition, this did not work out; but the Collier family, owners of the *Philanthropist,* published two other papers, the *American Manufacturer* and the *Baptist Minister,* and did, in 1828, make Whittier the editor of the first.

The *Manufacturer* was a weekly dedicated to the support of Henry Clay and the Whig party, especially to the policy of a high protective tariff. But Whittier, who, while still hoping for the editorship of the *Philanthropist,* had written to a friend that he would "rather have the memory" of a reformer "than the undying fame of Byron," promptly grafted the cause of prohibition onto that of a high tariff, and the first poem he wrote for his editorial column was an un-Byronic ditty entitled "Take Back the Bowl!"

In spite of this and other reformist excursions in the *Manufacturer,* Whittier knew his duty to the Tariff of Abominations enacted in 1828 and the "American System" of the Whigs. As one of Whittier's biographers, John A. Pollard, has pointed out, Whittier, in spite of the fact that he had been raised in the tradition of Jeffersonian democracy, failed to grasp the contradiction between Whig capitalism and his own inherited principles and assumed that what was good for New England loom-masters was good for New England in general and, in fact, for the human race at large. Whittier's Quaker pacifism made him regard Jackson, a soldier and duelist, as the "bloodthirsty old man at the head of our government," and blinded him to some of the economic and social implications of Jacksonian democracy; and so, for some years to come, Whittier continued to believe that Clay, as Pollard puts it, "really was a friend of the common man."

Meanwhile, Whittier helped in preparing a campaign biography of Clay, and came to edit two other pro-Clay papers, the *Gazette* of Haverhill and the *New England Weekly Review* of Hartford. He had made something of a reputation as a partisan editor, with a prose of biting sarcasm and a sense of political strategy. Though the poems poured out in unabated flow, his personal ambitions were more and more political. In fact, it is hard to believe that Whittier was really committed to poetry. The conclusion is not far short of inevitable that he was using his facility in verse as a device for success rather than using poetry as a way of coming to grips with experience. He wrote poems by the bushel and got himself extravagantly praised for them—and why not? He had become a master of the garrulous vapidity which was in general fashion.

But poetry was not enough. The joy of discovery and composition was not enough, nor even the recognition he was receiving. Whittier wanted more than recognition; he wanted some great, overwhelming, apocalyptic success, a success that he probably could not, or dared not, define for himself, a success that would be the very justification for life. "I would have fame visit me *now,* or not at all," he wrote Lydia Sigourney. Again, in a most extraordinary essay, "The Nervous Man," in 1833, he speaks through his character: "Time has dealt hardly with my boyhood's muse. Poetry has been to me a beautiful delusion. It was something woven of my young fancies, and reality has destroyed it. I can, indeed, make rhymes now, as mechanically as a mason piles one brick above another; but the glow of feeling, the hope, the ardor, the excitement have passed away forever. I have long thought, or rather the world hath *made* me think, that poetry is too trifling, too insignificant a pursuit for the matured intellect of sober manhood."

With some rational sense of his own limitations (he knew that what he knew was how to pile the bricks) was paradoxically coupled a self-pity and an air of grievance against the world that had not adequately rewarded the poet, by the age of twenty-five, with that overwhelming, life-justifying, undefinable, and apocalyptic success. So he wrote Lydia Sigourney that politics was "the only field now open." He turned to politics for the prize, not merely by clinging to Clay's coattails, to which he pinned wildly adulatory effusions such as "Star of the West," which became an effective campaign item, but by trying to run for office himself. In this period he made at least two unsuccessful attempts, and a letter soliciting support is significant.

Again, this letter emphasizes the *now:* "It [the election to Congress] would be worth more to me *now,* young as I am, than almost any office after I had reached the meridian of life." And the letter, which in fact was related to some rather dubious maneuvering, shows that Whittier, who had been outraged at Jackson and the spoils system, had secretly learned something—a "something" to which he must now give the moral disguise of unselfishness and loyalty: ". . . if I know my own heart, I am not entirely selfish. I have never yet *deserted a friend,* and I never will. If my friends enable me to acquire influence, it shall be exerted for *their benefit.* And give me once an opportunity of exercising it, my first object shall be to evince my gratitude by exertions in behalf of those who had conferred such favor upon me. . . ."

This, translated, means: you scratch my back, and I'll scratch yours.

For the moment, nothing came of Whittier's political projects, and nothing came of the love affairs that belong to the same period of his attempt to enter the great world. Whittier, in spite of a certain frailty, was tall, handsome, and attractive to women; and he himself was greatly attracted to women and was rather inclined to insist on the fact. But he remained a bachelor. In the series of love affairs, in the period before 1833, a pattern seems to emerge. The girls were non-Quaker, good-looking, popular, and above Whittier's station, both financially and socially; that is, the choice of sweethearts seems to have been consistent with his worldly and un-Quakerish ambitions. Some biographers take at face value Whittier's statement, made late in life, that he refused matrimony because of "the care of an aged mother, and the duty owed to a sister [Elizabeth] in delicate health." It is true that Whittier's father died in 1830, when the poet was only twenty-three, but his explanation of his bachelorhood does not quite square with the facts; he did not reject matrimony—the girls, with one possible exception, seem to have rejected him.[5] As an index to wounded self-esteem, frustrated ambition, and a considerable talent for boyish self-dramatization, we have this passage, which, though it dates back to 1828, cannot be without significance in relation to more than poetry:

[5]One girl, Eveline Bray, may not have turned him down, but have been turned down; but if Whittier did turn her down, he apparently did so not for aging mother and ailing sister, but for another girl whom he liked better. See Albert Nordell, *Quaker Militant.*

"*. . . I will quit poetry and everything else of a literary nature,* for I am sick at heart of the business. . . . Insult has maddened me. The friendless boy has been mocked at; and, years ago, he vowed to triumph over the scorners of his boyish endeavors. With the unescapable sense of wrong burning like a volcano in the recesses of his spirit, he has striven to accomplish this vow, until his heart has grown weary of the struggle. . . ."

There is no way to be sure what went on in Whittier's heart, or in his romances. In 1857, in a poem called "My Namesake," looking back on his youth, he said of himself:

> His eye was beauty's powerless slave,
> And his the ear which discord pains;
> Few guessed beneath his aspect grave
> What passions strove in chains.

Though Whittier was aware of the existence of the "chains," we cannot know exactly what they were. It may even be that Whittier, consciously choosing girls that fitted his "passions" and his vaulting ambition, was unconsciously choosing girls who would be certain to turn him, and his Quakerism, down. The whole thing is very tangled, and not less tangled for the fact that in spite of the courting of non-Quaker girls, he seems to have felt compelled to marry, if at all, within the sect. In 1829, writing about the pretty non-Quaker girls in Boston, he says: "The worst of it is if I ever get married I must marry a Quakeress with her bonnet like a flour dipper and a face as long as a tobacco yawl."

But what was to prevent him from seeking some pretty Quaker girl—or even a pretty Quaker girl who happened to be rich? Such creatures did exist, and the thought of a Quaker sweetheart did cross his mind, for in 1830, in the middle of his love affairs, he wrote a poem to a "Fair Quakeress," and praised her, whether she was real or imagined, for being "unadorned save for her youthful charms," and stated his conviction that beneath the "calm temper and a chastened mind" a "warmth of passion" was awaiting the "thrilling of some kindly touch." But that was as far as he got along this particular line of thought. Whittier did, it is true, have a protracted, complex relationship with one Quaker lady, Elizabeth

Lloyd, to whom we shall recur. But this was after he had given up his worldly ambitions and had made, as we shall see, his commitment to abolitionism as a way of life.

The change in the way of life may have made some difference in the kind of girl Whittier, in this second phase, found congenial: poetesses, dabblers in art, abolitionists, hero-worshipers, and protégés. But the old pattern of behavior did not change. In the same period when Whittier had written "The Nervous Man," to which I have already alluded, he composed another remarkable piece of what seems to be undeclared self-analysis; it is called "The Male Coquette," and it is hard not to believe that it predicted the role he was doomed to play until the end.

In any case, there was some deep inner conflict in Whittier, with fits of self-pity and depression, breakdowns and withdrawals from the world, violent chronic headaches and insomnia. A breakdown in 1831 sent Whittier from Hartford and his editorship back to Haverhill, and to such farming as his health permitted. In that period he set about reordering his life, trying to work out a life attitude and a purpose. Here, again, Garrison appeared. Already he had done a hitch in a Baltimore jail (unable to pay a judgment for libelously accusing a shipmaster of carrying a cargo of slaves), had founded, in January 1831, the *Liberator,* the most famous of abolitionist papers, and had written the pamphlet *Thoughts on African Colonization;* and these things had already had an effect on Whittier. Now, in the spring of 1833, Garrison wrote Whittier a direct appeal: "The cause is worthy of Gabriel yea, the God of hosts places himself at its head. Whittier, enlist!—Your talents, zeal, influence—all are needed."

When, a few weeks later, Garrison came to Haverhill and spoke at the Quaker meetinghouse, Whittier was ready now, as he put it, to knock "Pegasus on the head, as a tanner does his bark-mill donkey, when he is past service." Years later, after the Civil War, in the poem "The Tent on the Beach," Whittier wrote, with something less than full historical accuracy, of his shift in direction:

> And one there was, a dreamer born,
>   Who, with a mission to fulfil,
> Had left the Muses' haunts to turn
>   The crank of an opinion-mill,

> Making his rustic reed of song
> A weapon in the war with wrong.

A more candid account appears in a letter to E. L. Godkin, the editor of the *Nation:* "I cannot be sufficiently grateful to the Divine Providence that so early called my attention to the great interests of humanity, saving me from the poor ambitions and miserable jealousies of a selfish pursuit of literary reputation." And from, he added, "the pain of disappointment and the temptation to envy."

Whittier had, apparently, already suffered enough from those things, as well as from other wounds to ego and ambition, and the relief from suffering was what he must have been referring to when, late in life, he said that the question was not what he had done for abolitionism but what abolitionism had done for him.

Since for more than thirty years abolitionism was the central fact of Whittier's life, it is worth trying to say what it was, and what some of the assumptions behind it were. The difficulty here is, however, that abolitionism had many variants; and to make matters worse, abolitionism, like any vital force, was constantly changing its forms, with bitter factional struggles for power, prestige, and control of policy. But we may best try to understand its essential nature by focusing on the radical variety that is associated with the name of Garrison, remembering that Garrison's own views were not the same from beginning to end. And to understand Garrison's form of abolitionism, or even abolitionism in general, the simplest way to start is to say what it was not.

First, abolitionism was not a general Northern doctrine. The abolitionists were always, even during the Civil War, when the emancipation of slaves became a matter of public policy, a minority. In the earlier days, in fact, the mobbing of abolitionists was not uncommon in the North. Garrison himself was manhandled by the "broadcloth mob" of Boston—i.e., well-dressed businessmen—and Elijah Lovejoy was murdered, in 1837, in Illinois. Charles Follen, professor of German at Harvard, lost his post for being an abolitionist, and Governor Edward Everett of Massachusetts, who later was to make the two-hour oration at Gettysburg that preceded Lincoln's two-minute address, asked the legislature for laws to stamp out abolitionism. When, as late as 1862, the Hutchinson Singers entertained the troops of the Army of the Potomac by singing the words Whittier had written to the tune of Luther's "Ein Feste Burg Ist unser Gott," a hymn demanding the end of slavery, the performers were driven out of camp, and one of the Federal officers who helped them on their way was, in fact, reported to have said that he didn't like abolitionists any better than he liked Rebels—a perfectly logical position for a good Unionist.

Second, abolitionism was not anti-racism. If by racism we understand the idea that the Negro (or any nonwhite race) is inherently inferior, then racism was as prevalent in the North as in the South, and the opposition to slavery, whether as emancipationism or abolitionism, had no *necessary* connection with respect for, or acceptance of, the Negro. To dramatize this fact, we may point out that Lincoln, though an emancipationist, did not accept the idea of racial equality. In the light of the general historical and social background, it is not surprising that even an abolitionist *might* be, in one way or another, a racist; but it is true that there was less of this attitude among abolitionists than among the population at large, certainly of the more obvious kind.[6]

Third, abolitionism was not the same thing as emancipationism. It was a special form of emancipationism. For instance, Emerson, Melville, Lincoln, and Robert E. Lee were emancipationists, but they were not abolitionists. The most obvious difference between emancipationism and abolitionism lay in the intensity of feeling involved, and this difference was associated with the question of contexts in which the problem of slavery might be regarded. For an emancipationist, the problem of slavery, no matter how important it was conceived to be, was to be treated in a general context, social, political, moral, or theological. For instance, Jefferson, in looking to the gradual emancipation of the slaves, placed the problem in a context of social continuity and political stability. And

[6]Ironically enough, at the fundamental level of mere physical acceptance, there was a great deal less racism in the South than in the North, as the mixture of blood will amply demonstrate, and as many works of Southern literature, for instance the novels of William Faulkner, will document. Whittier, like most abolitionists, was opposed to miscegenation.

Lincoln, in taking the defense of the Union, not the freeing of the slaves, as the key issue in the Civil War, again considered the social and political contexts. But for an abolitionist the problem of slavery was paramount, central, burning, and immediate. The context did not matter.

Let us glance at this distinction in relation to theology. Behind both abolitionism and the antislavery impulse in general often lay Christian theology. Both the emancipationist and the abolitionist might well regard slaveholding as a sin, but for the latter in so far as he thought theologically, it was the prime and unforgivable sin. Benjamin Lay, a Quaker of the eighteenth century whom Whittier called the "irrepressible prophet," put it this way: *"As God gave His only begotten Son, that whosoever believed in Him might have everlasting life;* so the Devil gives his only begotten child, the *Merchandize of Slaves and Souls of Men,* that whosoever believes and trades in it might have everlasting Damnation."* Slavery, according to Lay, was the "greatest sin in the world"—the "very worst part of the old Whores Merchandize, *most filthy Whore of Whores, Babilon's Bastards."* This particular theological interpretation, by making slavery the "greatest sin,"[7] implied that all other issues had to be strictly subordinated, not only for the benefit of the slave but to save the soul of the abolitionist: if he connives with sin, he will be damned. The fear of connivance, furthermore, would rule out any attempt to work at practical solutions such as gradual emancipation or emancipation with compensation (none were, in fact, ever really tried and the elaboration and complication of debate about various schemes may have driven some antislavery people toward the basic simplicity of the abolitionist solution). In other words, a practical solution might be rejected because inconsistent with an abstract point, and this could lead to the rejection of all political action.

Associated with this in the rejection of political action was the notion that slavery was a violation of a "higher law,"[8] of which

[7]See, for instance, Hawthorne's "Ethan Brand" for a different primary sin.
[8]This is to be distinguished from the notion that slavery is a violation of "natural rights," though in practice the two notions might lead to the same line of action in defying the state. Here, the proponent of natural law would hold that the state cannot act to abridge natural rights. But the theological notion, with the conviction of personal revelation, gave the cutting edge and the intensity beyond the mere theory of natural rights.

government and other institutions, in so far as they in any way compromised with slavery, were in contravention. Such a "higher law" cannot, of course, be demonstrated; it can be known only by direct revelation to the individual. So, in a new form, appeared antinomianism, an issue that had plagued Christianity from earliest times and had continued significantly into colonial New England. The antinomian, in the early days of the church, might assume that because he had received the Christian revelation—"grace"—he could guiltlessly get drunk or commit fornication, and in the Massachusetts Bay Colony, Roger Williams and Anne Hutchinson, because of the "Inner Light" and the idea of the inwardness of regeneration, might claim wisdom perhaps superior to that of the Bible, and certainly to that of the synod of churches and the General Court. In any such case, the individual would set his revelation, his conscience, up against the community. This attitude would naturally lead to Garrison's gesture of publicly burning the Constitution as a "league with death and a covenant with hell," and, along with the notion of connivance with evil, to the notion that it was morally wrong even to try to work through institutions. But it must be observed that this is very different from maintaining that it is impractical or impossible to work through institutions. The "pure" Garrisonian might refuse to do so on grounds of principle, but even so, it must be recognized that the attitude toward political involvement was often fluctuating; and at different times, according to circumstances, the same individual might hold different attitudes. For instance, with the rise of the Republican party, a certain number of antislavery people who had previously abjured or despised political action began to accept it.

The notion of "higher law" and antinomianism had another corollary. Since slavery was a sin and a crime, the slaveholder, as a sinner, was denied, and as a criminal was outside of, the protection of law. This line of reasoning might lead to the fomenting of insurrection and the approval of massacre; and did lead to such legends as that Southerners liked to use skulls for drinking bowls, a legend in which Harriet Beecher Stowe and even Whittier believed, and which the poet refers to in "Amy Wentworth." More generally, the line of reasoning led to the vilification not only of all Southerners, but also of anybody else who failed to accept the abolitionist position, as murderers, thieves, adulterers, and whoremasters, to refer to some of the more amiable charges in vogue. An emancipationist like Lincoln was, to Wendell Phillips, the "slave-hound of Illinois," and even fellow abolitionists might come in for rough handling from those who had nearer relation with the Divine Will: "Among the true, inner-seal Garrisonians," as John Jay Chapman puts it in his sympathetic book on Garrison, "the *wrong* kind of anti-slavery was always considered as anti-Christ." Garrison, that master of vilification, visited as much of his spleen on Frederick Douglass, the ex-slave and fellow abolitionist, as he ever visited on a slave-master.

Abolitionism—at least one brand of it—thus set up against society, squarely and by principle, a naked and absolute individualism. This attitude struck not only at an evil in society, but at the roots of the democratic process, which is based on discussion, the recognition of the contexts of issues, and the assumption that the opponent on any issue is also a member in more or less good standing of society and of the human race; and it was this stripe of dogmatic individualism that Justice Oliver Wendell Holmes, who in 1861 had shared the views of the abolitionists, was to say he "came to loathe"—"the conviction that anyone who did not agree with them was a knave or a fool."

But this very attitude that seems to strike at the root of the democratic process must be recognized as one pole of the democratic process: the claim of the individual intuition to be heard in protest against an order established by a majority, or by vested interests with the toleration of the majority. Clearly, without respect for the criticism arising from the individual intuition, there can be no regeneration of institutions. And it is a sadly chastening experience to recognize that rational consensus eventuating in reform is rare, and that the historical process most often involves—and may *necessarily* involve—tragic collisions in which the individual intuition, dogmatically asserted, dynamically dramatizes certain essential values. The whole matter revolves around the question: Is the conscience at any given moment absolute, or is it conceived as less than absolute and, therefore, educable?[9]

[9]This whole question is a tangled one. The dictates of conscience are, in fact, likely to change from time to time (even Garrison changed his mind—i.e., his "conscience"—now and then), and in the face of such a fact how does one pick the moment when he can be *absolutely* certain that he is privy to God's will? And if

· · ·

In spite of the fact that many Quakers had been slaveholders and some, especially the seagoing Quakers of the southwest of England, had been in the slave trade (there was an English slave ship of the eighteenth century called *The Willing Quaker*), the tradition that Whittier directly inherited was that of Benjamin Lay and John Woolman, whose antislavery writings were fundamental documents in the history of abolitionism.[10] It was a tradition of brotherhood understood in quite simple and literal terms, and so his entrance into the abolition movement was a natural act, as was his repudiation of ambition and the reduction of poetry, so dangerously tied to the physical world and human passions, to the safe role of a mere "weapon in the war with wrong." But if abolitionism was for Whittier both a catharsis of, and a refuge from, his ambitions and his passions, the internal tensions in the movement, both philosophical and practical, set up a new problem. Whittier spent a large part of his active life trying to master, resolve, or mediate these tensions. He was a man of peace and a man of reason, and this world of abolitionism was no more cut to his measure than the old world he had repudiated. But he survived, and out of the struggle seemed to gain sweetness of spirit. Or did this struggle, by the fact that it absorbed the old struggles of ambition and passion, make possible the sweetness?

Whittier began his career as an abolitionist in 1833, by writing, and publishing out of his own thinly furnished pocket, a carefully stud-

---

two men of good conscience disagree, then what? In the ultimate sense, we can regard the dictates of a man's conscience—even if he himself regards it as a form of revelation and therefore absolute—as nothing more than the particular gamble he feels *obliged* to take with circumstances and history. History (at a certain moment—for history has a way of changing its mind) may say that the man's gamble was "right"; then the man gets a statue to his memory. But if history says that the gamble was "wrong," then the best the man can expect, in lieu of the statue, is a grudging recognition of his "courage" or "sincerity."

[10]Whittier celebrated the "meek-hearted Woolman" in a poem published in the *Thirty-Sixth and Final Annual Report* of the Philadelphia Female Anti-Slavery Society, 1870, and edited his *Journal* in 1871.

ied and well-argued pamphlet, *Justice and Expediency,* in which he expressed the conviction that the "withering concentration of public opinion upon the slave system is alone needed for its total annihilation." At the end of that year, he attended the convention in Philadelphia that founded the American Anti-Slavery Society, and had an important hand in drawing up the platform, which disavowed all violence and any attempt to foment servile insurrection. All his life it was a point of pride for him that he had been one of the original signers of this "Declaration."

From this time on, Whittier was constantly engaged in the cause of abolitionism, as a writer of both prose and verse, as a member, briefly, of the lower house of the Massachusetts legislature, as an editor of a series of antislavery papers, and as an organizer and speaker. He came to know contumely, the odor of rotten eggs, mob violence, and the struggle against physical fear. He also came to know the formidable wrath and contempt of Garrison.

Whittier had become more and more firm in his belief in political action, that is, in his belief that man is, among other things, a member of society. For instance, in a letter to his publisher, J. T. Fields, he rejected the radical individualism of Thoreau's *Walden,* which he called "capital reading, but very wicked and heathenish," and added that the "moral of it seems to be that if a man is willing to sink himself into a woodchuck he can live as cheaply as that quadruped; but after all, for me, I prefer walking on two legs."[11] Whittier saw man among men, in his social as well as in other dimensions, and as the proper object of appeal to reason rather than the target for contumely; and nothing could more infuriate the radical Garrison, who was publicly to accuse Whittier of being a traitor to principle. In fact, Whittier, a good Quaker, spent much of his energy, as I have said, in trying to mediate among factions of the movement, an effort that, in the end, came to nothing. The "political" wing of the original American Anti-Slavery Society split off to form the American and Foreign Anti-Slavery Society, and to this Whittier, in spite of his depression over the schism and estrangement from his old friend and benefactor, devoted his ener-

[11]Something of the root impulse that made Whittier reject Thoreau may have led to a revulsion from Whitman so intense that he flung *Leaves of Grass* into the fire.

gies for some years as an editor, propagandist, and political manipulator. In the last role, his great triumph was to get Charles Sumner to Washington, as a senator from Massachusetts.

As the tensions mounted during the 1850s, Whittier held as best he could to his principles of institutional reform and political action—and to his Quaker pacifism. He never compromised on the question of slavery, but he steadily insisted on viewing the question in human and institutional contexts, as for instance in the poem "Randolph of Roanoke," where he even speaks well of a slave-holder:

> He held his slaves; yet kept the while
> His reverence for the Human;
> In the dark vassals of his will
> He saw but Man and Woman!
> No hunter of God's outraged poor
> His Roanoke valley entered;
> No trader in the souls of men
> Across his threshold ventured.

When news of John Brown's raid on Harper's Ferry broke, Whittier wrote an article in which he expressed his "emphatic condemnation" of "this and all similar attempts to promote the goal of freedom by the evil of servile strife and civil war"—at the same time, however, he analyzed the danger which the South created for itself by trying to justify the internal contradiction between freedom and slavery in his system, and the tension in his feelings is indicated when he declared, at a meeting called at the time of John Brown's hanging, that he could not help but "wish success to all slave insurrections," for an insurrection was—and here he took a wild leap into a realm of transcendental logic—"one way to get up to the sublime principle of non-resistance." In other words, on this test matter of the raid on Harper's Ferry, Whittier—in his original editorial, at least—agreed with Lincoln and not with Emerson, Thoreau, Garrison, or the "Secret Six," the gentlemen who had provided John Brown with money and encouragement for his project.

There is, in fact, a general similarity between Whittier's views and those of Lincoln. As early as 1833, in his *Justice and Expediency*, Whittier pointed out the internal contradiction created by the presence of slavery in the United States, and declared that "Liberty and slavery cannot dwell in harmony together." He saw the psychological and economic issues raised by this coexistence of free and slave labor. He held the view that Christianity and civilization had placed slavery "on a moral quarantine"—in other words, he agreed with Lincoln that if the extension of slavery was stopped, it would die out in the slave states without forceful intermeddling. Though Whittier had some sympathy with those antislavery people who would resort to a Northern secession from the Union rather than connive in the annexation of Texas, he fundamentally saw the Union as necessary to the termination of slavery. As a basic assumption he held the view that the national problem was to "give effect to the spirit of the Constitution"—a notion which may be taken to describe the social history of the United States to the present time.

When the Civil War was over, Whittier saw, as many could not, that the war had not automatically solved the problem of freedom. Though rejoicing in the fact of emancipation, he could write, in a letter to Lydia Maria Child, that the "emancipation that came by military necessity and enforced by bayonets, was not the emancipation for which we worked and prayed."

When Whittier, at the age of twenty-six, came to knock "Pegasus on the head," the creature he laid low was, indeed, not much better than the tanner's superannuated donkey. In giving up his poetry he gave up very little. Looking back on the work he had done up to that time, we can see little achievement and less promise of growth. He had the knack, as he put it in "The Nervous Man," for making rhymes "as mechanically as a mason piles one brick above another," but nothing that he wrote had the inwardness, the organic quality of poetry. The stuff, in brief, lacked content, and it lacked style. Even when he was able to strike out poetic phrases, images, or effects, he was not able to organize a poem; his poems usually began anywhere and ended when the author got tired. If occasionally we see a poem begin with a real sense of poetry, the poetry gets quickly lost in some abstract idea. Even a poem as late as "The Last Walk

in Autumn" (1857) suffers in this way. It opens with a stanza like
this:

> O'er the bare woods, whose outstretched hands
> Plead with the leaden heavens in vain,
> I see, beyond the valley lands,
> The sea's long level dim with rain.
> Around me all things, stark and dumb,
> Seem praying for the snows to come,
> And, for the summer bloom and greenness gone,
> With winter's sunset lights and dazzling morn atone.

But the poetry soon dies, and the abstractions take over and continue relentlessly, stanza after stanza, to the end. Or we see how
"Abram Morrison," a shrewd and well-felt character piece, comes
to grief through diffuseness and blurred organization.

For a poet of natural sensibility, subtlety, and depth to dedicate
his work to propaganda would probably result in a coarsening of
style and a blunting of effects, for the essence of propaganda is to
refuse qualifications and complexity. But Whittier had, by 1833,
shown little sensibility, subtlety, or depth, and his style was coarse
to a degree. He had nothing to lose, and stood to gain certain
things. To be effective, propaganda, if it is to be more than random
vituperation, has to make a point, and the point has to be held in
view from the start; the piece has to show some sense of organization and control, the very thing Whittier's poems had lacked. But
his prose had not lacked this quality, or, in fact, a sense of the biting
phrase; now his verse could absorb the virtues of his prose. It could
learn, in addition to a sense of point, something of the poetic
pungency of phrase and image, and the precision that sometimes
marked the prose. He had referred to his poems as "fancies," and
that is what they were, no more. Now he began to relate poetry,
though blunderingly enough, to reality. And the process was slow.
It was ten years—1843—before Whittier was able to write a piece
as good as "Massachusetts to Virginia." It was effective propaganda; it had content and was organized to make a point. Here
Whittier had at least avoided his besetting sin of wandering and
padding, and we have only to set it in contrast to a piece like "The

Panorama" (which actually was much later) to understand its virtues.

Whittier had to wait seven more years before, at the age of forty-two, he could write his first really fine poem. This piece, the famous "Ichabod," came more directly and personally out of his political commitment than any previous work. On March 7, 1850, Daniel Webster, senator from Massachusetts, spoke on behalf of the more stringent Fugitive Slave Bill that had just been introduced by Whittier's ex-idol Henry Clay; and the poem, which appeared shortly after in the *National Era* of Washington, a paper of the "political" wing of the abolition movement,[12] laments the loss of the more recent and significant idol. "This poem," Whittier wrote later, "was the outcome of the surprise and grief and forecast of evil consequences which I felt on reading the seventh of March Speech by Daniel Webster. . . ." But here the poet remembers his poem, which does exploit dramatically surprise and grief, better than he remembers the facts of its origin; he could scarcely have felt literal surprise at Webster's speech, for as early as 1847, in a letter to Sumner, Whittier had called Webster a "colossal coward," because of his attitude toward the annexation of Texas and the Mexican war.

Here is the poem:

> So fallen! so lost! the light withdrawn
>   Which once he wore!
> The glory from his gray hairs gone
>   Forevermore!
>
> Revile him not, the Tempter hath
>   A snare for all;
> And pitying tears, not scorn and wrath,
>   Befit his fall!
>
> Oh, dumb be passion's stormy rage,
>   When he who might
> Have lighted up and led his age,
>   Falls back in night.

---

[12]In which Whittier's only novel—or near-novel—*Margaret Smith's Journal,* had appeared the previous year, and in which *Uncle Tom's Cabin* was to appear.

Scorn! would the angels laugh, to mark
   A bright soul driven,
Fiend-goaded, down the endless dark,
   From hope and heaven!

Let not the land once proud of him
   Insult him now,
Nor brand with deeper shame his dim,
   Dishonored brow.

But let its humbled sons, instead,
   From sea to lake,
A long lament, as for the dead,
   In sadness make.

Of all we loved and honored, naught
   Save power remains;
A fallen angel's pride of thought,
   Still strong in chains.

All else is gone; from those great eyes
   The soul has fled:
When faith is lost, when honor dies,
   The man is dead!

Then, pay the reverence of old days
   To his dead fame;
Walk backward, with averted gaze,
   And hide the shame!

The effectiveness of "Ichabod," certainly one of the most telling poems of personal attack in English, is largely due to the subtlety of dramatization. At the center of the dramatization lies a division of feeling on the part of the poet; the poem is not a simple piece of vituperation, but represents a tension between old trust and new disappointment, old admiration and new rejection, the past and the present. The Biblical allusion in the title sets this up: "And she named the child Ichabod, saying, the glory is departed from Israel" (I Samuel, 4:21). The glory has departed, but grief rather than rage, respect for the man who was once the vessel of glory rather than contempt, pity for his frailty rather than condemnation—these are the emotions recommended as appropriate. We may note that not only are they appropriate as a generosity of attitude; they are also the emotions that are basically condescending, that put the holder of the emotions above the object of them, and that make the most destructive assault on the ego of the object. If Webster had been motivated by ambition, then pity is the one attitude his pride could not forgive.

The Biblical allusion at the end offers a brilliant and concrete summary of the complexity of feeling in the poem. As Notley Sinclair Maddox has pointed out (*Explicator,* April 1960), the last stanza is based on Genesis 9:20–25. Noah, in his old age, plants a vineyard, drinks the wine, and is found drunk and naked in his tent by his youngest son Ham, who merely reports the fact to his brothers Shem and Japheth. Out of filial piety, they go to cover Noah's shame, but "their faces were backward, and they saw not their father's nakedness." Ham, for having looked upon Noah's nakedness, is cursed as a "servant of servants" to his "brethren."

The allusion works as a complex and precise metaphor: The great Webster of the past, who, in the time of the debate with Robert Young Hayne (1830) had opposed the slave power and thus established his reputation, has now become obsessed with ambition (drunk with wine) and has exposed the nakedness of human pride and frailty. The conduct of Shem and Japheth sums up, of course, the attitude recommended by the poet. As an ironical adjunct, we may remember that the Biblical episode was used from many a pulpit as a theological defense of slavery, Ham, accursed as a "servant of servants," being, presumably, the forefather of the black race.

We may look back at the first stanza to see another complex and effective metaphor, suggested rather than presented. The light is withdrawn, and the light is identified, by the appositive construction, with the "glory" of Webster's gray hair—the glory being the achievement of age and the respect due to honorable age, but also the image of a literal light, an aureole about the head coming like a glow from the literal gray hair. This image fuses with that of the "fallen angel" of line 27 and the dimness of the "dim, dishonored brow" in lines 19 and 20. In other words, by suggestion, one of the things that holds the poem together (as contrasted with the logical sequence of the statement) is the image of the angel Lucifer, the light-bearer, fallen by excess of pride. Then in lines 29–30, the light image, introduced in the first stanza with the aureole about the gray hair, appears as an inward light shed outward, the "soul" that had once shone from Webster's eyes (he had remarkably large and lustrous dark eyes). But the soul is now dead, the light "withdrawn," and we have by suggestion a death's-head with the eyes hollow and blank. How subtly the abstract ideas of "faith" and "honor" are drawn into this image, and how subtly the image itself is related to the continuing play of variations of the idea of light and dark.

From the point of view of technique this poem is, next to "Telling the Bees," Whittier's most perfectly controlled and subtle composition. This is true not only of the dramatic ordering and interplay of imagery, but also of the handling of rhythm as related to meter and stanza, and to the verbal texture. For Whittier, in those rare moments when he could shut out the inane gabble of the sweet singers, and of his own incorrigible meter-machine, could hear the true voice of feeling. But how rarely he heard—or trusted—the voice of feeling. He was, we may hazard, afraid of feeling. Unless, of course, a feeling had been properly disinfected.

In the "war with wrong," Whittier wrote a number of poems that were, in their moment, effectively composed, but only three, aside from "Ichabod," that survive to us as poetry.

"The Panorama," of 1855, though it is diffuse and not well organized, has strokes of shrewd observation, accurate phrasing, and controlled irony. For instance, here is the village of the Southern frontier, unkempt and slatternly, a combination of "vulgar newness" and "premature decay":

> A tavern, crazy with its whiskey brawls,
> With "*Slaves at Auction!*" garnishing its walls;
> Without, surrounded by a motley crowd,
> The shrewd-eyed salesman, garrulous and loud,
> A squire or colonel in his pride of place,
> Known at free fights, the caucus, and the race;
> Prompt to proclaim his honor without blot,
> And silence doubters with a ten-pace shot;
> Mingling the negro-driving bully's rant

With pious phrase and democratic cant,
Yet never scrupling, with a filthy jest,
To sell the infant from its mother's breast.

The "Letter from a Missionary of the Methodist Episcopal Church South, in Kansas, to a Distinguished Politician" not only marks a high point in Whittier's poetic education but may enlighten us about the relation of that education to his activity as a journalist and propagandist. The poem, as the title indicates, grew out of the struggle between the proslavery and the free-state forces for the control of "Bleeding Kansas." Though the poem appeared in 1854, four years after "Ichabod," it shows us more clearly than the earlier piece how the realism, wit, and irony of Whittier's prose could be absorbed into a composition that is both tendentious and poetic. The tendentious element is converted into poetry by the force of its dramatization—as in the case of "Ichabod"—but here specifically by an ironic ventriloquism, the device of having the "Letter" come from the pen of the godly missionary:

> Last week—the Lord be praised for all
>   His mercies
> To His unworthy servant!—I arrived
> Safe at the Mission, *via* Westport; where
> I tarried over night, to aid in forming
> A Vigilance Committee, to send back,
> In shirts of tar, and feather-doublets quilted
> With forty stripes save one, all Yankee
>   comers,
> Uncircumcised and Gentile, aliens from
> The Commonwealth of Israel, who despise
> The prize of the high calling of the saints,
> Who plant amidst this heathen wilderness
> Pure gospel institutions, sanctified
> By patriarchal use. The meeting opened
> With prayer, as was most fitting. Half
>   an hour,
> Or thereaway, I groaned, and strove, and
>   wrestled,
> As Jacob did at Penuel, till the power

Fell on the people, and they cried "Amen!"
"Glory to God!" and stamped and clapped
    their hands;
And the rough river boatmen wiped their eyes;
"Go it, old hoss!" they cried, and cursed the
    niggers—
Fulfilling thus the word of prophecy,
"Cursed be Canaan."

By the ventriloquism the poem achieves a control of style, a fluctuating tension between the requirements of verse and those of
"speech," a basis for the variations of tone that set up the sudden
poetic, and ironic, effect at the end:

P.S. All's lost. Even while I write these
    lines,
The Yankee abolitionists are coming
Upon us like a flood—grim, stalwart men,
Each face set like a flint of Plymouth Rock
Against our institutions—staking out
Their farm lots on the wooded Wakarusa,
Or squatting by the mellow-bottomed Kansas;
The pioneers of mightier multitudes,
The small rain-patter, ere the thunder shower
Drowns the dry prairies. Hope from man is not.
Oh, for a quiet berth at Washington,
Snug naval chaplaincy, or clerkship, where
These rumors of free labor and free soil
Might never meet me more. Better to be
Door-keeper in the White House, than to dwell
Amidst these Yankee tents, that, whitening, show
On the green prairie like a fleet becalmed.
Methinks I hear a voice come up the river
From those far bayous, where the alligators
Mount guard around the camping filibusters:
"Shake off the dust of Kansas. Turn to Cuba
(That golden orange just about to fall,
O'er-ripe, into the Democratic lap;)
Keep pace with Providence, or, as we say,
Manifest destiny. Go forth and follow
The message of *our* gospel, thither borne

Upon the point of Quitman's bowie-knife,
And the persuasive lips of Colt's revolvers.
There may'st thou, underneath thy vine and
    fig-tree,
Watch thy increase of sugar cane and negroes,
Calm as a patriarch in his eastern tent!"
Amen: So mote it be. So prays your friend.

Here quite obviously the ventriloquism is what gives the poem a "voice," and the fact instructs us how Whittier, less obviously, develops through dramatization a voice in "Ichabod." The voice of a poem is effective—is resonant—in so far as it bespeaks a life behind that voice, implies a dramatic issue by which that life is defined. I have spoken of the complexity of feeling behind the voice of "Ichabod," and in the present case we find such a complexity in the character of the missionary himself. At first glance, we have the simple irony of the evil man cloaking himself in the language of the good. But another irony, and deeper, is implicit in the poem: the missionary may not be evil, after all; he may even be, in a sense, "good"—that is, be speaking in perfect sincerity, a man good but misguided; and thus we have the fundamental irony of the relation of evil and good in human character, action, and history. Whittier was a polemicist, and a very astute one, as the "Letter" in its primary irony exemplifies. But he was also a devout Quaker, and by fits and starts a poet, and his creed, like his art, would necessarily give a grounding for the secondary, and deeper, irony, an irony that implies humility and forgiveness.

What I have been saying is that by repudiating poetry Whittier became a poet. His image of knocking Pegasus on the head tells a deeper truth than he knew; by getting rid of the "poetical" notion of poetry, he was able, eventually, to ground his poetry on experience. In the years of his crusade and of the Civil War, he was learning this, even though the process was, as I have said, slow. It was a process that seems to have been developed by fits and starts, trial and error, by floundering rather than by rational understanding. Whittier was without much natural taste and almost totally devoid of critical judgment, and he seems to have had only a flickering awareness of what he was doing—though he did have a deep awareness, it would seem, of his personal situation. As a poet he was trapped in the automatism and compulsiveness that, in "Amy Wentworth," he defined as the "automatic play of pen and pencil, solace to our pain"—the process that writing seems to have usually been for him. Even after a triumph, he could fall back into this dreary repetitiveness.

The mere mass of his published work in verse between 1843 and the Civil War indicates something of this undirected compulsiveness of composition that went on after he had decided to abandon poetry. In 1843 appeared *Lays of My Home;* in 1849, what amounted to a collected edition; in 1850, *Songs of Labor;* in 1853, *The Chapel of the Hermits and Other Poems;* in 1856, *The Panorama and Other Poems;* in 1857, the *Poetical Works,* in two volumes; and in 1860, *Home Ballads and Poems.* But in this massive and blundering production there had been a growth. In 1843 even poems like "To My Old Schoolmaster," "The Barefoot Boy," "Maud Muller," "Lines Suggested by Reading a State Paper," and "Kossuth" would have been impossible, not to mention "Skipper Ireson's Ride," which exhibits something of the élan of traditional balladry and something of the freedom of living language of "Ichabod" and the "Letter." But nothing short of a miracle, and a sudden miraculous understanding of Wordsworth and the traditional ballad, accounts for a little masterpiece like "Telling the Bees." There had been the technical development, but something else was happening too, something more difficult to define; Whittier was stumbling, now and then, on the subjects that might release the inner energy necessary for real poetry.

There was, almost certainly, a deep streak of grievance and undischarged anger in Whittier, for which the abolitionist poems (and editorials) could allow a hallowed—and disinfected—expression; simple indignation at fate could become "righteous indignation," and the biting sarcasm was redeemed by the very savagery of the bite. But there was another subject which released, and more deeply, the inner energy—the memory of the past, more specifically the childhood past, nostalgia, shall we say, for the happy, protected time before he knew the dark inward struggle, the outer struggle with "strong-willed men" (as he was to put it in "To My

Sister") to which he had to steel himself, the collapses, and the grinding headaches. Almost everyone has an Eden time to look back on, even if it never existed and he has to create it for his own delusion; but for Whittier the need to dwell on this lost Eden was more marked than is ordinary. If the simple indignation against a fate that had deprived him of the security of childhood could be transmuted into righteous indignation, both forms of indignation could be redeemed in a dream of Eden innocence. This was the subject that could summon up Whittier's deepest feeling and release his fullest poetic power.

Furthermore, if we review the poems after 1850, we find a subsidiary and associated theme, sometimes in the same poem. In poems like "Maud Muller," "Kathleen," "Mary Garvin," "The Witch's Daughter," "The Truce of Piscataqua," "My Playmate," "The Countess," and "Telling the Bees," there is the theme of the lost girl, a child or a beloved, who may or may not be, in the course of a poem, recovered. Some of these poems, notably "Maud Muller" and "Kathleen," involve the question of differences of social rank, as does "The Truce of Piscataqua" if we read blood for social difference, and "Marguerite" and "Mary Garvin" if we read the bar of religion in the same way. This last theme, in fact, often appears; we have it in "Amy Wentworth," "The Countess," and "Among the Hills," all of which belong to the mature period of Whittier's work, when he was looking nostalgically backward. But this theme of the lost girl, especially when the loss is caused by difference in social rank or the religious bar, even though it clearly repeats a theme enacted in Whittier's personal life, never really touched the spring of poetry in him except in "Telling the Bees," where it is crossed with the theme of childhood to mitigate the pang of the sexual overtones. The theme of the lost girl, taken alone, belonged too literally, perhaps, to the world of frustration. In life Whittier had worked out the problem and had survived by finding the right kind of action for himself, a "sanctified" action, and this action could, as we have seen, contribute to some of his best poetry; but more characteristically, his poetic powers were released by the refuge in assuagement, the flight into Eden, and this was at once his great limitation and the source of his fullest success.

For the poems specifically of nostalgia for childhood, we have "To My Old Schoolmaster," "The Barefoot Boy," "The Playmate," "The Prelude" (to "Among the Hills"), "To My Sister, with a copy of *The Supernaturalism of New England,*" "In School-Days," "Telling the Bees," and preeminently *Snow-Bound*. It is not so much the number of poems involved that is significant, but the coherent quality of feeling and, by and large, the poetic quality in contrast to his other work. As Whittier puts it in "The Prelude," he was more and more impelled to

> . . . idly turn
> The leaves of memory's sketch-book, dreaming o'er
> Old summer pictures of the quiet hills,
> And human life, as quiet, at their feet.

He was, as he shrewdly saw himself in "Questions of Life," an "over-wearied child," seeking in "cool and shade his peace to find," in flight

> From vain philosophies, that try
> The sevenfold gates of mystery,
> And, baffled ever, babble still,
> Word-prodigal of fate and will; . . .

As a young man hot with passion and ambition, and later as a journalist, agitator, and propagandist, he had struggled with the world, but there had always been the yearning for total peace which could be imaged in the Quaker meetinghouse, but more deeply in childhood, as he summarized it in "To My Sister":

> And, knowing how my life hath been
> A weary work of tongue and pen,
> A long, harsh strife with strong-willed men,
>   Thou wilt not chide my turning
> To con, at times, an idle rhyme,
> To pluck a flower from childhood's clime,
> Or listen, at Life's noonday chime,
>   For the sweet bells of Morning!

The thing from which he fled but did not mention was, of course, inner struggle, more protracted and more bitter than the outer with "strong-willed men."

Even the splendid poem "Ichabod," dealing overtly with Daniel Webster as a moral traitor to the cause of liberty, naturally echoes the characteristic regret for the loss of childhood and innocence. Literally, "Ichabod" deals with a "father" (Webster as the outstanding enemy of slavery) who betrays his children—his followers and admirers. The child must now confront reality. In regard to this theme and its recurrence, one may remember that the Biblical reference in this poem is to the drunken Noah who thus betrays his children—as Webster, we assume, is drunk with ambition.[13]

In the massiveness of the image, however, the father betrays the sons not only by wine but by death, for it is a death's-head with empty eye sockets that is the most striking fact of the poem. Here the evitable moral betrayal is equated, imagistically, with the inevitable and morally irrelevant fact of death. But by the same token, as a conversion of the proposition, the fact of death in the morally irrelevant course of nature is, too, a moral betrayal. The child, in other words, cannot forgive the course of nature—the fate—that leaves him defenseless.

In connection with this purely latent content of the imagery, we may remark that Whittier, in looking back on the composition of the poem, claimed that he had recognized in Webster's act the "forecast of evil consequences" and knew the "horror of such a vision." For him this was the moment of confronting the grim actuality of life. It was, as it were, a political rite of passage. Here the protector has become the betrayer—has "died." So, in this recognition of the terrible isolation of maturity, "Ichabod," too, takes its place in the massive cluster of poems treating the nostalgia of childhood that prevision *Snow-Bound.*

. . .

[13]In relation to the theme in Whittier's work of betrayed innocence and childhood, one may remember that Whittier's mother had died in December 1857.

On February 16, 1858, Whittier sent "Telling the Bees" (originally called "The Bees of Fernside") to James Russell Lowell at the *Atlantic Monthly,* saying, "What I call simplicity may be only silliness." It was not silliness. It was a pure and beautiful poem, somewhat overlong but informed by the flood of feeling that broke forth at the death of a mother.

> Here is the place; right over the hill
>   Runs the path I took;
> You can see the gap in the old wall still,
>   And the stepping-stones in the shallow brook.
>
> There is the house, with the gate red-barred,
>   And the poplars tall;
> And the barn's brown length, and the cattle-yard,
>   And the white horns tossing above the wall.
>
> There are the beehives ranged in the sun;
>   And down by the brink
> Of the brook are her poor flowers, weed-o'errun,
>   Pansy and daffodil, rose and pink.
>
> A year has gone, as the tortoise goes,
>   Heavy and slow;
> And the same rose blows, and the same sun glows,
>   And the same brook sings of a year ago.
>
> There's the same sweet clover-smell in the breeze;
>   And the June sun warm
> Tangles his wings of fire in the trees,
>   Setting, as then, over Fernside farm.
>
> I mind me how with a lover's care
>   From my Sunday coat
> I brushed off the burrs, and smoothed my hair,
>   And cooled at the brookside my brow and throat.
>
> Since we parted, a month had passed,—
>   To love, a year;
> Down through the beeches I looked at last
>   On the little red gate and the well-sweep near.
>
> I can see it all now,—the slantwise rain
>   Of light through the leaves,

The sundown's blaze on her window-pane,
    The bloom of her roses under the eaves.

Just the same as a month before,—
    The house and the trees,
The barn's brown gable, the vine by the door,—
    Nothing changed but the hives of bees.

Before them, under the garden wall,
    Forward and back,
Went drearily singing the chore-girl small,
    Draping each hive with a shred of black.

Trembling, I listened: the summer sun
    Had the chill of snow;
For I knew she was telling the bees of one
    Gone on the journey we all must go!

Then I said to myself, "My Mary weeps
    For the dead to-day:
Haply her blind old grandsire sleeps
    The fret and the pain of his age away."

But her dog whined low; on the doorway sill,
    With his cane to his chin,
The old man sat; and the chore-girl still
    Sung to the bees stealing out and in.

And the song she was singing ever since
    In my ear sounds on:—
"Stay at home, pretty bees, fly not hence!
    Mistress Mary is dead and gone!"

The setting of the poem is a scrupulous re-creation of the farm-stead where Whittier spent his youth, as Samuel T. Pickard, in his *Life and Letters of Whittier* reported in 1894. It was composed almost thirty years after Whittier had gone out into the world, and some twenty-two years after he had sold the home place and moved the family to Amesbury. Not only the same nostalgia that informs *Snow-Bound* is part of the motivation of this poem, but also the same literalism. But more than mere literalism seems to be involved in the strange fact that Whittier keeps his sister Mary—or at least her name—in the poem, and keeps her there to kill her off; and there is, of course, the strange fact that he cast a shadowy self—the "I" of the poem—in the role of the lover of Mary, again playing here with the theme of lost love, of the lost girl, but bringing the story within the family circle, curiously coalescing the youthful yearning for sexual love and the childhood yearning for love and security within the family circle. And all this at a time when Mary was very much alive.

Just as the shock of his mother's death turned Whittier's imagination back to the boyhood home and presumably released the energy for "Telling the Bees," so the death of his sister Elizabeth lies behind *Snow-Bound*. The relation of Whittier to this sister, who shared his literary and other tastes, who herself wrote verses (often indistinguishable in their lack of distinction from the mass of her brother's work), who was a spirited and humorous person, and who, as a spinster, was a companion to his bachelorhood, was of a more complex and intimate kind than even that of Whittier to his mother. She was, as Lucy Larcom,[14] a poetess of some small fame, observed in her diary, "dear Lizzy, his sole home-flower, the meek lily-blossom that cheers and beautifies his life"; and when she died, on September 3, 1864, Whittier said "the great motive of my life seems lost."

Shortly before Elizabeth's death there had been another crisis in Whittier's life, the end of his second and final romance with Elizabeth Lloyd, whom I have already mentioned. The relation with her was not merely another of his frustrated romances. He had known her for some twenty-five years, from the time when he was thirty. She was good-looking, wrote verses, painted pictures, believed ardently in abolition, and was a Quaker to boot. What could have been more appropriate.

She even fell in love with him, if we can judge from the appeals in letters written toward the end of her first connection with him: "Spirit, silent, dumb and cold! What hath possessed thee?" Or: "Do come, Greenleaf! I am almost forgetting how thee looks and seems." But Greenleaf was beating one of his strategic retreats; so

[14]Lucy Larcom was, apparently, also one of the ladies who were in love, to no avail, with the poet.

she cut her losses, got to work and made a literary reputation of sorts, married a non-Quaker and got "read out of meeting."

After her husband's death, however, Elizabeth Lloyd, now Howell, reappeared in Whittier's life. They became constant companions. Both suffered from severe headaches, but they found that if they caressed each other's hair and massaged each other's brows, the headaches would go away. Or at least Whittier's headache would, and he proposed to her. She refused him, but not definitively, and the dalliance went on. Even a quarrel about Quakerism did not end it. In any case, it did end, and in later years the lady nursed a grievance and spoke bitterly of the old sweetheart.

Whittier had scarcely escaped from Elizabeth Howell's healing hands when his sister Elizabeth died. If he still clung to the explanation that his long bachelorhood had been due to "the care of an aged mother, and the duty owed a sister in delicate health," its last vestige of plausibility was now removed. He was now truly alone, with no landmarks left from the Edenic past. There was only memory.

Before the end of the month in which Elizabeth died, Whittier sent to the *Atlantic* a poem which he said had "beguiled some weary hours." It was "The Vanishers," based on a legend he had read in Schoolcraft's famous *History, Condition, and Prospects of the American Indians,* about the beautiful spirits who fleetingly appear to beckon the living on to what Whittier calls "The Sunset of the Blest." To the Vanishers, Whittier likens the beloved dead:

> Gentle eyes we closed below,
>   Tender voices heard once more,
> Smile and call us, as they go
>   On and onward, still before.

The poem is, in its basic impulse, the first draft of *Snow-Bound.*

In a very special way *Snow-Bound* summarizes Whittier's life and work. We have already noted the obsessive theme of childhood nostalgia that leads to *Snow-Bound,* but as early as 1830, in "The Frost Spirit," we find the key situation of the family gathered about a fire while the "evil power" of the winter storm (and of the world) goes shrieking by. Whittier, too, had long been fumbling toward his great question of how to find in the contemplation of the past a meaning for the future. In "My Soul and I," of 1847, the soul that turns in fear from the unknown future to seek comfort in the "Known and Gone" must learn that "The past and the time to be are one,/And both are now."

The same issue reappears in "The Garrison of Cape Ann":

> The great eventful Present hides the Past; but
>   through the din
> Of its loud life hints and echoes from the life
>   behind steal in;
> And the lore of home and fireside, and the
>   legendary rhyme,
> Make the task of duty lighter which the true man
>   owes his time.

And it appears again in "The Prophecy of Samuel Sewall," of 1859.

As for the relation to the poet's personal life, *Snow-Bound* came not only after another manifestation of the old inhibition that forbade his seeking solace from Elizabeth Lloyd's healing hands—and this as he neared the age of sixty when the repudiation of the solace must have seemed catastrophically final; and not only after the death of the sister had deprived him of his "life-motive." It came, too, toward the end of the Civil War, when he could foresee the victory of the cause to which he had given his energies for more than thirty years and which had, in a sense, served as his justification for life and as a substitute for other aspects of life. Now the joy of victory would, necessarily, carry with it a sense of emptiness. Furthermore, the victory itself was in terms sadly different, as Whittier recognized, from those that he had dreamed.

If *Snow-Bound* is, then, a summarizing poem for Whittier, it came, also, at a summarizing moment for the country. It came when the country—at least, the North—was poised on the threshold of a new life, the world of technology, big industry, big business, finance capitalism, and urban values; and at that moment, caught up in the promises of the future, the new breed of American could afford to look back on their innocent beginnings. The new breed could afford to pay for the indulgence of nostalgia; in fact, in the new affluence, they paid quite well for it. The book appeared on February 17, 1866,[15] and the success was immediate. For instance, in April, J. T. Fields, the publisher, wrote Whittier: "We can't keep the plaguey thing quiet. It goes and goes, and now, today, we are bankrupt again, not a one being in crib." The first edition earned Whittier $10,000—a sum to be multiplied many times over if translated into present values. The poor man was, overnight, modestly rich.

The scene of the poem, the "Flemish picture" as Whittier calls it, the modest genre piece, is rendered with precise and loving care, and this had its simple nostalgic appeal for the generation who had come to town and made it, and a somewhat different appeal, compensatory and comforting, no doubt, for the generation that had stayed in the country and had not made it.

But the poem is not simple, and it is likely that the appeals would have been far less strong and permanent if Whittier had not set the "idyl" in certain "perspectives" of deeper interpretation. In other words, it can be said of this poem, as of most poetry, that the effect does not depend so much on the thing looked at as on the way of the looking. True, if there is nothing to look at, there can be no looking, but the way of the looking determines the kind of feeling that fuses with the object looked at.

Before we speak of the particular "perspectives" in which the poem is set, we may say that there is a preliminary and general one. This general perspective, specified by Whittier in the dedicatory note to his "Winter Idyl,"[16] denies that the poem is a mere

[15]Melville's book of poems on the Civil War, *Battle-Pieces,* appeared almost simultaneously, and was a crashing failure. As *Snow-Bound* seemed to dwell merely on the simplicity of the past, *Battle-Pieces* analyzed some of the painful complexities of the war and the present, and recognized some of the painful paradoxes in the glowing promises of the future: not what the public wanted to hear.

[16]Here is the beginning of the preparatory note: "The inmates of the family at the Whittier homestead who are referred to in the poem were my father, mother, my brother and two sisters, and my uncle and aunt both unmarried. In addition, there was the district school-master who boarded with us. The 'not unfeared, half-welcome guest' was Harriet Livermore, daughter of Judge Livermore, of New Hampshire, a young woman of fine natural ability, enthusiastic, eccentric, with slight control over her violent temper, which sometimes made her religious profes-

"poem." The poem, that is, is offered as autobiography, with all the validation of fact.

The reality of that literal world is most obviously certified by the lovingly and precisely observed details: the faces sharpened by cold, the "clashing horn on horn" of the restless cattle in the barn, the "grizzled squirrel" dropping his shell, the "board nails snapping in the frost" at night. This general base of the style is low, depending on precision of rendering rather than on the shock and brilliance of language or image; but from this base certain positive poetic effects emerge as accents and points of focus. For instance:

> A chill no coat, however stout,
> Of homespun stuff could quite shut out,
> A hard, dull bitterness of cold,
> That checked, mid-vein, the circling race
> Of life-blood in the sharpened face,
> The coming of the snow-storm told.
> The wind blew east; we heard the roar
> Of Ocean on his wintry shore,
> And felt the strong pulse throbbing there
> Beat with low rhythm our inland air.

Associated with this background realism we find a firm realism in the drawing of character. Three of the portraits are sharp and memorable, accented against the other members of the group and at the same time bearing thematic relations to them: the spinster aunt, the schoolmaster, and Harriet Livermore.

------

sion doubtful. She was equally ready to exhort in school-house prayer-meetings and dance in a Washington ball-room, while her father was a member of Congress. She early embraced the doctrine of the Second Advent, and felt it her duty to proclaim the Lord's speedy coming. With this message she crossed the Atlantic and spent the greater part of a long life in travelling over Europe and Asia. She lived some time with Lady Hester Stanhope, a woman as fantastic and mentally strained as herself, on the slope of Mt. Lebanon, but finally quarrelled with her in regard to two white horses with red marks on their backs which suggested the idea of saddles, on which her titled hostess expected to ride into Jerusalem with the Lord. A friend of mine found her, when quite an old woman, wandering in Syria with a tribe of Arabs, who with the Oriental notion that madness is inspiration, accepted her as their prophetess and leader. At the time referred to in *Snow-Bound* she was boarding at the Rocks Village about two miles from us."

The aunt, who had a tragic love affair but who, as the poem states, has found reconciliation with life, bears a thematic relation to both Elizabeth Whittier and Whittier himself. The schoolmaster, whose name Whittier could not remember until near the end of his life, was a George Haskell, who later became a doctor, practiced in Illinois and New Jersey, and died in 1876 without even knowing, presumably, of his role in the poem. As for Harriet Livermore, Whittier's note identifies her. The fact that the "warm, dark languish of her eyes" might change to rage is amply documented by the fact that at one time, before the scene of *Snow-Bound,* she had been converted to Quakerism, but during an argument with another Quaker on a point of doctrine asserted her theological view by seizing a length of stove wood and laying out her antagonist. This, of course, ended her connection with the sect. In her restless search for a satisfying religion, she represents one strain of thought in nineteenth-century America, and has specific resemblances to the characters Nathan and Nehemiah in Melville's *Clarel.* As a "woman tropical, intense," and at the same time concerned with ideas and beliefs, she is of the type of Margaret Fuller, the model for Zenobia in the *Blithedale Romance* of Hawthorne.

To return to the structure of the poem, there are three particular "perspectives"—ways in which the material is to be viewed. The first section (up to the first perspective) presents a generalized setting, the coming of the storm, the first night, the first day, and the second night. Here the outside world is given full value in contrast to the interior, especially in the following passage, which is set between two close-ups of the hearthside, that Eden spot surrounded by the dark world:

> The moon above the eastern wood
> Shown at its full; the hill-range stood
> Transfigured in the silver flood,
> Its blown snows flashing cold and keen,
> Dead white, save where some sharp ravine
> Took shadow, or the sombre green
> Of hemlocks turned to pitchy black
> Against the whiteness at their back.
> For such a world and such a night

> Most fitting that unwarming light,
> Which only seemed where'er it fell
> To make the coldness visible.[17]

The setting, as I have said, is generalized; the individual characters have not yet emerged, the father having appeared in only one line of description and as a voice ordering the boys (John and his only brother Matthew) to dig a path, with the group at the fireside only an undifferentiated "we" (line 156). This section ends with the sharp focus on the mug of cider simmering between the feet of the andirons and the apples sputtering—the literal fire, the literal comfort against the threat of literal darkness and cold outside.

Now, with line 175, the first perspective is introduced:

> What matter how the night behaved?
> What matter how the north-wind raved?
> Blow high, blow low, not all its snow
> Could quench our hearth-fire's ruddy glow.

But immediately, even as he affirms the inviolability of the fireside world, the poet cries out:

> O Time and Change!—with hair as gray
> As was my sire's that winter day,
> How strange it seems, with so much gone
> Of life and love, to still live on!

From this remembered scene by the fireside only two of the participants survive, the poet and his brother (Matthew), who are now as gray as the father at that snowfall of long ago; for all are caught in Time, in this less beneficent snowfall that whitens every head, as the implied image seems to say. Given this process of the repetition of the life pattern of Time and Change, what, the poet asks, can survive? The answer is that "Love can never lose its own."

After the first perspective has thus developed a new meaning from the scene of simple nostalgia by the fire, the poem becomes

[17]The brilliance of the last line coalesces and validates the whole scene.

a gallery of individual portraits, the father, the mother, the uncle, the aunt, the elder sister (Mary), and the younger (Elizabeth), the schoolmaster, and Harriet Livermore. That is, each individual brings into the poem a specific dramatization of the problem of Time. In the simplest dimension, they offer continuity and repetition: they, the old, were once young, and now sitting by the fire, with the young, tell of youth remembered against the background of age. More specifically, each of the old has had to try to come to terms with Time, and each portrait involves an aspect of the problem.

When the family portraits have been completed, the second perspective is introduced; this is concerned primarily with the recent bereavement, with the absent Elizabeth, and with the poet's personal future as he walks toward the night and sees Elizabeth's beckoning hand. Thus out of the theme of Time and Change emerges the theme of the Future, which is to be developed in the portraits of the schoolmaster and Harriet Livermore.

The first will make his peace in Time, by identifying himself with progressive social good (which, as a matter of fact, George Haskell had done by 1866). Harriet Livermore, though seeking, by her theological questing, a peace out of Time, has found no peace in Time, presumably because she cannot seek in the right spirit; with the "love within her mute" she cannot identify herself with the real needs of the world about her; she is caught in the "tangled skein of will and fate," and can only hope for a peace in Divine forgiveness, out of Time. After the portrait of Harriet Livermore, we find the contrast in the mother's attitude at the good-night scene: unlike Harriet she finds peace in the here-and-now, "food and shelter, warmth and health" and love, with no "vain prayers" but a willingness to act practically in the world. And this is followed with the peace of night and the "reconciled" dream of summer in the middle of the winter, an image of both past and future in the turn of Time.

With dawn, the present—not the past, not the future—appears, with its obligations, joys, and promises. Here there is a lag in the structure of the poem. When the snowbound ones awake to the sound of "merry voices high and clear," the poem should, logically, move toward its fulfillment. But instead, after the active intrusion of the world and the present, we have the section beginning "So days went on" (line 674), and then the dead "filler" for some twenty lines. Whittier's literalism, his fidelity to irrelevant fact rather than to relevant meaning and appropriate structure of the whole, here almost destroy both the emotional and the thematic thrust, and it is due only to the power of the last movement that the poem is not irretrievably damaged.[18]

The third "perspective" (lines 715–59), which ends the poem, is introduced by these eloquent lines:

> Clasp, Angel of the backward look
> And folded wings of ashen gray
> And voice of echoes far away,
> The brazen covers of thy book;

Then follow certain new considerations. What is the relation between the dream of the past and the obligations and actions of the future? The answer is, of course, in the sense of continuity of human experience, found when one stretches the "hands of memory" to the "wood-fire's blaze" of the past; it is thus that one may discover the meaningfulness of obligation and action in Time, even as he discovers, in the specific memories of the past, an image for the values out of Time. The "idyl" is an image, and a dialectic, of one of life's most fundamental questions that is summed up in the haunting simplicity of the end:

> Sit with me by the homestead hearth,
> And stretch the hands of memory forth
>   To warm them at the wood-fire's blaze!
> And thanks untraced to lips unknown
> Shall greet me like the odors blown
> From unseen meadows newly mown,
> Or lilies floating in some pond,
> Wood-fringed, the wayside gaze beyond;

[18]There are, in fact, other lags and fillers in the poem. For instance, there are repetitions in the two barn scenes (lines 21–30 and 81–92); it "happened" this way, so back we go to the barn for the retake. There are patches, too, where the mason piling bricks takes over from the poet, with monotonous versification; for instance, in lines 263–75, where the metrical pattern and the line stop the vital movement.

> The traveller owns the grateful sense
> Of sweetness near, he knows not whence,
> And, pausing, takes with forehead bare
> The benediction of the air.

As a corollary to the third "perspective" generally considered, Whittier has, however, ventured a specific application. He refers not merely to the action in the future, in general, in relation to the past, but also, quite clearly, to the Civil War and the new order with its "larger hopes and graver fears"—the new order of "throngful city ways" as contrasted with the old agrarian way of life and thought. He invites the "worldling"—the man who, irreligiously, would see no meaning in the shared experience of human history, which to Whittier would have been a form of revelation—to seek in the past not only a sense of personal renewal and continuity, but also a sense of the continuity of the new order with the American past. This idea is clearly related to Whittier's conviction, already mentioned, that the course of development for America should be the fulfilling of the "implied intent" of the Constitution in particular, of the American revelation in general, and of God's will. And we may add that Whittier, by this, also gives another "perspective" in which his poem is to be read.

Snow-Bound has been, and is, rarely read in Whittier's perspective. Its popularity depended on a merely sentimental view of the past and not as a view of the lively present—of the new America of the "Gilded Age"—the period when vast wealth seemed attainable and luxury of the most flashing order the reward of virtue.

If we leave *Snow-Bound,* the poem, and go back again to its springs in Whittier's personal story, we may find that it recapitulates in a new form an old issue. The story of his youth is one of entrapments—and of his failure to break out into the world of mature action. In love, politics, and poetry, he was constantly being involved in a deep, inner struggle, with the self-pity, the outrage, the headaches, the breakdowns. He was, to no avail, trying to break out of the "past" of childhood into the "future" of manhood—to achieve, in other words, a self.

The mad ambition that drove him to try to break out of the entrapments, became, in itself, paradoxically, another entrapment—another dead hand of the past laid on him. He cried out, "now, now!"—not even knowing what he cried out for, from what need for what reality. But nothing worked out, not love, or politics, or even poetry, that common substitute for success of a more immediate order. In poetry, in fact, he could only pile up words as a mason piles up bricks; he could only repeat, compulsively, the dreary clichés; his meter-making machine ground on, and nothing that came out was, he knew, real: his poems were only "fancies," as he called them, only an echo of the past, not his own present. And if he set out with the declared intention of being the poet of New England, his sense of its history was mere antiquarianism, mere quaintness: no sense of an abiding human reality. Again he was trapped in the past. All his passions strove, as he put it, "in chains." He found release from what he called "the pain of disappointment and the temptation to envy" only in repudiating the self, and all the self stood for, in order to save the self. He could find a cause that, because it had absorbed, shall we hazard, all the inner forces of the "past" that had thwarted his desires, could free him into some "future" of action.

So much for the story of the young Whittier.

But what of the old?

He had, in the end, fallen into another entrapment of the past. All action—and the possibility of continuing life—had been withdrawn: the solacing hands of Elizabeth Lloyd, the "great motive of . . . life" that the other Elizabeth represented, old friends such as Joshua Coffin, even the "cause" to which he had given his life and which had given his life meaning. Only memory—the past—was left. To live—to have a future—he had to re-fight the old battle of his youth on a new and more difficult terrain. He had to find a new way to make the past nourish the future.

It could not be the old way. The old way had been, in a sense, merely a surrender. By it, Whittier had indeed found a future, a life of action. But the victory had been incomplete, and the costs great; for we must remember that the grinding headaches continued and that the solacing hands of Elizabeth Lloyd had been, in the end, impossible for him.

The new way was more radical. That is, Whittier undertook to see the problem of the past and future as generalized rather than personal, as an issue confronting America, not only himself; furthermore, to see it *sub specie aeternitatis,* as an aspect of man's fate. And he came to see that man's fate is that he must learn to accept and use his past completely, knowingly, rather than to permit himself to be used, ignorantly, by it.

Having struggled for years with the deep difficulties of his own life, Whittier at last found a way to fruitfully regard them, and *Snow-Bound* is the monument of this personal victory. No, it may be the dynamic image of the very process by which the victory itself was achieved. But there is another way in which we may regard it. It sets Whittier into relation to an obsessive and continuing theme in our literature, a theme that most powerfully appears in Cooper, Hawthorne, Melville, and Faulkner: What does the past mean to an American?

The underlying question is, of course, why a sense of the past should be necessary at all. Why in a country that was new—was all "future"—should the question have arisen at all? Cooper dealt with it in various dramatizations, most obviously in the figures of Hurry Harry and the old pirate in *Deerslayer* and that of the squatter in *The Prairie,* who are looters, exploiters, and spoilers of man and nature: none of these men has a sense of the pride and humility that history may inculcate. How close are these figures to those of Faulkner's world who have no past, or who would repudiate the past, who are outside history—for example, the Snopeses (descendants of bushwhackers who had no "side" in the Civil War), Popeye of *Sanctuary,* Jason and the girl Quentin of *The Sound and the Fury* (who repudiate the family and the past), and of course poor Joe Christmas of *Light in August,* whose story is the pathetic struggle of a man who, literally, has no past, who does not know who he is or his own reality.

Whittier, too, understood the fate of the man who has no past— or who repudiates his past. This is his "worldling" of *Snow-Bound* (whom we may also take as an image of what the past might have been had the vainglorious dreams of his youth been realized), whom he calls to spread his hands before the warmth of the past in order to understand his own humanity, to catch the sweetness coming "he knows not where," and the "benediction of the air."

But, on the other side of this question, Whittier understood all too well the danger of misinterpreting the past—in his own case the danger of using the past as a refuge from reality. Faulkner, too, fully understood this particular danger and dramatized it early in *Sartoris* and later in "The Odor of Verbena." But the theme appears more strikingly and deeply philosophized in characters like Quentin Compson in *The Sound and the Fury* and Hightower in *Light in August.* But Faulkner understood other kinds of dangers of misinterpretation. Sutpen, with his "design" and no comprehension of the inwardness of the past, suggests, in spite of all differences, a parallel with Cooper's squatter in *The Prairie,* whose only link with the past is some tattered pages from the Old Testament that serve, in the end, to justify his killing of the brother-in-law (the pages having no word of the peace and brotherhood of the New Testament). But Faulkner's most complex instance of the misinterpretation of the past occurs with Ike McCaslin, who, horrified by the family crime of slavery and incest, thinks he can buy out simply by refusing to accept his patrimony: he does not realize that a true understanding of the past involves both an acceptance and a transcendence of acceptance.

If we turn to Melville, we find in *Pierre, or the Ambiguities* the story of a man trapped, as Whittier was, in the past and desperately trying to free himself for adult action, just as we find in *Battle-Pieces,* in more general terms, the overarching theme of the irony of history set against man's need to validate his life in action. And, for a variation on the general question, in *Clarel* we find the hero (who has no "past"—who is fatherless and has lost his God, and who does not know mother or sister) seeking in history a meaning of life, this quest occurring in the Holy Land, the birthplace of the spiritual history of the Western world; and it is significant that Clarel finds his only answer in the realization that men are "cross-bearers all"— that is, by identifying himself with the human community, in its fate of expiatory suffering—an answer very similar, though in a different tonality, to that of *Snow-Bound.*

With Hawthorne the same basic question is somewhat differently framed. We do not find figures with roles like those of Hurry Harry, the squatter, Joe Christmas, Hightower, or Clarel, but find, rather, a general approach to the meaning of the past embodied in Hawthorne's treatment of the history of New England. Nothing could be further than his impulse from the antiquarian and sentimental attitude of Whittier in his historical pieces or that of Longfellow. What Hawthorne found in the past was not the quaint charm of distance but the living issues of moral and psychological definition. What the fact of the past gave him was a distancing of the subject to gain an archetypal clarity and a mythic force. The sentimental flight into an assuagement possible in the past was the last thing he sought. He could praise the ancestors, but at the same time thank God for every year that had come to give distance from them. In his great novel and the tales the underlying theme concerns "legend" as contrasted with "action," the "past" as contrasted with the "future," as in the works of Cooper, Melville, and Faulkner; and sometimes, most obviously in "My Kinsman, Major Molineux," with this theme is intertwined the psychological struggle to achieve maturity, with the struggle seen as a "fate."

Whittier, though without the scale and power of Cooper, Hawthorne, Melville, and Faulkner, and though he was singularly lacking in their sense of historical and philosophic irony, yet shared their deep intuition of what it meant to be an American. Further, he shared their intuitive capacity to see personal fate as an image for a general cultural and philosophic situation. His star belongs in their constellation. If it is less commanding than theirs, it yet shines with a clear and authentic light.

Whittier lived some twenty-five years after *Snow-Bound* and wrote voluminously. But, as always, the flashes of poetry were intermittent: "Abraham Davenport," "The Prelude," "The Hive at Gettysburg," "The Pressed Gentian," "At Last," and "To Oliver Wendell Holmes." To these might be added the elegy on Conductor Bradley ("A railway conductor who lost his life in an accident on a Connecticut railway, May 9, 1873"), which may claim immortality of a sort scarcely intended by the poet—as a work of grotesque humor and unconscious parody and self-parody. The world would be poorer without this accidental triumph of what we may call inspired bathos. The opening stanzas run:

> Conductor Bradley, (always may his name
> Be said with reverence!) as the swift doom came,
> Smitten to death, a crushed and mangled frame,
>
> Sank, with the brake he grasped just where he stood
> To do the utmost that a brave man could,
> And die, if needful, as a true man should.
>
> Men stooped above him; women dropped their tears
> On that poor wreck beyond all hopes or fears,
> Lost in the strength and glory of his years.
>
> What heard they? Lo! the ghastly lips of pain,
> Dead to all thought save duty's, moved again;
> "Put out the signals for the other train!"

Whittier had lived into a world totally strange to him. The world of industrialism and finance capitalism, of strikes and strikebreaking, meant no more to him than it would have to Emerson. While a man like William Dean Howells saw the Haymarket case as a crucial test of justice, Whittier simply could not understand the issue.

But his fame was worldwide: the abolitionist, the hero, the humorist (for he was that, too, in his way), and, to top it all, a sort of minor saint in outmoded Quaker dress.

In Whittier's continuing bachelorhood, with a series of female friends and admirers, there ran a strain of flirtatiousness that more than one lady seems to have taken too seriously. The old fierce ambition had now shrunk to a small vanity that gratified itself in an excessive number of sittings for photographs and some devious tricks of self-advertisement, such as writing an interview with himself and disguising the identity of the interviewer, or doing the laudatory entry under his name in an encyclopedia of biography. So, too, the old passion that had striven "in chains" now flickered on in these little erotic charades. His ego needed these things even at the time when he had long since won the real battle against himself and fate.

. . .

Whittier died September 7, 1892, after a brief period of illness and a paralytic stroke. Toward the end, he was often heard to murmur, "Love—love to all the world." As he was dying, one of his relatives present by the bedside quoted his poem "At Last." He was buried in the section of the cemetery at Amesbury reserved for Friends. The grave was lined with fern and goldenrod, and the coffin was lowered to rest on a bed of roses. Nearby were the graves of the members of the family who had sat at the fireside of *Snow-Bound*.

His monument is *Snow-Bound*. It promises to endure.

THE THEMES OF
ROBERT FROST

$\mathscr{A}$ LARGE BODY OF criticism has been written on the poetry
of Robert Frost, and we know the labels which have been used:
nature poet, New England Yankee, symbolist, humanist, skeptic,
synecdochist, anti-Platonist, and many others. These labels have
their utility, true or half true as they may be. They point to something in our author. But the important thing about a poet is the kind
of poetry he writes. We are not interested primarily in his "truth"
as such—as label, as samplerwork—but in the degree to which it is
an organizing and vitalizing principle in his poem. For only in so
far as it operates as such a principle—in so far as the poem becomes
truly expressive—does the truth have meaning at all.

In any case, I do not want to begin by quarreling with the
particular labels. Instead, I want to begin with some poems and try

Presented as a Hopwood Lecture in 1947. First published in *Michigan Alumnus
Quarterly Review,* December 1947, and later in the University of Michigan Press
title *The Writer and His Craft,* edited by Roy W. Cowden, 1954. Included in *Selected
Essays,* 1958.

to see how their particular truths are operative within the poems themselves. I know perfectly well that there are some readers of poetry who object to this process. They say that it is a profanation, that they simply want to enjoy the poem. We all want to enjoy the poem. And we can be comforted by the fact that the poem, if it is true poem, will, like the baby's poor kitty-cat, survive all the pinching and prodding and squeezing which love will lavish upon it. It will have nine lives too. Further, and more importantly, the perfect intuitive and immediate grasp of a poem in the totality of its meaning and structure—the thing we desire—may come late rather than early—on the fiftieth reading rather than on the first. Perhaps we must be able to look forward as well as back as we move through the poem—be able to sense the complex of relationships and implications—before we can truly have that immediate grasp.

But we know that some poets flinch when faced with any critical discussion of their poems. The critic may so readily turn into the dogmatist who wants to extract the message from the poem and throw the poem away—just as the sentimentalist wants to enjoy his own feelings provoked by the poem and throw the poem away. Frost himself has been especially shy of the dogmatists and has not shown too much sympathy with a reader who, to quote him, "stands at the end of a poem ready in waiting to catch you by both hands with enthusiasm and drag you off your balance over the last punctuation mark into more than you meant to say."

Or we have the case of Yeats. An admirer sent Yeats an interpretation of one of his poems and asked if it was right. Yeats replied, grudgingly, that it was, but added that he did not think poets ought to interpret their own poems, or give the green light to the interpretations of other people, for this would serve to limit the poems.

A good poem is a massive, deep, and vital thing, but this does not imply that a poem is a stimulus to which any response, so long as it is intense, is appropriate. It does not mean that the poem is merely a body of material which the reader may fancifully reorder according to his whim. But it does imply that though the poem is a controlled focus of experience, within the terms of that control many transliterations are possible as variants of the root attitude expressed. (There are many ways to state the theme of a poem.)

To turn to the poems: The poets may make their protests and

reservations, but discussions will continue. As a starting point I am taking one of Frost's best-known and most widely anthologized pieces, "Stopping by Woods on a Snowy Evening." But we shall not be content to dwell exclusively on this poem, attractive as it is, for it will quite naturally lead us into some other poems. It will lead us to the other poems because it represents but one manifestation of an impulse very common in Frost's poetry. Here is the poem:

Whose woods these are I think I know.
His house is in the village though;
He will not see me stopping here
To watch his woods fill up with snow.

My little horse must think it queer
To stop without a farmhouse near
Between the woods and frozen lake
The darkest evening of the year.

He gives his harness bells a shake
To ask if there is some mistake.
The only other sound's the sweep
Of easy wind and downy flake.

The woods are lovely, dark and deep.
But I have promises to keep,
And miles to go before I sleep,
And miles to go before I sleep.

Now, the poem we are dealing with may be said to be simple— that is, the event presented is, in itself, simple and the poet says, quite simply, what the event presumably means. But this does not mean that the implications of the event are not complex; the area of experience touched upon by the poem is "suggestive" or "haunting." And all good poems, even the simplest, work, it seems to me, in exactly that way. They drop a stone into the pool of our being, and the ripples spread.

The poem does, in fact, look simple. A man driving by a dark woods stops to admire the scene, to watch the snow falling into the special darkness. He remembers the name of the man who owns the woods and knows that the man, snug in his house in the village, cannot begrudge him a look. He is not trespassing. The little horse is restive and shakes the harness bells. The man decides to drive on, because, as he says, he has promises to keep—he has to get home to deliver the groceries for supper—and he has miles to go before he can afford to stop, before he can sleep.

At the literal level, that is all the poem has to say. But if we read it at that level, we shall say, and quite rightly, that it is the silliest stuff we ever saw. That is what the Amazon queen in Shakespeare's *Midsummer Night's Dream* said to her husband as she watched the play Bottom and his fellows were giving in honor of her marriage. But Theseus, her husband, replied: "The best in this kind are but shadow and the worst are no worse if imagination amend them." We shall try to be a little less literal-minded than the Amazon queen and shall try to see what reality our little poem is a shadow of.

> Whose woods these are I think I know.
> His house is in the village though;
> He will not see me stopping here
> To watch his woods fill up with snow.

With that first stanza we have a simple contrast, the contrast between the man in the village, snug at his hearthside, and the man who stops by the woods. The sane, practical man has shut himself up against the weather; certainly he would not stop in the middle of the weather for no reason at all. But, being a practical man, he does not mind if some fool stops by his woods so long as the fool merely looks and does not do any practical damage, does not steal firewood or break down fences. With this stanza we seem to have a contrast between the sensitive and the insensitive man, the man who uses the world and the man who contemplates the world. And the contrast seems to be in favor of the gazer and not the owner— for the purposes of the poem at least. In fact, we may even have the question: Who is the owner, the man who is miles away or the man who can really see the woods?

With the second stanza another contrast emerges:

> My little horse must think it queer
> To stop without a farmhouse near

> Between the woods and frozen lake
> The darkest evening of the year.

Here we have the horse-man contrast. The horse is practical too. He can see no good reason for stopping, not a farmhouse near, no oats available. The horse becomes an extension, as it were, of the man in the village—both at the practical level, the level of the beast which cannot understand why a man would stop, on the darkest evening of the year, to stare into the darker darkness of the snowy woods. In other words, the act of stopping is the specially human act, the thing that differentiates the man from the beast. The same contrast is continued into the third stanza—the contrast between the impatient shake of the harness bells and the soothing whish of easy wind and downy flake.

To this point we would have a poem, all right, but not much of a poem. It would set up the essential contrast between, shall we say, action and contemplation, but it would not be very satisfying because it would fail to indicate much concerning the implications of the contrast. It would be a rather too complacent poem, too much at ease in the Zion of contemplation.

But in the poem the poet actually wrote, the fourth and last stanza brings a very definite turn, a refusal to accept either term of the contrast developed to this point.

> The woods are lovely, dark and deep.
> But I have promises to keep,
> And miles to go before I sleep,
> And miles to go before I sleep.

The first line proclaims the beauty, the attraction of the scene—a line lingering and retarded in its rhythm. But with this statement concerning the attraction—the statement merely gives us what we have already dramatically arrived at by the fact of the stopping—we find the repudiation of the attraction. The beauty, the peace, is a sinister beauty, a sinister peace. It is the beauty and peace of surrender—the repudiation of action and obligation. The darkness of the woods is delicious—but treacherous. The beauty which cuts itself off from action is sterile; the peace which is a peace of escape is a meaningless and, therefore, a suicidal peace. There will be beauty and peace at the end of the journey, in the terms of the fulfillment of the promises, but that will be an earned beauty stemming from action.

In other words, we have a new contrast here. The fact of the capacity to stop by the roadside and contemplate the woods sets man off from the beast, but in so far as such contemplation involves a repudiation of the world of action and obligation it cancels the definition of man which it had seemed to establish. So the poem leaves us with that paradox, and that problem. We can accept neither term of the original contrast, the poem seems to say; we must find a dialectic which will accommodate both terms. We must find a definition of our humanity which will transcend both terms.

This theme is one which appears over and over in Frost's poems— the relation, to state the issue a little differently, between the fact and the dream. In another poem, "Mowing," he puts it this way: "The fact is the sweetest dream that labor knows." That is, the action and the reward cannot be defined separately, man must fulfill himself, in action, and the dream must not violate the real. But the solution is not to sink into the brute—to act like the little horse who knows that the farmhouses mean oats—to sink into nature, into appetite. But at the same time, to accept the other term of the original contrast in our poem, to surrender to the pull of the delicious blackness of the woods, is to forfeit the human definition, to sink into nature by another way, a dangerous way which only the human can achieve. So our poem, which is supposed to celebrate nature, may really be a poem about man defining himself by resisting the pull into nature. There are many poems on this subject in Frost's work. In fact, the first poem in his first book is on this subject and uses the same image of the dark wood with its lethal beauty. It is called "Into My Own."

> One of my wishes is that those dark trees,
> So old and firm they scarcely show the breeze,
> Were not, as 'twere, the merest mask of gloom,
> But stretched away until the edge of doom.

I should not be withheld but that some day
Into their vastness I should steal away,
Fearless of ever finding open land,
Or highway where the slow wheel pours the sand.

I do not see why I should e'er turn back,
Or those should not set forth upon my track
To overtake me, who should miss me here
And long to know if still I held them dear.

They would not find me changed from him they
    knew—
Only more sure of all I thought was true.

Here the man enters the dark wood but manages to carry his
humanity with him; he remains more sure of all he had thought was
true. And thus the poem becomes a kind of parable of the position
of the artist, the man who is greatly concerned with the flux of
things, with the texture of the world, with, even, the dark "natural"
places of man's soul. He is greatly concerned with those things, but
he manages to carry over, in terms of those things, the specifically
human.

From "Into My Own" let us turn to a late poem, which again gives
us the man and the dark wood and the invitation to come into the
lethal beauty. This one is called "Come In."

As I came to the edge of the woods,
Thrush music—hark!
Now if it was dusk outside,
Inside it was dark.

Too dark in the woods for a bird
By sleight of wing
To better its perch for the night,
Though it still could sing.

The last of the light of the sun
That had died in the west
Still lived for one song more
In a thrush's breast.

Far in the pillared dark
Thrush music went—
Almost like a call to come in
To the dark and lament.

But no, I was out for stars:
I would not come in.
I meant not even if asked,
And I hadn't been.

In this woods, too, there is beauty, and an invitation for the man to come in. And, as in "Stopping by Woods on a Snowy Evening," he declines the invitation. Let us develop a little more fully the implications of the contrast between the two poems. The thrush in the woods cannot now do anything to alter its position. Practical achievement is at an end—the sleight of wing (a fine phrase) can do no good. But it still can sing. That is, the darkness can still be conquered in the very lament. In other words, the poet is prepared to grant here that a kind of satisfaction, a kind of conquest, is possible by the fact of expression, for the expression is, in itself, a manifestation of the light which has been withdrawn. Even in terms of the lament, in terms of the surrender to the delicious blackness, a kind of ideal resolution—and one theory of art, for that matter—is possible. (We remember that it was a thing for a man to do and not for a horse to do to stop by the other dark woods.)

But here the man, as before, does not go into the woods. He will not make those terms with his destiny, not, in any case, unless forced to do so. (The thrush cannot do otherwise, but a man can, perhaps, and if he can do otherwise, he more fully defines himself as man.) No, the man is out for stars, as he says. Which seems to say that man, by his nature (as distinguished from bird), is not dependent upon the day; he can find in the night other symbols for his aspiration. He will not lament the passing of the day, but will go out for stars.

I would not come in.
I meant not even if asked,
And I hadn't been.

What are we to take as the significance of this last little turn? Is it merely a kind of coyness, a little ironical, wry turn, without content, a mere mannerism? (And in some of Frost's poems we do have the mere mannerism, a kind of self-imitation.) Why had not the man been asked to come in? The thrush's song had seemed to be an invitation. But it had not been an invitation, after all. For the bird cannot speak to the man. It has not the language of man. It can speak only in terms of its own world, the world of nature and the dark woods, and not in terms of the man who is waiting for the darkness to define the brilliance of the stars. So here we have again the man-nature contrast (but we must remember that nature is in man, too), the contrast between the two kinds of beauty, and the idea that the reward, the dream, the ideal, stems from action and not from surrender of action.

Let us leave the dark-wood symbol and turn to a poem which, with other materials, treats Frost's basic theme. This is "After Apple-Picking," the poem which I am inclined to think is Frost's masterpiece, it is so poised, so subtle, so poetically coherent in detail.

> My long two-pointed ladder's sticking through a tree
> Toward heaven still,
> And there's a barrel that I didn't fill
> Beside it, and there may be two or three
> Apples I didn't pick upon some bough.
> But I am done with apple-picking now.
> Essence of winter sleep is on the night,
> The scent of apples: I am drowsing off.
> I cannot rub the strangeness from my sight
> I got from looking through a pane of glass
> I skimmed this morning from the drinking trough
> And held against the world of hoary grass.
> It melted, and I let it fall and break.
> But I was well
> Upon my way to sleep before it fell,
> And I could tell
> What form my dreaming was about to take.
> Magnified apples appear and disappear,

Stem end and blossom end,
And every fleck of russet showing clear.
My instep arch not only keeps the ache,
It keeps the pressure of a ladder-round.
I feel the ladder sway as the boughs bend.
And I keep hearing from the cellar bin
The rumbling sound
Of load on load of apples coming in.
For I have had too much
Of apple-picking: I am overtired
Of the great harvest I myself desired.
There were ten thousand thousand fruit to touch,
Cherish in hand, lift down, and not let fall.
For all
That struck the earth,
No matter if not bruised or spiked with stubble,
Went surely to the cider-apple heap
As of no worth.
One can see what will trouble
This sleep of mine, whatever sleep it is.
Were he not gone,
The woodchuck could say whether it's like his
Long sleep, as I describe its coming on,
Or just some human sleep.

The items here—ladder in apple tree, the orchard, drinking trough, pane of ice, woodchuck—all have their perfectly literal meanings—the echo of their meaning in actuality. And the poem, for a while anyway, seems to be commenting on that actual existence those items have. Now, some poems make a pretense of living only in terms of that actuality. For instance, "Stopping by Woods on a Snowy Evening" is perfectly consistent at the level of actuality—a man stops by the woods, looks into the woods, which he finds lovely, dark and deep, and then goes on, for he has promises to keep. It can be left at that level, if we happen to be that literal-minded, and it will make a sort of sense.

However, "After Apple-Picking" is scarcely consistent at the level of actuality. It starts off with a kind of consistency, but something happens. The hero of the poem says that he is drowsing off—and in broad daylight, too. He says that he has a strangeness in his sight which he drew from the drinking trough. So the literal world dissolves into a kind of dream world—the literal world and the dream world overlapping, as it were, like the two sets of elements in a superimposed photograph. What is the nature of this dream world? And what is its relation to the literal world, the world of real apples and the aching instep arch and the real woodchuck?

The poem opens with a few lines which seem to apply wholeheartedly to the literal world:

> My long two-pointed ladder's sticking through a tree
> Toward heaven still,
> And there's a barrel that I didn't fill
> Beside it, and there may be two or three
> Apples I didn't pick upon some bough.

It is all literal enough. We even observe the very literal down-to-earth word "sticking" and the casualness of the tone of the whole passage. In fact, it would be hard to say this more simply than it is said. Even the rhymes are unobtrusive, and all the more so because all of the lines except one are run-on lines. But let us, in the light of the rest of the poem, look more closely. The ladder, we observe, has been left sticking "toward heaven still." That is, as we have said, casual and commonplace enough, but we suddenly realize it isn't merely that, when we remember the poem is about the kind of heaven the poet wants, the kind of dream-after-labor he wants—and expects.

So, to break the matter down into crude statement and destroy the quality of the suggestive-in-the-commonplace, we have a kind of preliminary appearance of the theme which concerns the relation of labor and reward, earth and heaven. With our knowledge of the total poem, we can look back, too, at the next several lines and reread them: Maybe I missed something in my life, in my labor, the poet says, but not much, for I tried quite conscientiously to handle carefully every item of my harvest of experience, to touch with proper appreciation everything that came to hand. Maybe I did miss a few things, he seems to say, but I did the best I could, and on the whole did pretty well.

But now the harvest is over, he says, and the "essence of winter sleep is on the night, the scent of apples." He is aware of the conclusion, the successful conclusion of his effort, and in that awareness there is a strangeness in his sight. He is now looking not into the world of effort but the world of dream, of the renewal. It is misty and strange, as seen through the pane of ice, but still it has the familiar objects of the old world of effort, but the objects now become strange in their very familiarity. He is poised here on the frontier between the two worlds, puzzling about their relationship. But he can already tell, he says, what will be the content of the dream world, the world of reward for labor now accomplished.

> And I could tell
> What form my dreaming was about to take.
> Magnified apples appear and disappear,
> Stem end and blossom end,
> And every fleck of russet showing clear.

The dream will relive the world of effort, even to the ache of the instep arch where the ladder rung was pressed. But is this a cause for regret or for self-congratulation? Is it a good dream or a bad dream? The answer is not to be found in statement, for as far as the statement goes he says:

> For I have had too much
> Of apple-picking: I am overtired
> Of the great harvest I myself desired.

No, we must look for the answer in the temper of the description he gives of the dream—the apples, stem end and blossom end, and every fleck of russet showing clear. The richness and beauty of the harvest—magnified now—is what is dwelt upon. In the dream world every detail is bigger than life, and richer, and can be contemplated in its fullness. And the accent here is on the word contemplated. Further, even as the apple picker recalls the details of labor which made him overtired, he does so in a way which denies the very statement that the recapitulation in dream will "trouble" him. For instance, we have the delicious rhythm of the line

> I feel the ladder sway as the boughs bend.

It is not the rhythm of nightmare, but of the good dream. Or we find the same temper in the next few lines in which the poet returns to the fact that he, in the real world, the world of effort, had carefully handled and cherished each fruit, and *cherished* is not the word to use if the labor is mere labor, the brutal act. So even though we find the poet saying that his sleep will be troubled, the word *troubled* comes to us colored by the whole temper of the passage, ironically qualified by that temper. For he would not have it otherwise than troubled, in this sense.

To quote again:

> One can see what will trouble
> This sleep of mine, whatever sleep it is.
> Were he not gone,
> The woodchuck could say whether it's like his
> Long sleep, as I describe its coming on,
> Or just some human sleep.

Well, what does the woodchuck have to do with it? How does he enter the poem, and with what credentials? His sleep is contrasted with "just some human sleep." The contrast, we see, is on the basis of the dream. The woodchuck's sleep will be dreamless and untroubled. The woodchuck is simply in the nature from which man is set apart. The animal's sleep is the sleep of oblivion. But man has a dream which distinguishes him from the woodchuck. But how is this dream related to the literal world, the world of the woodchuck and apple harvests and daily experience? It is not a dream which is cut off from that literal world of effort—a heaven of ease and perpetual rewards, in the sense of rewards as coming after and in consequence of effort. No, the dream, the heaven, will simply be a reliving of the effort—magnified apples, stem end and blossom end, and every fleck, every aspect of experience, showing clear.

We have been considering the literal world and the dream world as distinct, for that is the mechanism of the poem, the little myth of the poem. But here it may be well to ask ourselves if the poet is really talking about immortality and heaven—if he is really trying to define the heaven he wants and expects after this mortal life. No, he is only using that as an image for his meaning, a way to define his attitude. And that attitude is an attitude toward the here and now, toward man's conduct of his life in the literal world. So we must make another transliteration.

This attitude has many implications. And this leads us to a rather important point about poetry. When we read a poem merely in terms of a particular application of the attitude involved in it, we almost always read it as a kind of cramped and mechanical allegory. A poem defines an attitude, a basic view, which can have many applications. It defines, if it is a good poem, a sort of strategic point for the spirit from which experience of all sorts may be freshly viewed.

But to return to this poem: What would be some of the implied applications? First, let us take it in reference to the question of any sort of ideal which man sets up for himself, in reference to his dream. By this application the valid ideal would be that which stems from and involves the literal world, which is arrived at in terms of the literal world and not by violation of man's nature as an inhabitant of that literal world. Second, let us take it in reference to man's reward in this literal world. By this application we would arrive at a statement like this: Man must seek his reward in his fulfillment through effort and must not expect reward as something coming at the end of effort, like the oats for the dray horse in the trough at the end of the day's pull. He must cherish each thing in his hand. Third, let us take it in reference to poetry, or the arts. By this application, which is really a variant of the first, we would find that art must stem from the literal world, from the common body of experience, and must be a magnified "dream" of that experience as it has achieved meaning, and not a thing set apart, a mere decoration.

These examples, chosen from among many, are intended merely to point us back into the poem—to the central impulse of the poem itself. But they are all summed up in this line from "Mowing," another of Frost's poems: "The fact is the sweetest dream that labor knows." However, we can step outside of the poems a moment and find a direct statement from the anti-Platonic Frost. He is comparing himself with E. A. Robinson, but we can see the application to the thematic line which has been emerging in the poems we have been considering.

> I am not the Platonist Robinson was. By Platonist I mean one who believes what we have here is an imperfect copy of what is in heaven. The woman you have is an imperfect copy of some woman in heaven or in someone else's bed. Many of the world's greatest—maybe all of them—have been ranged on that romantic side. I am philosophically opposed to having one Iseult for my vocation and another for my avocation. . . . Let me not sound the least bit smug. I define a difference with proper humility. A truly gallant Platonist will remain a bachelor as Robinson did from unwillingness to reduce any woman to the condition of being used without being idealized.

Smug or not—and perhaps the poet protests his humility a little too much—the passage does give us a pretty clear indication of Frost's position. And the contrast between "vocation" and "avocation" which he uses leads us to another poem in which the theme appears, "Two Tramps in Mud Time." The last stanza is talking about the relation of "love" and "need" as related to an activity—which may be transliterated into "dream" and "fact" if we wish:

> But yield who will to their separation,
> My object in living is to unite
> My avocation and my vocation
> As my two eyes make one in sight.
> Only where love and need are one,
> And the work is play for mortal stakes,
> Is the deed ever really done
> For Heaven and the future's sakes.

And we may notice that we have, in line with our earlier poems on the theme, the apparently contrasting terms "mortal stakes" and "Heaven."

In conclusion, I may cite "Desert Places," which is a late and more bleakly stoical version of "Stopping by Woods on a Snowy Evening," and "Birches," which is almost a variant of "After Apple-Picking." Here are the closing lines of "Birches":

> So was I once myself a swinger of birches.
> And so I dream of going back to be.
> It's when I'm weary of considerations,
> And life is too much like a pathless wood
> Where your face burns and tickles with the cobwebs
> Broken across it, and one eye is weeping
> From a twig's having lashed across it open.
> I'd like to get away from earth awhile
> And then come back to it and begin over.
> May no fate willfully misunderstand me
> And half grant what I wish and snatch me away
> Not to return. Earth's the right place for love:
> I don't know where it's likely to go better.
> I'd like to go by climbing a birch tree,
> And climb black branches up a snow-white trunk
> Toward heaven, till the tree could bear no more,
> But dipped its top and set me down again.
> That would be good both going and coming back.
> One could do worse than be a swinger of birches.

For the meaning, in so far as it is abstractly paraphrasable as to theme: Man is set off from nature by the fact that he is capable of the dream, but he is also of nature, and his best dream is the dream of the fact, and the fact is his position of labor and fate in nature though not of her. For the method: The poet has undertaken to define for us both the distinction between and the interpenetration of two worlds, the world of nature and the world of the ideal, the heaven and the earth, the human and the non-human (oppositions which appear in various relationships), by developing images gradually from the literal descriptive level of reference to the symbolic level of reference.

It may be said quite truly in one sense that this interpenetration, this fusion, of the two worlds is inherent in the nature of poetry—that whenever we use a metaphor, even in ordinary conversation, we remark on the interpenetration in so far as our metaphor functions beyond the level of mere mechanical illustration. But the difference between the general fact and these poems is that the interpenetration of the two worlds, in varying ranges of significance, is itself the theme of the poems. We can whimsically say that this does not prove very much. Even the most vindictive Platonist could not do very differently, for in so far as he was bound to state his Platonic theme in words—words, which belong to our world of fact and contingency—he would be unwittingly celebrating the un-Platonic interpenetration of the two worlds.

But there is a practical difference if not an ultimate one. We might get at it this way: The process the poet has employed in all of these poems, but most fully and subtly I think in "After Apple-Picking," is to order his literal materials so that, in looking back upon them as the poem proceeds, the reader suddenly realizes that they have been transmuted. When Shakespeare begins a sonnet with the question, "Shall I compare thee to a summer's day?" and proceeds to develop the comparison, "Thou art more lovely and more temperate," he is assuming the fact of the transmutation, of the interpenetration of the worlds, from the very start. But in these poems, Frost is trying to indicate, as it were, the very process of the transmutation, of the interpenetration. That, and what that implies as an attitude toward all our activities, is the very center of these poems, and of many others among his work.

NOTES ON THE POETRY OF

JOHN CROWE RANSOM

AT HIS EIGHTIETH BIRTHDAY

$\mathcal{N}$OTES—THAT IS all I am prepared to give, and the fact is strange. Strange, because since the first issue of the *Fugitive* magazine I have read, I think, every poem of John Crowe Ransom as it appeared, sometimes even in manuscript, and have memorized many of them. Once, some thirty-five years ago, I wrote an essay about them, which, after two or three years, was published. Between that time and this, I have looked back over it only once, and with distaste. Looking back at it again, I am confirmed in an old feeling that the piece did not really indicate the deeper reality I had sensed in the poems. Now that I am invited, for a happy occasion, to write something else on John Crowe Ransom, I find that even today I do not have the right topic, the name for the *thing,* whatever the thing may be, that has held me year after year.

There was, however, a period—when I was nineteen to twenty-five years old—when I rebelled against that power exercised by the

First published in *The Kenyon Review,* June 1968.

poems, and exercised, so unwittingly I may add, by their author. It was not merely that I, overwhelmed by the new poetry of Eliot, was puzzled and confused by the coldness of Ransom toward it: puzzled, confused, and at moments outraged, chiefly because of my passion for Ransom's own poetry. Nor was it merely that as I blundered into my own poetry I had to fight off, not always success-fully, what William Yandell Elliott, one of the Fugitives, had called "Johnny's bag of tricks," as well as T. S. Eliot's. Nor merely that the very coherence, intellectual and emotional, of Ransom's poetry was a painful reproach to my own attempts at poetry, which fact I blindly resented.

My rebelliousness stemmed, I now suppose, from a resentment against the cast of the author's mind which made such graceful gestures, enunciated such deep truths, and exercised such fascinat-ing authority for me, even as I knew, in despair, that I could never emulate that grace, live by those truths, nor accept such authority. My own nature was too volatile, awkward, and angry, and all the harmony and control embodied in the poetry and the man seemed to undercut life-possibility for me and deny life-need.

But the rebellion was imperfect. Even then I was still immersed in Ransom's poetry, and was gradually coming to understand that what continued to move me was not "Johnny's bag of tricks," and to understand, however dimly, that the pervasive theme of the poetry, even the very existence of the poetry, involved, in all its harmony, the disharmonies of life, mastering them without denying them. The writing of my old essay signified, I should now hazard, the end of the imperfect, and loving, rebellion against the poetry, as well as of the other more unconscious rebellion. By that time no longer a student but a colleague, even if a very junior one, and a friend, if a very overawed one, I discovered in that house a charac-teristic gaiety, and easy gallantry against the difficulties of life, a spirit of play which pervaded even the most serious concerns, and which merged, I am tempted to say, with a sense of ritual. All this was a revelation to me, who had lived by the excitements and violences of life rather than by acceptances; and was, no doubt, behind that fumbling little essay.

Now, looking again at the old essay, it occurs to me that what was wrong with it was a mechanical quality. I was so concerned to define a focal origin for the poetry that I sometimes confused the idea of such a focal origin with that of a formula. I was trying to find a mere pattern of ideas when I should rather have been trying to find a characteristic movement of mind—of being. My desire to fix on such a focal origin for Ransom's poetry sprang not merely from the youthful notion that there is a master key for everything, a magic word, but also from a need to place Ransom's poetry, which I had found indispensable to me, in relation to the Pound-Eliot strain, which dominated the age into which I had been born. And the need to do this may have had its roots in the fact that I myself, in trying to write poetry, and in thinking about poetry, was torn between the Pound-Eliot strain and another possibility, shadowy to me and undefined, which, though not like Ransom's poetry, then seemed nearer to it, in some way, than to anything else.

I do not now want to rewrite that fumbling old essay, but what I then thought I had found was that the irony of Ransom—his parables of men without sense of direction, of men who, incomplete, could not fathom or perform their natures—was derived from the same fragmented world as were *The Waste Land,* the *Cantos,* and *The Sound and the Fury.* In other words, if Ransom did not, like Pound, Eliot, and Faulkner, dramatize a world suffering from the then famous "dissociation of sensibility," and devise an allusive, fragmented style to illustrate the malaise, he at least offered, in his sequential narratives and orderly style, a diagnosis of the malaise as his subject, and found in the malaise the grounding of his characteristic irony of "chills and fever."

When I showed him the essay, he read it with attention, and then, with charming but (I thought) irrelevant friendliness, asked if he couldn't have his middle name back. The title, by some slip, was "The Irony of John Ransom"—and so "Crowe" got put back where it belonged. After some thought, he made a remark about hoping that his poems were worthy of the attention lavished upon them. Then he got up, strolled over to a window of his office, looked out for an instant, and as a kind of afterthought added that as far as "dissociation of sensibility" in the modern world went, he was rather inclined to think that man was, naturally, born as a kind of "oscillating mechanism." That was all.

The subject of my essay was, it seemed, politely declining to be saved for modernity. That much must have penetrated my density as I walked away with the manuscript in my pocket. He was saying, it occurred to me years later, that he was not writing about modern man, but about man. If modern man came in as a case in point (as modern man most surely did), it was under that rubric.

But meanwhile I kept remembering the phrase "oscillating mechanism." So that was what he saw as the underlying fact of his poems, the source of his style! With that in mind, I reread—and now reread—that first strange little volume, *Poems about God,* which appeared in 1919 by a "1st Lieut. Field Artillery, AEF." There are, in fact, several strange things about it.

The earliest piece in the book, "Sunset," was written in May 1916, and one strange thing here is that the author, who was twenty-eight, had never written a poem before. Another strange thing is that the poem is, in its own awkward way, concerned with the theme that was to prove central to Ransom's poetry: the haunting dualism in man's experience. Most bookish young men try their hand early at poetry. Why hadn't this one? Most poets have to work from poem to poem over a considerable length of time toward their central concern, have to discover it through their poetry. Why could this tardy poet hit so soon on his? There are, of course, no final answers to such questions, but we must risk some.

Here we must first hazard an answer to the second question, and that would be that Ransom had been living, consciously and unconsciously, with that central concern, in one form or another, for a long time and with great intensity. In other words, the underlying theme did not need to be discovered; it must have been there, and urgently.

To come to the first question, we may surmise that Ransom turned to poetry, even so tardily, because there was more than intellectual urgency involved. And here, as an aside, he had never written any prose either, beyond that required by the routines of his life. If the theme of the poetry had been, we can argue, of merely intellectual urgency, it would seem logical, in the light of his special philosophical training and interest, to suppose that he would have approached the issue by the way of prose speculation. In any case, the issue was not only there, it was not of merely intellectual and professional concern; it had been, and was being, lived into. It was, in fact, life, and, as life, not ever to be totally defined intellectually, a polarity of life having many manifestations, constantly changing its terms, a split in the human possibility, a tension among desires, among obligation, among pieties. From this the poetry would spring, because poetry gave the only way to deal with the issue.

Not that the first poem, or any poem ever to come, could resolve the issue. It could not even, in the end, name it. It could merely give one dramatic manifestation of the unnamed—or even unnamable—root-issue, just as subsequent poems could merely multiply and refine new manifestations. As Ransom once remarked, there is always something "inconclusive" about the endings of his poems— and how could it be otherwise if the very theme is one of ambiguities, of "oscillation," of a split in the self as well as in the world? If, however, the poetry could afford no conclusions, it could afford a release and a mastery through objectification; and afford, through the mounting variety of instances, the sense that the issue was not special to the self but built into the human condition, and could therefore more readily, in its commonness and inevitability, be confronted.

Here, however, we get ahead of ourselves, and in doing so, leave out of account the very things that make Ransom's poetry special and durable: the voice, the tone, the scrupulous distinctions and shadings of attitude, the wit and, even, the passion. Those things had not, of course, emerged in the first volume; certainly not as clearly as the thematic concern, however rudimentary that concern may there seem in comparison with later work. But though it was rudimentary in the first book, it was still put with considerable self-consciousness. The preface—which, dated France, May 13, 1918, is significantly the first published prose of the author—instructs us that the poet had decided that "God" was "the most poetic of all terms possible, was a term always being called into requisition during the great moments of the soul, now in tones of love, and now indignantly; and it was the very last word that a man might say when standing in the presence of that ultimate mystery to which all of our great experiences reduce." The poet, therefore, reached about in his experience and imagination for various occasions at which men call into requisition the great name. The name, however, was "taken here in ways" that were not "the ways of the fathers." So one obvious manifestation of the root-issue was the split between orthodoxy and unorthodoxy, between "belief" and "unbelief." Some of the poems directly concern this issue, and all indirectly. But another issue lurks in the background: in what way can the technical "unbeliever" still "believe"—still have reverence before "that ultimate mystery to which all of our great experiences reduce"? The division, here, is between those who have a reverence for, and appreciation of, life (whether technical "believers" or not), and those who do not—who are the truly secular, who, unlike Miranda in the poem "Men," cannot clap hands in "sudden joy" upon seeing the "dirty strangers" and cry out: "O brave new world!"

To this issue we must add another, that of the painfully dubious relation of body and soul. In "The Cloak Model," we find

> God's oldest joke, forever fresh
> The fact that in the finest flesh
> There isn't any soul.

Or we find the shock of the filthiness of flesh, of body as merely the medieval "sack of stercorry"—as in "Grace," when the pious hired man dies in his own vomit between the corn rows. In "Morning" we find the most explicit statement:

> Three hours each day we souls
> Who might be angels but are fastened down
> With bodies, most infuriating freight,
> Sit fattening these frames and skeletons
> With filthy food, which they must cast away
> Before they feed again.

I have remarked on some of the ways in which *Poems about God* is a strange little book, but the more one looks at it the stranger it gets. Strangely, all the writer's subsequent work is in little here. The prose book *God without Thunder* comes straight out of it, with its answer to the question of belief in the conception of myth. The criticism comes out of it. And the poems most explicitly. But let us remember the strange preliminary fact that the writer should have come back to Tennessee at all to write this book.

Frost deliberately went back to country New England in 1915 to "Yankee-fy" himself. We can readily understand the impulse of a writer like Frost, or Faulkner, to immerse himself in his special world. But Ransom, when he came back to Tennessee, had given no sign that he even vaguely thought of being a writer. He was aiming, if at anything, at being a teacher, had already, in fact, been teaching in a preparatory school in New England, and he was eminently well equipped—with his brilliant undergraduate record in America, his honors degree in "Greats" from Oxford, and his intellectual power—to distinguish himself in the graduate school of any of the Eastern universities, and thence proceed apace to the top of some academic career.[1] But he turned his back on opportunity and ambition and took an instructorship in a small Southern university, where salaries were low, teaching loads heavy, and promotions slow. He was not a man of random impulses, and it is not unlikely that the decision to turn away from the path dictated by common sense and ambition represented the scrutinized recognition of a deep need. Even if it is recognized that family responsibilities may well have prompted the decision.

Whatever dissatisfaction with the world of ambition and modernity forced him back, and whatever pieties drew him, he did not now enter a world where all that had been riven was made whole; and so we have *Poems about God.* About God, because reared in the atmosphere of belief, and with full awareness that men of philosophical learning and culture equal to his own had lived in belief, he, with his own skeptical cast of mind and faithfulness to experience, had to confront the problem of belief.[2] There was a split, the split indicated in the preface, between him and his traditional

[1]After serving in France as an officer of artillery in World War I, he did briefly attend the University of Grenoble, and even toyed with the idea of becoming a journalist, a notion he again flirted with about 1930.
[2]Shortly after *God without Thunder* appeared, he was to remark to me that a man of his turn of mind and temperament was scarcely the man to undertake such a book about Christian belief.

world, a split that, if we are to accept as autobiographical the poem "Plea in Mitigation" in the next volume, *Chills and Fever,* grew more complex with time, for he was, he says,

> a headstrong man, sentenced from birth
> To love unusual gods beyond all earth.
> And the easy gospels bruited hither and yon.

There was also a split in himself, a quarrel with the self, a drama of the self. Now, back in Tennessee, was the inherited scene for the action of such a drama, the place where the scene could, in fact, *be* the action. The scene could be the action in the deepest way, and what the drama quickly involved, by implication at least, was a whole tangle of issues.

The issues were, and remain, of great import in the modern world, but then they were set in a peculiarly restricted and unmodern environment. And here is a contrast between Ransom, Frost, and Faulkner on one hand, and Pound and Eliot on the other. Pound and Eliot deal with many of the same issues as do Ransom, Frost, and Faulkner, but they set the issues on a world stage, and the issues become aspects of their major theme of the crisis of culture. This expansiveness is precisely the opposite of the reductiveness of the others mentioned, for whom the great issues are most poignantly or forcefully dramatized in the local and small. In *Poems about God,* Ransom even bypassed the not very big city of Nashville, and its unimpressive modernities, and set his poems in memories of the rural world of his childhood.

Here the most common persona, sometimes specified, sometimes implied, is that of the farm boy following the plow or sweating with the harvest hands; it is also a reduction, as the Shropshire farm boy was one for Housman, the classical scholar turned poet (whose career may have given a suggestion to Ransom), or the New England farmer for Frost (who at that early date would scarcely have afforded Ransom any kind of model). Such dramatization of great issues by reduction is, of course, at the heart of the pastoral tradition: the irony of wisdom out of innocence, the clarity of the human outline when set in the light of nature, the shock of truth out of a presumed naïveté.

There was much naïveté in *Poems about God,* but for the purpose in hand it is the wrong kind, because it stems not from a coherent dramatization, not from a realized persona, but from a lack of dramatization. That is, though the poems belong to a special world, this world is given no proper "voice"; therefore, the reduction of a great issue often seems merely absurd, merely bathetic. What a farm boy might say is not what we will permit the twenty-eight-year-old scholar to say, and we don't quite know who is talking. To state matters another way, the trouble is that the poems have no style, no "voice."

But the basis on which Ransom was to discover a voice—and the right ratio between that voice and the self—was already inherent in *Poems about God,* in fictional memories of an earlier situation when he had taught school and heard his pupils droning over their Greek. Here is the second stanza of "The School":

> Equipped with Grecian thoughts, how could I live
> Among my father's folk? My father's house
> Was narrow and his fields were nauseous.
> I kicked his clods for being common dirt,
> Worthy a world which never could be Greek;
> Cursed the paternity that planted me
> One green leaf in a wilderness of autumn;
> And wept, as fitting such a fruitful spirit
> Sealed in a yellow tomb.

The resolution of the problem in the poem itself does not concern us here. What does concern us is the recognition of the difference between the son, with a head full of "Grecian thoughts," and the "common dirt" of "a world which never could be Greek." Here we do not have the farm boy as persona, but the displaced scholar.

Here is the grounding of the voice Ransom was to discover, and a right fiction for the persona, with, in the background, as both a model and a reproach, not the farmer-father of the poem but Ransom's own scholar-father, the translator of the Bible into Portuguese and the student of theology who by an act of faith and without condescension could make a full life for himself as a minister in churches of back-country South. The father, in other words, could live in that world, in both difference from it and identification with it.

The fiction behind *Poems about God* did not provide the basis for a style. This is not to say that such a fiction, theoretically regarded, might, if developed dramatically, not give a style. It is merely to say that it clearly did not give one to Ransom; with it, he was too close to his subject, and yet not close enough. Only by accepting his distance, by speaking not through the farm boy immersed in the world but as the young scholar with his head full of "Grecian thoughts," could he really "see" his subject: that is, by accepting the responsibility of a fuller use of his own sensibility and his own history, in another and more fruitful ratio of persona to the self.

We all know how, when one opens *Chills and Fever* (published in 1924, only five years after *Poems about God*), lines and phrases that never could have appeared in the earlier volume leap off the page. In "Spectral Lovers":

> He had reduced his tributaries faster,
> Had not considerations pinched his heart
> Unfitly for his art.

In "To a Lady Celebrating Her Birthday":

> This day smells mortuary more than most
> To me upon my post.

Of the tree in "Vaunting Oak":

> "Largely, the old gentleman is," I grieved, "cadaver . . ."[3]

In "Nocturne":

> The white moon plunges wildly, it is a most ubiquitous ghost . . .

---

[3]This line was revised (in *Selected Poems*) to read: " 'The grand old gentleman,' I grieved, 'holds gallantly. . . .' " And in the line from "Prometheus in Straits" the word *comfort* is revised to *practice.*

In "Prometheus in Straits":

And comfort my knees with red bruises of genuflection . . .

In "Captain Carpenter":

And made the kites to whet their beaks, clack, clack.

And let us not forget the famous "vexed" in "Bells for John White-side's Daughter" and the "thole" in "Here Lies a Lady."

Vocabulary, syntax, imagery, and rhythm, not to mention the range of reference and the varieties of dramatic context in individual poems, all constitute the voice which affirms the new persona and establishes the distance at which, as we have said, the subject was really to be "seen"; for in poetry a subject can be "seen" only if we can believe in the posited "see-er," and this is possible only if he is at such a distance from the subject that we can clearly distinguish him from it. The true drama, the true "insides," of a poem is in the act of the "seeing"—in the vital interrelation of the "see-er" and the "seen." So in these matters we must play with a paradox: *near* is *far,* and *far* is *near.* Nowhere may be *far* and *far* may be *near,* for this is a world where no rule is hard and fast.

In any case, in Ransom's poetry, the characteristic tenderness, the charity, the pitifulness appeared, paradoxically, only when the persona was more rigorously detached from the world of the subjects, when the "see-er" was located at a greater distance. Thus irony—the index of the distance, the mark of uninvolvement—made the tenderness, the involvement, possible. The tension between the irony and the tenderness, between the impulse to withdraw and the impulse to approach, became a fundamental aspect of the drama of the poetry.

Poems about God was very specifically rooted in the South, but what about the poetry of the new persona? Ransom has said that he never consciously set out to write "Southern" poetry—as Frost, it may be added, had set out, with his project of "Yankee-fying" himself, to write Yankee poetry. Ransom, in fact, discovered his new style, at a single stroke, in a poem that in the literal sense is about as far removed from the South, in place and time, as possible.

The poem is "Necrological," which had been suggested by the poet's reading of the death of Charles the Bold of Burgundy, whose body was left to the wolves outside the walls of the city of Nancy, which he had been beseiging. In the poem, a young friar comes out at night and ponders the field:

> The lords of chivalry were prone and shattered,
> The gentle and the bodyguard of yeomen;
> Bartholomew's stroke went home—but little it mattered,
> Bartholomew went to be stricken of other foemen.

In this poem appears for the first time the special "learned" vocabulary (and imagery, for often the two cannot be distinguished), the fields "white like meads of asphodel," the bodies "gory and fabulous," the firmament a "blue ogive." It is a vocabulary and imagery that give the whole poem the "distance" of events as on a tapestry, and are at the same time both romantic and anti-romantic, heroic and mock-heroic. But the focus of the poem is the young friar, who, in his person, dramatizes the issue. The "paternosters" have not stilled the "riddling" in his head, and he is drawn forth to ponder the scene, to try to find meaning in the fact of violence, suffering, love, devotion, courage, and death—the fact that all, in the end, seem to come to nothing, to be part of an aimless repetition, for the victor himself goes to "be stricken of other foemen." The friar has the perspectives of theology and history, but how can he relate them to each other, or to the brute facts of the world? Yet he must try to relate them; and once he has drawn the "crooked blade" from the dead man's belly, and fingers it, he, the unworldly man, is feeling himself into the role of those who act and suffer in the world, sitting so still he likens himself to those dead whom "the kites of heaven solicited with sweet cries." So he, the detached one, enters empathically the pathos of the world; and in the poem Ransom discovered, it would seem, not only the new stance and new style, but also the new persona, the first of many variants.

There were many poems to come in *Chills and Fever* that involve these variants of the persona, most notably "*Agitato ma non troppo,*" "Plea in Mitigation," "Tom, Tom, the Piper's Son," and

"Philomela." In *Two Gentlemen in Bonds,* of 1927, we find "Persist-ent Explorer," "Semi-Centennial," "Man without Sense of Direc-tion," and, one is tempted to add, "Antique Harvesters." These are poems about the nature and role of the poet—and, hence, of po-etry.

In one perspective they belong, in their own wry fashion, among the poems of the Romantics written to celebrate the poetic imagina-tion, poems like "Kubla Khan," *The Ancient Mariner, The Prelude,* and "Ode on a Grecian Urn." Man is the "persistent explorer" who, though he knows that the sound of the waterfall is not the voice of a god, and that water is only "the insipid chemical H_2O," will still let his "enemies" (the literalists) "gibe," and would throw this continent of literalism away and "seek another country." Man is, as the aging man of "Semi-Centennial" says of himself, a god with the "patrimony of a god," and though he cannot control the objective world, he knows that the "better part of godhood is design": he can still satisfy his "royal blood" by projecting his poems, his myths, his values upon the blankness of the world. This much, even though he, like the aging man, is sometimes "too tired" to work his magic.

I have said *man,* not *poet,* in discussing the last poem about the variants of the persona, for it is important to sense that in Ran-som's way of thinking, man to be fully man must in some way or another fulfill himself as poet, as a maker. Is it by accident that in the volume *Two Gentlemen in Bonds* the poem "Morning," which is not obviously about man as poet, comes immediately after "Persistent Explorer"? For the poems are theoretically linked, are complementary. In "Morning," then, Ralph wakes so gently that

> before the true householder Learning
> Came back to tenant in the haunted head
> He lay upon his back, let his stare
> Penetrate dazedly into the blue air
> That swam all round his bed,
> And in the blessed silence nothing was said.

In this moment of enchantment,

> He would propose to Jane then to go walking
> Through the green waves, and to be singing not talking.

But "he remembered about himself," his "manliness returned," the "dutiful mills of the brain" whirred again, and, suddenly rising, he "was himself again," and it was "simply another morning, and simply Jane." The other Jane who is not "simply Jane" must be created by the poet-Ralph—which is not to say that she, the other Jane, is more of a fiction than "simply Jane."

And this returns me to the idea that I might add "Antique Harvesters" to the list of poems that present variants of the persona. I refer to the revised versions, in *Selected Poems,* with a new stanza added at the end:

> True, it is said of our Lady, she ageth.
> But see, if you peep shrewdly, she hath not stooped;
> Take no thought of her servitors that have drooped,
> For we are nothing; and if one talk of death—
> Why, the ribs of the earth subsist frail as a breath
> If but God wearieth.

This stanza does flow naturally from what has gone before, and summarizes the preceding matter. But it adds an entirely new dimension. If the earth subsists merely in God's will—and by His love—then the "Lady" subsists only in what has been "done in love" for her; and, as corollary, we, her servitors, "are nothing" unless we create ourselves in the service "done in love." So this is a poem about creation, too, in a complex and deep way. It is also another poem in which, as in "Morning," man and poet are merged.

But "Antique Harvesters" is also the poem in which Ransom most specifically treats the South and regional piety, and this fact invites a side glance at the question of his "Southernness." One may somehow feel the poems to be very Southern, and yet only two, "Antique Harvesters" and "Old Mansion," more or less engage the subject. There are, in general, only faint vestiges of local color:

in "Lady Lost," the reference to the "West End," a section of Nashville; in "Two in August," the hackberry trees, which are characteristic of the region; in "Nocturne," the seersucker coat, which in the 1920s was as characteristically Southern as mint julep and the "Bonnie Blue Flag"; and, in "Dead Boy," the reference to "Virginia's aged tree" and the "county kin." This is a small showing for even so small a body of work as Ransom's, and most of the items are trivial. What we should look for is, in fact, not such items, but the language and the attitudes of the persona, and even the context in which the persona could be developed.

As for that context, I have already referred to the father, with his difference from, and identification with, the world of back-country South. But behind the father there would have stood many other figures—divines, scholars, statesmen—who had also borne an ambivalent relation to the actuality of America, who, by their learning and tastes, were anomalies in the raw land, but who, out of their learning, could, ridiculously or grandly, dream that raw land as a new Athens or a new Roman Republic with virtues to be kept forever untarnished, or even as a new City of God. Such men were different from, and, at the same time, identified with, their world.

But another kind of doubleness came in, too. For the images of the antique world that they carried in their heads—Jew, Greek, Roman—could, in ironical contrast, reduce the raw actual world to a pitiful triviality, or could, by the same token, elevate its rawness to the full dignity of its place in the story of Divine redemption or in the story of human liberty. This doubleness was built into the American, and specifically into the Southern, tradition, where it anachronistically lingered long after it had disappeared in more thriving regions. And this fact gives us another perspective in which to regard the poet's discovery of the persona, and by which to localize it as another dimension of irony.

For another context, it can be argued that Ransom's concern with the pathos of defeat, and with the spirit in which defeat can be borne, has some relation to the fact that the South is the only part of America that knows defeat, and that the poetry, at a considerable remove, echoes the Confederate disaster and all the ironies, casuistries, idiocies, and theological debates later provoked in the South by this inscrutable act of Divine Providence. By this reasoning,

then, even the battlefield of "Necrological" is not merely a medieval scene but a scene reflecting the Civil War, as the "riddlings" of
the Carmelite reflect those of a good Confederate pondering the
destiny of his land. So, with old Grimes, of "Puncture," as the
image of dignified acceptance of fate in contrast to the young companion who rails and could kick the dead; and in support of this
thesis, one may adduce the last two somewhat puzzling lines of the
poem:

> Smoke and a dry word crackled from his mouth
> And the wind ferried them South.

Even "Armageddon" may be read with a historical dimension,
with its ironies of inversions and interpenetrations applicable to the
struggle of 1861–65. Or, to take "Captain Carpenter," which treats
the tragic story of the common human lot and celebrates the common courage of man, it can be argued that, somewhat more indirectly, it treats the Confederate story, ironically reducing it by the
mock-heroic tone.

Further, the mock-heroic tone, here and elsewhere, may be taken
to represent an ironical reduction of official Southern rhetoric, an
echo which we get with different intent, an irony within an irony,
in "Antique Harvesters," in the stanza:

> We pluck the spindling ears and gather the corn.
> One spot has special yield? "On this spot stood
> Heroes and drenched it with their only blood."
> And talk meets talk, as echoes from the horn
> Of the hunter—echoes are the old men's arts,
> Ample are the chambers of their hearts.

And not only, one may guess, may the ironical reduction in
Ransom's style refer to official Southern rhetoric. It may also refer
to the pride of provincial learning in showing off its wares—the big
words and highfalutin references and elegant quotations in old-time
pulpits and editorials, on the hustings and the street corner.

Sometimes, more important than the mock-heroic strain, is another kind of echo in establishing the world of a poem. In this

connection, F. O. Matthiessen gives a very perceptive reading of "Antique Harvesters." After remarking on the "contemplative distance" set up by the word *antique* in the title, and by the *bank sinister* in setting the scene, he contrasts with these ironical "literary" devices other elements: in the words *runnel* and *meager,* we hear, he says, the "old-fashioned expressions, the Elizabethan or seventeenth-century usage that was brought to this country by the first settlers and that has disappeared now except for remote rural and mountain areas, especially in the South." And, as he adds, there are the "elaborate courtly phrases of an older public speech: 'Therefore let us assemble.'" Ransom has given here "essential traits" of the older culture of the South; but not only here. In "Blue Girls," how subtly work the word *seminary* and the phrase "your teachers old and contrary"! And what would "Conrad Sits in Twilight" be without the discreetly colloquial tone with which the last stanza opens?

In short, the Southernness of Ransom's poetry is a reflection of the dimensions of the persona, with both the tension and the loving interplay between a man and his heritage, the drama of "difference from" and "identification with."

It is hard, sometimes, to distinguish between poems in which the persona is actually the subject of a poem, is defined in a poem—as I have somewhat hesitantly taken "Antique Harvesters" to be—and those poems in which the persona is presented in the act of commenting on a subject; it is hard to know where to set the knife edge down. The only place where the author himself has set down the knife edge appears, in the volume *Two Gentlemen in Bonds,* in the distinction between the two groups labeled "The Innocent Doves" and "The Manliness of Men." The first section is clearly composed of poems about the gentle ones who are caught in the cleft stick of the world, the Blue Girls, Janet and her hen, and the Lost Lady. It is the second section that causes trouble, and the chief trouble is that we know that this author never causes trouble irresponsibly. He means the trouble to mean something. The section is not a mere catchall or grab bag, with a cute label stuck on.

But let us forget the label for a moment, and simply see what we find here. "Our Two Worthies" opens the section and "Equilibrists" closes it. What logic puts these poems here? The "Worthies" are Jesus the Paraclete and Saint Paul the Exegete, between whom, the poet says, let there be no "schism." But the schism is inevitable, between the "comforter" and the "explainer," the intuition and the word, the spirit and the organization, the City of God and the Church Militant.

As we look further, we find, in that *jeu d'esprit* "Survey of Literature," a sly tangential resemblance to the poem just cited: literature is made of what writers "had to eat and drink" (out of the raw experience of life), but it is also a thing of "consonants and vowels" (of all the more abstract aspects of language and technique). So here we have another "schism." But there are other "schisms" in the section—between the view held by the family and that held by the observer in "Dead Boy," between Grimes and the admiring narrator in "Puncture," between man and nature in "Semi-Centennial," between the husband and wife of "Two in August," among the birds in "Somewhere Is Such a Kingdom," between actuality and dream in such poems as "Persistent Explorer" and "Morning," between the two views of "dog" in the poem of that name, between the lovers in "Jack's Letter," between the literal and the poetic evaluations in "Antique Harvesters," between the obsession which the "Man without Sense of Direction" suffers and the natural peace he craves, between the two avatars of the "Amphibious Crocodile," between the official version of the Last Judgment in "Fresco" and all the forces released, including the widow's curse and Cleopatra's re-enactment of her wiles. And the last poem of the section, "Equilibrists," also deals with a "schism": the beautiful lovers are made for each other, but without even the memory which Paolo and Francesca might cherish in the whirl of the hot wind in the *Inferno,* they are caught like "two painful stars" in the "equilibrium" of their "prison world."

So all the poems in this section involve "schisms." The splits here are of two kinds, not always at the same level, but the recurrence, in variety, is the fundamental unifying fact of the section. In other words, here is a brief survey of the world man must live in and make his terms with, a more systematic presentation of what we have already found in *Chills and Fever.* But what relevance does this bear to the title of the section—"The Manliness of Men"? The answer is easy. This world of the "splits" is exhibited that we may see more clearly the way man, to fulfill his "manliness," must deal with it.

At first glance, certain poems in this section scarcely belong here, for instance, "Dead Boy" and "Jack's Letter." Both of these little pieces, beautiful and tender as they are, might seem better wrought for a place among "The Innocent Doves." But at second glance we see that the difference between such pieces and those of the first section is the intrusive presence of the observer, and the fact that the chief business of the poem is to show him in the effort of trying to come to terms with the situation. In "Dead Boy," the observer distinguishes between the two ways of regarding the boy, the view of the grief-stricken family and the literalistic view of one, like himself, from "the world of outer dark," who sees "the pig with a pasty face" as scarcely worth all this expense of emotion. But the observer will admit that he, in spite of his "rational" view, is moved, too; at least, he confesses ironically that he doesn't "love the transaction." He understands, in other words, that values are created, are relative not absolute, and in his understanding he grieves, as it were, with the grief of the family, not for the loss of the "pig," absolutely considered. Love, in one sense, creates the thing worthy of love—and of grief.

As a corollary of this, there is, in the course of the poem, a slight shift in the understanding of the bereavement. We start with "Virginia's aged tree" and "county kin" with some implication of family pride and vanity as components of the bereavement; not the nature and value of the dead boy but a "dynastic wound" would seem to be at stake. But at the end of the poem a shift of emphasis, slight but significant, has occurred. The "limbs" of "Virginia's aged tree" are aggrieved, not out of offended pride and vanity, but because there is a rupture of the elemental life process. The limbs are "shorn and shaken" in this rupture of their commitment to the ineffable blood continuity, in this outrage to a natural value beyond rational discussion. But this, as I have said, is only a corollary of the main idea, the creation of value by the fact of love.

In the same spirit we may look at "Jack's Letter." We may begin by setting it against another poem about a love letter, but a stranger kind of love letter, "Parting, without a Sequel," in the first section. At first glance, again, it would seem that "Jack's Letter" might well go back with the other poem, among "The Innocent Doves." Then we notice a difference. The touching subject in "Parting, without a Sequel" is presented on its own merits, as it were. We have the word issuing from the persona but we do not "see" the persona. In "Jack's Letter," the observer, however, significantly intrudes. Jack, we are given to understand, is no great hand as a letter writer, and what he says is not great matter. What, then, can such a letter mean to his distant beloved? It may mean everything, the observer intrudes to explain, if "she would lay it to her bosom." Doing that, she would "create" its meaning, and, as the poem implies, "create" Jack. And so we are back to the theme of "Dead Boy," and to those other poems from this section which we have previously discussed in relation to the persona, and to the topic of poetic creation, as the act by which man fulfills his "manliness," and proclaims his mastery over nature and fate.

Even the placement of the poems is sometimes of importance. "Jack's Letter" is followed by "Antique Harvesters," which seems so different, but is, if our earlier discussion of it is valid, a repetition, in another range, of the same theme of the creative power of love. In "Two in August," the distraught husband, after a nocturnal quarrel, goes out of the house and hears the night birds crying:

> Whether those bird-cries were of heaven or hell
> There is no way to tell;
> In the long ditch of darkness the man walked
> Under the hackberry trees where the birds talked
> With words too sad and strange to syllable.

Thus the poem ends with the ambiguous birds, to be followed by "Somewhere Is Such a Kingdom," in which the speaker of the poem affirms that when the birds ("of heaven or hell" in "Two in August") fall out and "croak and fleer and swear," he himself must seek

> Otherwhere another shade
> Where the men or beasts or birds

> Exchange few words and pleasant words.
> And dare I think it is absurd
> If no such beast were, no such bird?

Can we avoid the implication of this sequence? If the quarrel even of lovers is in the world (grounded in nature, even among "birds"), then our role as men in our manliness is to create the vision of a loving peace.

The sequence goes on. Now comes "Persistent Explorer," in which the hero, like the speaker in "Somewhere Is Such a King-dom," would "throw this continent away" (the world of actuality) and "seek another country": that is, would dream the dream that "manliness" demands. Then comes "Morning," which we have already discussed.

There is, too, a teasing relationship between "Puncture" and "Semi-Centennial" that could bear scrutiny; in fact, "Puncture" is altogether a poem in a peculiar relation to Ransom's work, teas-ingly tangential. The comic poems "Survey of Literature" and "Amphibious Crocodile" come together and thematically supple-ment each other. They are followed by "Fresco," which is comic, too, but more precariously and disconcertingly so. But what, then, of "Equilibrists," the famous piece which winds up this section? How literally are we to take "honor"? Literally, and also un-liter-ally? Surely, but what kind of "un-literalness," in what dimensions? And in the light of the cunning interlockings of the poems, should we not look curiously at the end of the poem just preceding "Equili-brists," and ponder the fact that here Cleopatra, on the Day of Judgment, renews "her harlotries"?—that is, ritually, as it were, re-enacts her necessary nature:

> But now in Heaven her harlotries were renewed,
> For she loosed the cerements wherewith she was gewed;
>
> Her side was buckled, but she undid the clasp
> And showed her small round bosom kissed by the asp.

Do we not have here another of Ransom's multifarious duali-ties—that lady who submits herself wholly to the flesh and that lady who, because of "honor" (whatever that word here may mean), cannot submit at all? But what does it come to in the end? What is the poet, the intrusive observer, really saying? Would it be possible to answer this question without keeping in mind the theme running throughout this section?

We have tried to indicate the thematic coherence of the section called "The Manliness of Men," and the interlocking relations among the poems composing it. This is not to imply necessarily that the section was planned in this spirit. The poems may well have been written before the poet made such a grouping.[4] In any case, in setting up the three sections of *Two Gentlemen in Bonds,* Ransom is bringing out into the open and refining a distinction implicit in the previous volume, a distinction important in any evaluation of his work. The poems of "The Manliness of Men" are the philosophical ones, those about the poet and his knowledge of, and appropriate attitude toward, the world he must live in. The poems in "The Innocent Doves" are about the victims of the world, who suffer without knowledge, without philosophy, in the world.

These victims are regarded with tenderness and pity, and, even if we come upon poems like "Blue Girls" or "Janet Waking" isolated in some anthology, there is the emotional impact. It would be hard to think of a poem superior to these in perfection of control and clarity of emotional outline. The poems seem perfectly self-sufficient in their dramatic force, for Ransom is a master of the withheld effect that releases a power at the very end, to linger with an increasing afterglow as in "Bells for John Whiteside's Daughter," or to burst suddenly forth as in "Vision by Sweetwater."

What kind of poem would "Vision by Sweetwater" be without the last two lines? It might be charming, beautifully rendered,

---

[4]It would be interesting to have the chronology of composition of the poems in this section, to know to what degree, if at all, the interlockings come from the fact that one poem seems to lead, as it were, to another. In the preface to *Selected Poems,* Ransom says that it would be difficult for him "to recover the exact order in which these [and presumably other] poems were composed," but he says in that book the "arrangement is substantially in that order." We know from Ransom's description elsewhere of his method of work that he usually did two or three poems in a little spurt. A thematic sequence?

nostalgic, haunting. But then comes the scream. With what power, with what complexity, it bursts forth here! Why is the boy "old suddenly"? For one thing, it is a scream hinting, in its very lack of specificity, at terror, loss, pain, containing all the tragic utterance and uncertainty that life may come to demand—bursting forth in sudden nakedness after the prattle of the girls in their "strange quick tongue." But what strangeness, to the boy, in their prattle has prepared him, and us, for the shocking strangeness of the scream? As a young boy, he is outside the world of the girls, fascinated but uncomprehending, shy but yearning toward their mystery, and when the scream bursts forth, it is charged not only with terror, loss, and pain, but with sexuality. It is a Dionysiac scream, a darker reality, bursting forth to violate the "innocent dream of ladies sweeping by," to chill into sudden silence the gay, innocent festival of the "bright virgins" moving by the water in their "delicate paces," as on a frieze.

What complexity and power lie, too, in the fact that we know nothing of the origin of the scream, not what provokes it, not from what throat it comes. This ignorance, and anonymity, is an index to the archetypal nakedness of the scream—merely scream, the ineluctable scream. It bursts forth in that nakedness from "one of the white throats" where it has been hidden—hidden as though lying in wait, or as though in guilt. Or both.

To continue, we may look at another detail: let us think of what the difference would be if the last line read

> From one of the white throats among which it hid,

and not, as now,

> From one of the white throats which it hid among.

When the poem comes to rest on the word *among,* the fact that the source of the particular scream (which throat?) is unknown is emphasized. The scream belongs, in one sense, not merely to a particular girl, a particular white throat, but could belong to any; and this is a way of saying that it belongs to all, and may, in the end, in the course of life, leap from each and all. The lingering rest on the word *among* universalizes the scream and therefore means, too, that the boy will hear it again. The speaker of the poem, now a man, looks back on that first scream, which, in ecstasy or pain, he now knows well, perhaps too well, and thus can bring his pity, with his knowledge and his sense of fate, into the poem.

Poem after poem exhibits this kind of delicacy and force, and invites us to investigate the strange paradoxical poise of effect. But however complete and self-fulfilling we may find a poem of Ransom's to be, to isolate it thus is to do more than common injustice. Isolated, the emotion is unmoored, ungrounded, even when in the poem itself there seems to be dramatic completeness. What is missed in isolation is the sense of the meaning of the persona, the sense of the nature and cost of the tenderness and pity, and the sense in which the irony that informs the utterance is, as Delmore Schwartz once put it, "an expression of the very painfulness of the emotion."

In isolating a poem, we lose something else, too, the sense of the blank backdrop of the world which ironically belittles, and even makes irrelevant, the story of an innocent one. By the same token, the poem has lost the full awareness of the nature of the act of tenderness, pity, empathy. For the act is, against that blank backdrop, as irrelevant and irrational, as devoid of meaning, as the fate of any innocent one. But as a last irony returning upon itself, the capacity for this act of pity is all that is available to man, to define himself; by its very gratuitousness, blankness, and irrationality, the act of pity affirms the "manliness" of man, his special power. It is, in short, the act of the creation of value.

Man and poet, life and poetry: this interrelation is central to the work of Ransom. And the interrelation has a special connection to two peculiar facts of his career. The first we have already discussed: the fact that he came to poetry late, and, coming late, struck immediately on his abiding themes as an aspect of his life-process. The second peculiar fact is stranger still. At the very height of his powers, he stopped writing poetry.

After the third volume, *Two Gentlemen in Bonds* (1927), Ransom was to write only five more poems: "Painted Head," "Prelude to an Evening," "Of Margaret," "What Ducks Require," and "Address to the Scholars of New England" (the Phi Beta Kappa poem at Harvard, in June 1939). All five, even the occasional poem, approach, or achieve, stylistic perfection, and though all deal with his old theme, all have new tonalities. Even "Painted Head," which most specifically restates the old themes of the "split," seems fresh, and "Prelude to an Evening," certainly one of his most masterful pieces, seems to promise, with deeper depth and resonances, a whole new phase of development. But the five poems were, in fact, an Indian summer: brilliant, but the end.

It is hard to know what happened. Or perhaps it seems hard to know only because it is so obvious. At some time in the mid-thirties—I cannot remember exactly what year, but certainly well before the Harvard poem—Ransom remarked to me that he thought he might write no more poetry. When I expressed surprise, he replied that he was sure that he could write more poems as good as, or better than, those already done, but he explained that he couldn't bear merely to repeat himself. He did not want to be a "pro" and merely build a reputation. He wanted to be an "amateur," he said. He had written his poems out of joy, he added, and did not want to have writing dwindle into a job. Then, after a moment of silence, he added, "Of course, if some day I find a new way in, I'll probably start writing again."

"Out of joy," he had said. At that time I did not understand what he really meant. Now I should say that he must have meant more than a special joy of composition; he must have meant that he saw poetry as a natural function of, an adjunct to, the process of living. And this idea, I think, can be distinguished from the idea that poetry is related to life, first as a way of commenting on, or discovering the meaning of, life, or second, as a substitute, or compensation, for life.

Long ago, back in the 1920s,[5] Ransom had said that as a poet he wanted "to find the experience that is in the common actuals"; that he wanted "this experience to carry (by association of course) the dearest possible values to which we can attach ourselves"; and that he wanted "to face the disintegration or multiplication of those values as religiously and calmly as possible."

This letter is, in fact, a remarkable description of exactly what

[5]In a letter to Allen Tate, quoted by John L. Stewart in *The Burden of Time*.

Ransom did accomplish in his poetry, but for present purposes I quote it because it illustrates how Ransom found his poetry in those "dearest possible values"—which are, I think he would say, the poetry of the life process. And if this is the case, then the writing of poetry would, in his view, be more secondary, more subsidiary to the overall business of living, because only a part of it. By this line of reasoning, the satisfaction found in the composition might well continue in other ways, from other sources: one might live one's poetry. And so we come back to the notion, found elsewhere in Ransom's prose, of living as the great art, and back, in a very special way, to the ancient notion of a good man's life as a poem.

Ransom did not, however, lose his interest in poetry in the ordinary, narrower sense. The drastic gesture of repudiation made by Rimbaud would be the last thing possible for Ransom, for his commitment to poetry, though fundamental, was of a different order from the commitment of a Rimbaud, for whom poetry was not a function of, but a surrogate for, life—a romantic absolute. Ransom has remained a reader of poetry, with a joyful relish in it; he has carefully and instructively revised his poems; and he is, of course, a hard theorist and critic of poetry.

Which brings us to the criticism. Allen Tate was, I believe, the first to point out, at the level of theory, the peculiar consistency between the poetry and the criticism of Ransom. But there is another kind of consistency that I want to emphasize here. To do this I must comment on the kind of criticism he has devoted himself to. It is a criticism concerned with philosophical groundings, with technical formulations, with structural definitions and analyses. As criticism, it has drawn back from the contours and colors of whatever poetic object was under discussion. It is, if you will, "abstract" in the extreme. And this would seem peculiar, even paradoxical; for one theme of the criticism, as of the poetry itself, is the need to assert the contours and colors of the "world's body" against "abstraction," against the violation of the world by the intellect. It would seem, however, that the critic who early saw "abstraction" as the enemy has, as is so often the case in all sorts of crucial struggles, as the poem "Armageddon" points out, taken on the qualities of the evil adversary.

This, however, is not true. Not true, because this criticism itself has, in a very special sense, its own existence as an "art," with all the concreteness and specificity implied by that fact. It is not merely that, by and large, Ransom's criticism is far better written than most, more precisely phrased, more urbane and witty. The style itself is merely an indication that the critical effort, which objectively considered seems devoted to salting the tail of an abstraction, is, when subjectively considered, an effort made by a whole man. Passion, wit, and sensuous delight are involved along with the cold intellection.

The style bespeaks an individual; and more significantly, even at its most rigorous, the critical effort may be felt as involving a social occasion, conversation with a glass in hand by the fireside, or on a summer afternoon under the maples, and the courtesies of the occasion are there. As the prose stems from the human depth and fullness behind the critical effort, so one recognizes in its rhythms and its wit, in its tone, the author's awareness of the reader as a friendly but independent other. The air is not that of a lecture, of a demonstration, but of a dialogue, of a collaborative quest. As a critic, then, Ransom most resembles Dryden. Ransom at his best, as Dryden at his, seems to understand criticism in its social dimensions, as an art, a dramatic art in fact, which implies the human context of the subject discussed and, too, the human context of the discussion itself. For Ransom, criticism, like poetry itself, is one of the ways of trying to live life with intelligence, logical scrupulosity, and moral rigor, but, withal, with gaiety, feeling, and respect for the human other. As in his poetry, so in his criticism, in the very act of anatomizing the splits and jags of life, Ransom would offer what healing of the splits and jags may be possible in the act of celebrating life.

For that is what Ransom's work, prose and poetry, sums up to: a celebration of life, as manifested in the virtues of charity and endurance, tenderness and gaiety. And in that work, we sense in what a context of hard realism and of unillusioned clarity of mind, and at what price, these virtues have been affirmed; and we find that in one sense this is the heart of the drama which informs and charges the whole. Some years ago, when the poet was a guest in my house, he kindly consented to read a few of his pieces to the company. After he had gone to bed, several people remained a little while, talking over the poems. One of them remarked on the precision, control, and tenderness. Another present, a lady, burst out: "But don't you see what passion and self-conquest lie behind all that?"

And I felt that she was right. This was what I had not realized when I wrote that little essay thirty years before.

How much of life does Ransom celebrate? That question, in one disguise or another, has been raised by many critics. This is the old, nagging question of scale and evaluation. Ransom has referred to himself as "small," as a "domestic poet"; and some critics, even some who admit his mastery of the medium, his subtlety and precision, and the clarity of emotion in his work, have insisted, almost angrily sometimes as though having been defrauded of something, on what they would call his "limited range," on his being a "minor poet."

That phrase is a tricky one. Its meaning, for one thing, depends on the tone of voice in which it is uttered—that is, on the motivation of the utterer. For another, its meaning depends on the context, specifically on what poets, and what kind of poets, the speaker would assume to be "major." Are Chaucer, Spenser, Shakespeare, and Milton the only major poets in English? What keeps Ben Jonson off the list? Can we add Wordsworth? If so, why not Coleridge? Or is the bulk of his work too small? Can a satirical poet like Pope or Byron be major? Can a poet who, because deeply ironical, does not make an overt commitment be called major? Can a poet close to us, like Eliot or Pound, be called major? Or must the work stand the test of time?

It is all a mare's-nest, and perhaps the only thing we can do is to be simple, and say with Ransom himself that for major poetry the "index is the amount of turnover produced in our gray stuff," adding, however, that there must be a corresponding amount of turnover in our guts, and that, as a corollary to those propositions, neither perfection nor intensity is enough and the poet's dramatizations must assert themselves in an appropriate magnitude.

Ransom is, then, a minor poet. But the important problem is always to determine if a poet is really a poet. And then what kind of poet a poet is, to discriminate his value. And Ransom offers a very special case. To consider it, we may turn back to the relation between the poems about "innocent doves" and those about the "manliness of men," recognizing that this distinction applies to all his work, both before and after the volume *Two Gentlemen in Bonds.* More than any poems about "the manliness of men," certain ones about the "innocent doves" offer a haunting power and a magic which Robert Lowell, in writing of Ransom, has equated with the "Celtic" strain in poetry that Matthew Arnold discriminates. For years I could not help puzzling over the seeming discrepancy between the small scale of a poem about an "innocent dove" and the abiding emotional force—a force that seemed to involve more "turnover of our gray stuff," and of our guts too, than the little poem overtly offered. Then I realized that the effect of a poem about an "innocent dove" depends to a considerable extent on the context provided by those about the "manliness of men," a context giving the philosophical and psychological grounding for, and interpretation of, the gesture of loving pity which the poem about an "innocent dove" is. To state it a little differently, the persona of a poem about an "innocent dove" is defined in the background by the poems about the "manliness of men," and only in so far as we understand the persona dramatized in those witty and learned poems, with their drier irony, do we appreciate the nature of the dramatization which the gesture of pity is.

To come at the matter again differently, in these "domestic" pieces the dramatizations do not directly assert themselves in an appropriate magnitude for "major poetry"; but by *implication,* if we set the individual poem in its full context, we see that the issues raised do approach the major—that is, are concerned with fundamental questions and, finally, with the tragic dilemmas of life. In this sense, Ransom more resembles a poet like Marvell than one like Herrick, to whom he is sometimes compared. Marvell is, of course, a minor poet; the dramatizations of, for instance, "The Garden" and "To His Coy Mistress" are not of "appropriate magnitude." But the poems do achieve tremendous resonance by the weight of implication. They are, as it were, exposed nerve ends of great issues, ends of nerves that run far back beyond the poems themselves. For a second comparison, we may turn to the philosopher-poet Coleridge, the haunting force of whose poems cannot be understood except in the light of his philosophy—not as illustrations of the philosophy but as life-thrusts toward the philosophy.

Why did Ransom elect the "domestic"? Did the fact, as some have seemed to imply, represent flight, withdrawal, repudiation? Or, on the other hand, wisdom, self-knowledge, compassion? Or is it the supreme strategy of an ironist who would delight in finding the large in the little, and the little in the large? Or the expression of a reverence for life that would cherish most the "common ancestrals"?

Perhaps we should say that the question is falsely put, that a man never "elects" such a thing; he can only live into it as the exfoliating sum of his life process embodying thousands of small choices and awarenesses. In any case, the poetry of Ransom is deeply consistent with his life story, the return to Tennessee, the criticisms of modernity, his contempt for ambition ("Ambition is a terrible thing," I once heard him say), his disinclination to becoming a "pro," the complex persona of the poetry, the paradox of the "artificial" style and philosophical weighting of the poetry on one hand, and the intensely personal quality on the other, the stoicism mixed with joy, a religious sense mixed with grateful delight, a sense of tragedy mixed with gaiety and the mock-heroic mode. Many years ago, speaking of a certain old man, he said, with a burst of feeling: "But there is always something tragic about old age." More lately, he has written in a letter: "Growing old, I find I love small, furry things, like kittens, more and more." So with everything else, poetry and philosophy, war and love, games, work in his garden, and friendship, he has lived into that, too.

He lived, in fact, through himself, into himself. And he has lived into a poetry which is completely and miraculously worthy of that self, and will abide. In the house of poetry there are many mansions, and this one, set high, with a long view, is swept and garlanded, and shines.

SECTION

IV

A POEM OF
PURE IMAGINATION:
AN EXPERIMENT IN READING

*T*HE DISCUSSION OF *The Ancient Mariner* always begins with reference to Mrs. Barbauld, that lady of "fine taste, correct understanding, as well as pure integrity," as Crabb Robinson called her. I suppose it is only reasonable to begin the discussion with Mrs. Barbauld, for if that "best specimen of female Presbyterian society in the country" is long since dust, her children, male and female, are legion and vocal. The famous remark to which her fine taste and correct understanding gave utterance had to do with a poem which, upon its appearance, had given offense to the judicious. A long time after the appearance of the poem itself, the poet, now a weak and lisping old man, recorded Mrs. Barbauld's remark, if we can believe the report in *Table Talk,* and his own comment upon it:

> Mrs. Barbauld once told me that she admired *The Ancient Mariner* very much, but that there were two faults in it—it was improbable,

First published in a 1946 edition of *The Rime of the Ancient Mariner,* Reynal and Hitchcock, Inc. Included in *Selected Essays,* 1958.

and had no moral. As for the probability, I owned that that might admit some question; but as to the want of a moral, I told her that in my own judgment the poem had too much; and that the only, or chief, fault, if I might say so, was the obtrusion of the moral sentiment so openly on the reader as a principle or cause of action in a work of such pure imagination. It ought to have had no more moral than the *Arabian Nights* tale of the merchant's sitting down to eat dates by the side of a well, and throwing the shells aside, and lo! a genie starts up, and says he *must* kill the aforesaid merchant, *because* one of the date shells had, it seems, put out the eye of the genie's son.

This passage, to which I shall return, gives Mrs. Barbauld her uneasy immortality.

I do not quote it, however, to pay the wonted tribute of a sneer. In fact, I am inclined to sympathize with the lady's desire that poetry have some significant relation to the world, some meaning. True, the kind of meaning prized by her female Presbyterian sensibility leaves something to be desired in the way of subtlety, if we are to judge from her own poems—from, for example, "An Inventory of the Furniture of Dr. Priestley's Study," "Inscription for an Icehouse," "Address to the Deity," or "To Mr. S. T. Coleridge, 1797," in which she advises the "youth beloved of Science—of the Muse beloved," to shun the "maze of metaphysic lore," where Indolence "fixes her turf-built seat." But it is easy to sympathize with her general point of view. The instinctive demand for significance is healthy, and one can especially sympathize with it after encountering a brand of hyperaesthetical criticism of our poem. This brand of criticism does not, to my knowledge, occur in the purlieus of bohemianism or in the shimmering pages of the *fin de siècle,* but rather, it flourishes in the very citadels of academic respectability, and in the works of some of the most eminent and sober students of Coleridge.

For example, one such critic, after stating that the passage concerning Mrs. Barbauld makes it forever clear that there was "no intention to give the poem a moral meaning," goes on to say: "Obviously, only the reader who cannot enjoy this journey into the realm of the supernatural finds it necessary to seek out a moral."[1]

There are two questions involved here: First, what did Coleridge

[1]The notes to this essay begin on page 400.

mean in the passage from the *Table Talk*? Second, what does Earl Leslie Griggs, the critic referred to above, mean by his remark? It so happens that Griggs has misread his text when he takes it as evidence that there is no "moral intention" in the poem. For Coleridge, according to his young kinsman Henry Nelson Coleridge, who recorded the *Table Talk,* did not say that the poem as it exists has no moral, but said that it suffers from the "obtrusion of the moral sentiment so openly." Nor did he say or even imply that the poem would be better if there were *no* moral. He merely said that the "obtrusion of the moral sentiment" is too "open." If the passage affirms anything, it affirms that Coleridge intended the poem to have a "moral sentiment," but felt that he had been a trifle unsubtle in fulfilling his intention. So all the critics who take this passage to argue that Coleridge intended *The Ancient Mariner* to be a poem without a theme, without relevance to life, have, like Griggs, reversed the undebatable sense of the text of the *Table Talk.*

Now, at the risk of a digression, I shall turn to the second question: What does Griggs mean by the word *moral* when he says that the poem has no "moral intention"? I take it that Griggs uses the word *moral* in a broad, general sense, equating it with theme understood as comment on human conduct and values. If he means something more specific, he has not given any indication of it. And if this broad, general sense is what he means, he is saying that the poem has no theme.

Presumably Griggs' remark is based on some theory of "pure poetry"—some notion that a poem should not "mean" but "be," and that the "be-ing" of a poem does not "mean." The actual statement he makes, however, does not concern his own, but Coleridge's theory of poetry: Coleridge, he says, had no "moral intention" and the poem has no theme. It may be that Griggs has stated his views a little unclearly and holds that special variant of the general theory of pure poetry which says that poetry (which is pure realization—however that may be interpreted) does make comments on life but that the truths it offers us are not worth listening to. But even that is a very different thing from asserting that a poet, Coleridge in this case, is not even undertaking to deliver an utterance about life. His theme may be a statement of error, but it is a statement. My first purpose in this essay is to establish that *The*

Ancient Mariner does embody a statement, and to define the nature of that statement, the theme, as nearly as I can.

It may be objected that Griggs does not, however, wish the word *moral* read in the broad, general sense which I have here provisionally adopted—that he intends such a narrow sense that room is left for all sorts of themes and meanings, just so long as they are not too painfully reminiscent of Sunday School. If that be objected, I can only appeal to the context of his statement. Why does he give us the simple alternatives of a "moral intention" and an enjoyable "journey into the realm of the supernatural"? And why does he dismiss so airily what he calls the "various efforts at interpretation," and specifically S. F. Gingerich's theory that the poem symbolizes the doctrine of necessitarianism? But I have dwelt on this matter only because it represents a point of view, about both *The Ancient Mariner* and poetry in general, which one frequently encounters. And certainly I do not wish to appear ungrateful to Griggs, to whom all admirers of Coleridge owe a great debt.

Nor do I wish to appear ungrateful to John Livingston Lowes,[2] whose views on this point will next engage us. Lowes seems to accept a very different premise from that of Griggs, for he says that "some interest deeply human, anchored in the familiar frame of things," was fundamental to Coleridge's plan. This "interest deeply human" turns out to be the idea of transgression and absolution, and of the train of consequence which persists even after absolution as what the Gloss terms "the penance of life." "You repent," says Lowes, "and a load is lifted from your soul. But you have not thereby escaped your deed. . . . It is the inexorable law of life."

This much, in itself, would seem to constitute a theme for the poem, a comment on human conduct and values. But Lowes now proceeds to reverse the direction of his argument—or if he does not do precisely that, he limits his reading of the function of the theme so that it is to be understood as having no relevance to actual life. The law of life appears in the poem, he says, merely to unify and "credibilize" the poem, because "we accept illusion only when in some fashion it bears the semblance of truth." He demands: "Has it still another end, to wit, edification?" He quickly adds that he is well aware of Coleridge's homiletical propensity, but he denies "edification" as being the poet's intention: "Nevertheless, to interpret the drift of 'The Ancient Mariner' as didactic in its intention is to stultify both Coleridge and one's self. For such an interpretation shatters the world of illusion which is the very essence of the poem."

The argument here is so vaguely put that it is difficult to understand precisely what the critic does mean. In one sense, it is quite true that the "intention" of the poet is not to "edify" the reader but to make a poem. In that sense, Lowes may be understood. But we must remember that in so far as the poem is truly the poet's, in so far as it ultimately expresses him, it involves his own view of the world, his own values. Therefore the poem will, for better or worse, have relevance, by implication at least, to the world outside the poem, and is not merely a device for creating an illusion. But this is precisely what Lowes proceeds to deny. The poem has, he says, no reference to reality: "And through the very completeness of their incorporation with the text of 'The Ancient Mariner,' the truths of experience which run in sequence through it have lost, so far as any inculcation of a moral through the poem is concerned, all didactic value." He supports this view by saying that "the 'moral' of the poem, *outside the poem,* will not hold water," because "consequence and cause, *in terms of the world of reality* are ridiculously incommensurable," and "punishment . . . palpably does not fit the crime."

What this amounts to seems to be this: (1) Coleridge introduces a theme into his poem merely as a structural device—he did not intend for it to be taken seriously. (2) We would not take it seriously anyway because it violates our moral sense—a man should not have to suffer so much just for shooting a bird.

These pronouncements lead me to a further statement concerning my purpose here: I shall try to establish that the statement which the poem does ultimately embody is thoroughly consistent with Coleridge's basic theological and philosophical views as given to us in sober prose, and that, without regard to the question of the degree of self-consciousness on the part of the poet at any given moment of composition, the theme is therefore "intended."[3] I shall also try to establish that the particular ground given by Lowes for the rejection of the relevance of the "moral" is based on a misreading of the poem—a reading which insists on a literal rather than a symbolic interpretation. In the end, I shall be attacking, in new terms, the position held by Griggs, for just as Griggs defines the poem as a journey into the supernatural for the sake of the journey, so Lowes defines it as an illusion for the sake of illusion. For them both, the poem is nothing more than a pleasant but meaningless dream.

The poem's "inconsequence is the dream's irrelevance," says the author of *The Road to Xanadu,* and thereby summarizes the view held by a large body of critics, who, either by way of praise or blame, have commented on the dreamlike quality of the poem. For such critics, as for Swinburne, Coleridge is one of the " 'footless birds of Paradise,' who have only wings to sustain them, and live their lives out in a perpetual flight through the clearest air of heaven." For these critics, *The Ancient Mariner* has no contact with reality. To support this view, that the poem is no more than a dream, they appeal to the report, in De Quincey's *Literary and Lake Reminiscences,* of Coleridge's remark that "before meeting a fable in which to embody his ideas, he had meditated a poem on delirium, confounding its own dream-scenery with external things, and connected with the imagery of high latitudes."

Let us examine the nature of this evidence. Coleridge presumably did connect his poem with dreams, just as he referred to his poem "The Raven," if we are to take Lamb's word, as a dream.[4] And we can well believe that a good deal of the *material* for the poem may have come from the poet's opium dreams. But the fact that Coleridge himself made this association between the poem and dreams does little to support the view that he thought of the poem as having no theme with a reference to reality. Coleridge's notion concerning dreams forbids that interpretation. "Dreams," he puts it in the *Table Talk,* "have nothing in them which is absurd and nonsensical." And again: "You will observe that even in dreams nothing is fancied without an antecedent *quasi* cause. It could not be otherwise." And in connection with speculations on the significance of dreams and visions: ". . . Who shall determine to what extent the reproductive imagination, unsophisticated by the will, and undistracted by intrusions from the sense, may or may not be concentred and sublimed into foresight and presentiment?"

There is no reason, however, for us to go to Coleridge's theory of dreams. De Quincey's sentence, in fact, betrays the critics who would use it to prove that Coleridge intended *The Ancient Mariner* to have no theme with a reference to reality, for the sentence says quite flatly that Coleridge's "ideas" preceded the "fable." In other words, at least according to De Quincey, there had been a general idea, a theme, in the poet's mind which finally found its appropriate medium of expression in the story of the "old navigator." And if the idea had an independent existence before an appropriate fable was hit upon, the idea must have had for the poet more than the structural importance assigned to it by Lowes. An idea can scarcely be said to function merely to unify and credibilize if nothing exists for it to unify and credibilize.

So much for one piece of evidence offered to support the view that the poem's "inconsequence is the dream's irrelevance." But there is another piece of evidence usually offered for this view—the passage from the *Table Talk* already quoted. I have pointed out how Griggs misreads one part of that famous passage. Let us look at it more closely. In it Coleridge refers to his poem as a work of "pure imagination," and it is this phrase which is most often offered to support the view held by Griggs, Lowes, and their school of readers. I am inclined to believe that they take the word imagination here at their own convenience and not in Coleridge's context and usage. They take it, as a matter of fact, in the casual and vulgar sense, as equivalent to meaninglessness or illusion; or if they don't take it in the casual and vulgar sense, they take it in terms of a poetic theory of illusion for illusion's sake which, as stated, denies significance to the word as fully as does the casual and vulgar sense.

Actually, a little reflection instructs us that the word was for Coleridge freighted with a burden of speculation and technical meaning. His theory of the imagination, upon which his whole art-philosophy hinges, "was primarily the vindication of a particular attitude to life and reality." And it would be strange if Coleridge, with his lifelong passion for accuracy of terminology and subtlety of distinction, had tossed away that sacred word which stood for the vindication of his most fundamental beliefs as irresponsibly as the merchant in the story of *The Arabian Nights* tosses away the "date shell."

To return to our argument, we must ask what is the burden of technical meaning with which Coleridge had freighted the word *imagination*? At the moment we shall not be concerned with a detailed exposition of Coleridge's theory, and certainly not with an account of the stages of its growth and clarification. We shall be, instead, concerned to see how Coleridge's concept would redeem works of pure imagination from the charge, amiable or otherwise, of being in themselves meaningless and nothing but refined and ingenious toys for an idle hour.

The key passage for this purpose is the famous one from the *Biographia Literaria,* but we shall group around it other passages drawn from various sources. Here is the key passage:

> The Imagination then I consider either as primary or secondary. The primary Imagination I hold to be the living power and prime agent of all human perception, and as a repetition in the finite mind of the eternal act of creation in the infinite I Am. The secondary Imagination I consider as an echo of the former, coexisting with the conscious will, yet still as identical with the primary in the kind of its agency, and differing only in degree and in the mode of its operation. It dissolves, diffuses, dissipates in order to recreate: or where this process is rendered impossible, yet still at all events it struggles to idealize and to unify.

It is the primary imagination which creates our world, for nothing of which we are aware is given to the passive mind. By it we know the world, but for Coleridge knowing is making, for, "To know is in its very essence a verb active." We know by creating, and one of the things we create is the Self, for a subject is that which "becomes a subject by the act of constructing itself objectively to itself; but which never is an object except for itself, and only so far as by the very same act it becomes a subject." It is irrelevant here whether we accept Coleridge's theory or regard all this, as did the vindictive Carlyle on his visit to the old sage, as a dreary, adenoidal mumbo-jumbo of "om-ject" and "sum-ject," a "mooning sing-song" of "theosophico-metaphysical monotony" in a "Kantean haze-world" populated by "dim-melting ghosts and shadows." The point, for present purposes, is that Coleridge attributes to imagination this fundamental significance.

We have been speaking only of what he calls primary imagination, the perception which produces our ordinary world of the senses. Even here we can observe that when "the imagination is conceived as recognizing the inherent interdependence of subject and object (or complementary aspects of a single reality), its dignity is immeasurably raised." But when we turn to his interpretation of the secondary imagination, that dignity is further enhanced. For here we leave creation at the unconscious and instinctive level and define it as coexisting with, and in terms of, the conscious will; here it operates as a function of that freedom which is the essential attribute of spirit.

Does Coleridge imply, however, that the poet in composing his poem acts according to a fully developed and objectively statable plan, that he has a blueprint of intention in such an absolute sense? To this question the answer is *no*. Several texts can be adduced on this point, for example, in "On Poesy": "There is in genius itself an unconscious activity; nay, that is the genius in the man of genius." But how can this be made to square with the key statement about the secondary imagination as "coexisting with the conscious will"?

Perhaps the answer could be found in an application of Coleridge's discussion of the Self, Will, and Motive. The common idea of will, he says, is the power to respond to a motive conceived of as acting upon it from the outside. But what is motive? Not a thing, but the thought of a thing. But all thoughts are not motives. Therefore motive is a determining thought. But what is a thought? A thing or an individual? Where does it begin or end? "Far more readily could we apply these questions to an ocean billow. . . . As by a billow we mean no more than a particular movement of the sea, so neither by a thought can we mean more than the mind thinking in some one direction. Consequently, a motive is neither more nor less than the act of an intelligent being determining itself . . ."[5] But will "is an abiding faculty or habit or fixed disposition to certain objects," and rather than motive originating will, it itself is originated in terms of that predisposition or permanent will.

It seems clear that the secondary imagination does operate as a function of that permanent will, and in terms of the basic concerns by which that will fulfills itself, but the particular plan or intention for a particular poem may be actually developed in the course of composition in terms of that "unconscious activity," which is the "genius in the man of genius," and may result from a long process of trial and error. "The organic form is innate," Coleridge writes in "Shakespeare, a Poet Generally"; "it shapes, as it develops, itself from within, and the fulness of its development is one and the same with the perfection of its outward form." Again, he says that the artist will not be successful unless he is impelled by a "mighty inward force," but he distinguishes this force, by implication at least, from plan or intention, for he goes on to say that the "obscure impulse" must "gradually become a bright and clear and burning Idea."[6] In other words, the plan and meaning of the work may be discovered in the process of creation. But it is to be remembered that this process is a function of the permanent will which constantly moves to fulfill itself in consciousness.[7]

It is possible that we have in Coleridge's theory of poetic creation a transposition into psychological terms of Plotinus' doctrine of creation:

> Consider the universe . . . are we, now, to imagine that its maker first thought it out in detail . . . and that having thus appointed every item beforehand, he then set about the execution? . . . All things must exist in something else; of that prior—since there is no obstacle, all being continuous within the realm of reality—there has suddenly appeared a sign, an image, whether given forth directly or through the ministry of soul or of some phase of soul, matters nothing for the moment: thus the later aggregate of existence springs from the divine world in greater beauty. There because There unmingled but mingled here. From the beginning to end all is gripped by the Forms of the Intellectual Realm: Matter itself is held by the Ideas of the elements and to those Ideas are added other Ideas and others again, so that it is hard to work down to crude Matter beneath all that sheathing of Idea. Indeed since Matter itself, in its degree, is an Idea—the lowest—all the universe is Idea and there is nothing that is not Idea as the archetype was. And all is made silently since nothing had part in the making but Being and Idea—a further reason why creation went on without toil. . . . Thus nothing stood in the way of the Idea . . . the creation is not hindered on its way even now; it stands firm in virtue of being All. To me, moreover, it seems that

if we ourselves were archetypes, Ideas, veritable Being, and the Idea with which we construct here were our veritable Essence, then our creative power too would toillessly effect its purpose: as man now stands, he does not produce in his work a true image of himself: become man, he has ceased to be All. . .[8]

However it works in poetic creation, the secondary imagination gives us more than poetry. The secondary imagination, as I. A. Richards puts it, "gives us not only poetry—in the limited sense in which literary critics concern themselves with it—but every aspect of the routine world in which it is invested with other values than those necessary for our bare continuance as living beings: all objects for which we can feel love, awe, admiration; every quality beyond the account of physics, chemistry, and the physiology of sense-perception, nutrition, reproduction, and locomotion; every awareness for which a civilized life is preferred by us to an uncivilized." But Richards, the child of the materialistic Bentham, with whom Coleridge, according to John Stuart Mill, had to divide the intellectual kingship of his age, is here casting into psychological terms what in Coleridge's thought appears often in theological and metaphysical terms;[9] and though Coleridge himself was constantly fascinated by what he called the "facts of mind" and defended the use of the word *psychological,* he was not content to leave the doctrine of the creativity of mind at the psychological level. There is a God, and the creativity of the human mind, both in terms of the primary and in terms of the secondary imagination, is an analogue of Divine creation and a proof that man is created in God's image. Furthermore, the world of Nature is to be read by the mind as a symbol of Divinity, a symbol characterized by the "translucence of the eternal through and in the temporal," which "always partakes of the reality which it renders intelligible; and while it enunciates the whole, abides itself as a living part in that unity of which it is representative." Reason, as opposed to the understanding, is, in Coleridge's system, the organ whereby man achieves the "intuition and spiritual consciousness of God," and the imagination operates to read Nature in the light of that consciousness, to read it as a symbol of God. It might be said that reason shows us God, and imagination shows us how Nature participates in God.

So, if we look at the phrase, a work of "pure imagination," in the light of Coleridge's theory of the imagination, we see that such a work would be one which not only, to borrow from Coleridge's portrait of the ideal poet, "brings the whole soul of man into activity, with the subordination of its faculties to each other according to their relative worth and dignity," and makes of the reader himself a "creative being" in the image of God, but also gives us a revelation, for "all truth is a species of Revelation." And so that phrase "pure imagination" as applied to *The Ancient Mariner* gives us little excuse to read the poem as an agreeable but scarcely meaningful effusion. Not only when Coleridge is theorizing does he insist upon "truth," upon "meaning." He often does so even in casual remarks upon particular poems or poets. For instance: "Not twenty lines of Scott's poetry will ever reach posterity; it has relation to nothing." Or: "How shall he fully enjoy Wordsworth, who has never meditated on the truths which Wordsworth has wedded to immortal verse?"

At this point I wish to anticipate a possible objection. It may be said that I am basing an argument for a certain interpretation of the poem on two passages, one from De Quincey and one from Henry Nelson Coleridge, which have only the status of hearsay testimony and are therefore without legal standing. It is true that we cannot know exactly what Coleridge said on either occasion, but it is not true that I am basing an argument upon these passages. I should be better pleased to leave them out of the discussion altogether and treat only of the poem itself and other material of indisputable authorship. Though I shall not base my own argument upon these passages, I am forced, however, to consider them in detail because they have been used now and again, for more than a hundred years, to support an interpretation of the poem which I consider fallacious. All I wish to put at stake here is this: If these passages of hearsay testimony are to be used at all, they will support my general contention.

I I

If *The Ancient Mariner* has a meaning, what is that meaning?

It is true that a poem may mean a number of different things. By this I do not intend to say that a poem means different things to different readers. This is, of course, true in one sense, but true, first, only in so far as the poet fails, as fail he must in some degree, in the exercise of his creative control, and second, in so far as each reader must, as a result of his own history and nature, bring to the poem a different mass of experience, strength of intellect, and intensity of feeling. In this second sense we may say that the reader does not interpret the poem but the poem interprets the reader. We may say that the poem is the light and not the thing seen by the light. The poem is the light by which the reader may view and review all the areas of experience with which he is acquainted.

I do not intend to say merely that a poem has different meanings for different readers, but that it may have different meanings for the same reader. For present purposes we may discriminate two senses in which this is true.

First, it is clear that a poem has different meanings when placed in different perspectives of interest. We may look at it as a document in the history of a language, in the history of literary forms, in the history of political ideas, or in a thousand other different perspectives, and in each of them discover a different kind of meaning. The significant factor in determining the difference among meanings in this sense is that the reader, from outside the poem, prescribes the particular perspective in which the poem is to be placed.

Second, a poem may have different meanings according to the different perspectives which are inherent in the poem itself and are not proposed from outside. But it may be objected that the difference between the *extrinsic* and *intrinsic* perspectives may not, in practice, really subsist. An illustration may clarify the distinction proposed. In the play *Julius Caesar* the topic of the transition from the Republic to the Empire appears. The same topic may be regarded in either the extrinsic or the intrinsic perspective. The decisive factor is this: If we regard it in the extrinsic perspective, we relate it to a body of facts and ideas many of which have not the slightest relation to the play. For instance, many of the facts pertinent to this perspective have been discovered and many of the ideas have been formulated since the date of composition of the play. If we regard the topic, however, in the intrinsic perspective, we relate the pattern which the topic receives in the play to other patterns in the play. For instance, the political theme (as we may call the topic as patterned in the play, as viewed in the intrinsic perspective) is related to the other themes, for instance, to the philosophical theme, which is here, I take it, primarily concerned with the question of free will and determinism. In other words, the various extrinsic perspectives disintegrate the play for their own special purposes; the various intrinsic perspectives merely define the themes which, it is assumed, the play unifies and makes mutually interpretive. Any substantial work will operate at more than one thematic level, and this is what makes it so difficult to define *the* theme of a profound creation; the root-idea will have many possible formulations and many of them will appear, or be suggested, in the work.

In *The Ancient Mariner,* I wish to distinguish two basic themes, both of them very rich and provocative, and I shall, in the course of my discussion, attempt to establish their interrelation.

One theme I shall call *primary,* the other *secondary.* I do not mean to imply that one is more important than the other. But the one which I shall call primary is more obviously presented to us, is, as it were, at the threshold of the poem. The primary theme may be defined as the issue of the fable (or of the situation or discourse if we are applying this kind of analysis to a poem which does not present a fable). The primary theme does not necessarily receive a full statement. In fact, in *The Ancient Mariner* it receives only a kind of coy and dramatically naïve understatement which serves merely as a clue—"He prayeth best, etc." But the theme thus hinted at is the outcome of the fable taken at its face value as a story of crime and punishment and reconciliation. I shall label the primary theme in this poem as the theme of sacramental vision, or the theme of the "One Life." The operation of this theme in the poem I shall presently explore.

As the primary theme may be taken as the issue of the fable, so the secondary theme may be taken as concerned with the context of values in which the fable is presented and which the fable may be found ultimately to embody, just as more obviously it embodies the primary theme. I shall label the secondary theme in this poem as the theme of the imagination. After having explored the operation of the theme of sacramental unity in the poem, I shall explore the operation of the theme of the imagination, and shall then attempt to define the significance of their final symbolic fusion in the poem.

Before proceeding to the investigation of these themes in the poem, I wish, however, to distinguish them from another type of theme which is sometimes emphasized in the discussion of this work. This type is the personal theme; it is concerned with those internal conflicts of the poet which may find expression in the poem. We have an example of this type of theme defined by Hugh I'Anson Fausset when he writes that the poem is "an involuntary but inevitable projection into imagery of his [Coleridge's] own inner discord. The Mariner's sin against Nature in shooting the Albatross imaged his own morbid divorce from the physical. . . ." Or we find more elaborately developed examples in Kenneth Burke's treatment, in *The Philosophy of Literary Form,* of the sexual and opium motives.

Without question there is an important relationship between such personal motivations and the poem finally created. The poem may very well represent, in one sense, an attempt to resolve such conflicts. The poem, read in this light, may give us a poignant chapter of biography, and as an image of human suffering and aspiration may move us deeply. But we may remember that the poem, even regarded in this light, is not an attempt merely to present the personal problem but an attempt to transcend the personal problem, to objectify and universalize it. And it is because of the attempt to objectify and universalize, that we can distinguish the themes inherent in the poem as such from the personal theme or themes which remain irrevocably tied to the man. The personal experience may provide motivations and materials, but in so far as it remains purely personal it does not concern us in the present context. Burke puts the matter very sensibly concerning his own studies of the personal themes of *The Ancient Mariner:*

> I am not saying that we need to know of Coleridge's marital troubles and sufferings from drug addiction in order to appreciate "The Ancient Mariner" and other poems wherein the same themes figure. I am saying that, in trying to understand the psychology of the poetic act, we may introduce such knowledge, where it is available, to give

us material necessary for discussing the full nature of this act. Many
of the things that a poet's work does for *him* are not things that the
same work does for us (i.e., there is a difference in act between the
poem as being-written and the poem as being-read).

For example, Coleridge's drug addiction may have given him the
psychological pattern underlying the crime of the Mariner and his
sufferings in the poem; we do not have to be drug addicts ourselves,
or to know that the poet was one, to respond to that psychological
pattern.

It is necessary to emphasize this distinction between the personal
and the objective themes, since the present poem, more than most,
has suffered from critics who have confused them in dealing with
it. Burke's sensible attitude has not been shared by, for instance,
Irving Babbitt or John Mackinnon Robertson, who says that Coleridge's work is "an abnormal product of an abnormal nature under
abnormal conditions." Robertson's attitude toward the poem, in so
far as his reasoning would equate special aspects of the poet's experience with the details of the poem itself, would seem to be the
equivalent of the fallacy of *argumentum ad hominem* in logic, and of
the fallacy in aesthetics of assuming identity of the material and the
thing created from the material, for it overlooks the universalizing
and normalizing process always inherent in the creative act.

To return to the matter of the objective themes: That more than
one theme should be involved, that the poem should operate on
more than one level, would be perfectly consistent with Coleridge's
emphasis on diversity within unity, and would be but one example
of the principle which Coleridge approves when he quotes the
remark "of the late Dr. Whitbread's that no man ever does anything from a single motive." The failure to realize this fact about
Coleridge's theory of composition has led a number of critics to try
to read *The Ancient Mariner* in terms of a two-dimensional allegory,
the sort of reading which gives us such absurdities as the point-to-
point equating of the Pilot with the Church and the Pilot's boy with
the clergy, or of the Hermit with the "idea of an enlightened
religion which is acquainted with the life of the spirit and aware of
the difficulties which beset it."

Coleridge's not infrequent remarks on allegory should have

warned the critics. The method of allegory—if by allegory we understand a fixed system of point-to-point equations—is foreign to his conception of the role of the imagination. "A poet's heart and intellect should be *combined*," he says, "intimately combined and unified with the great appearances of nature, and not merely held in solution and loose mixture with them, in the shape of formal similes." But a passage of greater significance on this point deals with the contrast between false and true religion:

> It is among the miseries of the present age that it recognizes no medium between literal and metaphorical. Faith is either to be buried in the dead letter, or its name and honors usurped by a counterfeit product of the mechanical understanding, which in the blindness of self-complacency confounds symbols with allegories. Now an allegory is but a translation of abstract notions into a picture-language, which is itself nothing but an abstraction from objects of sense. . . . On the other hand a symbol . . . is characterized by a translucence of the special in the individual, or of the general in the special, or of the universal in the general; above all by the translucence of the eternal through and in the temporal. It always partakes of the reality which it renders intelligible; and while it enunciates the whole, abides itself as a living part in that unity of which it is the representative.[10]

Allegory is, to adopt Coleridge's terms, the product of the understanding, symbol of the imagination.

Now, these statements by Coleridge raise the most profound and vexing aesthetic and, for that matter, epistemological questions, questions which I do not have the temerity to profess to settle. But we are committed to try to arrive at some interpretation, even provisional, of these statements, as applicable to his poetic practice. In trying to do this, we must, for the moment, accept Coleridge's terms as he uses them. For instance, it is not generally held that the "metaphorical" mode is mechanical—is a "translation of abstract notions into a picture-language." Rather, it is generally held that metaphor is the result of a vital and creative activity—that, as Susanne Langer puts it, "genuinely new ideas . . . have to break in upon the mind through some great and bewildering metaphor."

But Coleridge is using the word *metaphor* really to mean bad metaphor, i.e., a construction which has the form but not the function of metaphor. For the construction which exercises the proper function he reserves the word *symbol*.

Let us try to define some of the qualities which for him a symbol exhibits.

The symbol serves to *combine*—and he italicizes the word—the "poet's heart and intellect." A symbol involves an idea (or ideas) as part of its potential, but it also involves the special complex of feelings associated with that idea, the attitude toward that idea. The symbol affirms the unity of mind in the welter of experience; it is a device for making that welter of experience manageable for the mind—graspable. It represents a focus of being and is not a mere sign, a "picture-language."[11]

The symbol, then, is massive in the above sense. But it is massive in another sense, too. It has what psychoanalysts call condensation. It does not "stand for" a single idea, and a system of symbols is not to be taken as a mere translation of a discursive sequence. Rather, a symbol implies a body of ideas which may be said to be fused in it. This means that the symbol itself may be developed into a discursive sequence as we intellectually explore its potential. To state the matter in another way, a way perhaps more applicable to the problem of interpreting the present poem, a symbol may be the condensation of several themes and not a sign for one.

The symbol is focal and massive, but Coleridge introduces another quality into his description. He says that it is not mechanical (like allegory) and that it "partakes of the reality which it renders intelligible." The same thing is said here in two ways. What is said is that the symbol is not arbitrary—not a mere sign—but contains within itself the appeal which makes it serviceable as a symbol. Perhaps a distinction may help us here. A symbol may avoid being arbitrary in two ways: by necessity and by congruence.

By a symbol of necessity I mean the kind of symbol which is rooted in our universal natural experience. The wind in *The Ancient Mariner* is such a symbol. All phallic symbols, for example, are of this order. When Coleridge speaks of the poet's heart and intellect being intimately combined with the "great appearances of nature," he may be hinting at the idea of necessity. It is true, of course, that he takes these great appearances of nature to be revelatory of a supersensuous reality. For him Nature symbolizes God, though, as a matter of fact, there is also in Coleridge's thought the idea of a projective symbolism in Nature by which man realizes not God but himself. The problem of these two separate and perhaps contradictory ideas in Coleridge's thought on the symbolism of Nature need not concern us here. What does concern us here is that he apparently has some notion that the great appearances of Nature as symbols carry in themselves a constant, rich meaningfulness; in other words, he has some notion of the symbol of necessity. This would seem to be what is implied, too, by his statement that the symbol "partakes of the reality which it renders intelligible."

I would distinguish, tentatively, the symbol of congruence from the symbol of necessity by saying that the former does not come to us bearing within itself the reason for its appeal to us but is validated by the manipulation of the artist in a special context. For instance, Byzantium is a symbol in the poetry of William Butler Yeats, but without the special context which he creates and the special manipulation which he makes of Byzantium, it would never be a symbol for us. This does not mean that he could take any city—ancient Athens or modern Detroit—and make a symbol of it for the same purpose. Byzantium does offer him certain qualities which he can manipulate for the purpose in hand and fit into his special context: the naturalistic art of Athens, to take one aspect of his symbolic purpose, would not give him the forms he aspires to take when "once out of nature," nor would Detroit and the creations of Henry Ford afford the appropriate congruence. Byzantium offers him the congruence, but it is a congruence which he must discover for himself and validate for us.

In any case, the symbol, whether of necessity or of congruence, cannot be arbitrary—it has to participate in the unity of which it is representative. And this means that the symbol has a deeper relation to the total structure of meaning than its mechanical place in plot, situation, or discourse.

To summarize: The symbol is distinguished by being focal, massive, and not arbitrary. Allegory, in the special use of the term by Coleridge, is not focal or massive and is arbitrary. The distinction which Coleridge sets up may be a little clarified by comparison with the distinction stated more recently by C. S. Lewis, in *The Allegory of Love:*

> On the one hand you can start with an immaterial fact, such as the passions which you actually experience, and can then invent *visibilia* to express them. . . . This is allegory. . . . But there is another way of using the equivalence which is almost the opposite of allegory, and which I would call sacramentalism or symbolism. If our passions, being immaterial, can be copied by material inventions, then it is possible that our material world in its turn is the copy of an invisible world. . . . The attempt to read that something else through its sensible imitations, to see the archetype in the copy, is what I mean by symbolism or sacramentalism.

Coleridge and Lewis, as we learn from other discussions by Lewis, differ profoundly in their estimates of the artistic worth of allegory, but that is not relevant to the point here. The point here is that Lewis indicates, though he does not stress, the massive significance of symbol and the fact that it is not "invented" but discovered or read. And he goes on to make the interesting comment that the poetry of symbolism finds its greatest expression in the time of the Romantics. If this is true—and I think it is—it is strange that some critics should persist in reading the masterpiece of the Romantic poet who gives us most fully a theory of symbolism as though his poem were a simple, two-dimensional allegory. (I say "two-dimensional" here to avoid, if possible, a quibble about terms. If a reader should wish to maintain that allegory can be a system of focal and massive symbols, I would not quarrel with him. I would simply say that I am talking about "bad" allegory.)

What relevance does all this have for the reading of the poem? If we take the poem as a symbolic poem, we are not permitted to read it in the way which Coleridge called allegorical. We cannot, for instance, say that the Pilot equals the Church, or that the Hermit equals the "idea of an enlightened religion which is acquainted with the life of the spirit." The first of these readings is purely arbitrary. The second, though less arbitrary, simply ignores the massive quality of the episode involving the Hermit—considerations such as the Hermit's relation to nature, the function in returning the Mariner to human society, etc., and chiefly the tenor of the whole episode. This allegorical kind of reading makes the poem into a system of equivalents in a discursive sequence. But, as a matter of fact, we must read it as massive, as operating on more than one thematic level, as embodying a complex of feelings and ideas not to be differentiated except in so far as we discursively explore the poem itself. To take another example, we cannot blandly pass by such a crucial event as the shooting of the Albatross with merely a literal reading, the kind of reading which Lowes, among others, gives it—the kind of reading which makes the bird but a bird; the bird has a symbolic role in a symbolic pattern. Nor can we take the act of shooting the bird as merely wanton—or if wanton, in one sense, on the part of the Mariner, it is not to be taken as wanton on the part of the poet, and the nature of the act must participate in the truth of which it is a symbol.[12]

I I I

In the preceding section I have tried to indicate some reasons inherent in Coleridge's aesthetic theory for believing that *The Ancient Mariner* is to be read at more than one level, that it has more than one "meaning." In this section, I shall look at the poem in terms of what I have called the primary perspective or primary theme—the theme which is the issue of the fable.

The fable, in broadest and simplest terms, is a story of crime and punishment and repentance and reconciliation (I have refrained from using the word *sin,* because one school of interpretation would scarcely accept the full burden of the implications of the word). It is an example, to adopt for the moment Maud Bodkin's term, without necessarily adopting the full implications of her theory, of the archetypal story of Rebirth or the Night Journey. The Mariner shoots the bird; suffers various pains, the greatest of which is loneliness and spiritual anguish; upon recognizing the beauty of the foul sea snakes, experiences a gush of love for them and is able to pray; is returned miraculously to his home port, where he discovers the joy of human communion in God, and utters the moral "He prayeth best who loveth best, etc." We arrive at the notion of a universal charity, which even Babbitt admits to be "unexceptionable" in itself, the sense of the "One Life" in which all creation participates and which Coleridge perhaps derived from his neo-Platonic studies and which he had already celebrated, and was to celebrate, in other and more discursive poems.

Such an account as the above, however, leaves certain questions unanswered, and perhaps the best way to get at those questions is to consider the nature of the Mariner's transgression. Many critics, even Lowes, for example, dismiss the matter with such words as *wanton, trivial,* or *unthinking.* They are concerned with the act at the literal level only. In substance, they ask: Did the Mariner as a man have a good practical reason for killing the bird? This literal-mindedness leads to the view that there is a monstrous and illogical discrepancy between the crime and the punishment, a view shared by persons as diverse in critical principles as Lowes with his aestheticism and Babbitt with his neo-humanistic moralism. But we have to ask ourselves what is the symbolic reading of the act. In asking ourselves this question, we have to remember that the symbol, in Coleridge's view, is not arbitrary, but *must contain in itself, literally considered, the seeds of the logic of its extension—that is, it must participate in the unity of which it is representative.* And, more importantly, in asking ourselves this question, we must be prepared to answer quite candidly to ourselves what our own experience of poetry, and life, tells us about the nature of symbolic import; and we must be prepared to abide the risks of the answer. It would be nicer, in fact, if we could forget Coleridge's own theory and stick simply to our own innocent experience. But that, at this date, is scarcely possible.

This question—what is the nature of the Mariner's act?—has received one answer in the theory advanced by Gingerich that the Mariner does not act but is constantly acted upon, that "he is pursued by a dark and sinister fate" after having done the deed "impulsively and wantonly" and presumably under necessity. For Gingerich's theory is that the poem is a reflection of the doctrine of necessity which much occupied Coleridge's speculations during the years immediately leading up to the composition of *The Ancient Mariner:* "I am a complete necessitarian, and I understand the subject almost as well as Hartley himself, but I go farther than Hartley, and believe the corporeality of *thought,* namely that it is motion." So the first problem we must consider is to what extent Coleridge was actually a necessitarian, at least in the poem.

It would seem that Gingerich has vastly oversimplified the whole matter, by choosing texts on one side of the question only, and sometimes by ignoring the context of a text chosen. He ignores, for example, the fact that even during the period when Coleridge professed devotion to Hartley he was under the powerful influence of his mystical studies (in Plato, Plotinus, Bruno, Boehme, etc.), and that looking back, in the *Biographia,* on his period of error he could say: "The writings of these mystics acted in no slight degree to prevent my mind from being imprisoned within the outline of any single dogmatic system. They contributed to keep alive the *heart* in the *head;* gave me an indistinct, yet stirring and working presentiment, that all the products of the mere *reflective* faculty partook of Death." And in the sentence quoted by Gingerich in which Coleridge proclaims himself a complete necessitarian, the context has been neglected: Coleridge proceeds to make a joke of the thrashing which "a certain uncouth automaton," Dr. Boyer, had visited upon one of his charges, a joke which indicates an awareness that the acceptance of the doctrine of necessity and materialism doesn't take the pain out of the offended buttocks. But to be more serious, it is possible to reach into another letter of the same general period, a letter to John Thelwall, in December 1796, and find Coleridge saying flatly, "I am a Berkleyan." And this occurs in a long and passionate letter, really an essay, which is devoted to the attempt to convert Thelwall to Christianity; and in the course of the letter there is a fervid discussion of sin and repentance, concepts which Gingerich, extending certain texts from "Religious Musings" and other poems as a complete and tidy doctrine, denies to Coleridge. Gingerich even goes so far in his ardor to support his cause as to say that in "The Eolian Harp" (1795) Coleridge "conceives universal life as automatous," and proceeds to quote a few lines which in themselves might bear that interpretation. But he simply ignores the rest of the poem. The concluding stanza, which I shall present, follows immediately upon his chosen passage:

> But thy more serious eye a mild reproof
> Darts, O beloved Woman! nor such thoughts
> Dim and unhallowed dost thou not reject,
> And biddest me walk humbly with my God.

Meek daughter in the family of Christ!
Well hast thou said and holily disprais'd
These shapings of the unregenerate mind;
Bubbles that glitter as they rise and break
On vain Philosophy's aye-bubbling spring.
For never guiltless may I speak of him,
The Incomprehensible! save when with awe
I praise him, and with Faith that inly feels;
Who with his saving mercies healed me,
A sinful and most miserable man,
Wilder'd and dark, and gave me to possess
Peace, and this Cot, and thee, heart-honour'd Maid!

Here the conclusion of the poem repudiates as "shapings of the unregenerate mind" the very statements by which Gingerich would argue for a relatively systematic necessitarianism. And we may note further in this passage that we find quite positively stated the idea of sin, a thing which, according to Gingerich, is not in the necessitarian system or in Coleridge's thought. But we can go to a direct, non-poetic statement in his letters, made just after the completion of *The Ancient Mariner:* ". . . I believe most steadfastly in original sin; that from our mothers' wombs our understandings are darkened; and even where our understandings are in the light, that our organization is depraved and our volitions imperfect. . . ."[13]

The point I wish to make is this: We cannot argue that Coleridge was a systematic necessitarian and that therefore the killing of the Albatross is merely the result of the necessary pattern of things and is not to be taken as sinful *per se* or in extension. The fact seems to be that Coleridge was early moving toward his later views, that he was not, as he says, committed to any dogmatic system, and that, as Shawcross points out, the poems themselves "are sufficient to show us that his professed adherence to the necessitarian doctrines of his day was by no means the genuine conviction of his whole being." As early as 1794, he was, we may add, thinking of the mind as an active thing, the "shaping mind"; and if, in one sense, we grant the power of mind, we have broken the iron chain of necessity and the individual becomes a responsible agent and not the patient which Babbitt and Gingerich assume the Mariner to be. What

A. E. Powell, in *The Romantic Theory of Poetry,* says of Wordsworth, that he lived his philosophy long before he phrased it, is equally true of Coleridge, and in addition to his living into a transcendental philosophy through the practice and love of poetry, he lived into the guilt of opium long before the Mariner shot the Albatross: he knew what guilt is, and if he longed for a view of the universe which would absolve him of responsibility and would comfort him with the thought of participation in the universal salvation promised by Hartley and Priestley, there was still the obdurate fact of his own experience.

We have in these years, it seems, a tortured churning around of the various interpretations of the fact, and the necessitarian philosophy is only one possible philosophy in suspension in that agitated brew. And we even have some evidence that in the period just before the composition of *The Ancient Mariner*—before he had struck upon that fable to embody his idea—the poet was meditating a long poem on the theme of the origin of evil. Early in 1797, Lamb wrote him: "I have a dim recollection that, when in town, you were talking of the Origin of Evil as a most prolific subject for a long poem."[14] As a matter of fact, Coleridge never did "solve" his problem: he found peace simply by accepting the idea of Original Sin as a mystery.

In the *Table Talk* he says: "A Fall of some sort or other—the creation, as it were, of the nonabsolute—is the fundamental postulate of the moral history of Man. Without this hypothesis, Man is unintelligible; with it, every phenomenon is explicable. The mystery itself is too profound for human insight."

In his more elaborate and systematic treatment of the subject Coleridge adds another point which is of significance for the poem. Original Sin is not hereditary sin; it is original with the sinner and is of his will. There is no previous determination of the will, because the will exists outside the chain of cause and effect, which is of Nature and not of Spirit. And as for the time of this act of sin, he says that the "subject stands in no relation to time, can neither be in time nor out of time."[15] The bolt whizzes from the crossbow and the bird falls and all comment that the Mariner has no proper dramatic motive or is the child of necessity or is innocent of everything except a little wantonness is completely irrelevant, for we are confronting the mystery of the corruption of the will, the mystery which is the beginning of the "moral history of Man."

The fact that the act is unmotivated in any practical sense, that it appears merely perverse, has offended literalists and Aristotelians alike, and, for that matter, Wordsworth, who held that the Mariner had no "character" (and we may elaborate by saying that having no character, he could exhibit no motive) and did not act but was acted upon. The lack of motivation, the perversity, which flies in the face of the Aristotelian doctrine of *hamartia,* is exactly the significant thing about the Mariner's act. The act re-enacts the Fall, and the Fall has two qualities important here: it is a condition of will, as Coleridge says, "out of time," and it is the result of no single human motive.

One more comment, even though I have belabored this point. What is the nature of this sin, what is its content? Though the act which re-enacts the mystery of the Fall is appropriately without motive, the sin of the will must be the appropriate expression of the essence of the will. And we shall turn to a passage in *The Statesman's Manual.* Having just said that, in its "state of immanence or indwelling in reason and religion," the will appears indifferently as wisdom or love, Coleridge proceeds: "But in its utmost abstraction and consequent state of reprobation, the will becomes Satanic pride and rebellious self-idolatry in the relations of the spirit to itself, and remorseless despotism relatively to others . . . by the fearful resolve to find in itself alone the one absolute motive of action."[16] Then he sketches the portrait of the will in abstraction, concluding with the observation that "these are the marks, that have characterized the masters of mischief, the liberticides, the mighty hunters of mankind, from Nimrod to Bonaparte."

We may observe a peculiar phrase, the "mighty hunters of mankind, from Nimrod to Bonaparte," and in this blending of the hunting of beasts and the hunting of man—for Nimrod was himself both the mighty hunter and the founder of the first military state— we have an identification that takes us straight to the crime of the Mariner. The Mariner did not kill a man but a bird, and the literal-minded readers have echoed Mrs. Barbauld and Leslie Stephen: what a lot of pother about a bird. But they forget that this bird is more than a bird. I do not intend, however, to rest my case on the phrase just quoted from *The Statesman's Manual,* for the phrase itself I take to be but an echo from the poem at the time when the author was revising and reliving his favorite poem. Let us go to the poem itself to learn the significance of the bird.

In the poem itself the same identification occurs: the hunting of the bird becomes the hunting of man. When the bird first appears,

> As if it had been a Christian soul,
> We hailed it in God's name.

It ate food "it ne'er had eat," and every day "came to the mariner's hollo," and then later perched on the mast or shroud for "vespers nine." It partakes of the human food and pleasure and devotions. To make matters more explicit, Coleridge adds in the Gloss the statement that the bird was received with "hospitality" and adds, after the crime, that the Mariner "inhospitably killeth the pious bird of good omen." The crime is, symbolically, a murder, and a particularly heinous murder, for it involves the violation of hospitality and of gratitude (*pious* equals *faithful* and the bird is "of good omen") and of sanctity (the religious connotations of *pious,* etc.). This factor of betrayal in the crime is re-emphasized in Part V when one of the Spirits says that the bird had "loved the man" who killed it.

But why did the poet not give us a literal murder in the first place? By way of answering this question, we must remember that the crime, to maintain its symbolic reference to the Fall, must be motiveless. But the motiveless murder of a man would truly raise the issue of probability. Furthermore, the literal shock of such an act, especially if perverse and unmotivated, would be so great that it would distract from the symbolic significance. The poet's problem, then, was to provide an act which, on one hand, would not accent the issue of probability or shockingly distract from the symbolic significance, but which, on the other hand, would be adequately criminal to justify the consequences. And the necessary criminality is established, we have seen, in two ways: (1) by making the gravity of the act depend on the state of the will which prompts it, and (2) by symbolically defining the bird as a "Christian soul," as "pious," etc.

There is, however, a third way in which the criminality is established. We can get at it by considering the observation that if a man had been killed, we could not have the "lesson of humanitarianism," which some critics have taken to be the point of the poem. But we must remember that the humanitarianism itself is a manifestation of a deeper concern, a sacramental conception of the universe, for the bird is hailed "in God's name," both literally and symbolically, and in the end we have, therefore, in the crime against Nature a crime against God. If a man had been killed, the secular nature of the crime—a crime then against man—would have overshadowed the ultimate religious significance involved. The idea of the crime against God rather than man is further emphasized by the fact that the cross is removed from the Mariner's neck to make place for the dead bird, and here we get a symbolic transference from Christ to the Albatross, from the slain Son of God to the slain creature of God. And the death of the creature of God, like the death of the Son of God, will, in its own way, work for vision and salvation.

It may be instructive to see how another writer has treated these questions in presenting a similar story of the crime against a brute. I refer to Poe's "The Black Cat." In this story precisely the same issues appear, but where Coleridge leaves the issues in fluid suspension and leaves the nature of the crime defined only in the general symbolic tissue of the poem, Poe gives an elaborate analysis of the motivation and meaning of the act:

> And then came, as if to my final and irrevocable overthrow, the spirit of Perverseness. Of this spirit philosophy takes no account. Yet I am not more sure that my soul lives, than I am that perverseness is one of the primitive impulses of the human heart—one of the indivisible primary faculties, or sentiments, which give direction to the character of man. Who has not, a hundred times, found himself committing a vile or a stupid action, for no other reason than because he knows he should *not*? Have we not a perpetual inclination, in the teeth of our best judgment, to violate that which is *Law,* merely because we understand it to be such? This spirit of perverseness, I say, came to my final overthrow. It was this unfathomable longing of the soul *to vex itself*—to offer violence to its own nature—to do wrong for the

wrong's sake only—that urged me to continue and finally to consummate the injury I had inflicted upon the unoffending brute. One morning, in cold blood, I slipped a noose about its neck and hung it to the limb of a tree—hung it with the tears streaming from my eyes, and with the bitterest remorse at my heart—hung it *because* I knew that it had loved me, and *because* I felt it had given me no reason of offense—hung it *because* I knew that in so doing I was committing a sin—a deadly sin that would so jeopardize my immortal soul as to place it—if such a thing were possible—even beyond the reach of the infinite mercy of the Most Merciful and Most Terrible God.

All we have to do is to read Original Sin for Perverseness; and Poe himself carries us from the psychological treatment under Perverseness to the theological treatment under Sin.

There is another interesting parallel of treatment: the identification, in the crime, of the brute with the human. In the poem the identification is achieved symbolically, as we have seen. But in the story we must have more than this: the police are to arrest the hero and they will not arrest him for killing a cat, even if the killing is symbolically and spiritually equivalent to a murder. But Poe makes the symbolic transference, too. There are two cats, the first is hanged outright. The second cat, which takes the place of the first to plague the conscience of the hero and to frighten him with the white gallows mark on the breast, trips the hero on the stair to the cellar. The man then aims a blow with an axe at this cat, but his wife stays his hand. The blow intended for the brute is then delivered on the woman. The symbolic transference is made but is made in terms of psychological treatment.[17]

To return to the problems raised by the poem: We have not yet done with the matter of crime and punishment. There is the question of the fellow mariners, who suffer death. Here we encounter not infrequently the objection that they do not merit their fate. The tragic *hamartia,* we are told, is not adequate. The Gloss, however, flatly defines the nature of the crime of the fellow mariners: they have made themselves "accomplices." But apparently the Gloss needs a gloss. The fellow mariners have, in a kind of structural counterpoint (and such a counterpoint is, as we shall see, a characteristic of the poem), duplicated the Mariner's own crime of pride, of "will in abstraction." That is, they make their desire the measure of the act: they first condemn the act, when they think the bird had brought the favorable breeze; then applaud the act when the fog clears and the breeze springs back up, now saying that the bird had brought the fog; then in the dead calm, again condemn the act. Their crime has another aspect: they have violated the sacramental conception of the universe, by making man's convenience the measure of an act, by isolating him from Nature and the "One Life." This point is picked up later in Part IV:

> The many men, so beautiful!
> And they all dead did lie:
> And a thousand thousand slimy things
> Lived on; and so did I.

The stanza is important for the reading of the poem. The usual statement for the poem is that the Mariner moves from love of the sea snakes to a love of men (and in the broad sense this is true), but here we see that long before he blesses the snakes he is aware, in his guilt, of the beauty of the dead men, and protests against the fact that the slimy things should live while the beautiful men lie dead. In other words, we have here, even in his remorse, a repetition of the original crime against the sacramental view of the universe: man is still set over, in pride, against Nature. The Gloss points to the important thing here: "He despiseth the creatures of the calm."

There is one other aspect of the guilt of the fellow mariners worthy of notice. They judge the moral content of an act by its consequence; in other words, they would make good disciples of Bishop Paley, who, according to Coleridge, in *Aids to Reflection,* was no moralist because he would judge the morality of an act by consequence and not "contemplate the same in its original spiritual source," the state of the will. The will of the fellow mariners is corrupt. And this re-emphasizes the fact that what is at stake throughout is not the objective magnitude of the act performed— the bird is, literally, a trivial creature—but the spirit in which the act is performed, the condition of the will.

So much for the crime of the Mariner and the crime of his fellows. And we know the sequel, the regeneration of the Mariner.[18] In the end, he accepts the sacramental view of the universe, and his will is released from its state of "utmost abstraction" and gains the state of "immanence" in wisdom and love. We shall observe the stages whereby this process is consummated—this primary theme of the "One Life" is developed—as we investigate the secondary theme, the theme of the imagination.

I V

If in the poem one follows the obvious theme of the "One Life" as presented by the Mariner's crime, punishment, and reconciliation, one is struck by the fact that large areas of the poem seem to be irrelevant to this business: for instance, the special atmosphere of the poem, and certain images which, because of the insistence with which they are presented, seem to be endowed with a special import. Perhaps the best approach to the problem of the secondary theme is to consider the importance of light, or rather, of the different kinds of light.

There is a constant contrast between moonlight and sunlight, and the main events of the poem can be sorted out according to the kinds of light in which they occur. Coleridge underscores the importance of the distinction between the two kinds of light by introducing the poem by the motto from Burnet, added in the last revision of 1817 (in fact, the general significance of the motto has, so far as I know, never been explored). The motto ends: "But meanwhile we must earnestly seek after truth, maintaining measure, that we may distinguish things certain from those uncertain, day from night." The motto ends on the day-night contrast, and points to this contrast as a central fact of the poem. We may get some clue to the content of the distinction by remembering that in the poem the good events take place under the aegis of the moon, the bad events under that of the sun. This, it may be objected, reverses the order of Burnet, who obviously wishes to equate the "certain" or the good with day and the "uncertain" or bad with night. Coleridge's reversal is, I take it, quite deliberate—an ironical reversal which, in effect, says that the rational and conventional view expressed by Burnet seeks truth by the wrong light. In other words, Burnet becomes the spokesman of what we shall presently find Coleridge calling the "mere reflective faculty" which partakes of "Death."

Before we pursue this symbolism in the poem, let us look at moonlight in the larger context of Coleridge's work. Perhaps we shall find that it is serving, not only in *The Ancient Mariner* but elsewhere, the function defined by I. A. Richards: "When a writer has found a theme or image which fixes a point of relative stability in the drift of experience, it is not to be expected that he will avoid it. Such themes are a means of orientation."

As for the moonlight, more than one critic has noted its pervasive presence in Coleridge's work. Swinburne calls Coleridge's genius "moonstruck." And even Irving Babbitt goes so far as to say: "A special study might be made of the role of the moon in Chateaubriand and Coleridge—even if one is not prepared like Carlyle to dismiss Coleridge's philosophy as 'bottled moonshine.'" For the moon is everywhere, from the "Sonnet to the Autumnal Moon" of 1788 on through most of the poems, or many of them, trivial or great, sometimes with a specifically symbolic content, sometimes as the source of a transfiguring light which bathes the scene of *Christabel* or *The Ancient Mariner* or "The Wanderings of Cain" or "Dejection: An Ode" or "The Nightingale" of 1798 or the deep, romantic chasm of "Kubla Khan," and always she is the "Mother of wildly-working visions," as she is called in the sonnet mentioned, or the "Mother of wildly-working dreams," as she is called in "Songs of the Pixies" (1796). And in both the prose and verse, frequently when it is not the moon in this role it is some cloudy luminescence, the "luminous gloom of Plato," or "the slant beams of the sinking orb" of "This Lime-Tree Bower," or the glitter of the sunlit sea seen through half-closed eyelids in "The Eolian Harp."

We have, without question, a key image in Coleridge's moon, or Coleridge's half-light, and Coleridge himself has given us, in sober prose, a clue to its significance. Years later, looking back on the brief period of creative joy and the communion of minds which marked the years 1797 and 1798, he recalled the origin of the *Lyrical Ballads:*

During the first year that Mr. Wordsworth and I were neighbours, our conversation turned frequently on the two cardinal points of poetry, the power of exciting the sympathy of the reader by a faithful adherence to the truth of nature, and the power of giving the interest of novelty by the modifying colours of the imagination. The sudden charm, which accidents of light and shade, which moon-light or sun-set, diffused over a known and familiar landscape, appeared to represent the practicability of combining both. These are the poetry of nature.

Here the moonlight, or the dimming light of sunset, changes the familiar world to make it poetry; the moonlight equates with the "modifying colours of the imagination." To support this we have also the account given by Wordsworth in the *Prelude* of the night walk up Mount Snowden in the moonlight:

> When into air had partially dissolved
> That vision, given to spirits of the night
> And three chance human wanderers, in calm thought
> Reflected, it appeared to me the type
> Of a majestic intellect, its acts
> And its possessions, what it has and craves,
> What in itself it is, and would become.
> There I beheld the emblem of a mind
> That feeds upon infinity, that broods
> Over the dark abyss, intent to hear
> Its voices issuing forth to silent light
> In one continuous stream; a mind sustained
> By recognitions of transcendent power,
> In sense conducting to ideal form,
> In soul of more than mortal privilege.
> One function, above all, of such a mind
> Had Nature shadowed there, by putting forth,
> 'Mid circumstances awful and sublime,
> That mutual domination which she loves
> To exert upon the face of outward things,
> So moulded, joined, abstracted, so endowed
> With interchangeable supremacy,
> That men, least sensitive, see, hear, perceive,
> And cannot choose but feel. . . .

But to return to Coleridge's own testimony, not rarely we can find the moon appearing in the prose. For instance, we may glance at this passage in *Anima Poetiae* on symbolism: "In looking at objects of Nature while I am thinking, as at yonder moon dim-glimmering through the dewy windowpane, I seem rather to be seeking, as it were *asking* for, a symbolic language for something within me that always and forever exists, than observing anything new." How easily the moon, dim-glimmering, enters the conversation when his mind turns to the imaginative relation of man and Nature.

Let us see how this symbol functions in the poem, in connection with the theme of the imagination. We must remember, however, that here by the imagination we mean the imagination in its value-creating capacity, what Coleridge was later to call the secondary imagination.

We shall not go far into the poem before we realize that the light symbolism is not the only symbolism operating upon us. For instance, we shall encounter winds and storms at various important moments. Our problem, then, is not only to define particular symbolisms, but to establish the relationships among them—to establish the general import.

At the threshold of the poem, however, another consideration intrudes itself upon us. Certain images are first presented to us, and sometimes may appear later, at what seems to be merely a natural level. This question, then, will arise in the minds of certain readers: How far are we to interpret, as we look back at the poem, such apparently natural manifestations which at other times, at the great key moments of the poem, are obviously freighted with significance? In presenting the poem here, I shall undertake the full rather than the restricted interpretation. My reasoning is this: Once the import of an image is established for our minds, that image cannot in its workings upon us elsewhere in the poem be disencumbered, whether or not we are consciously defining it. The criterion for such full rather than restricted interpretation is consistency with the central symbolic import and, in so far as it is possible to establish the fact, with the poet's basic views as drawn from external sources. We can derive no criterion from the poet's conscious intention *at any given moment in the poem,* and this question is, in this narrow sense, irrelevant. (In its broader sense, it will be discussed later in this essay.) In any case, though here I shall undertake a full interpretation, if a reader should wish to interpret the poem in a restricted sense, I would not feel that my basic thesis was impaired. There is always bound to be some margin for debate in such matters.

The problem of the fullness of interpretation presents itself to us at the very outset of the poem. The voyage begins merrily under the aegis of the sun. Is our sun here merely the natural sun, or is it also the symbolic sun? But the question is more acute a stanza or two on, when the storm strikes and drives the ship south, the behavior of the ship being described in the powerfully developed image of flight from a pursuing enemy. Is this a merely natural storm, or a symbolic one as well? Let us linger on this question.

Later in the poem we shall find wind and storm appearing as the symbol of vitality and creative force. A storm, we recall, strikes as a consequence of the Mariner's redemption and brings him the life-giving rain. Is the first storm, then, to be taken with the same force, even though it is presented here in the imagery of a terrible enemy? I do not find the import here inconsistent with that of the storm at the Mariner's redemption. The storm at the redemption, though a "good" storm, is also presented in imagery of terror and power. The ambivalence of the storm is an important feature which is extended and developed later in the poem. But for the present, merely glancing forward to that final interpretation of the wind and storm, we can say that the first storm is an "enemy" because to the man living in the world of comfortable familiarity, complacent in himself and under the aegis of the sun, the creative urge, the great vital upheaval, this "bottomwind,"[19] is inimical.

When the storm has driven the ship south, we reach the second stage of the Mariner's adventure, the land of ice. This land is both beautiful and terrible, as is proper for the spot where the acquaintance with the imagination is to be made. Like the storm which drives the ship south, it shakes man from his routine of life. Man finds the land uncomfortable; he loses his complacency when he confronts the loneliness:

> Nor shapes of men nor beasts we ken—
> The ice was all between.

But out of this awe-inspiring manifestation of Nature, which seems at first to be indifferent to man, comes the first response to man—the Albatross—to receive the glad "natural" recognition of the mariners.

I have already indicated how the bird-man fusion is set up, how the bird is hailed in God's name, etc., how, in other words, the theme of the "One Life" and the sacramental vision is presented. Now, as a moment of great significance in the poem, I wish to indicate how the primary theme of the sacramental vision is for the first time assimilated to the secondary theme of the imagination. The Albatross, the sacramental bird, is also, as it were, a moon-bird. For here, with the bird, the moon first enters the poem, and the two are intimately associated:

> In mist or cloud, on mast or shroud,
> It perched for vespers nine;
> Whiles all the night, through fog-smoke white,
> Glimmered the white Moon-shine.

The sun is kept entirely out of the matter. The lighting is always indirect, for even in the day we have only "mist or cloud"—the luminous haze, the symbolic equivalent of moonlight. Not only is the moon associated with the bird, but the wind also. Upon the bird's advent a "good south wind sprung up behind." And so we have the creative wind, the friendly bird, the moonlight of imagination, all together in one symbolic cluster.

As soon as the cluster is established, the crime, with shocking suddenness, is announced. We have seen how the crime is to be read at the level of the primary theme. At the level of the secondary theme it is, of course, a crime against the imagination. Here, in the crime, the two themes are fused. (As a sidelight on this fact, we may recall that in "Dejection: An Ode," Coleridge gives us the same fusion of the moral and the aesthetic. In bewailing his own loss of creative power he hints, at the same time, at a moral taint. The "Pure of heart" do not lose the imaginative power, "this strong music in the soul.")

With the announcement of the crime, comes one of the most effective turns in the poem. As the Wedding Guest recoils from his glittering eye, the Mariner announces:

> . . . With my cross-bow
> I shot the Albatross.

And then the next line of the poem:

> The Sun now rose upon the right.

The crime, as it were, brings the sun. Ostensibly, the line simply describes a change in the ship's direction, but it suddenly, with dramatic violence, supplants moon with sun in association with the unexpected revelation of the crime, and with the fact, indicates not only the change of the direction of the ship but the change of the direction of the Mariner's life. The same device is repeated with the second murder of the Albatross—the acceptance of the crime by the fellow mariners. They first condemn the Mariner for having killed the bird "that made the breeze to blow," but immediately upon the rising of the sun, they accept the crime:

> Nor dim nor red, like God's own head,
> The glorious Sun uprist:
> Then all averred, I had killed the bird
> That brought the fog and mist.

As has been pointed out earlier, the mariners act in the arrogance of their own convenience. So even their condemnation of the crime has been based on error: they have not understood the nature of the breeze they think the bird had brought. But here we must observe a peculiar and cunningly contrived circumstance: the mariners do not accept the crime until the sun rises, and rises gloriously "like God's own head." The sun is, symbolically speaking, the cause of their acceptance of the crime—they read God as justifying the act on the ground of practical consequence, just as, shall we say, Bishop Paley would have done. They justify the crime because the bird had, they say, brought the fog and mist. In other words, they repudiate the luminous haze, the other light, and consider it an evil, though we know that the fog and mist are associated with the moon in the wind-bird-moon cluster at the end of Part I.

At this point where the sun has been introduced into the poem, it is time to ask how we shall regard it. It is the light which shows the familiar as familiar, it is the light of practical convenience, it is the light in which pride preens itself, it is, to adopt Coleridge's later terminology, the light of the "understanding," it is the light of that "mere reflective faculty" that "partook of Death." And within a few lines, its acceptance by the mariners has taken them to the sea of death, wherein the sun itself, which had risen so promisingly and so gloriously like "God's own head," is suddenly the "bloody sun," the sun of death—as though we had implied here a fable of the Enlightenment and the Age of Reason, whose fair promises had wound up in the bloodbath of the end of the century.

In the poem, however, at this point where the agony begins, we find an instructive stanza:

> And some in dreams assurèd were
> Of the Spirit that plagued us so;
> Nine fathom deep he had followed us
> From the land of mist and snow.

This Polar Spirit, as the Gloss will call him later, is of the land of mist and snow, which we have found to be adjuncts of the wind-bird-moon cluster; hence he, too, belongs to the same group and partakes of its significance. Two facts stand out about the present "carrier" of the imagination: his presence is known by dreams and his errand is one of vengeance. The first fact tells us that the imagination, though denied or unrecognized, still operates with dire intimations at a level below the "understanding"; "understanding" cannot exorcise it and its subconscious work goes on. The second fact tells us that, if violated and despised, the faculty which should naturally be a blessing to man will in its perverted form exact a terrible vengeance.

The fellow mariners do not, of course, comprehend the nature of the Spirit whose presence has been revealed to them in dreams. They have learned, by this time, that a crime has been committed and that vengeance is imminent. But they do not know the nature of the crime or their own share in the guilt. So in their ignorance they hang the Albatross about the Mariner's neck. Thus the second major stage of the poem concludes.

Part III consists of two scenes, one of the sun, one of the moon, in even balance. The first is the appearance of the specter-bark, which is in close association with the sun. There is the elaborate description of the sun, but in addition there is the constant repetition of the word, five times within twelve lines:

1. Rested the broad bright Sun
2. Betwixt us and the Sun
3. And straight the Sun was flecked with bars
4. Are those *her* sails that glance in the Sun
5. Are those *her* ribs through which the Sun[20]

The whole passage, by means of the iteration, is devoted to the emotional equating of the sun and the death-bark.[21]

Then the "Sun's rim dips," and we have the full and beautiful description of the rising of the "star-dogged Moon." But the moon does not bring relief; instead "At the rising of the Moon," as specified by the placement of the Gloss,

> Fear at my heart, as at a cup,
> My life-blood seemed to sip!

And immediately after, in the moonlight, the fellow mariners curse the Mariner with a look, and, one after another, fall down dead. The fact of these unhappy events under the aegis of the supposedly beneficent moon raises a question: Does this violate the symbolism of the moon? I do not feel that the poem is inconsistent here. First, if we accept the interpretation that the Polar Spirit belongs to the imagination cluster and yet exacts vengeance, then the fact that horror comes in the moonlight here is simply an extension of the same principle: violated and despised, the imagination yet persists and exacts vengeance. Second, we find a substantial piece of evidence supporting this view, in the parallel scene in Part VI, another scene of the curse by the eye in moonlight:

> All fixed on me their stony eyes,
> That in the Moon did glitter.

But this parallelism gives us a repetition with a difference. This event occurs after the Mariner has had his change of heart, and so now when the curse by the eye is placed upon him in moonlight, it does not avail; in moonlight now "this spell was snapt," and the creative wind rose again to breathe on the Mariner. In other words, the passage in Part VI interprets by contrast that in Part III. The moonlight, when the heart is unregenerate, shows horror; when the heart has changed, it shows joy.

In Part IV the penance of loneliness and horror, both associated with the crime against the imagination (loneliness by denial of the imagination, horror by the perversion of it), is aggravated with the despising of the creatures of the calm and with the curse in the eyes of the dead. Then, suddenly, we have the second moonrise:

> The moving Moon went up the sky,
> And no where did abide:
> Softly she was going up,
> And a star or two beside—

The Gloss here tells us all we need to know, defining the Mariner's relation to the Moon:

> In his loneliness and fixedness he yearneth towards the journeying Moon, and the stars that still sojourn, yet still move onward; and every where the blue sky belongs to them, and is their appointed rest, and their native country and their own natural homes, which they enter unannounced, as lords that are certainly expected and yet there is a silent joy at their arrival.

Life, order, universal communion and process, joy—all these things from which the Mariner is alienated are involved here in the description of the moon and stars. And immediately the description of the water snakes picks up and extends the sense of the stars. The snakes become creatures of light to give us another symbolic cluster:

> They moved in tracks of shining white,
> And when they reared, the elfish light
> Fell off in hoary flakes.

For the Gloss says here: "By the light of the Moon he beholdeth God's creatures of the great calm." And in the light of the moon we have the stages of the redeeming process: first, the recognition of happiness and beauty; second, love; third, the blessing of the creatures; fourth, freedom from the spell. The sequence is important, and we shall return to it. In it the theme of the sacramental vision and the theme of imagination are fused.

Part V, in carrying forward the next period of development consequent upon the Mariner's restored imaginative view of the world, continues, in new combinations, the sun-moon contrast, but here we move toward it by the refreshing rain and then the storm. In the Mariner's dream, which comes in the first heaven-sent sleep, we have the presentiment of the rain and storm, a dream which corresponds to the dream of the Polar Spirit which had hinted to the fellow mariners the nature of the crime: in both cases, at this instinctive, subrational level, the truth is darkly shadowed forth before it is realized in the waking world. In the Mariner's dream, before the real rain comes, the "silly buckets"[22] are filled with dew. Upon waking and drinking the rain, the Mariner, in his light and blessed condition, hears a roaring wind; then, as the Gloss puts it, there are "strange sights and commotions in the sky and the elements," presided over by the moon, which hangs at the edge of the black cloud. The moon of imagination and the storm of creative vitality here join triumphantly to celebrate the Mariner's salvation.

But here let us pause to observe a peculiar fact. The wind does not reach the ship, and the Polar Spirit, who had originally set forth on an errand of vengeance, provides the power of locomotion for the ship. Though he has been functioning as the sinister aspect of the imagination, he, too, is now drawn, in "obedience to the angelic troop," into the new beneficent activity. Not that he is to lose entirely his sinister aspect; we shall see that his vengeance persists, for the Mariner, in his role as the *poète maudit,* will show that the imagination is a curse as well as a blessing. But for the moment, though grudgingly, the Spirit joins the forces of salvation.

What now, we may ask, is the logic of this situation? If the wind were to drive the ship, the action would not be adapted to show the role of the Polar Spirit. Furthermore, if the wind were to drive the ship, the fusion of the natural and the supernatural in the terrible and festal activity below and above the sea would not be exhibited. And this is important, for here we have another moment of fusion of the primary and secondary themes: wind, moon, and Polar Spirit belong to the secondary theme of the imagination, but the "angelic troop," in obedience to which the Spirit acts, belongs properly to the primary theme, the theme of the "One Life" and the sacramental vision.

I have said that the angelic troop here serves to introduce the primary theme into the episode. Certainly, in the reanimation of the bodies of the fellow mariners, there is implicit the idea of regeneration and resurrection, and in this way the participation in the general meaning of the episode becomes clear. But the behavior of the reinspirited bodies, taken in itself, offers a difficulty. Taken at the natural level, the manipulating of the sails and ropes serves no purpose. Taken at the symbolic level, this activity is activity without content, a "lag" in the poem, a "meaningless marvel." And the spirits in the bodies give us an added difficulty. When day comes, they desert the bodies and as sweet sounds dart to the sun. The sun, under whose aegis the bad events of the poem occur, here appears in a "good" association.

Our problem of interpreting these "good" associations is parallel to that of dealing with the moon when it appears in "bad" association. I shall treat it analogously, by looking at it in the special context and not in isolation. This redemption of the sun—for we may call it that—comes as part of the general rejoicing when the proper order has been re-established in the universe. The "understanding," shall we say, no longer exists in abstraction, no longer partakes of death, but has its proper role in the texture of things and partakes of the general blessedness. It is, for the moment, "spiritualized." I say for the moment, for at noon, the hour when the sun is in its highest power and is most likely to assert itself in "abstraction," the sun resumes briefly its inimical role and prevents the happy forward motion of the ship:

> The Sun, right up above the mast,
> Had fixed her to the ocean.

As the Gloss explains here, this event takes place when the Polar Spirit, after having obediently conveyed the ship to the Line, still "requireth vengeance." In other words, the inimical force of the sun is felt at the moment when the power of imagination seems to be turning away vengefully from the Mariner. But this crisis is passed, for after all, the Mariner has been redeemed, and the ship plunges forward again with such suddenness that the Mariner is thrown into a "swound."

In his swound the Mariner receives a fuller revelation of his situation and of the nature of the forces operating about him. He learns these things, it is important to notice, in the dream—just as the fellow mariners had received the first intimation of the presence of the Polar Spirit through dreams. And the significance of this fact is the same: the dream is not at the level of the "understanding," but is the appropriate mode by which the special kind of knowledge of the imagination should be revealed.

It is in this dream that the Mariner for the first time receives an explicit statement of the relation of the Albatross and the Polar Spirit. Meanwhile the Gloss tells us that the Polar Spirit, having been assured that the Mariner will continue to do penance (as the Mariner himself learns from the Second Voice), returns southward. But the ship, which had been propelled by the Polar Spirit, continues on its way by another means, as the Second Voice describes. Do we have here an "unmeaning marvel," or is there some content to this business? An interpretation at this point probably demands more forcing than at any other, but there is, perhaps, a possible one consistent with the rest of the poem. The angelic troop and the Polar Spirit (the first associated with the primary theme, the second with the secondary theme) are both "supernatural"—as the Gloss somewhat superfluously remarks. But the Second Voice gives the Mariner, and us, a scientific, i.e., "natural," explanation of the progress of the ship. So we have here the supernatural powers (of the two orders) acting by the agency of the natural mechanism of the world—the supernatural and the natural conspiring together on the Mariner's behalf after his redemption.

There is, however, an additional item to be considered in the vision, the description of the moon and the ocean given by the Second Voice:

> 'Still as a slave before his lord,
> The ocean hath no blast;

His great bright eye most silently
Up to the Moon is cast—

If he may know which way to go;
For she guides him smooth or grim.
See, brother, see! how graciously
She looketh down on him.'

This is a fairly obvious definition of the role of the moon—the adored, the guiding, the presiding power.

After this definition in dream of the role of the moon, the Mariner wakes to find it shining and the dead men standing about with their moonstruck eyes fixing a curse upon him. This scene recalls two previous scenes of the poem. First, it recalls the other scene of the curse by the eye in moonlight before the redemption of the Mariner. Second, it recalls the main redemption scene when the Mariner blesses the snakes in the moonlight. With the first we have here a parallelism developing a contrast, and with the second a parallelism developing a repetition. For in this, we have a second redemption scene—the relief from the curse, which, the Gloss says, is "finally expiated." But as the spell is snapped, there is a moment in which the Mariner is fearfully bemused like one who knows

. . . a frightful fiend
Doth close behind him tread.

This last hint of the curse disappears with the rising of the strange breeze. It is not a "natural" breeze, for it does not ripple the water—it blows only upon the Mariner. The ship moves, but not by the breeze (presumably by the angelic troop, as before). It is the creative wind again, blowing only upon the Mariner, fanning his cheek, but also mingling "strangely" with his "fears"—a hint of the ambiguous power of the imagination. The rising of the breeze now, after this second redemption scene, corresponds to the rising of the great storm after the first redemption scene—a storm which, we must remember, was both terrible and festal in its aspect. The rising of the breeze now also recalls the first storm which drove the ship south in Part I—a parallelism by contrast, for the first storm was all "enemy" while the present breeze, though it mingles strangely with the Mariner's fears, is a sweet breeze.

Suddenly, under the sweet breeze, the Mariner descries the home port. Appropriately, it is drenched in the magnificent moonlight. But now we are to have another kind of light, too. By every corpse on deck stands a seraph-man with a body all of light as a signal to the land. So here, in the two kinds of light by which the return is accomplished, the men of light (associated with the primary theme) and the moon (associated with the secondary theme), we have a final fusion of the imagination and the sacramental vision.[23] We may, as it were, take them to be aspects of the same reality.

This fusion, with the beginning of Part VII, is restated by means of the figure of the Hermit, who is both priest of God and priest of Nature. We may look at the matter in this way: The theme of the "One Life," of the sacramental vision, is essentially religious—it presents us with the world, as the crew of the ship are presented with the Albatross, in "God's name." As we have seen, the poem is shot through with religious associations. On the other hand, the theme of imagination is essentially aesthetic—it presents us with the "great forms" of nature, but those forms as actively seized upon by the human mind and loved *not merely as vehicles for transcendental meaning but in themselves as participating in the reality which they "render intelligible."* The theme is essentially aesthetic, but it is also "natural" in the sense just defined as contrasted with the sense in which nature is regarded as the neutral material worked on by the mere "understanding." The Hermit, who kneels in the woods, embodies both views, both themes.

The Hermit, however, has another aspect. He is also the priest of Society, for it is by the Hermit, who urges the Pilot on despite his fears, that the Mariner is received back into the world of men. This rejoining of the world of men is not, we observe, accomplished simply by the welcoming committee. There is the terrific sound which sinks the ship and flings the stunned Mariner into the Pilot's boat. In the logic of the symbolic structure this would be, I presume, a repetition of the wind or storm motif: the creative storm has a part in re-establishing the Mariner's relation to other men.[24] Even if the destruction of the ship is regarded, as some readers regard it, as a final act of the Polar Spirit, to show, as it were, what he could do if he had a mind to, the symbolic import is not altered, for the Spirit belongs to the cluster of imagination which has the terrifying and cataclysmic as well as benign aspect. As a matter of fact, since the Gloss has earlier dismissed the Polar Spirit at the end of Part V, saying that he "returneth southward," it seems more reasonable to me to interpret the destruction of the ship as the work of the angelic troop, whose capacity to work marvels has already been amply demonstrated. And this reading gives us a fuller symbolic burden, too, and is consistent with the final fusion of themes which we observe in this general episode. At the level of the primary theme, the angelic troop wipe out the crime (i.e., the "criminal" ship and the dead bodies); at the level of the secondary theme, they do so by means of the "storm," which belongs to the symbolic cluster of the imagination.

V

By this reading of the poem the central and crucial fact is the fusion of the primary and secondary themes. And this means that the poem suddenly takes its place as a document of the very central and crucial issue of the period: the problem of truth and poetry. I do not mean to imply that this problem was first recognized by the Romantics. It had had a statement at least as early as the Platonic dialogue *Ion.* But with the English Romantics it was not only a constant topic for criticism, but was, directly or indirectly, an obsessive theme for poetry itself.

We have something of a parallel to this effort at making a marriage of poetry with truth, in the effort of the eighteenth century to establish a "holy alliance between science and religion," an effort which resulted in such works as Hartley's *Observations on Man* and Priestley's *Disquisitions,* which attempt to give the authority of science to the religious impulse. We can see, in fact, in Coleridge's early necessitarianism a continuation of this eighteenth-century effort. But the problem of poetry in the eighteenth century had been different; the poets then had felt, by and large, that poetry was at home in the world and in society and had its proper and well-defined function. The Romantic poets, on the other hand, felt that they had to justify their existence. However great the claims they made for poetry and however sweeping their gestures and rolling their periods, they made those claims because the need for justification was becoming acute. The claim they made was that poetry gives truth; or if they were as subtle as Coleridge, they sought to establish an intimate and essential connection between truth and poetry on psychological as well as metaphysical grounds. For the Romantics, as A. E. Powell says, poetry was a "form of knowledge, a form of action, the highest form of either; so high that it reached their object without their laboured process." As Keats said: "What the Imagination seizes as Beauty must be Truth." Over and over again, Blake affirmed that "Imagination is Eternity."

The problem of establishing a holy alliance between poetry and truth was, however, terribly complicated by the fact that truth itself was not one and simple. There were two truths, and they themselves might very well be in deadly competition: the truth of religion and the truth of science. The poets faced this situation in their various ways in a time when one body of opinion held that with the development of science, serious minds will turn from poetry, whose harmony "is language on the rack of Procrustes," whose sentiment "is canting egotism in the mask of refined feeling," whose passion "is the commotion of a weak and selfish mind," whose pathos "is the whining of an unmanly spirit," and whose sublimity "is the inflation of an empty head."

We know how Shelley responded to these words of Peacock with his *Defence of Poetry,* wherein he asserts that poetry "is at once the centre and circumference of knowledge; it is that which comprehends all science, and that to which all science must be referred." We know how Wordsworth had almost anticipated these very words. And we know that, though Coleridge may have had a deep-rooted instinctive distrust of science, he did aim at a glorious synthesis in which all breaches would be healed and all malice reconciled. And though the distrust of science may have existed, Coleridge could at the same time find in poetry itself a field for the study of the "facts of mind" and could, as in some of his criticism of Shakespeare, shift the emphasis from aesthetic to scientific (i.e., psychological) interest. But the main problem of reconciliation for Coleridge was that between poetry and religion, or morality, for since those were his twin passions, it was necessary for him to develop some vital connection between them if he was to be happy. His solution was, of course, one of detail and not part of the great synthesis of which he dreamed. For the age presented complications which could not, apparently, be resolved into such a system. "The fact is that the problem was," as Olwen Ward Campbell says, "gigantic, and the men were not more than great. And they seem to have suffered all of them from a kind of divided purpose and lack of conviction, which undermined their strength; part and parcel of the duality of the age. . . ."

The precarious solution which Coleridge attained was, of course, one aspect of his doctrine of the creative unity of the mind, which appears and reappears in his work and which is his great central insight and great contribution to modern thought. The opposition between thought and feeling he wished to abolish. As early as 1801, he could write to Thomas Poole: "My opinion is thus: that deep thinking is attainable only by a man of deep feeling, and that all truth is a species of revelation." And Coleridge was writing in that strain long before the composition of *The Ancient Mariner,* for instance, in a letter to John Thelwall in 1796: "I feel strongly and I think strongly, but I seldom feel without thinking or think without feeling." And he proceeds to connect this proposition with his own poetic style: "My philosophical opinions are blended with or deduced from my feelings, and this, I think, peculiarises my style of writing." He is simply developing this early view when he says, in connection with Shakespeare, that the poet is "a genial understanding directing self-consciously a power and an implicit wisdom deeper even than our consciousness." And this view of the process of composition was also Wordsworth's view as we have it in the Preface: ". . . the poems in these volumes will be found distinguished at least by one mark of difference, that each of them has a worthy *purpose.* Not that I always began to write with a distinct purpose formally conceived; but habits of meditation have, I trust, so prompted and regulated my feelings, that my descriptions of such objects as strongly excite those feelings, will be found to carry along with them a *purpose.* "

In all the quotations given above we find the idea that the truth is implicit *in the poetic act as such, that the moral concern and the aesthetic concern are aspects of the same activity, the creative activity, and that this activity is expressive of the whole mind.* Now, my argument is that *The Ancient Mariner* is, first, written *out of* this general belief, and second, written *about* this general belief.

As a poem written out of this belief, it aims to interfuse as completely as possible its elements, that is, to present its materials symbolically, or implicitly as an absorbed import held in suspension, rather than allegorically or overtly. As a poem written about this belief, it aims to present a fable in which the moral values and the aesthetic values are shown to merge. In other words, the poem is, in general, about the unity of mind and the final unity of values, and in particular about poetry itself. It is not remarkable that Coleridge should have written on this subject, for it was the subject of his "darling studies." He had long since written, to Thelwall: "Metaphysics and poetry and 'facts of mind,' that is, accounts of all the strange phantasms that ever possessed 'your philosophy' . . . are my darling studies." And here we have the metaphysics, the poetry, and the psychology blended, as they are in the poem itself.

The fusion of the theme of the "One Life" and the theme of imagination is the expression in the poem of Coleridge's general belief concerning the relation of truth and poetry, of morality and beauty. We find at the very turning point of the poem, the moment of the blessing of the water snakes, an explicit presentation of the idea. The sequence of events gives us, first, a recognition of the happiness of the water snakes in their fulfillment of being—they participate in the serene order of the universe. Like the stars and the moon which move unperturbed on their appointed business while the Mariner is fixed in his despair, the snakes, which appear, too, as light-giving, participate in the universal fullness of being. Seeing them thus, the Mariner can exclaim:

> O happy living things!

After this utterance, we have the recognition of the beauty of the water snakes under the aegis of the moon—that recognition being determined, we have seen, by the recognition of their place in the universal pattern:

> . . . no tongue
> Their beauty might declare:

Then love gushes from the Mariner's heart, the response at the level of instinctive feeling. Then he blesses them; that is, the instinctive feeling stirred by the recognition of beauty finds its formal and objective expression. But he blesses them "unaware," and the word may be important, corresponding in this little account of the natural history of a "poem" of blessing, composed by the Mariner, to Wordsworth's word *spontaneous* in his phrase "the spontaneous overflow of powerful feelings" and Coleridge's word *unconscious* in the statement, in "On Poesy," that "There is in genius an unconscious activity; nay, that is the genius in the man of genius." So we may have here, and I do not mean this too whimsically, the case of a man who saves his own soul by composing a poem. But what Coleridge actually means is, of course, that the writing of a poem is simply a specialized example of a general process which leads to salvation. After the Mariner has composed his poem of blessing, he can begin the long voyage home.

He gets home, in the moonlight, which, we recall, is the light of imagination, and in the end he celebrates the chain of love which binds human society together, and the universe. But even here the Hermit, who officially reintroduces him into human society, is a priest of Nature as well as a priest of God; and the relation between man and Nature is established by the imagination, and so the Hermit is also a priest of imagination. In other words, imagination not only puts man in tune with the universe but puts him in tune with other men, with society: it provides the great discipline of sympathy. The socializing function of the imagination was never lost sight of by the Romantics. The poet is the man speaking of men, Wordsworth declares, and Shelley says in the *Defence:* "The great instrument of moral good is the imagination," for it leads man to "put himself in the place of another and of many others," so that "the pains and pleasures of his species must become his own." Over and over again in that generation we encounter the idea, and the Mariner returns to proclaim how sweet it is to walk "with a goodly company."

If the Mariner returns to celebrate the chain of love which binds human society and the universe, the fact should remind us that the occasion is a wedding and his audience a wedding guest. But it is sometimes argued that the Mariner repudiates marriage, contrasting it with the religious devotion indulged in "with a goodly company."[25] Now the contrast is certainly in the poem, and is involved in one of the personal themes. But in the total poem we cannot take the fact of the contrast as being unqualified. At the level of doctrine, we do not have contrast between marriage and sacramental love, but one as image of the other. It is no accident that the Mariner stops a light-hearted reveler on the way to a marriage feast. What he tells the wedding guest is that the human love, which the guest presumably takes to be an occasion for merriment, must be understood in the context of universal love and that only in such a context may it achieve its meaning. The end of the poem gives a dramatic scaling of the love, in lines 591–609.

> What loud uproar bursts from that door!
> The wedding-guests are there:
> But in the garden-bower the bride
> And bride-maids singing are:
> And hark the little vesper bell,
> Which biddeth me to prayer!
>
> O Wedding-guest! this soul hath been
> Alone on a wide wide sea: . . .
>
> O sweeter than the marriage-feast,
> 'Tis sweeter far to me,
> To walk together to the kirk
> With a goodly company!—

The scale starts with the rude merriment, uninstructed and instinctive. Then the next phase, introduced by the significant word *but,* gives us the bride in the garden singing with the bridesmaids, retired from the general din and giving us, presumably, a kind of secular hymn of love. Then comes the vesper bell calling to prayer. The significance of the prayer is immediately indicated by the sudden statement that the Mariner's soul—and the use of the word *soul* here is important—has been alone on a wide sea: the Mariner now sees the chain of love which gives meaning to the marriage feast. In one of its aspects the poem is a prothalamion.

But we must ask ourselves more narrowly about the Mariner's situation, even as he proclaims his message of love. He is, we recall, a wanderer, with some shadow hanging over him of those two great wanderers, the Jew and Cain. His situation is paradoxical. Now from one point of view it is proper that the prophet of universal charity, even though he celebrates the village life of the goodly company walking to church together, should himself have no fixed address, for that would in a way deprive his message, symbolically at least, of its universality. But his wandering is not only a mark of his blessed vision: it is also a curse. So we have here a peculiar and paradoxical situation: the poem is a poem in which the poetic imagination appears in a regenerative and healing capacity, but in the end the hero, who has, presumably, been healed, appears in one of his guises as the *poète maudit.* So we learn that the imagination does not only bless, for even as it blesses it lays on a curse. Though the Mariner brings the word which is salvation, he cannot quite save himself and taste the full joy of the fellowship he advertises. Society looks askance at him. When he first returns home and is flung into the Pilot's boat (significantly by the creative storm), the ordinary mortals there are appalled: the Pilot falls down in a fit; the Pilot's boy "doth crazy go" and declares flatly that the Mariner is the devil himself; and even the Hermit has to conquer his mortal trepidations in prayer (though the priest ought to understand the artist as another person dedicated to ideal values). And even now, long after, the Wedding Guest has moments of terror under the glittering eye. The very gifts, the hypnotic eye, the "strange power of speech," set the Mariner apart.

Now, as we look back over the poem, we may see that this doubtful doubleness of the imagination has more than once been apparent. Creativity is a wind, a storm, which is sometimes inimical (as in the first storm in Part I) and is sometimes saving (as after the blessing of the snakes). But even in its most gentle manifestation, as the light breeze blows sweetly on the Mariner's brow on the voyage home, it "mingled strangely" with his "fears." There is always a strain of terror with the beauty, and in the end it is a shattering, supernatural blast which sinks the ship and delivers the Mariner to the waters of the home port even as the beneficent moon looks down.

The Mariner will be rescued and will pass like night from land to land. Let us linger on this phrase: like night. For even this tells us something. It gives us first the effortless, universal sweep, a sense of the universality of the Mariner's message which is carried from land to land. It tells us, too, by the easy, conventional equation of *dark* and *accursed* that the Mariner is the *poète maudit*. But night in this poem has a special body of associations, and with night we may have here, as a result of the long accumulation of night scenes, always with the association of the moon, a hint of the healing role of the imagination—a beneficent counterweight to the burden of the curse which is carried in the phrase. The phrase, in its special context, repeats, in little, the paradoxical situation of the Mariner.

Earlier I have said that we find in the blessing of the snakes a little fable of the creative process—the natural history of a poem of blessing. But in the end of the poem we have another fable of the creative process, and perhaps a fuller statement of Coleridge's conception of the poet, the man with the power which comes unbidden and which is an "agony" until it finds words, the power which wells up from the unconscious but which is the result of a moral experience, and in its product, the poem, the "tale" told by the Mariner, will "teach"—for that is the word the Mariner uses. It is a paradoxical process.

And that paradox, the paradox of the situation of the poet, was a central fact for Coleridge and his age. The cult of Chatterton was significant, from Coleridge's boyish "Monody on the Death of Chatterton," in 1790, to the production of Vigny's *Chatterton* on the night when, as Gautier said, one could almost hear the crack of solitary pistols. In *Adonais* we do not know whether the mark on the pale brow of the last of the mourners is that of Cain or Christ, in the "Ode" the poet falls upon the thorns of life, and in a letter to Mrs. Shelley appears the sentence: "Imagine my despair of good, imagine how it is possible that one of weak and sensitive nature as mine can run further the gauntlet through this hellish society of men." And Blake, who, as his letters and notebooks show us, frequently found himself at odds with the world, could complain:

> O why was I born with a different face?
> Why was I not born like the rest of my race?

Keats was, in one respect, like the waif, as Yeats said, looking into the window of the sweetshop. But where Keats is a gentle outcast,

Byron is a dark and theatrical one, practicing his wild glances before a mirror and hinting at horrid crimes. And when he describes himself, the outcast both noble-minded and accursed, he describes himself in *Lara* as a figure strangely like the Mariner, with, somehow, a mysterious message and a power to compel the listener like the power in the Mariner's glittering eye:

> None knew nor how, nor why, but he entwined
> Himself perforce around the hearer's mind;
> There he was stamped; in liking or in hate,
> If greeted once; however brief the date
> That friendship, pity, or aversion knew,
> Still there within the inmost thought he grew.
> You could not penetrate his soul, but found,
> Despite your wonder, to your own he wound;
> His presence haunted still; and from the breast
> He forced an all unwilling interest:
> Vain was the struggle in that mental net,
> His spirit seemed to dare you to forget.

But what of Wordsworth, who seems so respectably rooted in social centrality and who eschewed the opium phial of Coleridge and De Quincey, the bottle of Lamb, the rancors of Blake, the Satanic loves and heroic posturings of Byron, the languors of Keats, and the shrillnesses and self-pity of Shelley? I am not about to refer to Annette Vallon or to the youthful ardors of revolution. I refer to his critical theory. He says that a poet is a man speaking to men, and affirms the universal bond, as do his brother poets, for all that. But if we look close, we see that he also shares with his brother poets the fascination with the outcast, the outsider. He seeks poetry in the peasant, the idiot, the child. We know the reasons he gives, and sound ones they may be, for going to these figures, but we must not forget that these figures, too, are beyond the circle of respectable society. There is, it must be remembered, another point, which comes out of Wordsworth's description of the poet. He says, first, that the poet has a "more comprehensive soul" than other men, and second, that he is set off from them by a certain special endowment. The first notion refers to a difference in degree, but the second refers to a *difference in kind.* In developing this second notion, Wordsworth, like other Romantic critics, comments on the special nature of the aesthetic experience: the poet has, he says in the Preface, an "ability of conjuring up in himself passions, which are indeed *far from being the same as those produced by real events,* yet . . . do more nearly resemble the passions produced by real events than anything which, from the motions of their own minds merely, other men are accustomed to feel in themselves. . . ."

I am not prepared, on the basis of Wordsworth's insistence on the special quality of the creative experience, to call him, except fancifully, an example of the *poète maudit.* The imagination was for him a healing power, and his life was a strenuous effort to give others something of the benefit of this power and to make poetry genuinely social. Nevertheless, he did know something of the "distress," as he called it, which occasionally accompanied the exercise of the healing power, even if his distress was a little short of the Mariner's "agony." He says in *The Prelude* that the poet, "gentle creature as he is," has his "unruly times":

> . . . his mind, best pleased
> While she as duteous as the mother dove
> Sits brooding, lives not always to that end,
> But like the innocent bird, hath goadings on
> That drive her as in trouble through the groves;
> With me is no such passion, to be blamed
> No otherwise than as it lasts too long.

The dove that is goaded through the groves by its inward distress is a somewhat less compelling image than the Mariner who passes like night from land to land, but the idea is in both cases the same. But this description of the poet as cursed is not the only one in Wordsworth's work. In "Stanzas Written in my Pocket-Copy of Thomson's 'Castle of Indolence' " (1802) there is the description of a man who wanders the country in storm or heat or who sits for hours brooding apart from men.

> What ill was on him, what he had to do
> A mighty wonder bred among our quiet crew.

This man, who is compared to a "sinful creature, pale and wan," is in the end defined as a poet:

> But verse was what he had been wedded to;
> And his own mind did like a tempest strong
> Come to him thus, and drove the weary Wight along.[26]

So we have, even with Wordsworth, something of the paradox which haunted Coleridge with special vindictiveness all his life: the paradox implicit in the figure of the Mariner or in that other ambiguous figure in that other poem about the imagination:

> And all should cry, Beware! Beware!
> His flashing eyes, his floating hair!
> Weave a circle round him thrice,
> And close your eyes with holy dread,
> For he on honey-dew hath fed,
> And drunk the milk of Paradise.

V I

I have tried to show, by dwelling on details as well as on the broad, central images, that there is in *The Ancient Mariner* a relatively high degree of expressive integration. There may be lags and lapses in fulfilling the basic creative idea, but, according to my reading, these lags and lapses are minor. But one school of thought has always held that the lags and lapses are far from minor, that there is no pervasive logic in the poem. Wordsworth, of course, said as much, as did Mrs. Barbauld with her complaint of improbability, and Southey in his review of the piece in *The Critical Review.* Even Lamb, in defending the poem against Southey and declaring it to have the true power of playing "tricks with the mind," was constrained to admit that parts of the poem were "fertile in unmeaning miracles." And later, in defending the poem against Wordsworth's charge that it was not integrated, he again admitted that he disliked "all the miraculous parts of it."

We must remember that the poem to which all of the critics referred was not the poem as it stands before us today. I do not argue that it would have made any difference to Mrs. Barbauld, or even to Wordsworth, but Coleridge did arrive at, by the time of the publication in *Sibylline Leaves* (1817), two major changes: he added the Gloss, which should have made the structure of the poem clearer, and he revised the text. Whether or not Coleridge was led to these changes by the criticism of the obscurity and lack of logic, the revision of the text itself was in accordance with his own theory of composition, that the parts of a work should participate in the expressiveness of the whole. So we have, in the important omissions made in the last version, a purging of at least most of the "unmeaning miracles" of which Lamb presumably complained, the descriptions of Death on the specter-bark and of the burning arms of the spirits at the time of the homecoming.[27]

The charge of the lack of integration, however, still continues to be made. One recent critic, Newton P. Stallknecht, says, for instance, that "Coleridge gives us no inkling of a possible allegorical interpretation until we reach the middle of Part III and encounter the character *Life-in-Death.*" But by this critic and by others the problem is centered on the role of the supernatural in the poem. Stallknecht[28] says that "moralizing or the use of allegory in a ballad in which an imaginative use is made of the supernatural *for its own sake* is apt to seem out of place or even mechanical," and he then proceeds to define the split in the poem as one between the supernatural material and the moral which, he takes it, was grafted on the poem late in the process of composition.

This general view of the supernatural should, perhaps, be inspected in the light of Coleridge's statements regarding the place of his interest in the supernatural in his own development. We do not have, alas, the essay on "the uses of the Supernatural in poetry," which he confidently affirmed the reader would find prefixed to *The Ancient Mariner.* But we know of the childhood passion for marvels and mysteries, fairy tales and *The Arabian Nights,* and we know what value he put upon what Lamb called "that beautiful interest in wild tales" as an influence in forming the imaginative bent. For him they served the same purpose as those later and more respectable fairy tales of Plotinus and the other mystics to keep "the heart alive in the head" and save his mind from "being imprisoned within the outline of any single dogmatic system." Furthermore, we must recall the context in which the division of labor for the *Lyrical Ballads* was arrived at and in which Coleridge undertook to write the poems of a supernatural cast: the context was the passionate dialogue, protracted day after day, on the subject nearest the hearts of both the young men, the subject of the nature and function of poetry. It was a high theme for them, and in the discussion the supernatural partakes of the general seriousness: no subject for an idle shudder.

In the face of this situation, it is a little surprising to find it argued, as it is argued by Marius Bewley, that Coleridge's "motive, in the last analysis, was not substantially different from Mrs. Radcliffe's or Monk Lewis's," that the *frisson* is all except for some disjointed references to a moral preoccupation which appear in the poem only because the poet "could not help drawing in some measure from his full sensibility." But the moral element, even if it does appear thus disjointedly in the poem, "is forgotten, if indeed it was ever recognized as present; it is changed, choked out by theatrical fripperies." And he summarizes this interpretation by saying: "The moral value of the poem is sacrificed by the attainment of a somewhat frivolous distinction"—that of having successfully created an atmosphere of mystery.

Aside from the evidence in the poem itself against this view, a view not confined to Bewley's essay, one can go to Coleridge's own words concerning the use of the supernatural in those romances which Bewley takes the poet to emulate. Coleridge reviewed several of the Gothic romances, and was interested in them, but he demands in the midst of the atmosphere of terror and mystery a truth to nature, and though he recognizes in some of them moments of genius and a great deal of ingenuity, in general he estimates them "cheaply." He says: "The writer may make us wonder, but he cannot surprise us," if the order of nature is changed. "For the same reason a romance is incapable of exemplifying a moral truth." He continues: "The romance-writer possesses an unlimited power over situations; but he must scrupulously make his characters act in congruity with them. Let him work *physical* wonders only, and we will be content to *dream* with him for a while; but the first *moral* miracle which he attempts, he disgusts and awakens us." This was Coleridge's view in 1797, a few months before he began work on *The Ancient Mariner,* and it is highly improbable that in using materials similar to those of the romances, he would not have attempted to avoid the defects which he had observed in the romances themselves.

The chief defect which Coleridge had observed in the romances is that, being contrary to human nature, they have no "moral" content. Presumably what Coleridge tried to do in his poem was to use the materials of "physical wonders" as expressive of spiritual truth, the physically improbable as expressive of the spiritually probable. The notion stated by Coleridge in the review of Lewis's *The Monk* can be taken as implying an awareness of the various attacks on the probability of the poem, the most famous example of which appears in Wordsworth's famous note—the "events, having no necessary connection, do not produce each other." These attacks are all based on a concern with the "physical wonders" as such, a concern which neglects the "moral truth" in the experience of the human being who endures in the midst of the wonders.

Coleridge was aware of the attacks on the poem on the grounds of the improbability caused by the use of the supernatural, and when he came to the final revision he gave us, it would seem, his answer. It is in the long motto by Burnet, which calls special attention to the supernatural element in the poem. "I readily believe," Burnet says, "that in the universe are more invisible beings than visible." He continues:

> But who will expound to us the nature of them all, and their ranks and relationships and distinguishing characteristics and the functions of each? What is it they perform? What regions do they inhabit? Ever about the knowledge of these things circles the thought of man, never reaching it. Meanwhile, it is pleasant, I must confess, sometimes to contemplate in the mind, as in a picture, the image of this greater and better world: that the mind, accustomed to the little things of daily life, may not be narrowed overmuch and lose itself in trivial reflections. But meanwhile must we diligently seek after truth, maintaining just measure, that we may distinguish things certain from uncertain, day from night.[29]

It is worthy of note that this motto was added in the edition of 1817, long after the heyday of the first enthusiastic speculations on the Quantock Hills and now in the cold calculation of a critical middle age bent upon making the masterpiece more comprehensible. I have already indicated how the last sentence of the motto points to the night-day, moon-sun opposition in the poem, and ties with that basic symbol; and I take the use of the motto to be not a piece of whimsical mumbo-jumbo or a vain parade of learning, but a device for pointing at a central fact of the poem. It says that the world is full of powers and presences not visible to the physical eye (or by the "understanding"): this is a way of saying that there is a spiritual order of universal love, the sacramental vision, and of imagination; that nature, if understood aright—that is, by the imagination— offers us vital meanings. It is simply a way of underscoring the function of the supernatural machinery and atmosphere in the poem, a way of saying that it participates in the symbolic tissue of the poem.

For I take the poem to be one in which the vital integration is of a high order, not one of the "great, formless poems" which the Romantics are accused of writing,[30] and not a poem which would fit into T. S. Eliot's formula of the dissociated sensibility of the period. I take it to be a poem central and seminal for the poet himself. Though a philosopher has said that "it would be pedantry to look for philosophical doctrines" in these magical lines,[31] and though a literary scholar finds here "merely the aroma, the fine flavor," of the poet's meditations,[32] if we do look closely at the magical lines and look at them in the light of the poet's lifelong preoccupations, we may come to conclude, with Leslie Stephen, that "the germ of all Coleridge's utterances may be found . . . in the 'Ancient Mariner.' " It is central for Coleridge, but it is also central for its age, providing not a comment on an age, but a focus of the being and issues of that age. It is, in short, a work of "pure imagination."

VII

The type of critical analysis which I have just attempted always raises certain questions. I shall state them bluntly and in the terms in which they usually appear:

1. Assuming that certain interpretations can be "drawn out of" or "put into" the poem by an "exercise of ingenuity," how do we know that the poet "intended" them?

2. If the present interpretations are "right," (a) is the poem not obscure, since good and experienced readers of the past have "missed" them, or (b) how is it that such good and experienced readers, having missed the interpretations, have still been deeply affected by the poem?

These questions, it will be readily seen, have to do, in order, with the theory of poetic creation and the theory of poetic appreciation. To answer these questions properly would require a space not here at my disposal and a competence not at my command. But it is not to be expected that a reader will accept my interpretation if I am not willing to abide his questions. And so I shall indicate, at least, the lines along which I should try to frame answers.

I should begin by saying that the questions, *as stated,* are false questions. There are real problems concealed behind these questions, but these are false because they are loaded—they will not permit an answer which does not falsify the nature of the process under discussion.

Let us take the first one.

The falsity of the first question inheres in the word *intended* as the word is intended in the context. The implication here is that the process of poetic creation is, shall we say, analogous to the process of building a house from a blueprint: the poet has an idea, the blueprint, and according to it, plank by plank and nail by nail, he makes a poem, the house. Actually, the creation of a poem is as much a process of discovery as a process of making. A poem may, in fact, start from an idea—and may involve any number of ideas— but the process for the poet is the process of discovering what the idea "means" to him in the light of his total being and his total experience (in so far as that total experience is available to him for the purpose of poetry—the degree here varies enormously from poet to poet). Or a poem may start from a phrase, a scene, an image, or an incident which has, for the poet, a suggestive quality—what, for him in the light of his total being and total available experience, we may call the symbolic potential. Then the process for the poet is the process of discovering why the item has caught his attention in the first place—which is simply another way of saying that he is trying to develop the symbolic potential. Or the original item may lead by some more or less obscure train of association to another item which will become the true germ of the poem, and whose symbolic potential may supplant that of the first item.

However the process starts, it is, of course, enormously complicated. The degree of effort may vary from instance to instance (the poet may dream up his poem in a flash or it may be laboriously accreted like coral), and the degree of self-consciousness may vary from instance to instance (the poet may or may not in the process of creation interlard his symbolical thinking with discursive and critical thinking). As Coleridge said, and as many other poets and even scientists have said, the unconscious may be the genius in the man of genius. But this is not to define the process as an irrational process. What comes unbidden from the depths at the moment of creation may be the result of the most conscious and narrowly rational effort in the past. In any case, the poet always retains the right of rejecting whatever seems to violate his nature and his developing conception of the poem. And the process of rejection and self-criticism may be working continually during the composition of a poem. In the case of *The Ancient Mariner* we have good evidence that the poet was working in terms of a preconceived theme, and we know that the original composition required some months and that the process of revision required years.

Whatever the amount of possible variation from case to case in various respects, we can say that the process is a process of discovery which objectifies itself as a making. What the poet is trying to discover, then, is what kind of poem he can make. And the only thing he, in the ordinary sense, may "intend" is to make a poem. In so far as his process of discovery has been more than a rhetorical exercise, he cannot do otherwise than "intend" what his poem says, any more than he can change his own past as past, but he does not fully know what he "intends" until the poem is fully composed. A purpose "formally conceived" is not, as Wordsworth said, necessary, first to initiate the process of creation, or second, to give the finished poem a meaning ultimately expressive not only of the man but of his "ideas" in a restricted sense. But, Wordsworth went on to say, "habits of meditation have, I trust, so prompted and regulated my feelings, that my descriptions of such objects as strongly excite those feelings, will be found to carry along with them a *purpose.*"

If the poet does not have a blueprint of intention (and if he does happen to have it, we ordinarily have no access to it), on what basis may a poem be interpreted? What kind of evidence is to be admitted? The first piece of evidence is the poem itself. And here, as I have suggested earlier, the criterion is that of internal consistency. If the elements of a poem operate together toward one end, we are entitled to interpret the poem according to that end. Even if the poet himself should rise to contradict us, we could reply that the words of the poem speak louder than his actions.

But the application of the criterion of internal consistency cannot be made in a vacuum. All sorts of considerations impinge upon the process. And these considerations force on the critic the criterion of external consistency. But consistency in regard to what? First, in regard to the intellectual, the spiritual climate of the age in which the poem was composed. Second, in regard to the overall pattern of other artistic work by the author in question. Third, in regard to the thought of the author as available from nonartistic sources. Fourth, in regard to the facts of the author's life. These considerations cannot be applied in a mechanical fashion, that is, so as to confuse the material of the poem with the poem itself. If treated mechanically, the first, for example, will give us crude historicism, or the fourth will give us crude psychologism—both of which confound the material with the thing created, both of which deny the creative function of mind, both of which fail to provide any basis for distinguishing the excellent product from the conventional or inept. But treated as conditioning factors, as factors of control in interpretation, the considerations named above provide invaluable criteria.

I have said that both of the questions usually raised by the kind of interpretation I have attempted are false questions. They are false in themselves, without regard to the goodness or badness, the truth or falsity, of a particular interpretation. Just as the first question is false, as stated, because it is based on a misconception of the creative process, so the second is false because based on a misconception of the appreciative process. I shall repeat the second question: If the present interpretations are "right," (a) is the poem not obscure, since good and experienced readers of the past have "missed" them, or (b) how is it that they, having missed the inter-pretations, have still been deeply affected by the poem?

The trouble is that the word *missed* here falsifies the relationship between the reader and the poem. It implies a matter of yes-and-no. Actually, the relationship is not one of yes-and-no, but of degree, of gradual exploration of deeper and deeper levels of meaning within the poem itself. And this process of exploration of deeper and deeper levels of the poem may be immediate and intuitive. The reader may be profoundly affected—his sense of the world may be greatly altered—even though he has not tried to frame in words the nature of the change wrought upon him, or having tried to do so, has failed (as all critics must fail in some degree, for the simple reason that the analysis cannot render the poem, the discursive activity cannot render the symbolical). As for *The Ancient Mariner* itself, the great central fact of the poem, the fact which no reader could miss—the broken taboo, the torments of guilt and punish-ment, the joy of reconciliation—is enough to account for the first impact of the poem upon a reader. But beyond that, the vividness of the presentation and the symbolic coherence may do their work—as blessing sprang to the Mariner's lips—unawares. For the good poem may work something of its spell even upon readers who are critically inarticulate.

If this is true—if ideally appreciation is immediate and intuitive— why should critical analysis ever be interposed between the reader and the poem? The answer is simple: in order that the intuition may be fuller, that detail may be more richly and the central images more deeply realized. But in this case what becomes of immediacy of appreciation? Nothing becomes of it, if "immediacy" is read properly—if it is read as signifying "without mediation" of critical analysis and not as signifying "upon the first instant of contact." Let me put it in this way: A poem works immediately upon us when we are ready for it. And it may require the mediation of a great deal of critical activity by ourselves and by others before we are ready. And for the greater works we are never fully ready. That is why criticism is a never-ending process.

One last word: In this essay I have not attempted to "explain" how poetry appeals, or why. I have been primarily concerned to give a discursive reading of the symbol which is the poem, in so far as I can project the import of the symbol in such a fashion. I humbly trust that I am not more insensitive than most to the "magical lines," but at the same time I cannot admit that our experience, even our aesthetic experience, is ineluctably and vindictively divided into the "magical" and the rational, with an abyss between. If poetry does anything for us, it reconciles, by its symbolical reading of experience (for by its very nature it is in itself a myth of the unity of being), the self-devisive internecine malices which arise at the superficial level on which we conduct most of our living.

And *The Ancient Mariner* is a poem on this subject.

NOTES

1. *The Best of Coleridge,* ed. Earl Leslie Griggs (New York, 1934), p. 687.

2. The subtitle of *The Road to Xanadu* (Boston, 1927) is "A Study in the Ways of the Imagination." Actually, to employ the Coleridgean distinction (which Lowes explicitly repudiates) it should have been "A Study in the Ways of the Fancy," for in so far as Lowes treats the subject, we have only the "fixities and definities," the units of material employed by the poet in merely new combinations of material. Lowes does nothing to show what happens in terms of imaginative meaning to these items when immersed in the "deep well." He shows how, in a factual sense, these items are transmuted, how, for instance, the "disconsolate black albatross" of *Shelvocke's Voyage,* shot by the superstitious Captain Hatley in the hope of a fair wind, becomes the albatross in the poem, but he never shows how they enter into a meaningful structure, how they become organically related to each other.

3. Humphry House, in a sympathetic criticism of this essay (The Clark Lectures, Cambridge University, published under the title *Coleridge,* London, 1953), raises a pertinent question about my method. Coleridge's important critical work, he reminds us, "was all a good deal later than most of his important creative work. We cannot thus be sure how much of his critical opinion may be carried back into 1797–8 and brought to bear on his greatest poetry" (p. 92).

By way of explaining myself, I should appeal to the principle of presumptive coherence in development, the fact that, despite waverings and false starts, a writer's history usually shows us a basic line. (In appealing to such a principle, we have to be very honest with ourselves: we have to test our congruences very scrupulously, and reason from them only when their number is massive and the negative instances very few.) I am not, however, arguing that because Coleridge held a certain doctrine of the symbol in 1817, the year of the *Biographia Literaria* and *The Statesman's Manual,* a poem written in 1797–1798 would necessarily embody that doctrine in practice. The later statements would be relevant only in so far as we can hold that those later statements represented a development of a position essentially held at the time of the composition of the poem itself. Now, there is strong evidence that this is the case.

First, Coleridge says flatly that he had become aware of the special power of the imagination at an early date, his "twenty-fourth year." In the *Biographia Literaria* (I, 58–60), he describes the effect wrought upon him by the reading of a poem by Wordsworth, a poem which exhibited "the union of deep feeling with profound thought; the fine balance of truth in observing with the imaginative faculty in modifying the objects observed; and above all, the original gift of spreading the tone, the *atmosphere,* and with it the depth and height of the ideal world around forms, incidents, and situations, of which, for the common view, custom had bedimmed all the lustre, had dried up the sparkle and the dew drops" (p. 59). Then a little later in discussing the concept of the imagination, he refers to the subject as one to which a poem of Wordsworth's had "first directed my attention" (p. 64). The whole discussion of the origin of the *Lyrical Ballads* makes it clear beyond doubt that the basic conception of the imagination had been arrived at early. We also have the evidence of *The Prelude,* which grew out of these discussions—evidence that may be useful in the face of Coleridge's uneasy memory for dates.

Second, we have the evidence in certain poems. The shaping power of the mind is referred to in early poems, such as the sonnet "To Richard Brinsley Sheridan, Esq." (1795) and "Lines on a Friend Who Died of a Frenzy Fever" (1794). Shawcross points out that even in "Religious Musings" (1794) there is a volitional effort on the part of the finite mind.

Third, though Coleridge wrote *The Ancient Mariner* in 1797–1798, he worked closely on it in the period just before the publication of *Sibylline Leaves* (1817), which belongs to the same period as the *Biographia Literaria* and *The Statesman's Manual.* In other words, his careful revision of the poem apparently indicates that it satisfactorily embodies, or adumbrates, his theories of composition as held in 1817. The fact that he continued to nurse the hope of completing *Christabel* indicates the same thing about that poem. At the peak of his critical powers, and presumably under their aegis, Coleridge was revising *The Ancient Mariner.*

All in all, the evidence against this general view is based on the idea that the concept of the imagination was arrived at after the visit to Germany and the subsequent philosophical crisis. I do not deny that the crisis was real, but it seems to have resulted in a clarification of issues which had been brewing for a long time. Germany gave Coleridge form and authority, perhaps, but not the basic motivation for his final views. Yet even R. D. Havens (*The Mind of a Poet,* Baltimore, 1941), immediately after remarking on the fact that a poem by Wordsworth had provoked Coleridge to speculation about the imagination, proceeds to say that "this revolutionary conception of the imagination" was "probably derived from Kant" (p. 206). For a discussion of the date of Coleridge's study of Kant, and of the needs which led him to accept Kant, see René Wellek, *Kant in England* (Princeton, 1931), pp. 69–73.

Elsewhere in his book, Mr. House considers the idea that the poem itself "is part of the experience which led Coleridge into his later theoretic statements (as of the theory of the Imagination) rather than a symbolic adumbration of the theoretic statements themselves." It is certainly true that the poem is an element in the development of the critical theory; but it also seems true that the poem is a manifestation of that development. In practice I simply do not see how we can distinguish between these two things; they are aspects of a single process. What I am finally concerned to do, irrespective of any technical argument about the nature of symbolism, is to establish that the "import" of the poem is consistent with the declarations of the criticism, and to explore the significance of this consistency.

4. In a letter dated February 5, 1797, Lamb refers to the poem as "Your Dream" (*Complete Poetical Works of Samuel Taylor Coleridge,* ed. E. H. Coleridge [Oxford, 1912], I, 169). The poem is, in fact, a kind of parallel to *The Ancient Mariner* in so far as it concerns a violation of Nature: a woodsman cuts down a tree and kills a nest of young ravens, timber from the tree is built into a ship, and when a storm sinks the ship the father raven exults in his revenge. In the *Sibylline Leaves* version, Coleridge changed the end by the addition of two lines to take the curse off the statement that revenge was sweet:

> We must not think so;
>   but forget and forgive,
> And what Heaven gives life to,
>   we'll still let it live.

But in a manuscript note, Coleridge commented: "Added thro' cowardly fear of the Goody! What a Hollow, where the Heart of Faith ought to be, does it not betray? this alarm concerning Christian morality, that will not permit even a Raven to be a Raven, nor a Fox a Fox, but demands conventicular justice to be inflicted on their unchristian conduct, or at least an antidote to be annexed" (*ibid.,* I, 171). It is fruitless to invoke this note as evidence that Coleridge believed in the position adopted by Griggs and Lowes. When he here says that a raven might be left a raven, he means that the raven as outside the realm of human religion and morality is entitled to gloat over revenge. When Coleridge added the last two lines he did not add a "moral" to a poem which had previously had none; he simply made explicit the distinction between raven and man, and defined man's responsibilities more closely. Without the new lines, the poem had had a "moral"—and a very unsubtle one.

5. MX. B II, Alice Snyder, Coleridge on Logic and Learning (New Haven, 1929), p. 132.

6. "Preliminary Treatise on Method," *Encyclopedia Metropolitana* (London, 1845), I, 25.

7. See John Muirhead, *Coleridge as Philosopher* (London, 1930), pp. 142–48; and later discussion in this essay.

8. *Enneads,* V, I, 7: *The Divine Mind,* trans. Stephen Mackenna (London, 1926), IV, 81–82. Another important text on the matter of self-consciousness in creation appears in the account in Chapter xiv of the *Biographia Literaria* of the poet "described in ideal perfection." Here it is said that the secondary imagination is "first put into action by the will and understanding," and remains under "their irremissive, though gentle and *unnoticed control*" (italics mine).

9. The "huge ill-assorted fabric of philosophic and theological beliefs" can be read, according to Richards, as "an elaborate, transformed *symbol* of some parts of the psychology. . . . Coleridge constantly presents it [the philosophic and theological speculation] as though it were the matrix out of which he obtained his critical theories. But the critical theories can be obtained from the psychology without initial complication with the philosophical matter. They can be given all the powers that Coleridge found for them, without the use either literally, or symbolically, of the other doctrines" (*Coleridge on Imagination* [London, 1934], pp. 58–59).

10. *The Statesman's Manual,* p. 437. See also "Lectures of 1818," Sections on Allegory and on Spenser (*Coleridge's Miscellaneous Criticism,* ed. T. M. Raysor [Cambridge, 1936], pp. 28–33). One may remember, too, the terms in which Coleridge repudiated his own early poetry: his chief charge against it is that of being—though he does not use the word—allegorical. Muirhead (*op. cit.* p. 43) comments on the abstractions which populate the poems prior to 1797, and observes that in the great poems they are "wholly subordinated to the interest of the characters and incident." But, in realizing that the great poems are not simply allegorical, he goes to the other extreme and assumes, or momentarily seems to do so, that the poems therefore have no intellectual content. He concludes with a position like that of Griggs: "It would be pedantry to look for philosophical doctrines in their magical lines." One might retort that it is exactly the same kind of pedantry to look for meaning in the "magical" events of life itself.

But to turn to Coleridge's particular doctrine of symbolism, it seems to be developed under the shadow of Plotinus. The Universe, Plotinus says, "stands a stately whole, complete within itself, serving at once its own purpose and that of all its parts which, leading and lesser alike, are of such a nature as to further the interests of the total. It is, therefore, impossible to condemn the whole on the merits of the parts which, besides, must be judged only as they enter harmoniously or not into the whole, the main consideration, quite overpassing the members which thus cease to have importance." (Mackenna, *op. cit.* II, 2, 3; *ibid.,* II, 14–15.) But the whole

serves the "interests" of the parts. The following analysis can be trans-
posed into aesthetic terms: "In what sense can we then say that the individual soul is part of the universal soul? There comes to mind here an
analogy, the only one which, to speak of Plotinus, may be able to make
us understand the relation between the universal soul and the individual
souls. The theorem, he says, is part of the science, if one may speak thus;
but the theorem, and every theorem, is the science itself, in all its extension and its life: fixed there, reduced, concentrated in that point: but in
it all life is present, even if not explicitly expressed. Every scientific proposition receives life from all the science. . . . In the mind of the scientist,
or of any other person whatsoever, the theorem meanwhile has value in
so far as it is the entire science, regarded from one side only, in one of
its particular configurations. . . . So that, as the theorem may be called part
of the science and is nothing less, however, on reflection, than the science
itself, so the individual soul may be called part of the universal soul, which,
to consider well, is nothing more than the individual soul. And as the
theorem acquires consistency and life in the articulated complex of which
it forms a part, which is the scientific system, so the individual soul meanwhile affirms itself and empowers itself in so far as it is once more understood and once more understands the universal soul itself, from which
Plotinus thinks it proceeds. The theorem is all the science, but the science
in power, and the individual soul is all the universal soul, but in power"
(Cordelia Guzzo Capone, *La Psicologia di Plotino* [Napoli, 1926], p. 52;
translation mine).

11. I take it that this is what Susanne Langer means by the "unspeakable" in the import of the symbol. As applied to poetry, she puts it: "The
material of poetry is discursive, but the product—the artistic phenomenon—is not; its significance is purely implicit in the poem as a totality, as
a form compounded of sound and suggestion, statement and reticence,
and no translation can reincarnate that. . . . An artistic symbol . . . has more
than discursive or presentational meaning" (*Philosophy in a New Key* [Cam-
bridge, 1942], pp. 261–62). Elsewhere, she distinguishes between the
symbolic and the allegorical modes. In allegory, she says, "we have a
literal meaning—the key to this being the accepted meanings of the words
and sentence-forms—and a secondary meaning, which employs some features *of the primary* meaning," to express another structure. She continues:
"But allegory is a direct and obvious form of interpretation. For the
secondary meaning could really be literally expressed, being simply another story. It is verbally communicable, and does not really need the
literal story for its expression. . . . But to treat a myth [or symbol in the
sense used here] as an allegory in the strict sense is useless—for *all myths
expressing the same fundamental idea are allegories of each other,* but they are

formulations, exemplifications, not allegories of the concept they embody. Therefore, to treat a religious symbol, for instance, as an allegory of natural events, is merely substituting one language for another. The kernel of a myth is a remote idea, which is shown, not stated in the myth. It is only the myth which is stated in words" (*The Practice of Philosophy* [New York, 1930], pp. 156–58).

Following this line of thought, we can see that when one critic makes the Pilot's boy "equal" the clergy, to take an allegorical reading in the most absurd form, the critic is merely "substituting one language for another"—is merely trying, here very unconvincingly, to make another application of the principle behind the symbol which he should try to interpret. That is to say, the boy and the clergy are on the same level of "story." And this transposition of one for the other does little to carry us toward the "kernel" or "concept" or root-attitude of the poem, which, it is true, we can never wholly frame in words but which it is the business of criticism to carry us toward.

In this connection William Blake has a most instructive passage: "The Last Judgment is not Fable or Allegory, but Vision. Fable or Allegory are a totally distinct and inferior kind of Poetry. Vision or Imagination is a Representation of what Externally Exists, Really and Unchangeably. Fable or Allegory is Form'd by the daughters of Memory. Imagination is surrounded by the daughters of Inspiration, who in the aggregate are call'd Jerusalem. Fable is allegory, but what Critics call the Fable, is Vision itself. The Hebrew Bible and the Gospel of Jesus are not Allegory, but Eternal Vision or Imagination of All that Exists. Note here that Fable or Allegory is seldom without some Vision. Pilgrim's Progress is full of it, the Greek Poets the same; but . . . Allegory and Vision . . . ought to be known as Two Distinct Things, and so call'd for the Sake of Eternal Life. Plato has made Socrates say that Poets and Prophets do not know or Understand what they write or Utter; this is a most Pernicious Falsehood. If they do not, pray is an inferior kind to be call'd Knowing? Plato confutes himself" (from "Blake's Catalogue of Pictures," *The Writings of William Blake*, ed. Geoffrey Keynes [London, 1925], III, 145–46).

12. Humphry House (*op. cit.*, p. 108) says of my use of symbolism in interpreting the poem: "I suggest that if we accept the term 'symbol' we must allow a freer, wider, less exact reference; and that it is probably wiser to drop the term altogether. Mr. Warren himself fully allows for the possibility (even likelihood) that Coleridge did not *consciously* use symbols at all. This is consistent with Coleridge's recognition of the unconscious element in the workings of genius; but it does not therefore follow that there was a latent precision waiting for critics to elucidate."

There are several notions here. One is a technical consideration having to do with the use of the term *symbol.* I do not, as a matter of fact, feel wedded to the term: I mean it only as an image of deep import, using the word *image* in a broad sense to include event, etc. But if we discard the term *symbol,* we still have the problem of image and import. Aren't we back, for practical, immediate purposes, where we started?

Another notion above has to do with the discomfort at what is taken to be my exactness of reference and precision in interpreting the poem. I, like Mr. House, feel discomfort at the dry, schematic reading of this poem—or any poem. I, like Mr. House, take the import of this poem, and of individual items in the poem, to be massive and deep—"condensed," as I have said above; and like him I feel that when we come to the business of stating discursively that import we inevitably violate the richness of the poetic object as experienced. The violation is inevitable because we are transferring elements of the synthetic imagination into an incommensurable dimension of analysis. We are, however, committed, willy-nilly, to the attempt analytically to understand poetry: we are rational beings, and we take poetry to be, in its deepest sense, rational— that is, to have a structure, and a structure that reflects, embodies, and clarifies the secret structure of the human soul and human experience. The degree of consciousness in the creation of a poem is not necessarily relevant to its import; the real question is how fully, deeply—and veraciously because deeply—the poem renders the soul and the soul's experience, and thus enables us to understand it by living into its structure as projected in the structure of the poem. The only test of what, to use my critic's word, is "latent" in a poem is the test of coherence. (See Section VII of this essay.) In trying to determine what is latent, we may learn that the discipline of our ordinary analytic understanding, with its apparently, and often really, barren attempts at "precision," can sometimes be a step toward that deeper, fulfilling experience which we finally expect from the poem.

The same unease at my attempts at "precision" is implied elsewhere: "What happens in the poem is that the images gather their meaning by progressively rich associations, by gradual increment, and that exact equation is never fully demanded, even though the association is ordered and controlled" (p. 97). Now, I think this an admirable description of the poetic process—and a good Coleridgean one, to boot—and also an admirable description of the way a reader may very well experience a poem. But—and here is a big *but*—if the associations are "ordered and controlled," then aren't we committed to try to understand the nature of the order and control? This need not commit us to "exact equations," but it does commit us to the attempt to disentangle, or rather to precipitate from the solution which is the poem, the elements participating in the import of the poem. Furthermore, we must do this as "exactly" as possible, even while realizing the limitations of the dimension in which we necessarily work.

A more radical criticism of my treatment than that by Mr. House is implied in Elisabeth Schneider's very valuable and provocative *Coleridge, Opium and Kubla Khan* (University of Chicago Press, 1953). Her attacks on my views may be sorted out as follows:

(1) *Coleridge had no systematic theory of symbolism, and "naturally thought in other terms than those of dark symbol"* (p. 256).

To begin, not too seriously, the word *dark* here is a little forensic trick. But be that as it may, I don't think that the depth and coherence of a poem depend on a poet's theory—if they did, there would be very few deep and coherent poems. It is more likely, as a matter of fact, that the theory will develop from the poetry than the poetry from the theory, or that, at least, the writing of the poetry and the development of the theory will be aspects of the same process.

The import of a poem does not depend on critical theory, and its availability for the reader does not depend—and should not depend—on our acquaintance with the poet's critical theory as such. For whatever it may signify, I may say that my basic interpretation of *The Ancient Mariner* was arrived at before I had made a systematic study of Coleridge's theory of symbolism. Some elaboration of the interpretation occurred along the way, but I cannot say how much as a logical exfoliation of the idea as I lived longer with the poem or how much as a consequence of the study of Coleridge's theory. In any case, with humility in front of Miss Schneider's learning, I still do not find Coleridge's theory quite so irresponsible as she takes it to be. There are confusions, waverings, and lags in it, perhaps more than I am aware of, but even so, we cannot, it seems to me, deny the ideas and insights embodied in it.

(2) *The Ancient Mariner is not the sort of poem (presumably because it is developed from the ballad tradition) in which Coleridge would have expressed his serious ideas.* Miss Schneider says: "In *The Ancient Mariner* the verse itself seems more consonant with Coleridge's remark that the poem has too much moral than with any elaborate cosmic interpretation: its movement does not strike my ear as sufficiently grave to bear the weight of all the meanings that have been bestowed upon it" (pp. 259–60). I honestly don't know what Miss Schneider really means to say here. I believe that what follows is a fair summary of what she actually does say.

Coleridge says the poem has "too much moral."
It does have too much moral—presumably for a poem in the ballad tradition.
Presumably because it is a poem in the ballad tradition, its movement is not "sufficiently grave" to bear the weight of the moral (i.e., the "weight of all the meanings").

> *But it doesn't have any meanings anyway; they have merely been "bestowed"
> upon it, presumably by critics.*

So we get the final contradictory idea that the meanings have been
merely "bestowed"—even though we start by accepting Coleridge's remark that the poem really has "too much" moral. Or perhaps Miss
Schneider isn't making any connection between "moral" and "meanings."
In that case, we may not have self-contradiction, but what do we have?

Let us lay aside, however, the question of what the author wants to say
in the whole sentence, and fix on one of the individual ideas. Miss
Schneider says that her ear tells her that this verse is not "sufficiently
grave" to bear the weight of serious meaning. One might remark that if
Miss Schneider is going to resort merely to her ear, then we may all resort
merely to our ears and the devil take the hindmost. But more seriously,
does her ear really tell her that the following lines are not sufficiently grave
to bear serious meaning?

> O happy living things! no tongue
> Their beauty might declare:
> A spring of love gushed from my heart
> And blessed them unaware:

Or:

> O Wedding-Guest! this soul hath been
> Alone on a wide sea:
> So lonely 'twas, that God himself
> Scarce seemed there to be.

Miss Schneider does have a good ear, as her analysis of some of the
verse of *Kubla Khan* indicates, but here, anxious to grab another piece of
evidence for her argument, she cruelly slanders that innocent member.

Continuing in her line of argument, she says in her next sentence that
when Coleridge "planned to write on great or cosmic themes" he never
thought of using "minor poetic forms," and mentions some of his abortive
projects on a grandiose scale (p. 260). But the mere fact that Coleridge
couldn't write those epics seems to indicate, among other things, that his
mind didn't work that way. However much his ambition urged him to
draw up such projects, his genius simply wasn't of that order. Though his
genius wasn't up to the epics, there is no reason to assume that his native
seriousness—and ambition—was less when that genius did come to fulfill
itself on a more modest scale. And I see no reason to assume that a minor

poetic form, in this case the ballad, would not be found worthy of serious development and serious freighting. In fact, there is some evidence for this in Coleridge's admiration for Wordsworth, who often worked in terms of a very simple tradition.

(3) The Ancient Mariner *does not demand the kind of reading which I have tried to give it.*

Presumably Miss Schneider wants us to take the poem innocently. So do I: that is the only way to start to take any poem. But we have to see where our innocence will lead us—and we have to remember to keep on trusting our innocence all the way, down no matter how unexpected, and perhaps dark, a track. Miss Schneider says, however, that the track doesn't run very far in *The Ancient Mariner;* the poem doesn't demand much of our innocence. "Symbolic meaning" is not to be expected here.

"Symbolic meaning," she says, "becomes 'translucent' [only] when the poet alters the course of nature or heightens or distorts certain features of his subject in ways not accounted for by the surface meaning alone, when a particular emphasis not otherwise explicable is laid upon a word or image, or when his verse form takes on a special character that is intelligible only through a symbolic meaning" (p. 261). Are we to understand that Miss Schneider maintains that in *The Ancient Mariner* the poet does *not* alter the course of nature or distort any matters in a way not accounted for by the "surface meaning alone," and does *not* lay particular emphasis upon certain images in a way not explicable at the surface level? If she does maintain this, it would be nice to know what her "surface," or other, meaning of the poem would be, and I cannot but feel that some burden of proof is on her to give us a reading that proves no significant distortions or heightenings, or special emphases, to exist in the poem.

(4) Miss Schneider lumps the kind of reading which I have tried to do—"symbolic," if you will—with studies such as those of G. Wilson Knight and Maud Bodkin, and says that the "conscious symbol-seeking of critics or psychoanalysts," rarely succeeds in "salting the tail" of the "invisible bird," her image for the subconscious forces lurking beneath the "surfaces of our thought and feeling" (p. 260). Without reference to how well or how badly Mr. Knight, Miss Bodkin, and I have done our work, the point here is that Miss Schneider confuses two very different kinds of study, and this confusion, it seems to me, haunts all her theorizing, or implied theorizing, about the creative process. Mr. Knight and Miss Bodkin are, if I remember them correctly, trying to give a psychoanalytic reading of poetry; the symbols they are talking about are psychoanalytic symbols. What I am trying to do is to talk about poetic images and import—which may or may not overlap with the psychoanalytic symbols.

This matter is best discussed by thinking of the distinction between the reverie of wish-fulfillment and the reverie of any kind of creative activity. Miss Schneider makes the distinction: "The intense concentration of the act of composing does indeed bear some likeness to reverie. . . . But it is creative *will* that is at work and not the *wish*-fulfilment reverie of certain psychologico-aesthetic theories" (pp. 276–77).

I think that Miss Schneider is perfectly right here—and, incidentally, her notion of the will seems consistent with Coleridge's own. But we have to ask how the will works in relation to creative reverie. In a rough-and-ready, and tentative, way, I should hazard this: The poet wants to make a poem and is acting on his desire—is *willing* a poem. In his state of concentration certain things float into his mind; but these things are *unwilled,* for he cannot deliberately summon up any particular item; if he knew what to summon up, his work would already be done. He can envisage only the *kind* of thing, as it were, which he needs: he may see the shape of the blank spot, but he can't see—he can only feel—what ought to fill it. He can, however, reject by *will* whatever items are unsatisfactory, and he continues this process in the gradual envisagement of what he is creating. In general, he *wills* the poem. In particular, he *wills* the rejection of individual items.

In the wish-fulfillment reverie there is merely indulgence, no developing envisagement of a thing being created. The wish-fulfillment reverie is responsive only to the wish, and is merely an expression of the unconscious. The creative reverie, on the other hand, by envisagement and veto—by *will,* if you like—is responsive to various demands. It is, first, responsive to the "whole man"—to his total value-system, with its long-range as well as its short-range satisfactions. It may not adequately express this "whole man," and may even falsify him, but it cannot ignore him. Second, the creative reverie is responsive to the objective world, in respect to considerations of congruence, probability, association, etc. Third, the creative reverie is responsive to the laws of the medium, whatever that medium may be—paint, verse, mathematics, etc. The creative reverie is a massive, fluid process seeking objectification in a form that overpasses appetite.

To go further, the wish-fulfillment reverie is a surrender to the needs of the unconscious, while the creative reverie is, in the end, a liberation from the compulsiveness of the unconscious. This is not to say, however, that the creative reverie denies the needs of the unconscious, but that it gives new contexts to the images arising from the unconscious and criticizes projections of it, and in that process "liberates."

This is a way of saying that the unconscious does give materials on which the creative reverie works. The critical mischief starts when we confound those "materials" with the poem made from the materials. In any poem there may be lags, overlays, and undigested chunks of material, but the poem, in so far as it is a good poem, survives all this by the fact of having been "created." The study of the "materials," the sort of study which Miss Bodkin and Mr. Knight, for instance, have undertaken, may lead to enlightenment in so far as it enables us to distinguish between the material of the poem and the poem itself, to understand better how such material may be absorbed, and to understand better the process of its transformation into new meanings.

I heartily agree with Miss Schneider that a poem is not a form of automatic writing. It so happens that for years I had had a nagging suspicion that Coleridge's account of the origin of *Kubla Khan* oversimplified matters. I was prepared to admit that he may have had a dream start— possibly verbal—but my guess was that then, or later, he moved over into the more ordinary process of composition to finish up. I was the more prepared to admit this because I had once dreamed up part of a poem— alas, not *Kubla Khan*—and then finished it later in colder blood. So Miss Schneider's argument about the origins of *Kubla Khan* falls on ready ground; and I think her interpretation of the poem is masterly. But for the life of me I don't see how proving that Coleridge was not asleep when he dreamed up *Kubla Khan* proves anything except that Coleridge was not asleep. I don't see how it tells us anything about the nature of the creative process, or the nature of poetry.

13. Letter to George Coleridge, April 1798, *Letters,* I, 241–42. We also find a text on the matter of sin and grace in "Sonnet on Receiving a Letter Informing Me of the Birth of a Son." And if we look to the nightmare in Stanza VI of "Ode to the Departing Year," we find the same type of imagery which appears in the guilt dreams of "The Pains of Sleep," and which Meyer H. Abrams (in *The Milk of Paradise,* Cambridge, 1934) attributes to opium; the opium source of the imagery presumably means a guilt association. But see Schneider (*op. cit.*).

Thus far I have tried to show, in attacking the notion that the Mariner is passive and that the killing of the Albatross can therefore have no moral content, that Coleridge was not committed to necessitarianism in any sense which would make it inevitable in the poem. But there is another line of approach to the question. If it be assumed that Coleridge did accept the doctrines of David Hartley and Joseph Priestley, it still does not follow that the Mariner's act is without moral content, for we must do Coleridge the honor of supposing that he read the works of his masters a little more closely than some of the critics seem to have done. In Priestley's *Doctrine of Philosophical Necessity Illustrated* (Birmingham, 1782, pp. 142–64), there occurs a section entitled "Of the Nature of Remorse of Conscience, and of Praying for the Pardon of Sin, on the Doctrine of Necessity," which really develops Proposition XV of Chapter I of Part II of Hartley's *Observations on Man.* Priestley writes: "It is acknowledged that a necessarian, who, as such, believes that, strictly speaking, *nothing goes wrong,* but that everything is under the best direction possible . . . cannot accuse himself of having done wrong in the ultimate sense of the words. He has, therefore, in this strict sense, nothing to do with repentance, confession, or pardon, which are all adapted to a different, imperfect, and fallacious view of things. . . . In the sublime, but accurate, language of the apostle John, he will *dwell in love,* he will *dwell in God,* and *God in him;* so that, *not committing any sin,* he will have nothing to repent of. He will be *perfect, as his heavenly father is perfect."* But man does not live at that level of enlightenment and "because of influences to which we are all exposed" cannot constantly refer "everything to its primary cause." Therefore, he will "feel the sentiments of shame, remorse, and repentance, which arise mechanically from his referring actions to himself. And, oppressed with a sense of *guilt* he will have recourse to that *mercy* of which he will stand in need." Since no man, except for rare moments in the seasons of retirement and meditations, is ever more than an "imperfect necessarian," all men have the experience of sin and remorse, and the sin, for mortal man who cannot see the complete pattern, has a content, and the content is the "almost irrevocable debasement of our minds by *looking off from God, living without him . . .* and *idolizing ourselves and the world;* considering other things as *proper agents* and *causes;* whereas, strictly speaking, there is but *one cause,* but *one sole agent* in universal nature. Thus . . . all vice is reducible to idolatry. . . ." Thus at the level of mortal experience, the level at which the Mariner must live, his shooting of the Albatross would be an act of pride, of self-idolatry—the very word Coleridge uses later in describing Original Sin.

The point I am trying to make is, finally, this: Even on the view that Coleridge is influenced by the doctrines of the necessitarians, the killing of the Albatross still has, at the level of experience, a moral content and is not to be dismissed as merely a wanton or thoughtless act. It is an act for which, at the level of experience, man takes responsibility, for, as Priestley somewhat whimsically puts it, at the end of his chapter on guilt, "If . . . we cannot habitually ascribe *all* to God, but a part only, let it be (and so indeed it naturally will be) that which is *good;* and if we must ascribe anything to ourselves, let it be that which is *evil."*

There is, indeed, a shadowy relation between the vision of love to which the Mariner attains and the moments of vision which the necessitarians describe—the "self-annihilation" of Hartley—but the mystics had given Coleridge more rapturous descriptions of that state of bliss. Furthermore, the one thing that the poem does *not* establish is the notion that the crime and the subsequent horror are really part of a good; the Mariner never praises God for having given him the evil as a concealed good; instead, the horror of the crime and its consequences is never completely over-passed, and the agony of the Mariner continues to return at its uncertain hour. This is definitely not the way a poet of necessitarianism should end his tale.

14. *Letters of Charles Lamb,* ed. E. V. Lucas (London, 1935), I, 95. R. C. Bald ("Coleridge and *The Ancient Mariner:* Addenda to *The Road to Xanadu,*" in *Nineteenth-Century Studies* [*Ithaca,* 1940], p. 16) quotes from Lamb's letter and reports that Coleridge had already entered in his note-book (Gutch memorandum book, f. 21a) the topic for a projected poem: "The Origin of Evil, an Epic Poem." But Bald does not connect this with *The Ancient Mariner.* He says: "Some time in 1797, however, the subject changed; one of his other projects drew his attention to a more appropri-ate theme." But the case seems to be that Coleridge changed his subject, his fable, but not his theme.

There is also evidence of a more personal nature that Coleridge was obsessed by fear and guilt even before the full addiction to opium. For instance, there is his autobiographical note of January 11, 1805: "It is a most instructive part of my Life the fact, that I have been always preyed on by some Dread, and perhaps all my faulty actions have been the consequences of some Dread or other in my mind from fear of Pain, or Shame, not from prospect of Pleasure." And Coleridge lists the numerous dreads, from the boyhood horror of being detected with a sore head, through "a short-lived Fit of Fears from sex," to the "almost epileptic night-horrors in my sleep" (Bald, *op. cit.,* pp. 26–27).

Our knowledge of the poet's personal background helps us to define his dominant theme, but the critical argument can be rested on perfectly objective evidence in the poems themselves. Coleridge longed for the vision of universal love of "Religious Musings" or of the end of *The Ancient Mariner,* but we also have in "The Eolian Harp" the picture of the "sinful and most miserable man," who is "wilder'd and dark," and the nightmare in Section VI of the "Ode to the Departing Year," not to mention the later *Christabel,* "The Pains of Sleep," and *The Ancient Mari-ner* itself.

15. *Aids to Reflection,* pp. 268–90; quotation on p. 287. Coleridge's emphasis later on the mystery of Original Sin may find a strange echo in the famous remark about *The Ancient Mariner* in the *Table Talk,* to the effect that the poem, as a work of pure imagination, should have had no more moral than the tale in *The Arabian Nights* of the "merchant's sitting down to eat dates by the side of a well, and throwing the shells aside, and lo! a genie starts up and says he must kill the aforesaid merchant *because*

one of the date shells had, it seems, put out the eye of the genie's son." But this account of the story of "The Genie and the Merchant" from the First Night, is not accurate. In fact, the careless date shell had killed the son of the genie. When the merchant begs for pity, the genie exclaims: "No mercy! Is it not just to kill him that has killed another?" And when the merchant then pleads his own lack of evil intention, the genie replies, "I must kill thee since thou hast killed my son." What is important here may be that the story referred to from *The Arabian Nights* is not merely a tale of the miraculous, but is one dealing with a random act and its apparently incommensurable punishment, much on the order of that in *The Ancient Mariner.* The mystery of sin and punishment is again before us. There is even a faint hint of a theological parallel with Christianity, the avenging Father and the Son who suffers at the hand of man. One can see why, perhaps, this particular story sprang to Coleridge's mind. But what did he mean by the statement about the moral and the use of this story as an example? He never said, we must remember, that his own poem should be meaningless or be without a "moral." He simply said that the moral should be less obtrusive. Then he offers an example of a story wherein a mysterious factor in life is caught up without any rationalization. It may be objected that Coleridge, after all, didn't have the story straight. The error, of course, may well have been that of Henry Nelson Coleridge, who had the habit of putting down after reaching home the remarks of his distinguished kinsman (see Preface to *Table Talk*), and whose memory of *The Arabian Nights* may well have been less perfect than that of Coleridge, to whom the book had been at one time almost a devotional work. But assuming that the error is Coleridge's, we do not necessarily assume that he mistook the fundamental, mysterious drift of the tale. For a discussion of the moral significance of the story, see House, *op. cit.,* pp. 90–92.

16. P. 458. If we transfer the terminology here to the pattern of *The Ancient Mariner,* we can describe the poem as the progression of the will from abstraction and self-idolatry to the state of immanence which expresses itself as wisdom or love—those being, as Coleridge says in the passage, two aspects of the same power, the "intelligential" and the "spiritual." We may observe that, in the poem, the punishment for the sin of self-idolatry, for the resolve of the will to find in itself alone "one absolute motive," is fitted with Dantesque precision to the nature of the crime. It is, in fact, a mere extension of the crime. It is loneliness. And when the Mariner bites his own arm for the blood to drink, we have the last logical extension of "self-idolatry" converted to its own punishment.

17. The crime presented in *The Ancient Mariner,* the crime of self-assertion in the face of Law, was of peculiar appeal to the Romantics. *"Le sentiment presque ineffable, tant il est terrible, de la joie dans la damnation,"* says

Baudelaire in his essay on *Richard Wagner et Tannhauser à Paris.* Another example is Shelley's interest in the crime of incest and his comments on the "poeticality" of the topic. The crime against an animal is, of course, a special case of this self-assertion, the perversity of pride. Baudelaire, in his essay on Poe, quotes his own translation of the passage given in the text from "The Black Cat" (*Revue de Paris,* March and April 1852). Flaubert's *Légende de saint Julien l'hospitalier* is another example of this twisted rendering of the Hymn of Saint Francis or the "jubilate Agno" of Christopher Smart.

18. What of the crew? The poem says the souls "fled to bliss or woe," and that is all we have in explicit terms. But the bodies remain to be inspirited by the angelic troop. Marius Bewley ("The Poetry of Coleridge," *Scrutiny,* VIII, 406–20) comments that this episode bears a reminiscence of the Incarnation and the Resurrection, and is a further emphasis on the controlling principle of love which springs from God. But he might have gone further and pointed out that, in the general structure of the poem, these associations define the inspiriting of the corpses as an act parallel to the spiritual rebirth experienced by the Mariner. It is another example of the repetition and counterpoint in the organization of the poem. But Bewley's whole view is that the poem is basically incoherent.

19. "I never find myself alone with the embracement of rocks and hills . . . but my spirit courses, drives, and eddies like a leaf in Autumn; a wild activity of thoughts, imaginations, feelings, and impulses of motion, rises up within me; a sort of *bottom-wind,* that blows to no point of the compass, comes from I know not whence, but agitates the whole of me; my whole being is filled with waves that roll and stumble . . ." (quoted by A. E. Powell, *The Romantic Theory of Poetry* [London, 1926], p. 99). Here Coleridge uses the storm at sea as an image to describe the state of imaginative excitement provoked by the contemplation of nature—the storm he welcomed and was to long for in the later years when the wind blew no more. I am indebted to Maud Bodkin (*Archetypal Patterns in Poetry* [Oxford, 1934], pp. 35–36) for the original suggestion for the interpretation of the wind and storm in the poem. She writes: "So, also, the image of a ship driving before the wind is used by him to express happy surrender to the creative impulse. 'Now he sails right onward,' he says of Wordsworth engaged upon *The Prelude,* 'it is all open ocean and a steady breeze, and he drives before it.' In *The Ancient Mariner* the magic breeze and the miraculous motion of the ship, or its becalming, are not, of course, like the metaphor, symbolic in conscious intention. They are symbolic only in the sense that, by the poet as by some at least of his readers, the images are valued because they give—even though this function remains unrecognized—expression to feelings that were seeking a language to relieve their

own inner urgency. . . . We find graven in the substance of language testimony to the kinship, or even identity, of the felt experience of the rising of the wind and the quickening of the human spirit. 'Come from the four winds, O breath, and breathe upon these slain, that they may live.' Behind the translated words, in the vision of Ezekiel, we can feel the older meaning, strange to our present-day thought, in which the physical wind, and the breath in man's nostrils, and the power of the Divine Spirit, were aspects hardly to be differentiated." But I do not see, in the light of the poem's organization or in that of Coleridge's "Dejection" (which employs quite explicitly the wind image for creativity), that we have to assume, with the author of *Archetypal Patterns,* the image not to be symbolic in conscious intention.

The image, of course, is not uncommon in other Romantic poetry. In Shelley, for instance, it appears as the paradoxical wind, destroying to create, in the "Ode." And in *A Defence of Poetry* we find the calm-wind opposition used precisely as in *The Ancient Mariner:* "We are aware of the evanescent visitations of thought and feeling sometimes associated with place or person, sometimes regarding our own mind alone, and always rising unforeseen and departing unbidden, but elevating and delightful beyond all expression . . . it is as it were the interpenetration of a diviner nature through our own; but its footsteps are like those of a wind over the sea, which the coming calm erases."

20. Though not in connection with the present topic, the italicized *her* in these lines is puzzling. A reasonable explanation is suggested by Frederick Pottle in a letter to the present writer: "In the version of 1798 there was an understandable contrast between *his* Death's bones and *her* the Woman's lips, *her* looks, *her* locks, and I have wondered whether the italicized *her* in the preceding stanzas (referring to the ship) did not get in by mistake. If so, the mistake was made at the very beginning, and not corrected in the many opportunities that S. T. C. had for revision."

21. It may be objected that the light of sunset is also, according to the passage from the *Biographia Literaria,* the light of the imagination. I am inclined to think that such an objection here would be legalistic, for Coleridge in the passage from the *Biographia* is thinking of a dimming light, a trick of light and shade, and the setting sun here has a "broad and burning face," and, according to the Gloss at this point, there is "No twilight within the courts of the sun." I take it that the Gloss is Coleridge's own way of anticipating the above objection, at the same time as he explains, somewhat superfluously, the statement that the dark comes at one stride.

22. Kenneth Burke is quite properly struck by the suggestive force of the phrase "silly buckets." His interpretation involves what he takes to be

the role of the Pilot's boy as a scapegoat for the Mariner's curse. He writes: "But his (the boy's) appearance in the poem cannot be understood at all, except in superficial terms of the interesting or the picturesque, if we do not grasp his function as a scapegoat of some sort—a victimized vessel for drawing off the most malign aspects of the curse that affects the 'greybeard loon' whose cure has been effected under the dubious aegis of moonlight. . . . I remember how, for instance, I had pondered for years the reference to the 'silly buckets' filled with curative rain (dew). I noted the epithet as surprising, picturesque, and interesting. I knew that it was doing something, but I wasn't quite sure what. But as soon as I looked upon the Pilot's boy as a scapegoat, I saw that the word *silly* was a technical foreshadowing of the fate that befell this figure in the poem. The structure itself became more apparent: the 'loon'-atic Mariner begins his cure from drought under the aegis of a moon that causes a silly rain, thence by synecdoche to silly buckets, and the most malignant features of this problematic cure are transferred to the Pilot's boy who now doth crazy go" (*The Philosophy of Literary Form* [Baton Rouge, 1941], pp. 287–88).

Burke emphasizes the relation of the moon and opium, and does not regard the moon as the presiding symbol of the concept of imagination at the level of an objectified, infusive theme. As for the role of the Pilot's boy, I do not feel it necessary to regard him as a scapegoat, though I do not think that this falsifies the tenor of the poem. I would make only this reservation: such an identification would be a significant connection, as I shall later point out, with the idea of the Mariner as the *poète maudit.*

But the phrase "silly buckets": We can go at this by looking at the cluster of meanings involved in the history of the word, meanings which would have been vitally present for Coleridge and the shadows of which can be detected in contemporary usage. The old meanings of *saelig-seely,* the sense of fortunate, blessed, happy, innocent, weak, still haunt the word, and fuse with the other meaning. In the poem the phrase comes in the first dream of blessedness, innocence, and happiness, just after the Albatross has dropped into the sea, and in the dream even the inanimate objects, but those associated with the longed-for water, receive the touch of this blessedness—and incidentally, this blessing of the buckets by the Mariner, for it amounts to that, repeats his blessing of the snakes, so that even the inanimate objects share in the new sacramental vision. As for the senses of weakness and stupidity in the word, we have the condition of the buckets as empty and worthless. Throughout, of course, there is the man-bucket transference, empty bucket and thirsty man (lonely, accursed, foolish, weak man) that become full and blessed.

23. "Lines Left upon a Seat in a Yew Tree," which appears in *Lyrical Ballads* and which, though begun as early as 1788 or 1789, had received

its final form in 1797, bears on the general question discussed here, in relation both to the sin of the Mariner and to the imagination. The poem ends with the following lines:

> If Thou be one whose heart the holy forms
> Of young imagination have kept pure,
> Stranger! henceforth be warned; and know that pride,
> Howe'er disguised in its own majesty,
> Is littleness; that he who feels contempt
> For any living thing, hath faculties
> Which he has never used; that thought with him
> Is in its infancy. The man whose eye
> Is ever on himself doth look on one,
> The least of Nature's works, one who might move
> The wise man to that scorn which wisdom holds
> Unlawful, ever, O be wiser, Thou!
> Instructed that true knowledge leads to love;
> True dignity abides with him alone
> Who, in the silent hour of inward thought,
> Can still suspect, and still revere himself,
> In lowliness of heart.

Here quite clearly the sin of pride is a sin against imagination, the equation made in *The Ancient Mariner.* As Ernest de Selincourt points out (*The Poetical Works of William Wordsworth* [Oxford, 1940], I, 329), Coleridge, who heard the poem in June 1797, was much affected by it. In July he wrote to Southey (*Letters* I, 224), though without specific reference to this poem: "I am as much a Pangloss as ever, only less contemptuous than I used to be when I argue how unwise it is to feel contempt for anything." George Wilbur Meyer (*Wordsworth's Formative Years* [Ann Arbor, 1943], p. 207) connects Wordsworth's *The Borderers* (conscious pride in Oswald, unconscious pride in Marmaduke) with the doctrine of "The Yew Tree," and says of the influence on Coleridge: "The strength of the impression which Wordsworth's philosophy of love made upon Coleridge may be approximately estimated when we observe that Coleridge expressed the same philosophy in *Osorio,* and in 'The Rime of the Ancyent Marinere,' where, it will be remembered, the wedding guest receives this good advice:

He prayeth well who loveth well, etc."
Mr. Meyer does not make any further connection of the poem with *The Ancient Mariner,* and apparently does not make this connection except with the stanzas of the moral tag.

24. The interpretation of the poem given thus far is in some points

similar to those given by earlier readers. George Herbert Clarke ("Symbols in 'The Ancient Mariner,' " *Queen's Quarterly*, XL, 27–45) emphasizes the importance of the sun-moon opposition and makes this the key symbol of the poem, but he interprets the sun as the "God of Law" and the moon as the "God of Love," and with the first associates the Polar Spirit and the First Voice, and with the second the Hermit and the Second Voice. I feel that this view is a justifiable one, but that the exploration of the symbols has been stopped at a stage which leaves much of the poem unaccounted for, and which actually falsifies certain incidents in the poem—for example, those involving the Polar Spirit, which should be connected with the moon-cluster and not with the sun-cluster. Another study which emphasizes the importance of the sun-moon opposition is by Kenneth Burke (*op. cit.,* pp. 24–33, 33–66, 93–102). He notes that punishment is under the sun, and recovery and forgiveness under the moon. But his concern is with the personal themes, and not with the other types of theme. In this particular study he is primarily concerned with the creative process and not with the thing created, though, of course, it is difficult to treat one without treating the other. In any case, he makes some extremely valuable comments on *The Ancient Mariner* and "The Eolian Harp."

In neither of the above studies is the theory of the imagination connected with the poem. But that idea does appear in two other studies, one by Dorothy Waples and one by Newton P. Stallknecht. Miss Waples ("David Hartley in 'The Ancient Mariner,' " *Journal of English and Germanic Philology,* XXXV, 337–51) takes the view that Coleridge denied the moral of the poem in his conversation with Mrs. Barbauld because the moral is Hartleyan, in her view, and Coleridge had repudiated Hartley. She interprets the poem as a strict, two-dimensional allegory of the Hartleyan progression, by association, from imagination, through ambition, self-interest, sympathy, and theopathy, to the moral sense. After the killing of the bird, imagination introduces the Mariner to fear; ambition and shame are involved in the repudiation of the Mariner by his fellows, who hang the bird at his neck; his acquaintance with death and horror appeals to self-interest and refines it to repentance; the incident of the snakes shows the development of sympathy; the return to the power of prayer indicates the transition to theopathy; the return to human society affirms the moral sense. There are several lines of comment due here. First, the author plainly misreads, as do a number of other critics, what Coleridge actually said in the *Table Talk.* He did not repudiate the moral of the poem, he simply said that its "obtrusion" was too open. So she starts her argument from a false premise. Second, she makes Coleridge a doctrinaire follower of Hartley in a way which denies the rich complexity of his development. Third, her narrow allegory leaves large tracts of the poem unaccounted for. Why, for example, does the Polar Spirit pursue the ship? What do the various storms have to do in the poem? Is there any symbolic content for the sun-moon opposition? Why does the Mariner, if he has achieved the moral sense, have to wander the world with his recurring agony? She does use the imagination as a starting point for her interpretation, but it is the imagination according to Hartley, and not according to Coleridge, which is a very different kettle of fish. According to Hartley, the pleasures of the imagination, "the first of our intellectual pleasures, which are generated from the sensible ones by association" (*Observations on Man* [London, 1834], p. 475), belong primarily to youth, and are of value only as they lead, as a kind of bait, to higher pleasures. It follows that Hartley has a contempt for and fear of the arts as connected with "evil communications," the "pagan show and pomp of the world," and vanity and waste of time. They are only disinfected when "devoted to the immediate service of God and religion in an eminent manner," and when "profane subjects" are abjured (p. 481). It is unnecessary to develop the point that this view, which makes the imagination a mode of memory, is absolutely opposed to the theory of the relation of art and morality held by both Wordsworth and Coleridge at the time of the composition of the *Lyrical Ballads.* In any case, if *The Ancient Mariner* involves the concept of the imagination, the Coleridgean imagination presides, as the moon, over the end of the poem, and is not something which merely serves as a starter and is abandoned after its usefulness is over.

Stallknecht ("The Moral of the *Ancient Mariner,*" *Strange Seas of Thought* [Durham, N. C., 1945], pp. 141–71: slightly revised version of an article "The Moral of the 'Ancient Mariner,'" PMLA, XLVII, 559–69) presents a much more valuable consideration of the poem. His thesis is that it, like *The Prelude* (1805, Bk. xi, lines 75 ff. and 133 ff.), gives the account of the world apprehended through the lower faculty of mere reason as a universe of death and then the redemption from the horror of this mechanistic interpretation by the discovery of the imaginative love of nature, which "strengthens the human spirit, raising it also to a life of moral freedom and happiness" (p. 148). I think that this is a good statement of the general background of the poem if the critic does not mean to imply that in *The Ancient Mariner* the imagination does not participate in the final freedom and happiness and is overpassed. My criticism of the essay is primarily directed at the application of his view to the poem itself. The critic treats the idea of the poem as a late excrescence, really separate from the "fine dramatic use of incident" and the "simple and lively imagery" and the materials drawn from the books of travel; for him the poem is not "dominated by a subtle moral." In other words, he limits his interpretation to: "(1) the incident of Part IV where the spell begins to break . . . and (2) the last stanzas, wherein the Mariner is rewarded with a deep sense of human love and sympathy" (p. 151). The intention of my essay, however, is to demonstrate that the poem taken as a whole is meaningful.

Stallknecht argues that since Coleridge, in the account of the origins of the poem (*Biographia Literaria,* Chapter xiv), makes no reference to any meaning in the original plan, and since Wordsworth suggested the shooting of the Albatross, Coleridge had no intention of a meaning for his poem when he began it and did not discover one until he had reached the third and fourth parts. On the first part of his argument, we can merely appeal to the poetic theory of both Coleridge and Wordsworth—a point discussed elsewhere in this essay. The fact that Coleridge did not give an abstract statement of his idea, or did not say that the poem was intended to have one, may prove nothing more sinister than that Coleridge did not envisage a reader who would entertain the theory that poetry may have no meaning and still be poetry; and anyway, it is not to be taken as a proof that the poem as finished twenty years later would still have all the lags and meaninglessness attributed to it by Stallknecht. (A poem may have such defects, but we have to discover them by going to the poem and not by going to some remark about the origin of the poem or to a discussion of its mere materials—so much philosophy, so much supernatural machinery, so much dramatic incident, all weighed out like so much bread, cheese, and pickle for a sandwich.)

As to the second part of his argument—that Coleridge did not discover a meaning until he reached the middle of the poem—there is some evidence that the general idea which was finally embodied in the poem had been occupying Coleridge's mind for some time. Aside from the general discussions of the subject recounted in the *Biographia Literaria,* we can point to three items: First, De Quincey's remark that Coleridge told him that he had at first intended to embody his "idea" in a dream poem involving imagery drawn from high latitudes; second, Lamb's letter to Coleridge about the epic on the origin of evil (see Note 14); and third, Coleridge's statement in the preface to "The Wanderings of Cain" that the crime of Cain involved a crime against "sense" (a crime concerned with man's proper relation to nature) and that *The Ancient Mariner* was written "instead" of the poem about Cain, the other accursed wanderer. These two items of evidence indicate that Coleridge had had in mind the general idea embodied in *The Ancient Mariner* and that it involved a crime against nature. It does not matter, then, that Wordsworth happened to suggest the particular piece of narrative machinery, the shooting of the Albatross, which was to embody the idea. Further, at what point in the process of composition Coleridge happened to grasp his total vision of the poem is irrelevant; the important thing is that we can go to the poem and discover the embodiment.

25. Burke, *op. cit.,* p. 71; Hugh I'Anson Fausset, *Samuel Taylor Coleridge* (London, 1926), p. 166.

26. I am indebted to Frederick Pottle for this piece of evidence.

27. The following stanzas are omitted. The description of death:

> His bones were black with many a crack,
>   All black and bare I ween;
> Jet-black and bare, save where with rust
> Of mouldy damps and charnel crust
>   They're patch'd with purple and green.
>
> A gust of wind sterte up behind
>   And whistled thro' his bones;
> Thro' the holes of his eyes and the hole of
>   his mouth
>   Half-whistles and half-groans.

The return:

> The moonlight bay was white all o'er,
>   Till rising from the same,
> Full many shapes, that shadows were,
>   Like as of torches came.
>
> A little distance from the prow
>   Those dark-red shadows were;
> But soon I saw that my own flesh
>   Was red as in a glare.
>
> I turn'd my head in fear and dread,
>   And by the holy rood,
> The bodies had advanc'd and now
>   Before the mast they stood.
>
> They lifted up their stiff right arms,
>   They held them strait and tight;
> And each right-arm burnt like a torch,
>   A torch that's borne upright.
> Their stony eye-balls glitter'd on
>   In the red and smoky light.

28. *Op. cit.,* p. 150.

29. The translation used here is from the edition of the poem by Carleton Noyes (New York, 1900).

30. A. E. Powell (*op. cit.,* pp. 1–14), in following Croce's distinction between classic and romantic art as given in *I Problemi,* describes the romantic artist as one who values content more than form, who "has a practical as well as an artistic interest in his matter," who "prizes emotional experience for its own sake, and aims at enlarging men's power to experience" (p. 1). But this is a dangerous distinction in practice, for it tends to lead to an arbitrary definition of form, to a conception corresponding to Coleridge's notion of "superimposed form" as opposed to "organic form," or Blake's notion of mathematic form as opposed to living form. Dr. Boyer taught Coleridge that poetry has "a logic of its own, as severe as that of science" (*Biographia Literaria,* I, 4), and Coleridge's total effort in criticism may be taken as tending toward a description of that logic, or that formal principle. And it is a very dangerous and narrow conception of form that would equate it with mere syllogistic deployment of argument in a poem, with neatness of point and antithesis, or consecutiveness or realism of action. Who can maintain Pope's *Essay on Man* has form and that Keats's odes do not?

31. Muirhead, *op. cit.,* p. 43.

32. S. F. Gingerich, "Coleridge," *Essays in the Romantic Poets* (New York, 1924), p. 29.

ABOUT THE AUTHOR

ROBERT PENN WARREN was born in Guthrie, Kentucky, in 1905. After graduating summa cum laude from Vanderbilt University (1925), he received a master's degree from the University of California (1927), and did graduate work at Yale University (1927–28) and at Oxford as a Rhodes Scholar (B. Litt., 1930).

Mr. Warren has published many books, including ten novels, sixteen volumes of poetry, and a volume of short stories; also a play, two collections of critical essays, a biography, three historical essays, a critical book on Dreiser and a study of Melville, and two studies of race relations in America. This body of work was published in a period of well over half a century—a period during which Mr. Warren also had an active career as a professor of English.

All the King's Men (1946) was awarded the Pulitzer Prize for Fiction. The Shelley Memorial Award recognized Mr. Warren's early poems. *Promises* (1957) won the Pulitzer Prize for Poetry, the Edna St. Vincent Millay Prize for the Poetry Society of America, and the National Book Award. In 1944–45 Mr. Warren was the second occupant of the Chair of Poetry at the Library of Congress. In 1952 he was elected to the American Philosophical Society; in 1959 to the American Academy of Arts and Letters; and in 1975 to the American Academy of Arts and Sciences. In 1967 he received the Bollingen Prize in Poetry for *Selected Poems: New and Old 1923–1966,* and in 1970 the National Medal for Literature, and the Van Wyck Brooks Award for the book-length poem *Audubon: A Vision.* In 1974 he was chosen by the National Endowment for the Humanities to deliver the third Annual Jefferson Lecture in the Humanities. In 1975 he received the Emerson-Thoreau Award of the American Academy of Arts and Sciences. In 1976 he received the Copernicus Award from the Academy of American Poets, in recognition of his career but with special notice of *Or Else—Poem/Poems 1968–1974.* In 1977 he received the Harriet Monroe Prize for Poetry and the Wilma and Roswell Messing, Jr. Award. In 1979, for *Now and Then,* a book of new poems, he received his third Pulitzer Prize. In 1980 he received the Award of the Connecticut Arts Council, the Presidential Medal of Freedom, the Common Wealth Award for Literature, and the Hubbell Memorial Award (The Modern Language Association). In 1981 he was a recipient of a Prize Fellowship of the John D. and Catherine T. MacArthur Foundation. In 1986 he was designated as this country's first official Poet Laureate. Mr. Warren lives in Connecticut with his wife, Eleanor Clark (author of *The Bitter Box, Rome and a Villa, The Oysters of Locmariaquer, Baldur's Gate, Eyes, Etc.: A Memoir,* and *Gloria Mundi*). They have two children, Rosanna and Gabriel.